W9-DEW-439

THE NIGHT
IS WATCHING

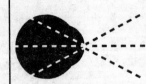

This Large Print Book carries the
Seal of Approval of N.A.V.H.

THE NIGHT IS WATCHING

HEATHER GRAHAM

THORNDIKE PRESS
A part of Gale, Cengage Learning

Detroit • New York • San Francisco • New Haven, Conn • Waterville, Maine • London

LIBRARY OF CONGRESS CATALOGING-IN-PUBLICATION DATA

Graham, Heather.
    The night is watching / by Heather Graham. — Large Print edition.
        pages cm. — (Krewe of Hunters Series) (Thorndike Press Large Print Core)
    ISBN 978-1-4104-5864-3 (hardcover) — ISBN 1-4104-5864-4 (hardcover) 1. Murder—Investigation—Fiction. 2. Arizona—Fiction. 3. Large type books. I. Title.
PS3557.R198N53 2013
813'.54—dc23   2013013742

Published in 2013 by arrangement with Harlequin Books S.A.

5202 9708 6/13

Printed in the United States of America
1 2 3 4 5 6 7 17 16 15 14 13

For Nan and Joe Ryan and my one and only but really great trip to Tombstone with them!

PROLOGUE

Mornings were quiet in Lily, Arizona.

A pity, Sloan Trent thought, walking up the two steps to the raised sidewalk of the town's main street. He felt tourists were missing out, because these summer mornings were beautiful, retaining the night's chill, while the days were often blazing.

Not surprisingly, the street was called Main Street. Sometimes, when the wind picked up, tumbleweeds actually swept down the street, along with little clouds of dust. The tourists loved it — except on the few rainy days that turned the dirt road into a mud slide, which clearly explained the raised wooden sidewalks of the 1880s.

The entire town was built of wood; only a few of the newer dwellings on the outskirts were brick or concrete. When Lily was built, lumber had been the easiest material to acquire, so everything was made of wood. Even the jail.

It was probably a miracle that Lily had never burned to the ground. But, small and barren though it might be, the town was a survivor. Just naming it Lily had been a piece of optimism, but when Joseph Miller had first come in hopes of finding gold way back in the 1850s, he'd named the place for his grandmother — not because she'd been beautiful or sweet, but because the Irishwoman had been blessed with the greatest tenacity he'd ever known, according to his memoir.

And Lily, Arizona, was a town that had held on tenaciously through good and bad, fair times and foul.

Sloan looked down the broad dusty road that had been preserved. Lily had almost been a ghost town, in the *truly deserted* sense; at one time, in the early 1900s, only three places of business had remained open, and since one had been the sheriff's office and jail, there'd really just been two mercantile establishments, both hanging on by a thread. Those two had been the Paris Saloon and the theater, the Gilded Lily. Of course, staying afloat at that time in this dry Western town off the beaten track, on the road between Tucson and Tombstone, was a struggle, and the Gilded Lily had offered pretty tawdry entertainment in the guise of

8

theater. Clearly, the place had been successful.

And because miners, ranchers, opportunists and downright outlaws enjoyed the services of the main saloon across the street and the bar in the theater, the jail did a booming business, as well.

Today, there weren't many shoot-outs. There weren't even many drunken brawls. It was strange to be sheriff back here after being with the Houston, Texas, police force. And strange to be head of a six-man — including one woman — force when he'd previously worked with hundreds of fellow officers.

But he'd come back to be with his grandfather when they'd first found out about his illness, and then stayed with him, tended to him, while the cancer slowly killed him. And now . . .

Now, he didn't have the heart to leave again.

Ah, yes, here he was in Lily, Arizona, taking care of not-so-major crime!

And that, he reminded himself, was why he'd left the new sheriff's office down the highway and come into the tourist end of town. There was another report from the old sheriff's office and jail, which was now being operated as a restaurant and bed-and-breakfast, known, naturally, as the Old Jail. It was featured on all the "haunted" shows that continually played on cable stations. Another "theft" had occurred.

The nineteenth-century office and jail sat next to the Gilded Lily, while the Paris Saloon and the old stables were across the street. While it was small in comparison to major tourist destinations like Tombstone, Lily had made something of a comeback. The other side of the saloon, in an old barbershop, had become a state-of-the-art salon and spa, and next to it, in the old general store, was a place called Desert Diamonds — a souvenir shop that also boasted a pizza parlor, ice cream and a barista stand. It was also a small museum. Grant Winston, proprietor, had been around since practically the Dark Ages and he displayed his old newspapers and artifacts in a special climate-controlled room in the back.

Main Street was hopping as a tourist destination. The old stables offered horse-back riding, day tours and haunted night tours. They'd even arranged a few Styro-foam "relics" out in the desert to heighten the pleasure.

Shaking his head at the marvels of modern commerce, Sloan paused for a minute.

A breeze had picked up suddenly, and a large clump of sagebrush went skidding down the road before him. He was struck by the feeling that something was about to change — that dark forces were coming to life in Lily, Arizona.

He couldn't help grinning at his ridiculous feeling that the sudden chill in the air and the sweep of sagebrush could be a forewarning of some kind of evil.

He opened the door of the bed-and-breakfast. The old sheriff's desk was now the check-in counter, and the deputy's desk held a sign that read Concierge.

Because, of course, in Lily, Arizona, you needed a concierge.

But the concierge did double duty, working the morning coffee and continental breakfast station that was laid out in the old gun room and pitching in when the gun room turned into a restaurant. The food wasn't bad and there was often a need for reservations, since the room held only six tables.

"Sheriff, thank God you're here!"

Mike Addison, owner and manager of the Old Jail, was at the sheriff's desk. He stood quickly when Sloan walked in.

"I came right over, Mike," he said. "What is it this time?"

"The couple in Room One! You know, Hardy's cell," Mike said dramatically. "They were robbed last night!"

"What happened?"

"They woke up this morning — and their wallets had been stolen. I wouldn't believe it myself, Sloan, if they weren't such fine people and if they weren't so honestly upset. The husband says they were over at the Gilded Lily, they saw the show, had one nightcap and came back. As you know, only our guests have keys to the front and the cells. I swear, I can't figure out how someone could have gotten into their room!"

Mike was in his thirties, tall, lean and earnest. He'd come out from Boston, having been a lover of all the Old West movies he'd seen growing up, thanks to cable channels. He'd bought the jail from old "Coot" Stevens, who'd first turned it into a B and B. Mike had worked hard to maintain its historic aspects and make it a nice place to stay. While the rooms were extremely small — they'd started out as cells, after all — they featured beds with luxurious mattresses, exceptional air-conditioning and tales of the outlaws who'd lived and died in the area, some in the cells and some at the scaffolding on Main Street.

"Where are they?" Sloan asked.

"The breakfast room. I offered to spike their morning coffee, they were so upset. Jerry and Lucinda Broling."

Sloan nodded and went in. The walls were covered with various weapons and rifles dating from the early 1800s to the 1960s. The tables were stained wood, which gave the place atmosphere and was easy to clean.

The young couple in question certainly looked dejected enough as they sat at the table, heads bowed and shoulders slumped. They appeared to be in their late twenties. Jerry Broling glanced up with hope in his eyes as Sloan entered. "It's the sheriff, honey. He'll do something. Everything will be fine, you'll see!" he said.

Lucinda, a blonde with cornflower-blue eyes, smiled tremulously. She'd been crying.

"How do you do? Sloan Trent," he said, introducing himself. "So, you think you were robbed during the night. In your room?"

"It had to be!" Lucinda insisted. "We went to the show — it's very funny, by the way — and afterward we stopped at the bar in the Gilded Lily."

"We had Kahlua and cream," Jerry said.

"I had Tia Maria. *You* had Kahlua and cream." Obviously, the robbery had made

13

them both irritable.

"Neither of us drank a lot," Jerry said. "We —"

"*I* hadn't been drinking at all," Lucinda broke in. "Jerry was draining a few beers in the saloon during the show."

"I wasn't even slightly buzzed." Jerry's tone was hard.

Lucinda waved a hand in the air. "I paid for the drinks."

"And that's the last time you saw your wallets?" Sloan asked. "At the saloon and the bar?"

"Mine never came out of my pocket. It should've been in my jeans this morning," Jerry said.

Lucinda waved a hand in the air. "I'd been using my credit card. Jerry hadn't paid for anything all day. *His* might have been anywhere. But I know that my wallet was in my purse when I went to bed."

Sloan nodded thoughtfully. "I understand you were in Room One."

"I've already searched it," Jerry told him.

"We even pulled the mattress up," Lucinda said.

"Did you ask at the Gilded Lily?"

"Well, they're not open this early, are they?" Jerry asked.

"Not for business, but they have rehears-

14

als, meetings . . . The costumer goes in to sew up rips and tears and so on."

Mike was at the door. "I called. Spoke to Henri Coque. They're up and about, working down in the old storage room digging up more wigs. He went up to the bar area and searched through everything. Couldn't find any credit cards. Talked to everyone he could, but no one handed in a lost wallet."

"So, you were in Trey Hardy's cell," Sloan said.

They nodded. "Excuse me. I'll give the place a search, too, if you don't mind."

The couple looked at him doubtfully. "Sheriff, there's a thief in this town," Lucinda said.

"A low-down, no-account pickpocket!" Jerry muttered.

"Stop trying to sound like some Old West bank robber," Lucinda groaned.

"Lucinda —"

Sloan left the squabbling couple, passed through the barred wooden door to the cells and walked down the length of the hallway. The door to Room One, the Trey Hardy cell, was open.

Hardy had been a true character in his day. A Confederate cavalry lieutenant who had lost everything during the Civil War, he'd started robbing banks. He was a hero

15

to some back in Missouri — just like Jesse James. He'd stolen from the carpetbaggers to give back to the citizens. He'd been dashing and handsome, and when things had gotten hot for him in Missouri, he'd gone farther. But in Lily he came up against another ex-Confederate, Sheriff Brendan Fogerty. Fogerty felt that the war was over, and ex-Reb or not, Hardy wasn't stealing from the citizens of Lily, Arizona. He'd taken Hardy in after winning a fistfight on Main Street. Hardy had promised to come willingly if Fogerty bested him. To a cheering crowd, he had turned himself in when Fogerty had pinned him. Sadly, unknown to Fogerty, his deputy, Aaron Munson, had a long-standing beef with anyone who'd fought against the Union. Before Hardy could be brought to trial, Munson shot Hardy down in his cell, only to be dragged out to the street and lynched himself by a furious mob enamored of the handsome Hardy.

While Munson haunted Main Street, Hardy was said to haunt the jail and the cell where he had died.

The doors to the cells were wooden with barred windows. They were entered with large jail keys that had to be returned — lest the guest be charged a hefty fee. In the

16

age of the plastic slot card, the Old Jail was a holdout. But entering a cell with a big jail key held greater charm.

The door wasn't locked, so Sloan stepped inside. The couple had done a pretty thorough job of searching. Drawers were still open and the mattress lay crookedly on the bed.

Sloan turned back to make sure he hadn't been followed. There was a security camera in the hall but he knew that was just for show; Mike never remembered to change the tape. He seldom had trouble. Guests seemed to love talking about the shadowy apparitions they'd seen in the halls or the "cold spots" that had moved into the room, et cetera, that went with staying at such a place. He walked to the dresser; it was heavy. A wide-screen TV sat on it, along with the bust of an Indian chief.

Sloan waited a minute, then shook his head, said quietly, "Give it up. Return the wallets."

He heard the rasp of something against the wall. Turning, he saw that that there were two wallets on the floor. They might have been wedged behind the dresser and wall — and fallen when he tugged at the dresser.

He picked them up and headed to the

door, then looked back into the room. "You know, Hardy, shadows in the night, cool. Your few ghostly appearances — great. But quit with the money, the keys and the wallets, huh? All these people think you're the next best thing to Jesse James. Don't go ruining your wonderful reputation."

For a moment, Sloan thought he saw him. Hardy seemed to be standing there, still wearing a gray jacket and a sweeping gray hat with a plume, a cross between a Western outlaw and a disenfranchised soldier. He had a neatly clipped golden beard and his eyes were bright. He saluted Sloan.

Shaking his head, Sloan walked back to the breakfast room and set the wallets on the table.

The couple gaped at him incredulously. "They were wedged behind the dresser," he said.

"Oh, thank you!" Lucinda gushed.

"Yeah, man, thanks!" Jerry said.

"Check them, make sure everything's in them," Sloan said.

"You said you searched everywhere!" Lucinda accused Jerry.

"Hey, you were in the room, too!"

She'd barely finished speaking when they heard it.

The sound was terrible; it seemed to come

18

from the earth itself. It was a scream — one that might have been piercing except that it was muffled.

It came again and again . . .

"What the f—" Jerry began, leaping to his feet.

"Oh, my God!" Lucinda cried, trembling.

Even Sloan felt as if ice trickled down his spine.

And then he realized the source of the scream. There was nothing unearthly about it. It was simply coming from the basement of the theater next door.

Sloan strode quickly from the Old Jail and down the few steps to the swinging, slatted doors that led into the Gilded Lily. He saw the long bar and the rows of seating to the side of it and the stage at the far end.

"Hey!" he called out, seeing no signs of life.

He hurried behind the bar to the stairs that went down to the basement and storm cellar, now a depository for over a hundred and fifty years' worth of costumes, props, scenery and other old theater paraphernalia.

He heard the scream again as he rushed down the steps.

The muted light blinded him for a moment. The basement was divided into a main room and three side rooms, separated by foundation walls.

He blinked and adjusted his vision. A woman stood alone at the back of the main basement room. She held an old burlap cover that had apparently protected shelves holding wigged mannequin heads. She was young, blonde and pretty, and he recognized Valerie Mystro, the current ingenue in residence at the Gilded Lily Theater Company.

"Valerie!"

She didn't hear him when he called her name. She was staring in horror at something on the shelf.

Sloan strode over to her and took her by the shoulders. She looked at him blankly, as if not seeing him at first.

"Valerie!"

She trembled. "Sloan!" she said, and swallowed.

"Valerie, what is it? What's wrong?"

She lifted a shaky finger and pointed at the row of old carved wooden wig heads.

They were creepy, Sloan agreed. Each had been painted with a face. Some pouted, some just stared, some seemed to laugh. A few of the newer heads were made of plastic or Styrofoam.

And at the end of the row . . .

There was one that bore a dark curly wig

tied with a red ribbon. Dark curls fell over the forehead.

But the head wasn't carved from wood. Nor was it plastic or Styrofoam.

It was a human skull, a skull stuck on a wooden spike. The jawbone had fallen and lay on the ledge.

That made it appear as if the skull itself was screaming.

As if evil was indeed alive in the world and had come to Lily, Arizona.

1

Jane Everett was entranced.

She'd been to a ghost town or two in her day, but never a functioning ghost town.

But then, of course, Lily, Arizona, had never really been a ghost town because it had never been completely deserted. It had just fallen by the wayside. It had seen good times — when the mines yielded silver and there'd been a hint of gold, as well, and the saloons and merchants had flourished — and it had seen bad times when the mines ran dry. Still, it had the look of either a ghost town or the set of a Western movie. The main street had raised wooden side-walks and an unpaved dirt street. Muddy when it rained, she was certain, but that was seldom in this area.

The car her boss, Special Agent Logan Raintree, had hired to bring her to town let her out in front of the Gilded Lily, where she'd be staying. The driver had set her bag on the wooden sidewalk, but she waited a minute before going in, enjoying a long view of the street.

There were a number of tourists around. She heard laughter from across the street and saw that a group of children had come from a shop called Desert Diamonds and were happily licking away at ice cream cones. Farther down, a guide was leading several riders out of the stables; she could hear his voice as he began to tell them the history of the town.

But the theater itself was where she was heading so she turned and studied it for a moment. Someone had taken pains to preserve rather than renovate, and the place appeared grand — if *grand* was the right word. Well, maybe grand in a rustic way. The carved wooden fence that wound around the roof was painted with an array of lilies and the name of the theater; hanging over the fence and held in place with old chain were signs advertising the current production, *The Perils of Poor Little Paulina*. Actors' names were listed in smaller print beneath the title. She knew the show was a parody of the serialized *Perils of Pauline* that had been popular in the early part of the twentieth century.

No neon here, she thought, smiling. They

were far from Broadway.

She'd read that the Gilded Lily had hosted many fine performers over the years. The theater had been established at a time when someone had longed to bring a little eastern "class" to the rugged West; naturally, the results had been somewhat mixed.

As she stood on the street looking up at the edifice, a man came flying out the latticed doors. Tall and square as a wrestler, clean-shaven and bald with dark eyes and white-winged brows, he bustled with energy. "Jane? Jane Everett? From the FBI?"

"Yes, I am. Hello."

"Welcome to Lily, Arizona," he said enthusiastically. "I'm Henri Coque, artistic director of the theater for about a year now and, I might add, director of the current production, *The Perils of Poor Little Paulina.* We're delighted to have you here."

"I'm delighted to be here," she responded. "It's a beautiful place. Who wouldn't want to come to a charming, Western, almost ghost town?"

He laughed at that. "I'm glad to hear that, especially since I'm the mayor here, as well as the artistic director. Lily itself is small. Let me get your bag, and I'll show you around the theater and take you to your room. I hope you're all right with staying here. Someone suggested one of the chain hotels up the highway, but everyone else thought you'd enjoy the Gilded Lily more."

"I'm happy to be here," Jane assured him. "I can stay at a chain hotel anywhere."

She *was* happy. They'd been between cases when Logan had heard from an old friend of his — a Texas cop, now an Arizona sheriff — that a skull had appeared mysteriously in the storage cellar of a historic theater. It had sounded fascinating to her and she'd agreed to come out here. The local coroner's office had deemed the skull to be over a hundred years old and had determined that handing it over to the FBI was justified, so that perhaps the deceased could be identified and given a proper burial. Like most law enforcement agencies, the police here were busy with current cases that demanded answers for the living.

The skull, she knew, was no longer at the theater. She would work at the new sheriff's office on the highway, but she was intrigued by the opportunity to spend time at the historic theater, learn the history of it and, of course, see where the skull was found.

That was the confusion — and the mystery. No one remembered seeing the skull wearing the wig before. Granted, the theater had been holding shows forever; it had

26

never closed down. And people had been using the various wigs down there forever, too. From her briefing notes, Jane knew that everyone working at the theater and involved with it had denied ever seeing the skull, with or without a wig. It seemed obvious that someone had been playing a prank, but Jane wasn't sure how identifying the person behind the skull — given that he or she had been dead over a hundred years — would help discover who'd put it on the rack.

The sheriff, Sloan Trent, had wanted to send the skull off to the Smithsonian or the FBI lab, but the mayor had insisted it should stay in Lily until an identification had been made. So, Sloan had requested help from his old friend, Logan Raintree, head of Jane's Texas Krewe unit of the FBI teams of paranormal investigators known as the Krewe of Hunters. And that had led to Logan's asking Jane, whose specialty was forensic art, to come here. The medical examiner who'd seen the skull believed it was the skull of a woman and he had estimated that she'd been dead for a hundred to a hundred and fifty years.

"Come, Ms. — or, I guess it's Agent — Everett!" Henri said, pushing open the slatted doors and escorting her into the Gilded

Lily. "Jennie! Come meet our forensic artist!"

Jane tried to take in the room while a slender woman wearing a flowered cotton dress came out from behind the long bar behind some tables to the left. The Gilded Lily, she quickly saw, was the real deal. She felt as if she'd stepped back in time. Of course, her first case with her Krewe — the second of three units — had been in her own hometown of San Antonio and had actually centered on an old saloon. But the Gilded Lily was a theater *and* a saloon or bar, and like nothing she'd ever seen before. The front tables were ready for poker players, with period furniture that was painstakingly rehabbed. To the right of the entry, an open pathway led to the theater. Rich red velvet drapes, separating the bar area from the stage and audience section, were drawn back with golden cords. The theater chairs weren't what she would've expected. The original owners had aimed for an East Coast ambience, so they, too, were covered in red velvet. The stage, beyond the audience chairs, was broad and deep, allowing for large casts and complicated sets. She saw what appeared to be a real stagecoach on stage right and, over on stage left, reaching from the apron back stage rear, were railroad tracks.

"Hello, welcome!"

The woman who'd been behind the bar came around to the entry, smiling as she greeted Jane. She thrust out her a hand and there was steel in her grip. "I'm Jennie Layton, stage mother."

"Stage *mother*?" Jane asked, smiling.

Jennie laughed. "Stage manager. But they call me stage mother — with affection, I hope. I take care of our actors . . . and just about everything else!" she said.

"Oh, come now! I do my share of the work," Henri protested.

Jennie smiled. "At night, we have three bartenders, four servers and a barback. And we have housekeepers who come in, too, but as far as full-time employees go, well, it's Henri and me. And we're delighted you agreed to stay here."

"I thought the theater history might help you in identifying the woman," Henri said.

"Thank you. That makes sense. And it's beautiful and unique."

"Lily *is* unique! And the Gilded Lily is the jewel in her crown," Henri said proudly.

"Well, come on up. We have you in the Sage McCormick suite," Jennie told her, beaming.

The name was familiar to Jane from her

reading. "Sage McCormick was an actress in the late 1800s, right?"

"All our rooms are now named for famous actors or actresses who came out West to play at the Gilded Lily," Henri said. "Sage, yes — she was one of the finest. She was in *Antigone* and *Macbeth* and starred in a few other plays out here. She was involved in a wonderful and lascivious scandal, too — absolutely a divine woman." He seemed delighted with the shocking behavior of the Gilded Lily's old star. "I'll get your bag."

"Oh, I'm fine," Jane said, but Henri had grabbed it already.

"Tut, tut," he said. "You may be a very capable agent, Ms. Everett, but here in Lily . . . a gent is a gent!"

"Well, thank you, then," Jane said.

Jennie showed the way up the curving staircase. The landing led to a balcony in a horseshoe shape. Jane looked down at the bar over a carved wooden railing, then followed Jennie to the room at the far end of the horseshoe. This room probably afforded the most privacy, as there was only one neighbor.

"The Sage McCormick suite," Jennie said, opening the door with a flourish.

It was a charming room. The bed was covered with a quilt — flowers on white —

and the drapes were a filmy white with a crimson underlay.

"Those doors are for your outdoor balcony. It overlooks the side street but also gives you a view of the main street, although obstructed, I admit," Jennie said.

"And the dressing room through here . . ." Henri entered with her bag, throwing open a door at the rear of the spacious room. "It's still a dressing room, with a lovely new bath. Nothing was really undone. The first bathrooms were put in during the 1910s. We've just updated. And, you'll note, this one retains a dressing table and these old wooden armoires. Aren't they gorgeous?"

They were. The matching armoires were oak, with the symbols of comedy and tragedy carved on each side and on the doors. "They were a gift to Sage when she was here," Henri said reverently. "A patron of the arts was so delighted that he had these made for her!"

Jane peeked beyond. The bathroom was recently updated and had a tiled shower and whirlpool bath. The color scheme throughout was crimson and white with black edging.

"This is really lovely. Thank you," Jane said again.

"It's our best suite!" Henri gestured

expansively around him.

"How come neither of you are in here?" Jane asked, smiling. "And what about your stars? I don't want to put anyone out."

"Oh," Jennie said. "Our 'stars' tend to be superstitious. They're in the other rooms on this level." With a quick grin she added, "And Henri and I are quite happy in our own rooms . . ."

Jane waited for her to say more.

Henri spoke instead. "Sage McCormick . . ." His voice trailed off. "Well, theater folk are a superstitious bunch. I mean, you know about her, don't you?"

"I know a little," Jane said. "She disappeared, didn't she?"

"From this room," Jennie explained. "There's all kinds of speculation. Some people believe she was a laudanum addict, and that she wandered off and met with a bad end at the hands of outlaws or Indians. Laudanum was used like candy back then. Lord knows how many people died from overusing it. Like today's over-the-counter pills. Too much and —"

"And some people believe she simply left Lily with her new love — supposedly she intended to elope — and changed her identity," Henri said impatiently. "Prior to that, she'd met and married a local man ey had a child together."

ally? But she still kept her room at the
d Lily?" Jane asked.

f course. She was the *star.*" Henri
e as if this was all that needed to be
.

Anyway, the last time anyone reported
ing her was when she retired to this room
ter a performance," Henri went on.

"Her esteemed rendition of *Antigone*!"
ennie said.

"What about the husband? Was he a suspect?" Jane asked.

"Her husband was downstairs in the bar, waiting for her. He was with a group of local ranchers and businessmen. One of her costars went up to get her, and Sage was gone. Just . . . gone. No one could find her, and she was never seen again," Jennie told her.

"Oh, dear! You're not superstitious, are you?" Henri asked. "I understood that you're a forensic artist but a law enforcement official, too."

Jane nodded. "I'll be fine here."

"Well, settle in, then. And, please, when you're ready, come on down. We'll be in the theater — I'll be giving notes on last night's performance. Join us whenever you're ready."

"I wouldn't want to interrupt a rehearsal."

"Oh, you won't be interrupting. The show is going well. We opened a few weeks ago, but I have to keep my actors off the streets, you know? You'll get to meet the cast, although the crew won't be there. This is for the performers. As Jennie mentioned, the cast lives at the Gilded Lily while performing, so you'll meet your neighbors."

"Thank you," Jane said, and glanced at her watch. "Sheriff Trent is supposed to be picking me up. I'll be down in a little while."

"Oh! And here's your key," Henri said, producing an old metal key. "The only people here are the cast and crew —"

"And bartenders and servers and a zillion other people who've come to see the show or have a drink," Jennie added drily. "Use your key."

"I will," Jane promised.

Henri and Jennie left the room. Jane closed the door behind them and stood still, gazing around. "Hello?" she said softly. "If you're here, I look forward to meeting you, Sage. What a beautiful name, by the way."

There was no response to her words. She shrugged, opened her bag and began to take out her clothing, going into the dressing room to hang her things in one of the armoires. She placed her makeup bag on the dressing table there, walked into the bathroom and washed her face. Back in the bedroom, she set up her laptop on the breakfast table near the balcony. Never sure if a place would have Wi-Fi, she always brought her own connector.

Jane decided she needed to know more about Sage McCormick, and keyed in the name. She was astounded by the number of entries that appeared before her eyes. She went to one of the encyclopedia sites, assuming she'd find more truth than scandal there.

Jane read through the information: Sage had been born in New York City, and despite her society's scorn for actresses and her excellent family lineage, she'd always wanted to act. To that end, she'd left a magnificent mansion near Central Park to pursue the stage. She'd sold the place when she became the last surviving member of her family. Apparently aware that her choice of profession would brand her as wanton, she lived up to the image, marrying one of her costars and then divorcing him for the embrace of a stagehand. She flouted convention — but was known to be kind to everyone around her. She had been twenty-five when she'd come out to the Gilded Lily in 1870. By that point, she'd already appeared in numerous plays in New York, Chicago and Boston. Critics and audiences alike had adored her. In Lily, she'd instantly fallen in love with local entrepreneur Alexander Cahill, married him almost immediately — and acted her way through the pregnancy that had resulted in the birth of her only child, Lily Cahill. On the night of May 1, 1872, after a performance of *Antigone,* Sage had gone to her room at the Gilded Lily Theater and disappeared from history. It was presumed that she'd left her husband and child to escape with a new lover, an outlaw known as Red Marston, as Red disappeared that same evening and was never seen in Lily again, nor did any reports of him ever appear elsewhere. Her contemporaries believed that the pair had fled to Mexico to begin their lives anew.

"Interesting," Jane murmured aloud. "So, Sage, did you run across the border and live happily ever after?"

She heard the old-fashioned clock on the dresser tick and nothing else. And she remembered that she'd promised to go downstairs. The sheriff was due to pick her up in thirty minutes, so if she was going to meet the cast, she needed to move.

Running into the dressing room, she ran her brush through her hair, then hurried out. As she opened the door to exit into the hall, she was startled to see a slim, older woman standing there with a tray in her hands. The tray held a small plug-in coffeepot, and little packs of coffee, tea, creamers and sugar.

"Hello!" the woman said. She looked at Jane as though terrified.

"Hi, I'm Jane Everett. Come on in, and thank you."

The woman swallowed. "I — I — I . . . Please don't make me go in that room!" she said.

Jane tried not to smile. "Let me take that, then. It's fine. You don't have to come in."

The woman pressed the tray into Jane's arms, looking vastly relieved. Jane brought it in and set it on the dresser. She'd find a plug in the morning.

When she turned around, the woman was still standing there. She wore a blue dress and apron and had to be one of the house-keepers.

"Thank you," Jane said again.

Suddenly, the woman stuck out her hand. "I'm Elsie Coburn. If you need anything, just ask me."

"Elsie, nice to meet you," Jane said, shaking her hand. She couldn't help asking, "How did this room get so clean?"

"Oh." Elsie blushed and glanced down. "I make the two girls clean this room. They do it together. They're okay as long as they don't work alone. Bess was in here one day and the door slammed on her and none of us could open it. Then it opened on its own, so . . . well, we don't have to clean it that often, you know? No one stays in this room. One of those ghost shows brought a cast and crew in here and the producer was going to stay in the room all night but he ran out. . . . People don't stay in that room. They just don't."

"Oh, well, I'm sorry that my coming here caused distress."

Elsie shook her head. "No, no, we're happy to have you. If you don't mind . . . please don't mention that you had to bring your own tray in."

"Of course not," Jane assured her. "Why did the producer of the ghost show run out in the middle of the night?"

"He said *she* was standing over his bed, that she touched him, that —"

"She? You mean Sage McCormick?"

Elsie nodded.

"But what made him think she wanted to hurt him?"

"What?" Elsie was obviously mystified.

Jane smiled. "I thought ghost shows tried

to prove that places were haunted."

"This whole *town* is haunted. Bad things, really bad things, have happened over the years. The ghost-show people got all kinds of readings on their instruments. And the Old Jail next door! People leave there, too, even though they don't get their money back if they do. This place is . . . it's scary, Agent Everett. Very scary."

"But you live and work here," Jane said gently.

"I'm from here, and I don't tease the ghosts. I respect them. They're on Main Street, and they're all around. I keep my eyes glued to where I'm going, and that's it. I do my work and I go home, and if I hear a noise, I go the other way." She rubbed her hands on her apron. "Well, a pleasure to meet you. And we're glad you're here."

"Me, too. And don't worry about cleaning the room — no one has to clean it while I'm here. I'll just ask you to bring me fresh towels every couple of days. How's that?"

Elsie looked as if she might kiss her.

She nodded vigorously. "Thank you, miss. Thank you. I mean, thank you, Agent Everett."

"Jane is fine."

Flushing, Elsie said, "Jane." She turned and disappeared down the hall, heading for the stairs. Jane closed her door, locking it behind her as she'd been told to do.

When Sloan arrived at the Gilded Lily, the servers had yet to come in for the night. He had to knock on the doors — the solid doors behind the latticed ones that had been preserved to give the place its old-time appearance — to gain entry. The bar didn't open until five.

Jennie let him in, smiling as she did. Jennie was always in a good mood. "Sloan, hi. You're here for Jane?"

So . . . Agent Everett was already on a first-name basis with people at the Gilded Lily. But then again, was she like most agents, or was she an artist — with the credentials to work on FBI cases? He gave himself a mental kick; even though he'd made the call to Logan that had brought her to town, Sloan wasn't pleased about her being here, but he wasn't sure why.

Yes, he needed to find out who the skull belonged to. But logically, in his opinion at least, the skull should have been sent off to a lab where such things were done or to the experts at a museum. In the end — after arguing with Henri Coque about procedure — Sloan had been the one to call Logan to ask for a forensic artist and Logan had sent

40

her. He'd trusted Logan to send him a good artist, but he was also aware that Logan was a different kind of lawman.

Sloan was, too.

He and Logan had shared secrets that they hadn't let on to others. Working cases together, they'd both had occasion to follow leads *because they'd spoken to the dead.*

Sloan didn't walk around interacting with spirits all the time. But there'd been occasions . . . He and Logan had recognized the ability in each other. And they'd been good partners.

True, he sometimes argued that the dead *he* saw were his particular form of talking to himself. And while it might seem that talking to the dead should solve everything, it didn't work that way. But now Logan wasn't a Ranger anymore; he was a fed. And he was the head of a unit. A special unit that was informally called the Texas Krewe.

Jane Everett was part of that Krewe. Did that mean she shared Logan's secrets? Or that she knew about Sloan? He doubted it. Logan never spoke to anyone about anyone else's business. But, somehow, Jane Everett made him uneasy.

Was he worried that she was only an artist — and not really much of a law enforcement agent?

Or was he worried that she was an artist *and* an agent and might find *him* incompetent?

He'd just had an odd feeling that they needed to get the skull out of Lily. It was almost as if the skull could be a catalyst for bad things to come.

Ridiculous, he told himself. Still, he didn't like it.

But *he'd* been the one to call Logan Raintree.

In keeping with what Sloan knew about his old friend, he wasn't surprised, when he'd looked up his recent work, that Logan's Krewe worked with strange, supernatural cases.

In fact, it was one reason he'd decided to approach him.

Because there's more to this than meets the eye and it may be important — but do I really want to know? he asked himself. He'd called Logan because he wondered if they might need help from the dead while not wanting it to be true.

"Yes, I'm here for Agent Everett," he told Jennie.

"Come in," she said. "The cast is down by the stage apron. She's been meeting them all."

"Sure." Thankfully, there weren't any

other pressing issues in Lily at the moment.

He followed Jennie into the theater.

The group had gathered around the stage. Valerie Mystro, who had found the skull, was leaning casually against the show's hero, Cy Tyburn, a tall, blond, all-American-looking actor from Kansas. Alice Horton, dark-haired, dark-eyed, sultry and buxom, the show's vamp, was seated on the stage next to Brian Highsmith. Brian was dark-haired, as well; his green eyes bright against the near-black of his hair. Smiling, he appeared to be totally nonevil, although he played the show's villain. Henri looked happy, standing in front of the newcomer, Jane Everett, who was seated next to Alice.

Even in the group of beautiful twenty-to-thirty-year-old actors, Jane Everett stood out. She was seated, so he couldn't judge her height, and she was wearing a typical pantsuit — one he might expect to see on a working federal agent. The slight bulge was apparent at her rib cage; she was wearing a shoulder holster and carrying her weapon, which was probably just as regulation as her black pantsuit and white shirt. But she wore her hair loose and it was a striking shade, the deepest auburn he'd ever seen. And when she looked up at his arrival, he saw that she had the most unusual eyes he had ever seen, as well. They were amber. Not brown. Not hazel. Amber.

As he entered, she stood. Whatever they'd been discussing, they'd all gone quiet as he walked in.

"Sloan! We've just met Jane," Valerie said happily. She giggled. "I told her how terrified I was when I *found* the skull, but then, she's an FBI agent — I'm sure she would have behaved perfectly normally."

"Maybe not. A skull can startle anyone," Jane Everett said.

"Oh, you haven't met yet!" Valerie said. "I'll introduce you. Agent Jane Everett, meet our town's sheriff, Sloan Trent. Sloan, this is Agent Everett."

"It's Jane, please," Jane said, standing to shake his hand. She was on the tall side, he noted. Probably about five-nine, since she was wearing neat low pumps and seemed about five-ten or so against his six-three frame. She had a beautiful face, absolutely elegant and classical. He imagined that once they were gone, the show's leading ladies would be discussing her . . . assets. She appeared to be lean and trim, but even in her regulation attire, she seemed to have the curves to suggest a well-honed body.

So this was the artist Logan had sent to sketch his skull?

44

It wasn't *his* skull, he reminded himself. But the skull had belonged to a living, breathing human being and it was part of his town's history. As far as he knew, anyway. And if it wasn't — if Jane Everett's rendering of the long-dead woman couldn't be identified — someone had dug it up from somewhere to play a gruesome prank on the show's cast or crew.

It just should have gone to Washington or a museum, he thought again.

He understood why Henri had insisted it stay in Lily. He wanted to know who'd gotten hold of the skull — and who'd put it in the basement storage room of the Gilded Lily.

"Sheriff Sloan Trent," he said, accepting her hand and nodding to the others in acknowledgment. They all greeted him in turn, either as Sloan or as Sheriff — as if that was his given name. There wasn't a lot of formality in Lily.

"I'm here to take you to our offices. We have a room prepared for you to work in. I hope you'll find everything you need."

She nodded. "I bring most of my own supplies," she said, patting the black case she carried over her shoulder. "We should be fine. Thank you, Sheriff."

"My pleasure, Agent Everett. You ready?"

45

"I am."

There was a chorus of "lovely to meet you" and "nice to make your acquaintance" and other cordial statements as they left the stage area and headed out, along with "See you later, Sloan!"

He led the way to his SUV — then hesitated. He'd been raised to open doors for ladies, but wasn't sure what the protocol was with an agent. He decided he'd be damned if he was going to change. He opened the passenger door. She thanked him as she slid in.

An awkward silence followed as he drove down Main Street, then along the paved road that passed by a smattering of houses and ranches on small plots, and finally larger tracts as he traveled the six miles from the heart of Lily to the modern "downtown" area of town.

She broke the silence.

"So, Logan said he sometimes worked with you in Texas. But you're from Lily?" she asked.

"I am," he told her.

"It's really remarkable," she said. Her voice seemed strained; she was obviously trying to be pleasant and cheerful. "The town, I mean — not that you're from it."

"It's remarkable in its preservation, I sup-

46

pose. Tombstone is similar, but far better-known. The gunfight at the O.K. Corral and all that," he said. "We had our share of outlaws, but none that caught the American imagination like Wyatt Earp and his brothers. Of course, Wyatt Earp wrote books that fostered the popular conception of the Old West."

"Ah, but Lily has the Gilded Lily," Jane said.

"And Tombstone has the Birdcage." He glanced her way. "But the Gilded Lily has never been closed. It's been an operating theater since it first opened. And while the Birdcage had its 'cages' or 'cribs' in balconies so its ladies of the night could entertain during performances, the Gilded Lily *pretended* to be a totally legitimate theater. The working ladies only entertained clients in their rooms upstairs — and that was to keep from losing clientele to the saloon and 'entertainment' center across the street. Of course, the Gilded Lily tried for a higher class of clientele," Sloan said.

She laughed softly. "Convenient where they placed the Old Jail. Right next to the Gilded Lily . . ."

"Within shouting distance," he agreed.

"And across the street from the saloon."

"Either way, you could walk prisoners into

47

a cell within a few hundred feet," he said. He glanced at her. "You're from Texas?"

"Yes," she said. "San Antonio," she added. "Though I did work with different agencies around the state until I joined Logan's Krewe."

"You always wanted to be an artist?" he asked.

She shrugged. "I was always drawing," she said.

They'd reached the sheriff's office. He pulled into the lot in front.

The office wasn't really that small — not when you considered the size of the town. The building had been constructed in the 1930s by someone who'd evidently been to Toledo, Spain, and fallen in love with the medieval architecture. There was a tower on either front corner, and the roof was tile while the exterior was brick. The parking lot held room for at least twenty cars — someone had been optimistic about the growth of Lily. To the left, where the offices were located, were a bank, a coffee house, a Mexican restaurant and an Italian restaurant. To the right was an Asian restaurant and a Brazilian steak house, along with the area's mall — an enclosure of about eight shops. Lily could proudly say that there were three national chain stores among them.

The biggest excitement in town had occurred when they'd acquired one of the country's largest burger chains, which had chosen to locate in the mall. Keeping offices in old adobe homes or the occasional professional building were a few lawyers, accountants, doctors and decorators. The high school was just half a mile back toward the old town.

"Not such a small place," she said cheerfully as he parked and they exited the car.

"Small enough that the skull should have been sent to a lab," Sloan murmured.

He realized that his antagonism toward her became apparent with his careless words when she made a barely perceptible movement, stiffening. She stood by the car, looking at him, and he saw the hardness that came into her eyes.

"I'm really proficient at what I do, Sheriff. You don't need to worry that my work will be lacking in any way."

He could have said something to try to smooth her ruffled feathers; he didn't. He just shrugged. "Since this isn't a new murder, I'm sure your work will be more than sufficient."

He felt the chill of her eyes. "Sheriff, I will certainly try very hard to do work that's sufficient."

He hadn't meant to make matters worse. On the other hand, he could hardly have been more rude. Once again, an explanation or an apology might seem lame, so he indicated the door and said, "That didn't come out the way I meant it. I'm sure you're excellent at what you do. Come in and meet the staff — all two of the rest of our day crew."

She turned, not waiting for him, and entered through the front door.

Deputy Betty Ivy was on duty at the desk when they came in. Again, someone had been overoptimistic about the growth of Lily. There were three offices for senior law officials, but since they only had six law officials all told — three on days, three at night, reduced to two at various hours to avoid overtime — one office was usually empty. Betty often manned the front desk during the day. Lamont Atkins, an easygoing man in his mid-forties who managed to maintain more control with a quiet voice than any swaggering might accomplish, also worked the day shift. Lamont started his day by touring around in town; he liked to show that the sheriff's department was ever-vigilant. Chet Morgan rounded out his day crew.

As they walked in, Jane Everett breezed

right up and introduced herself to Betty with professional charm before Sloan could make the introductions. From his office behind the entry, Chet Morgan rose and came out to join them by the front desk, grinning and friendly as he met Jane.

"We've set up the skull in the interrogation room," Betty said, standing. "I've got a scanner in there, camera connected to the computer, sketch pad . . . I've watched a few forensic programs, so I thought you might want to take a lot of pictures and do whatever you do to get that 3-D image thing going. I mean, the computer has a camera, but I wasn't sure how you'd move it around to get the right angles, so . . . well, anything you need, we'll do our best to get for you."

"That's perfect, thank you. Actually, more than perfect. I have my own instruments for measurements. I'll probably do what I call an imagination sketch today — just what I see from the skull," Jane told her. "It's late, and I've come in from the D.C. area, so I'm a little travel-weary. Tomorrow, I'll start with the measurements."

"I'm intrigued to see your work!" Betty said enthusiastically.

Betty was a good woman — and a good deputy. When he'd come back to Lily, Sloan had been surprised that she hadn't wanted the job of sheriff herself. A widow with two grown children, she'd worked for the department most of her adult life. But she hadn't wanted the responsibility of being sheriff. She had iron-gray hair, cheerful blue eyes and a way of handling the occasional drunk or kid working on a misspent youth with unshakeable stoicism and a calm demeanor. She had the ability to convince both drunks and adolescents that they weren't going anywhere — they'd pay the price for their transgressions before a judge and no fast-talking lawyer was getting them out of the clink that night. Sloan had told her that being sheriff of Lily wasn't really a matter of heavy responsibility but Betty had said, "Oh, Sloan, small towns can still have big problems. I like being a deputy. You run for sheriff. I'll vote for you!"

"Ms. Everett — Agent Everett!" Chet said, quickly correcting himself. "Anything you need, you let me know!"

Chet was only twenty-six. He was staring at Jane Everett as if Marilyn Monroe had risen from the grave and floated into their offices. He was as good and solid a deputy as Betty, just . . . young. Tall, a bit awkward, Chet had served in the military as a sharpshooter before returning to Lily — and a parade in his honor. Lily was small; the return of a serviceman was an occasion to be celebrated.

"Agent, come with me, if you will," Sloan said. "I'll show you your workroom. And the skull."

"Well, show her the kitchen and where to find coffee, too, huh?" Betty said, frowning at Sloan before turning to smile at Jane again. "We've got sodas, coffee, snacks, you name it. Kitchen's the first door on the left down that hall and you help yourself to anything. Oh, and you have an intercom in there. If you need me for anything, just push the button and call me."

Jane thanked Betty and Chet and followed Sloan down the hall. He opened the door to Interrogation Room A. They also had Interrogation Rooms B and C, but they'd never actually used A to interrogate anyone, much less B or C.

He opened the door and turned on the lights. There was a desk with a computer and they'd also set up a graphic arts easel with a large sketch pad for their guest. As she'd said, Betty had supplied their guest with a camera, computer, scanner, tracing paper, "tissue markers," wire and mortician's wax. The skull itself had been set in the middle of a conference table in the center of the room; it was on a stand, minus the wig and with a few adjustments. Sloan hadn't known much about reconstructing a lifelike image from a skull, but Betty had done some research and had some help from a professor friend in Tucson. The skull had been angled to the best of the professor's ability at a "Frankfurt plane," or the anatomical position of the skull as it naturally sat on the body.

The jawbone, disarticulated, lay in front of it, just as it had when it was found.

Jane seemed to have eyes for nothing but the skull. She walked right up to it, studied it for a moment and then picked up the jaw, testing the jagged lines that connected it.

"The M.E. was right," she murmured. "It's very old." She glanced at Sloan. "If this was someone who'd died more recently, the structure would have more integrity. The years gone by create these soft spots. If you pressed too hard along one of these lines, it could just fall apart. I would agree that it's the skull of a woman — probably in her late twenties or early thirties, judging by the fusion of the bones. She took good care of her teeth, since there's very little decay."

For a moment, she closed her eyes. She seemed to be in a trance; she looked like a medium standing there, as if she could communicate with the bone.

Irritated, he cleared his throat.

"Can I get you anything?" he asked her.

She turned to look at him, and she seemed equally irritated. "Sheriff, you are, after all, the *sheriff*. A very busy man. I'm sure I can find my own way around the office. I'll help myself to coffee . . . if you don't mind."

"We change to the night crew at five," he told her. "Please wrap up your work for the day by then. I'll get you back to the Gilded Lily and then pick you up in the morning, about 8:00 a.m. — if that works for you."

She nodded. "Yes, that's fine."

He left her and returned to his office, the one directly behind Betty's desk. There were several folders waiting for him. He picked up the first — the arrest report for Arty Johnson. Arty was an old-timer with a penchant for drinking too much. He'd wind up banned from the Gilded Lily and the saloon, but he was really a decent guy, and he'd quickly work his way back into the good graces of the management. Last week, Arty had gotten a little carried away and joined the cast onstage at the Gilded Lily. Henri Coque, incensed at the time, had demanded that he be arrested. Arty had slept it off in one of the five cells, and then Sloan had driven him home. Arty had rued his behavior all the way.

He set the file aside. Hopefully, Henri wouldn't press charges.

He picked up the next file, shaking his head. Jimmy Hough, local high-school senior and football star, was in the cells now. His father owned a beefalo farm; the meat hadn't become as popular in the east as they'd expected, but Caleb Hough still made a fortune selling his hybrid meat. Jimmy had taken his father's Maserati out for a spin and crashed into Connie Larson's Honda. When he was picked up, he'd been as high as a kite — not even Lily, Arizona, escaped the drugs that continued to ravage schools.

Logan decided this was a good time to type up reports.

An hour passed as he dealt with paperwork. Then he became aware of a commotion out front. He looked up. Caleb Hough was accosting Betty, reaming her out for putting his son's future at risk.

Sloan got up and went out to meet the big man. Caleb wore his wealth as if it were clothing. Maybe that was what happened to self-made men, at least in areas like this, where the population was sparse.

"Trent!" Hough bellowed as Sloan walked out. "You had the audacity to order your deputy McArthur to keep my kid in jail overnight. It was just a fender bender! Jimmy has a future — he's a star! He's being scouted by colleges across the country. If my boy has a record —"

"Hough, I had my deputy keep your boy in here when he was picked up because he was three sheets to the wind. I would think you'd want him learning something about accountability. No, he's not a bad kid, and I don't want to see him with a record. I didn't just throw him in and forget him, either. I asked Doc Levin in to check on him. I also had a good conversation with him and with Connie Larson. Jimmy didn't leave the scene, and he was concerned about hitting Connie. I kept him overnight because, for one, he needed to sober up. Two, he needed a lesson. I let him out this morning, since Connie doesn't want charges pressed and there were no witnesses, and I believe that he's a good kid. However . . . he knows I'm watching him now, even if you aren't. I warned him that if he takes one step in the wrong direction, I'll throw the book at him. He's charged with careless driving. Now, get the hell out of here before I charge *you* with something."

Hough scowled at him furiously. "Who do you think you're talking to? Who do you think you are, putting in your two cents on how to raise my boy?"

"He won't be a boy in a year, Caleb. He'll be of legal age — and if he doesn't learn his lessons now, he'll face some real problems."

"This isn't the end of this!" Hough warned him.

"Let's hope it is. For your son's sake," Sloan told him.

Hough seemed about to explode. But he turned on his heel and stalked out. Sloan followed him to the door and saw Jimmy Hough standing in front, looking as if he wanted to crawl into a hole. His father walked up to him and slammed the back of his head. Sloan reached for the door but felt Betty's hand on his arm.

"Let it go. The kid's okay. Maybe he'll survive the old man," she said quietly.

He nodded and went back to his office. Betty followed him. "He is pretty powerful, you know, with all his money. Maybe you don't want to be enemies."

"If money can buy this office, Betty, I don't want it," Sloan said.

"He's going to cause you trouble."

"I should have charged the kid with a DUI," Sloan muttered. "I didn't because Jimmy was so remorseful and no one was hurt — and because I figured he did deserve a second chance."

"And there were no witnesses," Betty reminded him. "And Connie's not going to file charges."

As they spoke, the door opened and he saw that Declan McCarthy, his senior-ranking night deputy, had arrived. It was time for the shift change.

He shoved his folders into a desk drawer, anxious to leave. "Let's call it a day, Betty. Declan is here."

Declan came in cheerfully. He'd started off working as an officer in Detroit. He frequently said that he found Lily, Arizona, to be like a little piece of hot, dry heaven.

Betty went out to report on the day, but there wasn't much. Sloan closed his computer and went to retrieve Jane Everett.

He knocked on the door before opening it. She was sitting in front of the easel and had just finished a drawing.

Sloan paused, staring at the rendering she'd done. It was only a sketch, but she'd done a remarkable job of capturing *life*. The woman on the page seemed vibrant — on the verge of speaking. Jane had her hair tucked in a bun, a few tendrils escaping to fall over her forehead. She wore a secretive smile as if she held some tidbit of information that she *might* be convinced to share with others.

The oddest thing was that he sensed something familiar about her. . . .

"Sheriff? Ready to go?" she asked briskly.

"That's her?" he asked. "You're already done?"

She shook her head. "No — well, yes and no. I attached the jaw and did some of the easier work. That's my preliminary, a bit of a guesstimate. This is what you might call a special science, because it's a combination of science and art. It's two-dimensional. You take photographs, feed them into the computer, fill in the tissue-depth approximations for race, age and sex and get a computer mock-up. In the sketch, I worked with images of the skull, using printouts and tracing paper, and this is what I came up with. Tomorrow, I'll start with the tissue markers — build in the most likely muscle and tissue depths measurements, and begin physically reconstructing. This is just my first imagining."

"That's pretty remarkable," he said. He couldn't take his eyes off the image she'd created. He gave himself a mental shake. "Yes, I'm ready when you are."

Jane picked up the coffee cup she'd apparently gotten from the kitchen, collected her bag and moved toward the door. She stopped. He was still in the doorway, he re-

60

alized, staring at the drawing she'd done, wondering why he felt he knew the woman in the drawing.

"Sheriff?"

He stepped aside. She exited the room ahead of him, and he heard water running as she washed her coffee mug. He was still gazing at her rendering of a woman's face.

He made himself turn away and leave.

Back in the front office, he introduced Jane to Declan McCarthy, Scotty Carter, the night man on the desk, and Vince Grainger. Now she'd met his entire department.

Once outside, he again opened her car door, before he walked around to his own.

They didn't speak. He didn't try to make small talk.

He couldn't dislodge the mental image he now had of a living, breathing woman.

Except that she was long dead.

And nothing remained of her except her skull.

2

The Gilded Lily's bar and restaurant was open for business when Sloan Trent dropped Jane off. The inner doors that had been locked earlier were now wide-open, and the slatted doors invited travelers to enter — just as they had for over a hundred years. Jane walked in, quickly noting there was no one around that she'd already met. She was assuming the actors she'd encountered that morning were getting into costume or makeup or perhaps finishing dinner somewhere else. In any event, she didn't recognize a single person in the bar.

A waitress in a prairie costume, her hair covered by a bonnet, greeted her as she came in. "Dinner, miss? Or did you just wish to sit at the bar?"

Jane smiled. "Neither. I'm going upstairs. I'm staying here for a few days."

"Oh!" The young woman smiled. "I'm Liz. You're the artist. Welcome. If you want

to eat, call down to the bar. We can run something up if you want privacy. And if not, well, come on down! I know you're here to work on a project, but you should take some time to see the place. Desert Diamonds across the street has great books and weird little treasures. The spa is terrific. The Old Jail is a neat place to stay — really scary. I live in town, but I rented a room there once. Oh, and you have to get down to the basement in the Gilded Lily. Henri took me through once." She paused and laughed. "They wouldn't need to do anything to set it up as a haunted attraction! They have old wig stands with painted and carved faces that can totally creep you out and a room filled with old film and theater stuff. Mannequins and wooden cutouts. Some of the mannequins were dressmakers' dummies. Some were theatrical displays and some were movie props. One of the directors in the 1950s had Hollywood connections and started collecting them."

"Sounds like a museum," Jane said.

"It could be!" Liz told her. "The theater is a treasure trove of history. And, honestly, the food here is good!"

"Thanks. I can't wait to see it all — and I'll be down in a bit."

"Great!"

Jane headed for the stairs. She needed a few minutes to gather her composure before returning into public again. There were times when federal agents didn't get along well with the local law and yet, in her experience, everyone just wanted a solution to the crime. She was surprised by the simmering hostility that seemed to lie beneath the sheriff's not-entirely-cordial exterior. So, he thought they should have packed up the skull and sent it off. Fine. Turned out it wasn't his call. The mayor had wanted to hang on to it.

On the other hand, she and Trent had Texas in common. It wasn't as if she hadn't dealt with a few rugged macho-man cowboy types in Texas, but Sloan Trent personified every aspect of that image. Physically *and* in his attitude and manner. He was six-three or so, broad-shouldered, with the kind of ruggedly sculpted face that instantly made him larger than life.

He didn't have to behave as though he'd been burdened with an adolescent.

Add to that the fact that he'd worked with Logan, so surely he knew that the Krewe units were *different*. That they were called in when it seemed a sixth sense, an awareness of the unusual, was needed. Even within their own branch of the FBI — although they were respected for their record of solving cases — they were often known as ghostbusters.

They could live with it. They knew that many of their fellow agents looked at them with a certain amount of awe, as well.

Maybe that was Sheriff Trent's problem. Maybe he thought she'd create an image and then insist on a séance or something to put their dead woman to rest.

Actually, the whole situation was annoying. Because, like it or not, she found him extremely attractive — and she worked with a lot of extremely attractive men. She gritted her teeth; she hated the fact that she was drawn to him and that, despite all common sense, she found him compelling on many levels.

Sexual among them.

"I won't be here that long!" she told herself. She was a federal agent with a good reputation. She wasn't naive and she wasn't going to accept unprofessional behavior from anyone, attractive or not.

When she entered her room and closed the door, she said aloud, "So, the sheriff is an ass. I've put up with worse."

She was startled when her hairbrush came flying out of the dressing room and nearly smacked her in the head.

65

Her regulation weapon was holstered and she instantly drew, flicking off the safety. She walked cautiously into the dressing room but there was no one there and nothing else was out of place. She walked into the bathroom, but again, saw nothing.

Returning to the bedroom, she holstered her weapon. "Interesting," she said aloud. "I assume you're Sage McCormick, although, of course, I could be wrong. If I said anything that offended you, I'm sorry. I'll keep my opinions to myself."

The room yielded nothing.

She kicked off her shoes, removed her jacket and holster and plopped down on the bed. It had been a long day of travel, since she'd started off at the crack of dawn, East Coast time. She was tired. She lay there for a few minutes with her eyes half-open, wary now of the room. But nothing else happened. Finally, she decided she wanted a shower, and if she was going to have a shower and get something to eat, she needed to rise before she fell asleep and found herself waking, starved, at three or four in the morning.

She placed her gun and holster in the bedside drawer, went through her closet for fresh clothing and hurried into the bathroom. The whirlpool was tempting, but it

would send her right to sleep and she had to switch time zones. Instead, she got into the shower and emerged ten minutes later, feeling nicely refreshed.

Still in the bathroom, she dried off, then wrapped the towel around herself and looked in the mirror. It was solidly misted from the steam. But as she picked up a face-cloth to clear it, she paused. An eerie sensation swept over her.

She wasn't alone.

And as she stood there, writing appeared in the mist.

BEWARE

She froze. She'd long accepted that there was a thin veil between life and death and that restless spirits could linger behind for any number of reasons. And yet, despite everything, despite every Krewe case she'd worked and those she'd been involved with for the San Antonio police, she still felt a moment's primal fear. Her heart thudded. Her breath caught.

The writing began again.

TRICKSTER

"Beware of a trickster," she said, exhaling as she did. "Who is the trickster?" she asked softly.

But, this time, she wasn't to be answered. "Talk to me, please. If there's something I should know . . ."

No more writing appeared in the mist on the mirror.

She didn't touch it. She brushed her teeth and looked again. Nothing more than the two words she'd already seen.

She left the bathroom, closing the door so the mist would remain awhile longer, and dressed in casual clothes for the evening to come. She debated staying in the room, but by the time she'd brushed her hair, the fog had cleared in the bathroom mirror and no other incidents had occurred.

Jane figured she'd go downstairs for dinner. She stood in the middle of the room. "I know you're here," she said. "If you have something to tell me, please do."

No objects flew, the air didn't grow cold, nothing happened at all.

And still, Jane was certain that she was being watched. And judged.

She made her way downstairs, and when she reached the lower level, she noticed that the velvet curtains were drawn and that laughter was coming from the theater section of the Gilded Lily. She turned and saw that there were still a few diners at the tables and a mix of locals and tourists at the bar; she assumed the locals were the men in work wear rather than the designer jeans and denim shirts or T-shirts and cutoffs the tourists tended to wear. Women, of course, were harder to peg. Several wore casual dresses and others were in pants or jeans and T-shirts.

She sat at a table that she thought must be in Liz's station, since she was delivering food to a family at a nearby table. She was right. As she studied the menu, Liz breezed by with a smile. "Hi, glad you came down! Okay," she said, lowering her voice, "I don't suggest the fish. We have farm-raised tilapia and it's kind of blah. Are you a vegetarian? We do a cheese and broccoli risotto that's absolutely delicious. But, hey, we're in meat country. The beefalo is pretty darned good, either as a steak or in a burger. And then, of course, there's Tex-Mex. We have excellent fajitas, tacos, burritos . . ."

"The risotto sounds great," Jane said.

"Oh, you are a vegetarian."

"No." Jane shook her head. "It just sounds good for tonight."

Liz was going to give her the full list of wine choices to complement her meal but Jane didn't think she wanted her perceptions dulled in the least that night. "I'll have an iced tea, thanks."

"Sure thing!" Liz said. "Be right back. Oh, take a peek at the show if you like — just slip through the curtain. We've all been told that you have free rein of the place and to make you as happy as we can."

"That's really nice. Thank you," Jane told her.

Liz grinned and hurried off, and Jane decided to check out the show. As she stepped through the divide in the curtain, she saw that there was a full house and moved to the side to hover in the background.

"Oh, no, oh, no! What shall I do, what shall I do?" Valerie Mystro was crying out as Jane entered. Valerie was tied to the train tracks on the stage, struggling against the ropes that held her there while a train whistle sounded in the background.

"I'm coming, my heart, I'm coming!" Cy Tyburn cried in return. He'd been tied to the old stagecoach across from the tracks.

"Save her! Save her!" someone from the audience called out enthusiastically.

Cy stopped and looked at the audience, arching his brows. "Well, duh!" he said, bringing a rise of laughter from the crowd.

Jane laughed herself as he tried to drag the stage-coach toward Valerie.

"The knife!" Valerie shrieked.

"The knife?" Cy asked.

"The one strapped to your ankle, idiot!"

70

someone yelled from the audience.

"Oh, yeah . . . yeah!" Cy said.

The play was ridiculous, Jane could see, but tremendous fun, and the audience seemed to love it. Cy cut himself loose, then ran over and freed Valerie as the audience urged him on.

Valerie spoke loving words of appreciation, while he gazed into her eyes adoringly. The two ran offstage together just as a train pulled out from behind the curtains. Alice, in full vamp mode, was standing in the front of the locomotive, hissing as she saw that she'd lost her victims. The audience booed her until she stepped down, played with them, telling them she was really a good girl caught in terrible circumstances. Then she launched into a musical number in which she told the audience why everyone should love a vamp. Watching, Jane smiled. It was a cute show, suitable for all ages. The physical humor had broad appeal and the sets were impressive.

She felt a tap on her shoulder. Liz had come in to get her.

"Take your time, but your food is on the table," she said cheerfully. "And," she whispered, "all hell breaks loose when the show lets out!"

Jane whispered a thank-you and watched

a few more minutes of the show. As Alice's musical number ended, Cy Tyburn, naive and innocent hero, came back on-stage. He tried to warn Alice about the evil machinations of the villain, Brian Highsmith, and Alice listened with wide-eyed adoration. They shared the number "You Make a Bad Girl Even Better at Being Badder."

It was clever, and Jane decided that the next night she'd make a point of seeing the whole show. She quietly left the theater and returned to her table. A metal cover had been placed over her plate to keep her meal warm and, as she lifted it, she glanced at the stairs.

A woman was standing on the upper landing, her hand resting on the stair rail. She was dressed in late-Victorian attire, in a dark green travel suit with a slight bustle and a tailored jacket over a high-buttoned blouse. A green hat was worn at an artistic angle, her dark hair neatly tied at her nape. Her facial structure was elegant, handsome. She stared down at Jane, and for a moment, Jane thought she was an employee who worked in the bar or food area — or perhaps sold tickets or souvenirs. But as she watched Jane, she raised her hand from the rail, adjusted a glove and slowly faded away, her eyes on Jane all the while.

"Maybe he's just clinging to history," Jane suggested.

"He's got a notion that he can create some kind of great romantic story that will make the theater and the town even more appealing. You know, hit up the travel sites and magazines and so on."

"Is that really such a bad thing?" Jane asked.

Liz delivered an iced tea to Sloan and he thanked her. "I don't know. I just think that there are labs better situated to deal with this."

"In my brief, I read that no one has any idea how the skull got where it was."

"That's right. Henri is always saying that one day he'll get all the 'treasures' in the basement organized. Some of the things down there really are priceless. Old cutouts for advertising and promo, dressmakers' dummies, mannequins — some are wire, some are wooden, some are cardboard. Some are junk and some are certainly collector's items. The problem is, it's such a hodgepodge, the actors seldom go down there. Now, the wigs are used, they hadn't been in about a year. What happened was that the show was about to open and Valerie's wig had been damaged, so she went to see what else they had down there

75

until it could be fixed. But . . . if she hadn't needed a wig, the skull could have sat there for weeks or months or who knows how much longer. They hadn't been touched in ages, so . . ."

"There was powder residue on it so I assume you tested for prints?" Jane asked. "Or was it just seen as an act of mischief — not really worth investigating — since no real crime was committed? At least, not a current crime."

"Mischief, but the kind of mischief that infuriated Henri. Yes, we tested for prints and found none. It had been wiped clean. I mean, there weren't even prints from way back when. Nothing at all. Someone wore gloves and knew enough to wipe it down."

"So, you're thinking maybe it was someone who'd been in law enforcement?" Jane asked skeptically.

He laughed. "No! I was thinking someone who's seen a cop or forensic show at some time during his or her life — and that's practically everyone. The woman's been dead for over a hundred years, so as you said, we're not looking at current crime. Also, Henri wants to exploit the skull — great for tourism. I also think he wants to know *who* it belonged to. That might help him figure out who put a wig on the skull, and he wants to know that so he can fire his or her ass."

"You believe whoever did it had to be an actor or crew member or Gilded Lily employee?"

"It's not like the place is locked up tight all the time. It's unlikely that anyone *not* associated with the theater would have wandered in with a skull in hand to hide it under a wig in the basement," he told her, shrugging. "So, yes, it had to be someone already here, someone trying to cause trouble."

"Someone like . . . a trickster," Jane murmured.

"A trickster?" Sloan asked, looking at her curiously. "Yes, I guess."

"Ah, beware tricksters."

"Pardon?"

"Nothing, just thinking out loud," she said. "It's hardly a good . . . joke when you consider that the skull once belonged to someone living and breathing."

"Maybe after so many years that didn't matter much to whoever put it there."

"Are you investigating?"

"We did investigate," Sloan replied. "Like I said, we dusted for prints. We checked out the basement area. Naturally, we did a thorough search. We wanted to make sure

77

there were no more bones down there. But whoever messed around with the skull wiped it clean, and prints in the basement would mean little because everyone goes down there from time to time. Not necessarily for a wig, but there are boxes of fabric, costumes pieces, props, you name it. So, other than me questioning the cast, crew and staff, there wasn't all that far we could go. Everyone here denied ever seeing the skull before."

"I guess you're at a dead end, if you'll forgive the pun. And I understand that Henri Coque might want to know who put the skull there."

"Everyone — other than the person who put it there, of course — wants to know who did it. Who the trickster, as you called him, might have been."

"Someone with a warped sense of humor, I guess."

Sloan frowned at her. "I'm surprised Logan let you come here. Don't you and your group usually deal with felonies, serial killers, major crime?"

"Yes."

"So how could he spare you?"

"I'm an artist. You needed an artist. If something major occurs, he'll call me back in. Frankly, I'm surprised myself. You don't want me here, for whatever reason, but you called Logan."

"I thought I explained that," he said, a little testily. "I know Logan. I trust him. If we *had* to have someone in here, I'd prefer to go with a professional sent by someone I know."

"Power struggle!" she teased.

"Not at all. Henri is a politician, I'm just a lawman. But I wanted it done right." He hesitated. "Henri wanted to call in a local artist who does landscapes, caricatures and the like. When I suggested calling a friend who could recommend a legitimate forensic artist, we came to a compromise."

"Ah," she said.

"So, I wound up with a member of Logan's own Krewe."

"So you did."

He didn't offer an opinion as to whether that was what he'd wanted or not. He knew Logan, so he had to know something about their Krewes. She'd already guessed as much. But he didn't ask the questions they usually got. Questions like "Aren't you known as the bureau's 'ghost-busters'?" Or "Shouldn't you be off chasing ghosts somewhere?" Or one of her personal favorites: "Did the ghost do it? Or was it the butler? Or the butler's ghost? Ha-ha!"

Yes, he had to realize that Krewe units were considered "special" or "specific."

But he didn't ask her another question. Liz arrived with his meal and they both began to eat, concentrating on their food. After a while, the silence grew awkward, even though there seemed to be an expectant quality in the very air between them. He was definitely way too attractive, and the sexual draw she felt toward him made her uneasy.

Jane felt that she had to speak. "You were close to Logan?" she asked.

"Logan didn't tell you anything about me?"

"Just that you were a friend he knew from Texas, and you needed a forensic artist here in Lily. He gave me a short brief on the situation, on the Gilded Lily and the town."

"We worked well together. I was with the police force in Houston. He was a Ranger, which, of course, you know. We met when we ended up combining forces to capture a spree killer who was making his way through the state," Sloan told her. "That was before Logan joined the bureau. But I take it you worked with him before then, too?"

"I did. I wasn't with any agency. I was brought in whenever a forensic artist was needed."

"So, when you were a little girl, you knew you wanted to grow up and do facial reconstructions for law enforcement?" he asked. There was a curl to his lip. He did have a sense of humor.

"I started off the usual way. I was into nudes," she said drily.

He gave her a full-fledged smile at that. "Sorry. I guess I did ask that rather caustically."

"I always drew, and I had a flair for faces. When I was in college, one of my professors was asked to help with a reconstruction on a burn victim. I was fascinated by his ability to take a skull and return it to life through the image he created. I didn't go right into forensics, though. I graduated, and then apprenticed on an anthropological dig in Mexico. And . . . well, Texas is a big state. I helped various departments fairly frequently. Logan was approached by a man named Jackson Crow, who managed the first Krewe, and I was called in. We worked a sad and gritty case in San Antonio, and next thing I knew, I was in the academy at Quantico."

"Life does take us along unexpected paths sometimes," he said. He sounded far more open than he'd been earlier in the day.

"You seemed disturbed by my sketch,"

81

she said.

He shrugged. "I can't put my finger on it, but your sketch reminded me of someone."

"At this point it's not really accurate, you know. It's just the way I work. Tomorrow, I'll have measurements, do a second sketch and begin to build up the face. With what we know and what we can guess, that should give us a better sense of a person's appearance. Some of it remains guesswork, of course, but you'll have more of a likeness when I'm done. But you *can't* know the woman. The skull is over a hundred years old. If it was from someone more recently dead, it wouldn't be as delicate."

"No, I haven't been around for a hundred-plus years," he said with a slight laugh.

"True, but I understand you've been in law enforcement for quite a while. Did you always want to be a cop?" she asked.

"Yep."

"You're from here. However, you started your career in Texas?"

"I went to Texas A & M University and then into the academy."

"You left Houston to come back here," she said.

"My parents died when I was a kid. I was raised by my grandfather. He was dying. I came home to be with him."

"I'm sorry."

"Thanks. He had a good life and lived well. Didn't deserve to die the way he did, but then no one does. The cancer was brutal."

"And you stayed here in Lily," she said.

He had a rueful smile that could almost be described as charming. "Well," he mused slowly. "I took the job of sheriff. Right now they'd be stretching to find someone to take my place. I have deputies who'll be up to it soon enough."

"Still . . . Houston, Texas. Lily, Arizona. You must've become accustomed to dealing with gangs, murder . . . you name it."

"Lily is a change," he agreed. "In a way, a damned nice change. Back in the very early days — the Civil War and after — you had a fair share of bar brawls, shoot-'em-ups and rancher-outlaw entanglements. Then, a decade or two after the war, there were men working the silver mines out in the caverns. Those were rough days. There was a sheriff way back — but no real sheriff's department, and the sheriff had to be an ex-outlaw himself to handle the trigger-happy gunfighters out here. Now, of course, we have our small-town department and the larger county department. The towns had their own sheriffs back then and county help

83

amounted to praying that the militia might be on hand or the regular military if things went really badly. But then the outlaw days pretty much petered out in the twenties. We had a few more modern bank-robber types pass through in the thirties. In the forties, when a lot of local men went off to war, the town almost closed down. Now . . ." He paused with a shrug. "Now, we get a few bar brawls, a few fender benders, occasionally a domestic situation. But Lily's a safe place. We have law-abiding citizens and tourists for the most part."

"So, you stay because you love Lily, you love the peace and tranquility or . . . ?"

"Or I burned out in Houston?" he asked her.

"I didn't say that."

"It's easy to burn out in Houston," he said mildly. "But no, I didn't burn out."

"If you were friends with Logan and worked with him, you were probably pretty intense as a cop," Jane said.

"Intense? I think it's a requirement. Anyway, I liked working in Houston. And I don't mind being the sheriff in Lily. There is a lot here that's good. I like the history, and the fact that my family's from this area. Anyway, who knows what the future will hold?"

The velvet curtains were drawn back by an usher as they spoke; people surged out of the theater area and into the bar.

"Time for me to go," Logan said, rising. He dug into his pocket and left a large bill on the table. "I'll pick you up in the morning. Eight-thirty? We have a car you can use while you're here if you want, but it's down at the sheriff's office."

"Thank you. I'll build up the skull tomorrow, get a more realistic look at measurements and have a more accurate image of soft-tissue depth, at least," she told him.

"Thanks," he said. "You should see the show while you're here."

"I did watch a few minutes of it before you arrived. It's really cute."

"Catch the haunted hayride, too."

"Sounds like fun. Maybe I will."

People were spilling out of the theater. He glanced at the crowd and grimaced. "Kind of a long day. I'm out of here. Good night."

"Good night."

He made a quick escape, and Jane soon realized why. It had been a full house and forty or fifty people were milling in the bar. It seemed a nice crowd; the show made people laugh and put them in a pleasant mood. Some people were going across the street to the saloon — too crowded at the

Gilded Lily. She could see that the theater was good for all the businesses in the area. It brought those who then stayed at the Old Jail or other local bed-and-breakfast places or hotels and it brought people to shop and visit restaurants and use the stables.

Liz came sailing by to ask her if she wanted anything else before the crowd got crazy. Jane said no.

"I told you, you're totally on the house," Liz said, looking at the money.

"Sloan left that."

"That man!" Liz groaned. "He always tips way too much. Well, Lily is his town, and he tries to make sure we all do well here. Wish he'd stay around!"

"You don't think he's going to stay in Lily?" Jane asked.

Liz shook her head. "No. Not forever, anyway. He's popular here. He's a man's man, you know?" She laughed. "He doesn't smoke, but I could've seen him as the Marlboro Man, sexy and rugged and good-looking. Don't you think?"

"He's a very attractive man," she replied, trying to sound noncommittal.

"Be still, my heart!" Liz said, and then laughed again. "Oh, well. You sure you don't want anything else — more tea, some coffee or maybe decaf?"

"No, no, I'm fine, thank you. I'm going to call it a night." She reached for her purse; her food might be free, but she wasn't letting a server work for nothing.

"Don't you *dare* leave money. Next time, you can give me a tip if you want. Sloan tipped enough for five tables," Liz told her. "Seriously, don't you put down a dime!"

Jane didn't want to insult the woman and she was afraid that insisting might just do so. "All right, thank you. But, please —"

"Next time!" Liz said.

Liz moved on, efficiently taking orders from the crowd now seeking chairs and bar stools.

Jane didn't see Henri Coque, Jennie or any of the actors yet — just the people who'd been in the audience. She headed for the stairs. She glanced around to see if the slightest hint of an apparition might appear; none did. She was convinced, however, that she'd seen the image of a woman there earlier.

The ghost in her room? The spirit of Sage McCormick?

And had Sage been busy in the bedroom while she was gone?

Jane turned the key in her lock, opened her door, flipped on the light and looked around. Nothing seemed to have changed in the room. "Hello," she said softly.

"Hey!"

The shout came from the hall. Startled, Jane swung around. Brian Highsmith was opening the door to the room beside hers. "You all right, Jane? Were you expecting to greet the resident ghost? If you're worried, I can check out the room for you."

Brian was serious; he seemed worried that she might be frightened, even though he knew she was an FBI agent.

"Just because you know how to use a gun," he said, walking down the hall toward her, "doesn't mean you might not be afraid of the theater's reputation."

"Brian, I'm pretty sure every old building has a reputation for being haunted."

"But this is *Lily.*"

"Yes, yes, it is."

He paused, looking a little disappointed. "You don't understand. This town . . . well, it saw a lot of violence. The whole place is haunted, inside and out. Are you positive you don't want me to check that there's nothing — no one — in your room?" He leaned against the wall, presenting her with a come-on smile. Was he trying to use this as a pickup line? Did he think she'd ask him to protect her, so he could offer to sleep by her side?

He was dark and handsome, and although he played the villain, he had a pretty-boy flair to him. She was disturbed to realize she was comparing him to Sloan Trent. Trent was far more seductive, even in his awkward courtesy when he'd pondered opening a door for her. She liked his looks, but she was still debating his reversal, from hostility to polite and genial conversation this evening. Well, he'd wanted a seat to have dinner. It could be as simple as that.

"Jane?"

"Oh, no, Brian, thanks. I had my door locked. I'll be fine."

"You're not afraid of ghosts?"

"Not tonight. I'm too tired."

"You really should take the haunted hayride trip tomorrow night," he advised. "You'll hear about all the ghosts haunting this town. Pretty scary."

It was the second time she'd been told she should try out that particular Lily attraction. Maybe she would. She'd enjoy learning more about the history of the town.

She smiled at Brian. He was young and earnest — if a bit too persistent. "And yet," she said, "you seem to be okay. As do the other actors."

"Well, we're not sleeping in *her* room," he said.

"I'll take my chances tonight."

"If you need me, just holler. I'll be here in a second," he assured her.

"I appreciate that," she told him. "But I'm quite tired. Traveling all day, you know. I'm sure the room is empty — and that I'll go right to sleep. A lot of people believe Sage ran away to Mexico, right? If so, she's not here."

"Okay, but don't forget. Just scream if you need me. Some people *don't* believe she ran off."

"I'll do that," she promised solemnly.

With a reluctant nod, he returned to his room down the hall as Jane entered hers and closed the door.

She'd much rather deal with a ghost than a young would-be lothario.

She leaned against the door for a moment, and then moved away, quickly turning to lock it.

Experience had taught her. The living were usually far more dangerous than the dead.

Usually . . .

3

Sloan's house wasn't but a mile down Main Street where it crossed Arizona Highway 101. Although it was in the countryside, it was also within walking distance of the Gilded Lily. Only two properties sat between him and the old town. One belonged to Silvia Mills — eighty-eight and spry — and the second belonged to Mike Addison, who now owned the old sheriff's office and jail bed-and-breakfast. Mike was seldom at his property; his ranch overseer was a good man of mixed Mexican, American and Indian descent, Barry Garcia. Neither Mike nor Silvia ever had any trouble at their properties.

Sloan's house was ranch-style and had been built in the 1860s, first as a one-room log structure, and then gradually, as the years had gone by, as a far larger home. The front door still opened into the main section of the house, a parlor with leather and wood furniture, Indian artifacts, a stone fireplace and a stone counter that separated it from the kitchen. Beyond that was a screened-in porch with a pool; to the left were two bedrooms and to the right was a master suite. It was a comfortable home and had always been in his family. Wherever he chose to go in the future, he'd hang on to the house. Johnny Bearclaw, an Apache who'd come to help his grandfather before Sloan made it home, still lived here. Johnny's wife had died of cancer and he had no children; running Sloan's property and working with the horses seemed to be a good life for him. He had an apartment above the barn, which was about an acre back on the land. He looked after the house and grounds and the two buckskin quarter horses Sloan kept, Kanga and Roo.

It was late. Sloan had been out far longer than he'd expected, not thinking he'd actually stop by the Gilded Lily for dinner. But as he'd driven through town from the sheriff's office, the theater had beckoned him — mainly because he was fascinated by their visiting artist.

And he did have to eat. That was a fact. He knew he'd been rude, so maybe taking a few minutes to be . . . not rude would be a smart idea. He reminded himself that Logan would never have sent him his own Krewe member if she weren't good. He'd gone to Logan because they both knew there were forces in the world that weren't obvious, that weren't necessarily *seen* by everyone. Logan had sent him Jane, therefore Jane was good.

It wasn't *good* that bothered him.

It was the fear that finding the skull was all some kind of catalyst, that something evil had begun — or come to the surface — when the skull was found. Dread had been building within him and he'd sensed it, felt it in the air, almost smelled it . . . but been unable to pin it down.

Maybe that was why he'd wanted the damned skull out of town!

They weren't dealing with a current tragedy, accident or murder. Whatever had happened to the living, breathing person they now sought to identify, it had happened way before they could make an arrest or bring any responsible party to justice. So why his concern?

He didn't know.

He walked into the kitchen and opened his refrigerator. For a moment he froze, brought to full attention as something plopped onto the counter next to him.

He refrained from pulling his gun and

smiled to himself, shaking his head.

"Cougar. Where were you? Sleeping on top of the fridge?"

He stroked the pitch-black cat with the huge gold eyes that sidled up to him.

"Sorry, how inconsiderate of me. I've eaten, you haven't. Hang on, okay?"

Sloan found the cat's bowl, which was shoved up against the cabinets beneath the sink, and filled it with cat food, then checked the automatic water dispenser he had for his pet. It was still almost full.

"You needed sustenance and that comes first. I was just going for a beer."

The cat meowed; he was darned loud for a cat. Very talkative. He'd found Sloan, rather than the other way around. One day, he'd been on the doorstep and Sloan had taken him in. The fliers he'd posted around town hadn't produced an owner, nor had the ad he'd placed in the paper. Cougar had become his. He was huge, maybe part Persian or Maine coon, and he deserved the name "Cougar."

Once the cat was cared for, Sloan pulled a beer from the refrigerator and went back to the parlor.

He eased into one of the two plush leather chairs that sat in front of the fire, although tonight he didn't have a fire going. He closed his eyes for a minute; when he opened them again, he saw that he wasn't alone.

The man who sat next to him was ageless. His hair was long and dark and barely graying. He wore jeans, a calico shirt and a cowboy hat. His facial structure was fine and proud, his expression stoic at all times.

It wasn't Johnny Bearclaw. Johnny never entered without knocking.

It was the "visitor" he'd first met when his grandfather was dying. Longman. In talking, he'd learned that Longman had ridden with Cochise and had been his great-great grandfather on his mother's side. He had come for his grandson, Sloan's grandfather — and to see that his great-great grandson learned how to help the living cross the great plain to the great lands beyond.

Only, when Sloan's grandfather had died and crossed the plain, Longman had not. He chose to remain behind and torment Sloan. At least that was how Sloan saw it.

He managed to keep from groaning out loud. He held his silence, waiting for the spirit of his ancestor to speak.

Longman didn't say anything for a while. He stared at the hearth as if a fire was crackling.

"Evening," Sloan said at last, raising his

95

beer to Longman, who nodded gravely, then continued to stare as if deep in thought, mesmerized by dancing flames that weren't there.

"An artist is doing a rendering of the woman whose skull was discovered up at the theater," Sloan began. "She's a very good artist." She was. "I don't know why, but I feel I've seen the woman in her drawing, and it bothers me. But that's impossible." He didn't add that he was bothered by Jane Everett, as well. She could be all business, and yet courteous at the same time. She'd clearly gone through all the right training. She was truly stunning and he had to admit he was attracted to her in a way that was definitely physical but much more. Maybe it had to do with how she moved and spoke, or the depth of passion and care that seemed to lie beneath the surface.

He was worried about her. Again, he didn't know why. She was no doubt proficient at protecting herself.

Longman looked at him. "And?" he asked.

"And . . . and that's it. Oh, there's the usual. Caleb Hough is acting like an idiot over his son being arrested. The kid is okay, though."

"But you're worried."

96

"Yeah, I'm worried." He didn't say that Hough wasn't his major concern at the moment; it was Jane Everett. Strip away the FBI appearance, the tailored business attire, and Jane Everett looked as if she could be a model for an elegant line of lingerie.

That didn't explain why he was afraid for her. In fact, there was no reason for anyone to be afraid in Lily. The town had kids who drank too much and a few adults, like Caleb Hough, who thought they were money kings. There weren't even any high school gangs in Lily and, for the most part, Native Americans, African Americans, Hispanics and old Euro-Americans — everyone — got along just fine.

Longman turned back to the hearth. "When you feel the wind, my boy, it means it is blowing from somewhere. Remember that. Too often, we forget that we need to pay heed to the sights and sounds that tease the air. If you feel wind, Sloan, then you must look for the storm, for surely it is coming."

"A storm? To Lily? When?" Sloan asked.

"A storm, a change, a shake-up. The ground is always quiet before the earth erupts. First, men feel a rumble, and if they don't heed the warning, they fall through the cracks."

Great. Really great. All he needed was a cryptic ancestor. Longman was on his mother's side. His dad's people had been a no-nonsense mix of English and Norwegian. But, of course, this land had been in his mother's family for generations. Longman was his mother's great-grandfather, and it was her father who'd raised him. This house was on old Apache land, it was natural, he supposed, that his last full-blooded Apache ancestor should come to his parlor to watch invisible flames.

Then, of course, his dad's family had its share of the unusual, as well. The bad, the good — and those who'd just disappeared into thin air.

As if reading his mind, the specter of his dead great-great grandfather looked at him thoughtfully. "You think you've seen the woman in the picture because you have. You've seen pictures of her many times — even old photographs. In fact, those pictures have been seen by everyone in Lily. You believe they found the skull of Sage McCormick, your father's great-grandmother."

Yes, it *had* been in his mind. Of course!

"You knew her?"

"I often saw her perform from the back of the theater. I was allowed in. We were tolerated in Lily — my people, I mean. When

98

the wars still raged and Native peoples were rounded up, many of us were part of the community here. I remember when Sage McCormick came to Lily. I remember her presence onstage. I remember her laughter, and that she was kind. I remember when she fell in love with your father's great-grandfather, and I remember her daughter, your father's grandmother, as she grew up."

"So that's it," Sloan said. "I knew the picture because I'd seen the woman Jane depicted dozens of times. She's my great-great grandmother. And I've avoided ac-knowledging this — because I never wanted to know how she died. It's the distant past now, but I guess the stories always made me want to believe she went to Mexico and lived happily ever after in a world where she could be herself." He sighed. "And if there *is* a ghost in her room at the Gilded Lily, I wanted to believe that it wasn't her — or that she returned there after her death. Does that make sense?"

There was no answer. Sloan looked over at the chair. Longman was gone.

Maybe he had never been there. Sloan didn't know. He had never known if he cre-ated spirits with whom he could earnestly debate the dilemmas in his own mind or if they actually existed.

But now . . .

Cougar, still in the kitchen, suddenly let out a screech. The cat was almost as good as a watchdog. Sloan jumped to his feet. He headed straight to the kitchen and saw that the cat was standing by the door to the screened-in porch, his back arched.

Sloan strode across to the door, set his hand at his waist over his gun, and yanked the door open.

No one there.

He looked out at the far stretches of his property. Sparse trees grew here and there, low and scraggly. His land stretched out in back until it came to a row of foothills that skirted the mesa where Lily was situated. To the left, he saw the stables and the paddocks, and all seemed quiet. A light burned upstairs in Johnny Bearclaw's apartment. He heard one of the horses whinny.

He had ten acres — a big enough spread if someone wanted to hide there.

He walked out to the stables, turning on lights as he entered. Kanga and Roo whinnied again as he approached their stalls, stepping up to the gates to receive attention. Sloan patted the horses, speaking to them softly. Kanga was almost twenty, and she was as friendly as a dog and loved human interaction. Roo was "the young un," at twelve. He was Kanga's only offspring, bred from Fierce Fire, an award-winning running quarter. Sloan wasn't much on rodeos, but occasionally he brought Roo out to show. He didn't enter competitions, but Roo could turn on a dime, and Sloan liked to let him strut his stuff now and then.

The horses didn't seem skittish. Then again, they did like human contact and Sloan had enough visitors out here that they wouldn't be skittish if they'd heard someone walking around the yard.

Maybe the cat had seen demons that haunted his feline mind.

As he stood by the stalls, his cell phone rang. He answered it quickly.

"Hey, you down there?" Johnny Bearclaw asked.

"Yeah, it's me, Johnny."

"You been there awhile?"

"No, I just came out. The cat was freaking out over some noise or other," Sloan said.

"I was about to come down," Johnny announced.

"You heard something?"

"It sounded as if the horses were a little restless. I'll be right there."

Sixty seconds didn't pass before Johnny came hurrying down the steps from the overhead apartment. He wasn't a tall man;

he stood maybe five-ten, but he was barrel chested and had broad shoulders and huge hands. Johnny could tenderly serve a dying man soup — or tackle the meanest bronco. His dark eyes were narrowed as he said, "Oddest thing. I just had the feeling someone was around. Strange as hell. Then heard Kanga there neighing and stomping. I saw the light spill out over the paddocks and called you. Does anything seem to be amiss?"

Sloan shook his head. "Let's take a look around for the hell of it, though."

"Could've been a coyote who thought better of it. 'Course, we don't have any chickens around here, anyway. A coyote would have figured that out pretty fast," Johnny said.

"We'll split up. I'll go east, and you take the west," Sloan told him.

Some brush on either side separated Sloan's property from his neighbors, but like him, his neighbors had paddocks and stables; they all put up picket fences in front of their homes, but they didn't bother with gates. No one cared if someone rode over someone else's land.

That meant there wasn't far to go and not many places to look.

Sloan met Johnny at the rear of the stables.

"If someone was snooping around, they're not here now," Johnny said. "My money is on a coyote."

"You're probably right." Sloan looked off into the night. Behind them, the foothills were purple in the moonlight.

" 'Course, if anyone *was* around here and they knew the place and wanted to disappear . . ." Johnny began.

"They could just head out back behind the hills," Sloan finished.

"Not much there now but desolation," Johnny said. "The old mine entrances were blown out with dynamite years ago."

"Coyote," Sloan said. "Thanks, Johnny. Get some sleep."

"Yeah, you, too, Sloan. Everything going all right?"

"Yep."

"That artist come in?"

"Yep."

"She any good?"

"Yes, very good. Well, see you tomorrow, Johnny."

"Hey, bring her on out. The horses could use some more exercise."

"Yeah, maybe," Sloan agreed.

He waved good-night to Johnny and returned to the house. He seldom set the alarm, but he did that night.

When he lay down to sleep, he felt a thump at the foot of the bed. He smiled. There was nothing unearthly about that thump; it was Cougar, settling down for the night.

He wondered why he still felt so disturbed. He'd probably had a hunch from the beginning that the skull might have belonged to Sage McCormick. The story had seemed off to him — women might leave their husbands, but from what he'd read about Sage, she wasn't the type to walk out on a child.

Still, she had been dead for a hundred years.

But, like Henri, he was concerned. Why had the skull shown up *now*? Where had it been?

And where was the rest of Sage McCormick?

He thought that when he slept he might be plagued with dreams of the late 1800s — dreams in which outlaws rode down Main Street in a cloud of dust and flying sagebrush. Or that he'd dream of the Gilded Lily, a dream in which Sage McCormick took the stage, belted out a musical number . . . and then demanded that he find the rest of her body.

He didn't dream anything of the kind.

Instead, he saw Longman seated cross-legged on the top of a sand-swept dune. Jane Everett stood next to him. She wasn't in her bureau suit; she wore a long white gown that might've been appropriate in the late 1800s or in a show . . . like *The Perils of Poor Little Paulina.* Her hair was flowing around her face and shoulders, caught in the same breeze that swept the white gown around her body. She was listening intently to Longman. Sloan wanted to tell her that Longman wasn't real, that he was a ghost or a figment of his — Sloan's — imagination. He was a small portion of all that had made up Sloan's past, a man he'd heard about from his family, one who was wise and careful and ready to face the world with his slow wisdom, whatever the world might bring.

Jane didn't know that, couldn't know it, and yet her features were both troubled and animated as the two conversed. She needed to find something out, and it seemed she believed Longman would help her.

She continued to stand next to Longman, heedless of herself, of her environment.

Sloan was mounted on Kanga, far below them, and as he watched, a shadow composed of desert sand began to sweep out of the earth and form a barrier between him and the other two, Jane and Longman. It grew darker as it rose in a frenzy — and it seemed to form the image of a man as it whirled closer and closer to where Longman sat and Jane stood. He shouted out in warning but they didn't hear him. He spurred Kanga, but no matter how hard he rode, the danger moved ahead of him. He had to reach them before the swirling dark shadow enveloped them. . . .

He woke with a start. He was sweating as he lay there, as if his physical exertion had been real.

Sloan looked around his darkened room. Nothing had changed. The cat, curled at his feet, stared at him with his wide eyes.

Sloan glanced at the clock on his bedside table and saw that only minutes had passed since he'd gone to bed. Wonderful — he was dreaming about a woman who'd come to town for a few days. Granted, the population here was small. But . . .

She would be an unusual and striking woman regardless of where she was. He would've found her intriguing and sensual, and his libido would have been piqued anywhere he might have met her. He just hadn't admitted it yet.

With a groan, he threw his head back on the pillow. He was dreaming about Jane

Everett. He would've expected a great dream about hot sex on a balmy beach. But no, he was dreaming about dark forces swirling around, ready to engulf them all.

It was going to be a long night.

As usual when she went online, Jane found herself browsing far longer than she'd intended. She discovered that she had a ton of email waiting for her.

One was from Logan. Everything okay out there?

Yes, fine. I'll finish up in a few more days, she typed. She went on to describe the town of Lily, and the people she'd met. She refrained from saying much about his friend, the sheriff. At the end she added, Anything on the rise? Do I need to be back sooner?

She shut down the computer; if there'd been an emergency, Logan would have called her.

She rose, stretched and looked around the room. Nothing in it had changed, nothing had moved and she hadn't heard even a creak in the old floorboards around her. The clock on the mantel told her she'd managed to spend several hours on the computer.

Too easy to do.

She stood and walked into the dressing room and then the bathroom.

The mirror was clear; no words remained, not even the hint of a smudge.

Jane slid out of her clothing and into a pair of pajamas that consisted of a tank top and loose trousers. She pulled the bedcovers down and noticed that a blanket lay on the trunk at the foot of the bed. It didn't seem cold in the room so she left it where it was. The bed stretched out invitingly. She hadn't lied when she'd told Brian how tired she was.

When she lay down to sleep, she hesitated for just a minute.

"Good night," she said softly. "And I apologize for anything I might have said about Sheriff Trent. He seems upset about what's going on. I believe he's a decent human being."

Once again, nothing moved or changed in the room. Jane closed her eyes and wondered if she'd stay awake all through the night, waiting to see if something was going to happen.

She tossed and turned and half woke in the wee hours of the morning, feeling a chill. She was too tired to actually get up and do anything about it. She thought about the blanket, but she couldn't make herself move.

Moments later, she felt warm again and

fell into a deep and peaceful sleep.

The alarm on her phone went off at 7:00 a.m.

She woke up. Light was filtering through the drapes and she lay there luxuriously for a few minutes, surprised that she'd slept so well.

Rising, she showered, brushed her teeth and dressed in a black pantsuit, a blue shirt, her holster and gun and jacket.

It wasn't until she picked up her computer bag and supply box that she looked back at the bed.

The blanket lay there, neatly stretched out over the bedspread. The blanket that had been on the trunk.

The blanket she hadn't reached for because she'd been too tired to move.

She *must* have moved. She must have retrieved it in her sleep.

But she hadn't.

She couldn't help shivering. Yes, even knowing that some remained behind in spirit when death had claimed their earthly forms, she could still feel that eerie sense of disquiet, of fear.

But she'd learned long ago to accept it.

And really . . .

What a nice gesture.

"Thank you," she said aloud. "Thank you

so much. I was cold, and you made me warm, and I had a great sleep."

There was no response, but she hadn't expected one. Yet as she walked to the door, a rush of cold air swept by her. If felt as if something, someone, was hurrying through the dressing room.

She started to follow. As she did, there was a knock at her door.

She glanced at her watch; she was late. Wonderful. Sheriff Trent had felt compelled to come up and make sure she was ready.

"Just a minute!" she called.

She followed the draft that had seemed to touch her and walked into the dressing room.

This time, there was no steam coming from the bathroom. She didn't need to go that far.

There was a message on the mirror at the dressing table. It was written in her lipstick; it looked as if it had been written in blood.

TELL THEM THE TRUTH

Puzzled rather than scared, she ignored the chill that seemed to touch her.

The truth about what?

"But I don't know the truth," she said.

She watched as the tube of lipstick she'd left out on the table began to float in the air and write out more letters.

YOU WILL
BEWARE
TRICKSTER

"Jane?" a woman's voice called from outside her room. So not Sloan, after all.

"Coming!" she said.

She hurried to open the door and found Alice Horton. In jeans, a tank top and sneakers — her hair scooped up into a ponytail — Alice looked way more like the girl next door than she did a wicked vamp. But, of course, she was an actress, and she seemed to be pretty good. She could probably play just about any character.

"Hey, Alice," she said. "How are you?"

"Fine, thanks. I thought I'd come up and get you. Jennie talked Sloan into having a cup of coffee, but he's getting a little restless," Alice told her.

"Thank you. I'm on my way. Give me one second."

Jane left the door open and went back for her purse and bag; she hesitated and dashed into the bathroom, anxious to see if there was another message.

There was.

HELP PLEASE HELP US

As he drove to the station, Sloan was smiling to himself. He didn't realize his passenger had noticed until she asked, "What's so amusing, Sheriff?"

He glanced her way quickly, glad of the dark glasses that hid his eyes.

"Oh, nothing."

"You're grinning from ear to ear," Jane said.

"I'm sorry. I won't do it anymore."

Jane let out a sigh of aggravation. "Come on, now you *have* to tell me what you were thinking. It's only fair!"

"First I should tell you I'm not rude or macho or politically incorrect — most of the time."

She laughed. "Okay, I believe you. But now I know there's a really politically incorrect thought running through your head, so you have to tell me."

"Uh, well . . . you're not what I was expecting. Not what I figured you'd, um, look like. Being a Krewe member and all . . ." His voice trailed off.

"Pardon?"

"Never mind!"

"No! Tell me!"

"You make me think of a TV show. Like those crime shows where the medical examiner is a beautiful woman who whispers gentle things to her corpses. You know, like, 'You poor, poor baby, what did they do to

you?' Or a crime show where the c   a
are dressed by Versace or some ot   a
signer."

She stared at him as if she were abo
explode.

"I didn't mean to be offensive, Ag
Everett. It was a compliment," he insist
"You're just — I mean, you must be a liti
aware that you're . . . beautiful."

She gazed at the road ahead, a slight smile
playing on her lips. "Well, that part of your
statement is quite charming, so thank you.
But I *don't* whisper sweet nothings to
corpses," she assured him. "And I only wish
I had a wardrobe by Versace."

He winced. "I'm sorry. I guess, even if we
know better — and I do — we all expect a
forensic artist to be an old man like Dr.
Bunsen Honeydew from the Muppets or . . .
I'm not helping myself here, am I?" he
asked.

"No."

"Let me try again. Agent Everett, you look
very nice today."

Her smile still teased at her lips as she
turned to him. "Hmm. Does that mean I
looked like hell yesterday?"

"No. I just . . . hey, sorry. I told you! I
shouldn't have said anything."

Her smile became an honest laugh. "It's

ll right. I prefer to avoid stereotypes — as
an artist and a law enforcement officer. But
you . . ."

"Me?"

"Yeah, Sheriff. You. Spend much time at
the rodeo? Or, wait — walking down Main
Street for a quick-draw contest with a bad
guy?"

"What?"

"Well, you know, you look the part. Rugged Western hero. Gunslinger. Tough guy."

He grinned. "So *I'm* a stereotype?"

"Oh, you definitely could be. But . . . are
you?"

He didn't have to answer; they'd arrived
at the sheriff's office. But even as he exited
the car, Deputy Chet Morgan came hurrying out of the office. "Heidi Murphy just
called, and she sounded pretty hysterical.
She took a group out on a trail ride and
they found a body."

"A body? Did she call 9-1-1 for an ambulance?" Sloan asked quickly.

"She did, and an ambulance is on its way
out. But Heidi was insistent that there's no
need. Says the corpse is practically mummified and that she knows dead from alive. I
was going to head out there."

"I'll take it, Chet. Why don't you hold
down the fort with Betty and Agent Ever-

ett," Sloan told him.

Mummified? Were remains from the past showing up all over the place?

"I'd like to ride with you on this, if you don't mind," Jane said.

She was wearing her sunglasses and her perfect face was stoic. Sloan thought of the dream that had plagued him the night before.

"It's better if you stay here, get your work done."

She didn't have an argument and she knew it as well as he did. She was a federal agent on loan, and a body in the desert was his territory. He'd be calling in the county coroner, and if someone had been killed recently, the state police would probably come in on it, too. But . . . she was a fed.

"Please. I understand. But I'd really like to ride along on this," she said.

He wished she hadn't been so polite, that the tone of her voice hadn't shown her complete respect for her position — and his.

The dream had been ridiculous. Brought on by the fact that he'd been back home too long without meeting a woman who really appealed to him. So, just because he was afraid for her, and because he was so attracted to her, he was about to be a jerk.

He checked himself. "Sure. If you wish. Chet, where are they?"

"They're by that replica Apache village. She was working with a second guide, Terence McCloud, and she's having him take the tour on back. She'll be waiting for you. And I'll warn you — she's freaking out. She didn't want to hang out by a corpse."

"I'm on my way."

He started back to the car without saying anything to Jane.

She followed him, slipping into the passenger seat as he held the door.

Once in the car, he turned to her. "This isn't just a ride-along. It really means *ride*. The trail area where Heidi found the corpse is out back from where my home is. We'll drive to my place and get the horses. You ride, don't you?"

He hoped she'd say no.

"Yes, I ride."

Of course she did.

He called Johnny Bearclaw as he drove, asking him to saddle Kanga and Roo.

"Kanga and Roo?" Jane asked as he rang off.

"I didn't name them," he said. "My grandfather got them from an old friend years ago. Kanga is a mare, Roo is her colt. They're good horses," he said briefly.

They *were* good horses. Despite that, over the years, one or the other of the two had lost a rider — they could turn so sharply. They never hurt anyone; riders just slid off.

He wondered if he was hoping she'd take a tumble . . . and not be able to come with him.

At his property, he walked around the house and straight to the stables, where Johnny had both horses saddled and ready to go.

Sloan introduced Johnny and Jane. They were cordial to each other, and Johnny smiled, honestly happy to meet Jane. She was easy and relaxed, and Sloan was forced to admit that he was the only one who seemed to be awkward with her.

She admired Kanga and Roo and, naturally, Johnny was pleased.

"We need to get moving," Sloan said. "I'll take Roo. Johnny, give Jane a hand up, will you?"

The horses were both seventeen hands tall. He swung up on Roo, leaving Jane to ride his beautiful grande dame. She tended to be a slightly smoother ride. Roo sometimes thought he was still a colt.

Jane politely accepted Johnny's hand but straddled Kanga with agility. She knew how to ride, just as she'd said.

He kneed Roo, and they started off at a long, smooth lope to the rear of his property and onto the trails beyond that led through the foothills. She followed easily at his pace. A half mile into the ride, through desert, rocks and scraggly brush, they connected with the standard trail the stables used for their rides.

They passed one of the entrances to the old silver mines, then the Old Trading Post set up by the stables, where no one actually worked but a few vending machines could be found, and finally reached the Apache village the stables had created as a halfway point on the ride. Although the Apache had never lived in this little array of tepees, they'd set up some placards that accurately described life for Natives of the area; they'd also been hired to fashion the tepees and fireplaces, drying racks and weapon stands that formed the village.

He saw Heidi sitting forlornly on a rock near the placard that gave a history of Geronimo. She held her horse's reins loosely and looked as if she was on the verge of tears.

"You're here! Thank God! Oh, Sloan, you're here!" she said, rising. Heidi was thirty-three, thin and athletic with short-cropped blond hair and dark brown eyes.

An excellent rider, she often borrowed Roo when she entered barrel-racing competitions. Although Sloan had no interest in being part of a rodeo, he didn't mind lending Heidi his horses. She was calm, assured and competent, not to mention friendly and garrulous — a great tour guide. She didn't own the stables or the tour company, but she did the managing and scheduling.

He dismounted, aware that Jane was doing the same behind him.

"Heidi, you called 9-1-1? Where's the body?"

"We're right in the middle of no-road-ville. I'm assuming the med techs are coming by horse-drawn wagon. But I told them — oh, they were being ridiculous. They kept telling me to try emergency procedures, artificial respiration. Sloan, he's dead. I mean, *dead.* I am not putting my lips on a corpse!"

"Heidi, they weren't here. Their job is to save lives," Sloan told her. "Where —"

"Over here, Sloan," she interrupted, walking around behind another pile of rocks. She glanced back at Jane. "Uh, hello."

"This is Agent Everett," Sloan said.

"Oh, hi, nice to meet you. You're the artist, right? You make faces out of skulls."

"Something like that," Jane said.

119

Sloan had reached the corpse. He stopped, staring at it incredulously.

As Heidi had reported, the corpse was just about mummified. Brown leathery skin stretched so tightly over the skull and bones that it seemed like an eerie caricature. A dusty old hat sat on the corpse, which was propped up against a rock almost as if he'd sat down to take a nap — and never awakened. He was dressed in dust-covered pants, an old shirt and a vest; it appeared that he'd been buried beneath the sand for years and dug up to sit on the trail.

"See! And they wanted me to do mouth-to-mouth resuscitation! Gross! He's — I mean, he's real, right?"

Sloan hunkered down to study the corpse more closely. Jane knelt beside him, studying the dead man in silence.

"The clothing is certainly old. Handmade, I think," Jane said. "I'm not an expert on this, but it does look like the cloth is incredibly fragile — almost disintegrating — and that this man has been dead for years. . . ."

Right. He might well have died around the time Sage McCormick disappeared — only to appear again in Lily as a skull more than a hundred years later. What the hell was going on here? Another macabre joke? Or were these dead showing up for a different reason?

"Who would do this?" Heidi demanded. "Who would dig up this poor guy and put him here? It's so creepy! I can't believe I stayed here waiting for you. I thought. . . I was so afraid he'd move. I never could have stayed if it was night!"

Sloan took a pen from his pocket and gingerly touched a darkened spot on the shirt. It was difficult to see clearly, but it seemed that the corpse had taken a slug in the chest.

"Poor fellow was shot a hell of a long time ago," Jane noted.

Sloan felt a vibration and heard the rumbling of the horse-drawn wagon as it arrived on the scene. Two emergency techs jumped out of the covered wagon that was kept at the stables for emergencies in the desert. They could also bring helicopters, but most often, the wagon made its way to the desert. He knew many of the county techs but not all, and he didn't know these two.

Sloan stood. The men approached, both of them staring at the corpse.

"Well," the older one said.

"I told you I couldn't revive him!" Heidi said.

"This is a waste of time for us," the younger man said. He looked at Sloan. "I'm sorry, I mean . . . well, this is unusual."

"Why did no one believe me when I said *dead, dead as a doornail*?" Heidi asked.

"Heidi, sometimes people think they've found a dead person when people are unconscious or in a coma. We always try to hope for life first," Sloan said. He introduced himself and Jane, and the med techs did the same.

"I don't know what protocol is here," the older man, who'd introduced himself as Gavin Bendle, said. "I get the feeling this guy's been dug up as some kind of a joke. I almost feel as if . . . we should just rebury him here. No muss, no fuss."

"I say bring him to the medical examiner's office. They can make the call there," Sloan said. "You've already got the wagon out. I'm sure historians and anthropologists will want to examine the corpse before . . . before he's reburied, I guess."

"This is *Lily,*" the younger man, Joe Rodriguez, murmured.

Sloan laughed. "Right. And the town has no morgue. Our dead go to the county."

"Can I go back?" Heidi asked hopefully.

No one answered her. They were all staring at the corpse.

"I'm afraid to try to move it," Joe admitted.

122

"Might break," Gavin agreed.

"Maybe we should get some kind of scientist out here," Joe said.

"Maybe I could go back?" Heidi asked again.

Sloan turned to Heidi. "Of course. I'll get a formal statement from you later."

"A formal statement?" Heidi repeated. "I took out a trail ride. I saw this corpse sitting here. I called it in. That's my formal statement."

"He's pointing," Jane said suddenly.

"What?" Sloan asked.

"See how his hand is lying there? It looks as if someone arranged him so his fingers are pointing . . . in that direction," she said.

She rose, walking in the direction in which the fingers pointed.

Sloan followed her. He didn't see anything at first. Neither did Jane. She seemed perplexed.

"He's *definitely* pointing this way," she said.

"The tepee," Sloan suggested. The tepee that stood a few feet from him was real; it just hadn't ever been lived in by an Apache. Sloan ducked down and entered. There were cold ashes where a central fire would have burned. Indian blankets were rolled against the sides, and old cooking utensils

123

had been set up as if ready for use.

It took a moment for his eyes to adjust. Then Sloan realized he was breathing in a scent he'd learned all too well over the years.

The scent of death.

He walked toward one of the blankets and tugged at it.

A corpse rolled out.

He felt Jane behind him. She didn't scream, but behind her, Heidi let out a terrified yelp. "Oh, my God! It's another dead man!"

Gavin and Joe came in behind her.

"No!" Heidi said. "Oh, God!"

"It's a fresh one," Gavin muttered.

And so it was.

They had an old corpse. . . .

Pointing the way to a new one.

What the hell was going on in Lily?

4

Sloan pulled out his penlight to examine the man and try to determine who he might be and how he'd died. He didn't want to disturb the corpse any more than he needed to, until the medical examiner arrived.

The corpse was dressed in dirty denim jeans and a cotton shirt. He was wearing work boots, and Sloan noted that his hands and nails were dirty, as if he'd been doing manual labor. He judged him to be about forty years of age, but he'd never seen him before. At first, the cause of death wasn't apparent. Then Sloan noted that the red on the blanket was deeper because of the blood that had escaped from a bullet hole in the back of the man's head. He dug into his pocket for the gloves he hadn't needed yet in Lily but carried anyway because of his days in Houston. He checked the man's pockets, but he wasn't carrying a wallet or any form of identification.

"You know him?" Jane asked.

"No."

Heidi was standing there, hyperventilating.

"Heidi, you don't need to be here. Gavin, can you and Joe take the old corpse back to town and over to the county morgue and then get a medical examiner out here for me — and a crime-scene unit? Jane, can you get Heidi back to the stables? You can use the patrol car to return to the office. Looks like I'll be out here for a few more hours."

Jane nodded. "Sure," she said. "Heidi?"

But Heidi didn't seem to hear.

"I knew him! I knew him. I knew him, oh, God, I knew him!" Heidi cried.

Sloan rose and took her by the shoulders. "Heidi, calm down." He led her out of the tepee. "Who is it?"

"Um, um . . . his name was Jay. Jay something. He stayed at the Old Jail the other night. He was alone. He came and took the trail ride. Alone. His name'll be on a form back at the stables. Everybody has to sign a form before they get on one of the horses. He was just a tourist, I'm pretty sure."

Gavin and Joe walked behind Sloan. "We'll get the old corpse back and send out the investigators," Joe said dully.

Sloan nodded. He was still looking at Heidi. "So you took him on a trail ride. The usual?"

"Um, it was three days ago. I took him on a night ride. No, wait. He went on two trail rides. He went during the day and then again at night. Oh, God, oh, God, oh, God . . ."

"Heidi, let's go back to the stables," Jane said. She glanced at Sloan, evidently realizing that the biggest help she could offer was taking Heidi off his hands. She put an arm around her. "Come on now. Are you going to be able to ride?"

"Her horse knows this trail and the way back to the stables better than I know my way around my own house," Sloan said.

"Call if you need me," Jane told him. "Heidi, come on."

Sloan watched her go, berating himself. He'd actually wanted her to be an incompetent rider; he guessed that for some reason he'd wanted her to do badly at something.

Now he was grateful. She was a well-trained federal agent. She also happened to be a beautiful one.

He walked over to where Gavin and Joe had managed to slide a board beneath their century-old mummified corpse and lift it into the wagon, apparently causing no harm to the remains.

"We'll get crews out here as fast as we can," Joe promised.

"I'll be here," Sloan said.

He watched as they crawled in the wagon and Joe picked up the reins. Jane helped Heidi onto her bay, mounted Kanga smoothly and turned to wave to him.

He lifted his hand. "Thank you," he said, though he doubted she could hear him.

But she nodded. He didn't hear her, either, but he thought she said, "See you tonight."

When they were gone, he returned to the area of the tepee. Unfortunately, they'd all done a lot of tracking around before they'd realized they had a current murder on their hands.

Sloan inspected the area carefully. In the end, he decided they hadn't messed up any tracks or caused the crime scene any real harm.

The dead man — Jay, whatever his last name might be — had been forced to his knees, Sloan surmised. He'd been shot, execution-style, right where he'd knelt. The blanket had soaked up most of the blood.

Why the hell would anyone take a casual tourist out to the desert and execute him?

"Because, son, he wasn't a casual tourist,"

he heard.

He turned around. Longman was with him. He seldom saw Longman except in his own house.

Sloan nodded.

"I will wait with you," Longman told him.

He smiled, glad that Longman hadn't decided to reveal himself to Heidi. Poor Heidi would've had a heart attack and he might have had another corpse on his hands.

"Thank you," he said. He pulled out his phone and called the office, telling Chet to get down to the stables and the Old Jail and find out everything he could about the dead man they knew only as Jay.

And then he waited.

Soon enough, he heard the whir of a copter.

He closed his eyes and remembered the strange feeling he'd had the day he'd gone to the Old Jail over the stolen wallets.

He remembered the change in the air.

The skull in the theater basement.

And he remembered his dream.

The dark cloud of evil wasn't coming his way.

It was already here.

Heidi might have been in shock for a few minutes, but riding back to the stables, she talked nonstop. "It's horrible. Just horrible. That poor man! Shot dead. He was nice — and he actually tipped after the ride. So he comes here on vacation and he winds up dead in the desert. That's so horrible. Oh, Lord, I thought an *old* corpse was horrible. A new one is so much worse. I wonder who the old corpse is? You know, not much happens in Lily. Seriously, thank God we're not *that* far from Tucson in one direction and Phoenix in the other, because we're pretty dead these days. Oh, God, not dead! That's not what I meant. I mean . . . there were all kinds of murders way back in the day. Right after the Civil War and into the era of all the cowboys and miners. Back then, I think it was a couple of killings a week. But that was the wild, wild west, you know?"

Jane knew. It was just that her own mind was racing and she was only half paying attention to Heidi, which didn't seem to matter.

"We had our famous outlaws — sheriffs, deputies *and* outlaws. Trey Hardy was the big one around here. He robbed banks after the Civil War. He was a Reb and when the war was over, his family had nothing, but he was like a Robin Hood — giving money and food to everyone around him. Except, of course, robbing banks is illegal. He was finally taken into custody by Sheriff Brendan Fogerty. Problem was, his deputy, Aaron Munson, *hated* Hardy — although I don't think he really knew him — and he murdered Hardy in his cell. But people *loved* Hardy, and they were furious, so they wound up lynching Aaron Munson right in front of the jail on Main Street. So Hardy's supposed to haunt his old jail cell, just like Munson's supposed to haunt the street. Oh! Wow! What if we found Trey Hardy's body? Or Munson's? No, wait, that can't be. They're buried up on Dead Horse Hill, in the graveyard there. Unless someone dug them up. But Hardy supposedly wore parts of an old Rebel cavalry lieutenant's uniform. And Munson . . . he'd probably be in a deputy's uniform. No, wait, maybe they didn't have them back then. . . ."

Jane could have turned to Heidi and said that, yes, ghosts seemed to be teeming in Lily, Arizona. And that was probably true, but what could the ghosts have to do with a man being shot in the desert? And what was the point of scaring Heidi even more than she already was?

"You're so calm!" Heidi said, admiration brimming in her eyes.

"Sad to say, I've seen a few corpses," Jane told her. *And sadder to say, I've had conver-*

sations with some.

"Nothing happens here — nothing! And now a skull, an old corpse *and* a new corpse!" Heidi marveled.

Thankfully, they reached the stables soon after that. And with almost perfect timing, her phone rang. It was Sloan; he'd called to make sure they'd gotten back without incident.

She assured him that they had. "Is there anything I can do?" she asked.

"A crime-scene unit is out here, and I have Betty and Chet on finding out who our dead man is, where he came from and how he might've gotten himself shot in the desert," Sloan explained. "Our old corpse, as Heidi calls him, is on his way to the county morgue. If you're up to it, take the patrol car back to the station and work on the skull."

She smiled at that.

If she was up to it.

"I'm in town. I'll clean up, grab something to eat, then head over to your place to get the car and go back to the office. It's still early."

"Sure. Like I said, I have a car for you. It's at the office, so once you're there, you can leave whenever you want. I'll give Johnny Bearclaw a call and tell him you'll need my backup keys. Oh, and thank you for dealing with Heidi."

"No problem. She was traumatized. I can well imagine. I remember the first time I saw a corpse. Don't you remember what it was like?"

He was quiet a minute. "There've been so many now. Anyway, thanks."

His voice seemed to wrap around her. Impatiently she gritted her teeth as they ended the call. It was better to think of him as a jerk. She didn't need a one-night affair with cowboy.

Or maybe she did. Work had consumed her since the Krewe had come together. She'd had a life. Once.

She shook her head. They were dealing with the dead — not just the "old" dead, but the "new" dead.

And she was daydreaming about sex. . . .

She walked toward Heidi, who was watering her bay. "Heidi, can I leave Kanga here? I'll be back in an hour or so, then I'll ride her over to Sloan's."

"Sure. She'll be fine here," Heidi said.

"Thanks."

She left Heidi and walked across the street. The door to the theater was open, although it was still early. When she went in, she found Valerie Mystro behind the bar

133

making herself a cup of coffee at the espresso machine.

"Hey!" Valerie said, turning around and hurrying to the bar when she saw Jane. "I heard someone was murdered out in the desert. How horrible! I don't think I ever met the man, but I heard that he was here in town. That's so scary — almost as scary as finding the skull."

"How do you know all of this already? I just got back with Heidi."

"Oh, well, this is a small town, remember? I was across the street at the saloon earlier, having lunch with Alice and Brian. And the people who'd been on the ride came in and told us about the weird mummified man they'd seen. And then Terence came in because they were closing the stables for the rest of the day. And Chet — Sloan's deputy — had just been at the stables to get the information on the dead man. Seriously, Jane, this is a small town. If you sneeze, everyone knows about it."

"I see."

"It's so strange! I'm from Philadelphia. There's something going on there all the time. But when you're in a small place like this, well — it's different. And this is scary. Of course, in a way, the whole place is scary." She glanced around and lowered her

134

voice. "I don't know how you can stay in that room upstairs!"

"It's a nice room." She smiled. "I like staying there. In fact, I want to."

"But it's *haunted.* I know that for a fact."

"Oh?"

Valerie nodded with assurance. "I actually think Henri put you in there on purpose."

"Because he hoped he'd scare me?"

"I guess you don't scare easily, do you?" Valerie asked her. "But you *should* be scared."

"Why? What has this ghost done?"

Valerie was shocked. Her pretty face wrinkled in confusion. "Done? Well, it's a ghost, for one. But I tell you, people have run out of that room. They say Sage McCormick shows up in the middle of the night, looking at them. They wake up — and there she is, watching them sleep."

"She's never hurt anyone, has she?"

"Well . . . I'm sure she has. Indirectly. She makes them nervous wrecks and then they trip and fall and . . . People are weird! Some come here because they *want* to see her, but she scared the producer of a ghost show right out of here. And over at the Old Jail, Trey Hardy is still there, you know. He moves people's things around. And he just plain scares them, too!"

135

"But you're not afraid to stay at the theater?"

"No one died in my room or became overly attached to it." Valerie's eyes widened. "This is horrible timing. Silverfest is next weekend. The money it brings in helps keep the town going for the whole year."

"What happens at Silverfest?"

"Everyone dresses up in old frontier wear. We have a horse parade down Main Street, we perform all day and night as our characters. All the kids in town and half the adults dress up, too. And down by Sloan's property there's a rodeo. Oh, and we have a shootout on Main Street. It's fun, and brings in a ton of money." She paused. "Too bad it isn't Goldfest, but it's not, it's Silverfest. They found way more silver than they did gold. And there was the gold heist, so I guess we don't celebrate gold."

She suddenly seemed to remember her coffee. "Want some coffee? This machine is great. American, caffe latte, cappuccino and mochaccino!"

"Sure. Actually, I could use something to eat."

"Oh, that's right. Sloan came for you so early. We have a refrigerator with sandwich meat, if you want, or I'll run across the street with you. There's pizza, there's the

136

saloon —"

"A sandwich will be fine. I'm going to have to get back to work," Jane said.

"Let me make it for you. Salami, ham or turkey? And do you like cheese?"

While Valerie rummaged around under the bar, Alice joined them and then so did Brian and Ty, all talking about the two corpses.

A minute later, Henri Coque joined them, as well.

He didn't want a sandwich; he walked around the bar and poured himself a large Scotch.

"What the hell?" he said, gulping down the shot. "Who's digging up old corpses — and why? And why shoot a tourist?" He shook his head with disgust, then sighed. "I guess people can be ghoulish. Maybe these corpses will make us more popular this Silverfest. Let us pray!" He lifted his glass to the beautiful nineteenth-century, oval-framed portrait of a woman over the bar. "To you, my love! May we prosper, despite chaos! What is the world coming to here in Lily?"

"Or going back to?" Valerie asked, shivering.

Jane frowned and studied the painting. There was a sharp similarity between it and the sketch she'd drawn.

She frowned, looking at Henri.

"That's Sage McCormick?" she asked, but she already knew the answer.

"Our beautiful ghost!" he said reverently. "Yes, indeed, that is Sage McCormick!"

Jane studied the old painting. It portrayed the woman she'd seen on the landing. Sage McCormick had rich dark curls that surrounded her face. Her eyes were large and gray, framed by rich lashes. Her lips were generous and curled into a secretive smile. She did, indeed, have the look of a queen — a sweeping, emoting drama queen. And yet . . . there was something about her eyes. She would have done well in their modern world, Jane thought. She was a bit of a wild child, a rebel. A woman before her time.

"Ah, Sage! Bless this place!" Henri said, overemoting himself. "May you help us prosper, indeed, because we cannot let this theater fail, can we?"

"At least it's a slow week," Dr. Arthur Cuthbert, one of the county medical examiners, told Sloan. "I have a died-at-home-alone octogenarian on my schedule and that's it. I can keep the old fellow on ice awhile longer. My diener — assistant — is just cleaning up our tourist, Mr. —" he paused, checking his

138

notes "— Mr. Jay Berman. However, I'm willing to bet he died from a .45 caliber to the back of the head."

"Looks likely," Sloan said. He hadn't worked with Cuthbert before, and he wasn't sure of a medical examiner who made quick suppositions. What seemed obvious . . . Well, things weren't always what they seemed. He might be judging too hastily, though, he told himself.

Whoa, there, Sloan. Getting testy these days.

However, Detective Liam Newsome with the county joined him at the autopsy. He'd arrived at the crime scene when the forensic units were finishing up. Newsome was a decent cop, an oddly thin little man with sharp eyes and a sharper mind. They'd worked a hit-and-run on the town line when Sloan had first returned to Lily.

When the three of them headed into the autopsy, Sloan's opinion of Cuthbert began to change. Cuthbert was precise, speaking to him and Detective Newsome and into a recorder all the while. Their dead man, Berman, had been approximately five-eleven and two hundred pounds. He had suffered no defensive wounds, which seemed consistent with the fact that he'd probably been kneeling. His attacker had likely walked behind him and pulled the trigger almost point-blank, judging by the powder burns. When he was done with the initial work, Cuthbert told Sloan he'd have the stomach contents analyzed, which would help narrow down the time of death. His informed guess was between two and four in the morning. When the lab reports came back, he'd send all the information to both Sloan and Liam at their respective departments.

"So, our tourist came to Lily and was shot execution-style," Newsome said as they exited the morgue together. "You ever seen anything like that before?"

"Not in Lily." Sloan had seen the style of killing, but that had been when he was dealing with known drug lords and their minions and in a big city rather than a little town where it seemed everyone knew everyone. Even the tourists. He pulled out his phone, looking at the information Betty had sent. "My deputies traced his identity — he'd given the management his credit card at the Old Jail and at the stables — and they've been checking his movements since he got to town. He's from New York. Flew out to Tucson and drove to Lily late last week after picking up a rental car at the airport. He said he was on his own and just loved all the stories he'd heard about the Old West.

He went to the show one night and took a couple tours with the stables. That's all I've got at the moment. Appears he was friendly with everyone he met and seemed like a regular guy on vacation. I'll start making further inquiries, try to find out if anyone got anything more from him."

Newsome nodded. "I'll work on the home angle. Maybe he was running from New York. Maybe his killer was never in Lily. Any word on the rental car?"

"No. Betty called the rental agency. No tracking device on his car. It was a new Nissan XTerra. Silver-gray." Sloan looked down at the page and gave Newsome the license number.

"I'll get a trace on it," Newsome said.

Sloan nodded. "I'll start with our locals."

"We'll see if he had family or friends — *acquaintances* — in New York who might've known if he had a different reason for coming out here. You had any trouble with drugs lately?"

"No more than the usual. Kids, mostly," Sloan told him.

The two parted ways at the morgue. Sloan headed back to his office, stopping at Old Town first.

Mike Addison was at the desk in the Old Jail. He already knew about everything that

141

had happened in the desert.

The fact that news traveled like wildfire in a small town had its good points; he didn't have to explain what he needed to know.

"Sloan, don't it just beat all?" Mike asked him. "I'm so sorry to hear about this. That Jay seemed like an all-right guy."

"Tell me about him, Mike. Tell me everything he said and did while he was here."

"Hell, I don't room with my guests!" Mike said. "He checked in, and he talked to me about things to do in town. I told him to see the show and take tours from the stables. If he didn't ride, he could do the haunted hayride at night. He was really a nice guy."

"Why was he out here on his own?"

"Said he was a history buff, that he'd read all about Arizona and Lily."

"Where did he stay?" Sloan asked. "Which room?"

"Well, you can imagine. A guy like that."

Sloan prayed for patience. "Mike, I don't want to imagine. Just tell me which room he stayed in."

"The Trey Hardy cell. He was the guest in that cell right before the young couple who lost their wallets."

"And he checked out?"

Mike nodded. "Let's see. It's Tuesday now. . . . He came in last Tuesday night,

142

checked out Thursday morning. Our young couple got here Friday afternoon — and, well, you know about Saturday. Their wallets disappeared, they freaked out and left that day after you found the wallets. No one stayed there on Saturday night. They were supposed to be there another few days. I have it booked again starting Thursday night. Everything in and near town is booked as of Thursday. The Silverfest activities start on Friday, so folks will be coming in big numbers."

"Let me have the key, Mike. I want to take another look in there."

"Here you go!" Mike handed him the key.

Sloan went to the Trey Hardy cell. Nothing looked any different than it had when he'd been in there a few days ago to search for the wallets that had "disappeared."

He sat on the bed. Mike's housekeeping staff was good; the cell was immaculate. He wasn't sure what he thought he'd find in the cell but he began to go through the drawers. They were empty — except for a King James version of the Bible.

He sat back down on the bed, wondering what Jay Berman could have been up to that had gotten him executed out in the desert.

It was while he was sitting there that the door to the tiny bathroom suddenly flew open. "So, Hardy, there *is* something I'm missing, huh?" he asked.

He figured that one day the ghost would actually make an appearance. He never knew if he imagined the vague image he sometimes saw or if it was real. Longman always appeared as a solid entity to him. He'd never been sure if he was crazy or not; he'd decided he'd consider himself functional, if crazy, and learn to live with what he either did or didn't see.

But now, it seemed that whether a ghost or his mind was suggesting it, he needed to investigate the small bathroom that had been built into the cell.

Shower, sink and toilet were almost on top of one another. The tile floor was clean and the wastebasket under the sink had been emptied. A mirror hung over the sink and a small cabinet, which had been nailed over the toilet, held the usual tiny containers of lotion, shampoo, conditioner and soap.

And a tissue box.

Sloan picked up the box. There were remnants of a piece of paper beneath it. Apparently, someone had set a note there to keep it from falling into the sink. Somehow, it had gotten damp and ripped, leaving behind the little corner of paper.

144

All that remained were a few blurred words. He frowned as he studied them.

DES DIA

It could only mean one place. Desert Diamonds. And it might not mean anything at all; Mike might have told Jay Berman that Desert Diamonds was where he could go to have pizza, coffee or buy souvenirs.

He looked into the mirror and froze. To his astonishment, he saw more than his own reflection there. For a moment, it was as if someone stood behind him, looking into the mirror, as well, meeting his eyes.

It was Trey Hardy, his plumed hat set jauntily on his head. He looked at Sloan grimly and nodded.

He didn't speak.

He disappeared, fading away until he was nothing but a memory.

Or a sure sign of insanity.

It was late in the day when Jane finally returned Kanga to Sloan's stable and took the patrol car back to the station. Betty was just about to leave.

"Jane!" she said, pausing to greet her before walking out. "How's the work going?"

"The work — oh, it's going very well."

"I wish I knew more about what you do!"

Betty said enthusiastically. "It's science *and* it's art!"

Jane smiled. "I'm lucky. I love my job. The form of the human skull shapes the face, but it's the soft tissue that really creates the unique appearance of each human being."

"How accurate can you be? When did people learn how to do this?" Betty asked.

"Pretty accurate. A lot is in the hands of the artist, especially where coloring comes into play, though nationality or ethnic background can often be determined by the skull. There was a French anatomist named Paul Broca who was the first to use scientific methods to create images of the living from the dead, showing the relationship between the bone and the soft parts. That was in the late 1800s," Jane told Betty. "This is probably more than you wanted to know, so stop me if I'm boring you."

"No, I'm fascinated. I didn't know any of this."

"Okay, you asked for it! Anyway, Broca defined the differences between different ethnic groups. Then there was a German anatomist, Hermann Welcker, who went on to measure the soft tissue in male cadavers and found nine 'median points' from which to work. All this was then enhanced by a Swiss anatomist, Wilhelm His, who worked with cadavers and used the nine median points and six lateral points to further the ability to re-create the appearance of life when nothing's left but bone. As you can tell, I love it. And thanks to technology, what we can do grows all the time. Scientists and artists have worked together through the years to identify remains when all other hope of identification is gone."

"That's really important," Betty said. She cocked her head to one side. "So, you're an artist. Are you an agent, too?"

"Yes, I'm an agent. Anyone in a Krewe — part of the FBI's behavioral sciences group — has to go through the academy."

"Good!" Betty said. "I love to see other women in law enforcement. Can you shoot?"

"Fairly decently, yes," Jane said.

That made Betty smile. "Well, you're a wonderful asset to have here. I'm sorry. We're usually a great place. And you got here for one of our very rare episodes of violence. Murder," she added softly.

"Bad things can happen anywhere. But that doesn't make the town bad."

Betty smiled again, obviously pleased at the compliment. "Yeah, you're right. Bad things — that's just life, huh? I'm so glad that you're enjoying your time here." She gave an easy shrug. "Well, I'm off. The night crew is on." She winked. "Not as good as the day crew, but they're okay."

Jane laughed, waving as Betty went to her car.

Jane put Sloan's keys in his desk, got the keys to the little Kia that had been rented for her use and then spent a few hours working with the soft-tissue markers on the skull. After about two hours, however, she felt she'd have to pick up again the next day. She was just too tired to concentrate and she didn't want to read a measurement wrong. True, the measurements were averages that had been determined through the years by many different anatomists and scientists. But every face was unique, something artists needed to remember as they worked, always letting the skull itself be the guide.

The problem now, of course, was that she was pretty sure she was looking at the earthly remains of Sage McCormick. Or part of them, at any rate. She'd seen the painting, and she'd seen her sketch. That was definitely going to influence her. But did that really matter? She'd done the two-dimensional drawing before she'd seen the painting above the bar and learned it was Sage McCormick.

She surveyed her work so far. Not much. The skull and markers by themselves did very little to form a human face.

Before leaving, she paused to look at the sketch she'd created the day before. The woman she'd depicted based on the skull had been beautiful. Of course, she'd given her the sparkle in her eyes and the look of friendly mischief that seemed to radiate from her smile.

Sage McCormick. It was the same expression she had in the painting. Maybe, Jane told herself, she'd been subconsciously aware of the painting when she'd checked in. But she didn't think so; she hadn't really seen it until she was sitting there today with Valerie and Henri.

Sloan Trent had seemed startled by the image — disturbed by it, even. But then, he'd seemed disturbed by Jane herself at the time, so she hadn't gotten an explanation from him.

She covered her work with a muslin cloth. She was almost done with it and would start the buildup with clay to produce muscle structure the following day. She left the interrogation room and walked to the front. Now that the sheriff's office had a murder to deal with, she doubted there'd be much interest in what she was doing.

Tired, Jane glanced at her watch and saw that it was past nine. When she reached the front office, she was pleasantly greeted by Scotty Carter, who was at the desk. He was the youngest of the crew here, she thought; he appeared to be about twenty-five, with a facial structure that suggested a Native American background.

"How are you doing, Agent Everett? If you need anything, you let us know, okay? We try not to interrupt you when we know you're working," he told her.

"I've been fine, thank you," she said, equally polite. "Did you hear from the sheriff?" she asked.

The deputy nodded. "He's in town now. Sloan won't be taking any time off now that we've had a murder here. Things like that don't happen in Lily very often. Well, I mean, it used to — the streets ran red with blood, as they say — but that was more than a century ago."

"Have you learned anything about the dead man?" she asked.

Scotty hesitated, looking up at her with dark brown eyes. "It's an ongoing murder investigation, you know. Although," he added, frowning, "you are a federal agent. . . ."

Jane smiled. "Don't worry. You don't need

to tell me anything. I'll just ask how things are going when I see the sheriff."

"You got your car keys, right? You going to be okay getting around?"

"I'll be fine," she assured him.

Outside, the town seemed exceptionally quiet. The stars overhead had never looked brighter, but she realized that was partly because there was little air pollution. As she pulled onto the road to town, she thought that just as the stars had never looked brighter, the road had never seemed as dark. It wasn't a long drive, and as she neared town, the darkness seemed to break in a pool of misty light — all the light shimmering from the theater and the saloon and the curio store, Desert Diamonds. She parked behind the theater in the paved lot.

As she walked around to the dirt road in front, she heard laughter and conversation. Murder in Lily or not, the show, as shows traditionally must, had gone on.

It had apparently concluded, since there were people spilling out onto the street, on their way to the saloon or to Desert Diamonds for pizza. That afternoon she'd learned that the saloon stayed open until 1:00 a.m., while Desert Diamonds closed at eleven, staying open to catch the late-night snackers and souvenir-shoppers who might be leaving the theater.

Coming around the Old Jail, Jane paused. A man was standing in the road as people walked past and around him; he was staring at her. He wore a Confederate jacket, old-fashioned cotton trousers and a plumed cavalry hat. He had long curling hair beneath the hat, and she thought he might be an actor who'd come in to work with the theater ensemble.

But even as she returned his stare, she saw someone brush by without noticing him. Someone else passed by — walking right through him.

He wasn't real. Or he *was* real, just not really there.

She hurried toward him, sensing that he was curious about her — or curious about the fact that she'd seen him. But when she reached the street, he was gone, as if he'd been absorbed into the crowd.

Then she saw him enter Desert Diamonds. She followed.

That afternoon she'd grabbed a cold drink at the little pizza parlor in the front corner of the establishment but she hadn't taken time to explore because she'd wanted to bring Sloan's horse back to his stable and get to the sheriff's office.

Now she looked around. The coffee shop

was to the right, the pizza parlor to the left. The ice cream parlor was in back, and in between, she saw every kind of souvenir that could be imagined in an old frontier town. Kids' bow-and-arrow sets, badges, tour books, maps, stuffed toy horses, cows, bulls, buffalo, armadillos, snakes and more — filled the many shelves and covered the tables.

Jane started walking up and down the aisles, trying to figure out where her ghost had gone, but she didn't see him — just the endless supply of souvenirs. Shot glasses, mugs, cactus juice, hot sauce and kitchen utensils crowded one aisle. T-shirts, towels and spaghetti-strap dresses another. She'd gone down three rows when she was startled to run straight into Sloan.

He instinctively set his hands on her shoulders to steady her.

"Looking for a killer in the T-shirt section?" she asked, surprised that she felt a little awkward.

He raised his eyebrows. "You're shopping for shot glasses that say 'Lily, Arizona'?"

No, I followed a ghost, she thought.

Jane shook her head. "It's a curio shop. I was curious. And excuse me, but I was there when you found a corpse this morning. Sorry, two corpses. So, yes — I'm *really*

153

curious. What are you doing here?"

"Exploring the possibilities," he told her.

"Oh?"

He studied her face, then shrugged. "Look, it's late. I haven't eaten in a while —"

"Neither have I," she said flatly.

He had the grace to smile. "Well, ma'am," he said, exaggerating his drawl, "I just gotta get outta town for a while. I'm heading to my place. Come on out if you wish and I'll fill you in."

"Sure. I remember how to get there. It's pretty easy around here with only one road."

"I'll drive," he insisted.

"That's ridiculous! You'd have to come back here to drop me off."

"There *has* been a murder, you know," he reminded her.

"I'm a federal agent," she reminded him.

"You want to talk?" he asked. "If so, I drive."

She sighed. "Fine. Stay up all night driving me around."

He shrugged again. She saw that he had two books in his hands and he stopped by the clerk to pay for them before they left, assuring the clerk — who, of course, knew about the desert corpses — that they were on it, and he didn't believe anyone else was

154

in danger, but that, of course, they should all be careful and stay in groups to be safe.

"Seriously," he said when they were in his patrol car, "why were you prowling around the shop at this time of night?"

"I just finished work for the day."

He paused, frowning. "You went in to work on the skull after getting Heidi home, getting Kanga back to the stables and . . . and after this morning?"

"That's what I'm here for," she said lightly.

"Oh, yeah. I guess I forgot," he murmured.

"Out of sight, out of mind."

Gazing ahead at the road, he smiled at that.

"So why were you shopping for tourist books in your own town?" she asked him.

"Our victim."

"Oh?"

"Yep. I came in to see Grant Winston — the old guy who owns Desert Diamonds. Jay Berman, the victim in the desert, bought the same two books I've just purchased. Seems he was big on Lily's history. All he talked to anyone about was the old legends. Apparently, a few locals, including Caleb Hough, have been in buying the same books. Anyway, right now, I'm trying to learn whether Jay Berman was looking for something out here. Something the history or the old legends might help me figure out."

"I'm sure there are lots of legends — and a lot of pretty violent history," Jane said. "So far, I've heard about Sage McCormick. Who disappeared." She turned to face him. "And I'm also sure *you* think the sketch I did of our skull suggests it belonged to Sage McCormick."

His jaw tensed.

"Yes," he said after a moment.

"I don't understand. Why does that bother you so much?"

He let out a sigh. "I guess it shouldn't."

"But it does."

He glanced over at her. "Remember, Agent Everett, I'm a man from these here parts," he said, exaggerating his accent once again. "Sage McCormick was my great-great grandmother. Not that I knew her, or that my parents did. Call me sentimental, but I still don't like to think she might have been viciously murdered — and that her body is scattered all over the place!"

He swung his eyes back to the empty road, but he was aware of her shocked reaction. Which quickly turned into a nod of understanding.

"That explains a great deal," she murmured.

He didn't ask what.

5

It was difficult to believe he'd just met Jane Everett, or that it could be this easy to sit at his house with her, discussing the case. She'd spent a few minutes stroking Cougar and, naturally, the cat had reveled in the attention.

Johnny Bearclaw had left pulled pork in the oven and a salad in the refrigerator; there'd been plenty for two. When they'd finished cleaning up, they sat at the table together and he went on to tell her everything he knew about their victim.

"Jay Berman didn't have any relatives in New York. He took off from Oklahoma twenty years ago and never looked back. Both parents are dead now and his only family's estranged. He had no rap sheet in New York, but he didn't seem to have any friends, either, which makes me think he was lucky — he just never got caught. He worked part-time as a mechanic in a shop and lived in a studio up past Harlem. It's not possible to support yourself in New York City with only the money from a part-time job. No one that any of the New York authorities managed to track down seemed to know anything about him, so I suspect he moved in the underworld. Petty theft, that kind of thing. He had a legitimate Social Security number and paid taxes. But other than that . . ."

"So some guy who didn't have any friends in New York came on vacation to Lily, Arizona, and wound up being shot in the back of the head," Jane said thoughtfully. "Why?"

She was leafing through the books he'd purchased at Desert Diamonds.

"He was looking for something," Sloan said. "Okay, that's speculation on my part, but I'm willing to bet he was. And I'm trying to find out what."

"At Desert Diamonds?"

"These books are replica editions. *The Great Gold Heist* is actually a compilation by a historian in the 1890s who put together a book composed of newspaper reports on the disappearance of a stagecoach carrying gold — right around the time Sage disappeared. The second is written by Brendan Fogerty, the sheriff in the town when all this was going on. Certain incidents, although they occurred about the same time, weren't believed to be connected in any way."

"Still, it's interesting. Sage disappears, the gold disappears — and they weren't connected?"

"Sage disappeared two weeks before the gold did. And while she was known for her Bohemian lifestyle, she was never suspected of being a gold thief."

"I'm assuming people went out to look for the missing stagecoach?"

"They did. They never found the gold, the stagecoach and horses, the driver or the two armed guards hired to watch over it. No wreckage, no bodies — nothing," Sloan said.

"And Sage disappeared two weeks before," Jane repeated.

"Yes."

"What about the man she supposedly left with?"

"Red Marston?"

"Yes."

"Well, he was considered a shady character. But he disappeared — or took off — at the same time. He was apparently good-looking and he had the reputation of being a womanizer."

"Could they have hidden out for those two

weeks — waiting for the stagecoach to leave?" Jane asked.

"Sure. Anything could have happened. This was back in the 1870s. We have a few records, and plenty of oral legends. But they're pretty much supposition because people were making assumptions back then just as they do now."

Jane yawned. She seemed suddenly startled, looking out to the living room area.

He looked, too. Longman was in his chair by the fire.

Sloan glanced sharply at Jane, but she'd already returned to the book.

He felt something cold slip over him as he watched her.

Logan Raintree's unit was known for its *unusual* cases.

Did they really search for ghosts?

And find them?

She stood up. "I guess I should get back. Especially if we're going to be worth anything in the morning."

He didn't move; instead he frowned at her. "You see him, don't you?" he demanded. "It's true — you and your team do paranormal investigations!"

"We're a legitimate unit. We've gone through all the proper training, and we've been extremely effectual. And I'm damned good at what I do," she said defensively.

"You just saw Longman," Sloan said.

She was silent as she returned his stare.

"Longman?" she asked. Her voice was thin.

He shook his head. "All this time . . . I've wondered if he's in my mind. But you just saw him. Admit it."

She sighed. "Yes, I saw him." She turned around. "He's gone now. At least, I don't see him anymore."

"Why didn't you *say* you saw him?" Sloan asked her. "Before I brought it up?"

"How was I supposed to know *you* saw him?"

"He's real. I mean, he's a real ghost," Sloan said.

"Who is he?"

"One of my great-great grandfathers on my mother's side."

"Do you have any other great-great grand-parents hanging around?" she asked.

"Sage?"

"Sage."

Sloan sat down. "They say she haunts the old theater. I've never seen her. I've always thought that everything I've heard about Sage supposedly haunting the theater had to do with people acting crazy. They scare themselves silly. People think they hear

162

something or a shadow moves in the night — and they're out of there." His eyes narrowed. "Have *you* seen her?"

"I don't know for sure. I've seen . . . I've seen a woman standing on the stairs. At any rate, I thought she was there. And in my room . . . things do move." She smiled. "Actually, I think she might be there. I was angry, I went in and I said that the sheriff was an ass and —"

"You said I was an ass — out loud?" he broke in.

She raised one shoulder. "Sorry. Yes. You *had* acted like an ass. I mean, after all, you were Logan's friend, Logan sent me here and you were a jerk."

Sloan kept his expression noncommittal. "And then?"

"My brush flew at me."

He couldn't help smiling and he wondered if it could be true — that Sage McCormick was watching out for him.

"Do you have any special talents?" he asked Jane. "Can you make contact with her?"

She hesitated, looking at him. "Sloan, they *choose* to make contact with us. We can let them know we're open to it, but . . . I really have to get some sleep," she finished softly.

He nodded. "All right. Let me get you back."

"I could've just driven."

"A man's just been killed in this town. You shouldn't do anything to put yourself at risk."

"I can shoot. I'm not the best, but I'm pretty good."

He smiled, reaching for his keys. "I can shoot, too. But I plan on being extremely careful until we find out exactly what happened to Jay Berman."

He found it was difficult driving her back. Not the driving — the sitting next to her. He couldn't stop thinking about the fact that she'd seen Longman.

She had surely seen others. Including Sage. Maybe. She knew, she understood . . .

He wanted to keep a distance between them, build a wall that kept him from having to recognize how different that made them.

And yet he was equally drawn to Jane Everett. To her scent, the quickness of her smile, the incredible color of her eyes. Big mistake, he told himself. She was only here to create a likeness based on a skull.

Which now seemed moot. He knew they'd found Sage McCormick.

When they arrived at the theater, she

opened her door as he opened his. He waited as she came around the car to where he stood by the driver's seat. She didn't speak for a moment.

"Sloan . . . she wrote to me."

"What?"

"She wrote to me. Sage McCormick wrote to me."

"She sent you a letter?" he asked skeptically.

Jane shook her head. "No, I took a shower, and she wrote in the mist on the mirror. She said *beware* and *trickster.* And she wants me to tell you the truth about something, but I have no idea what. Maybe she wants you to know that it's her skull. She's been cryptic, to say the least."

"There was writing on your mirror — writing in the shower mist?"

"Yes."

"And you're sure it was Sage McCormick?"

"No, I'm not."

"Do you think someone came into your room? The . . . trickster, perhaps?"

"No, I don't. I'm careful about locking doors. I may not have come from law enforcement like some members of my team, but I learned a lot and saw a lot," she told him. "I'm very careful," she said again.

He was silent. It was strange to think that a woman who had become both famous and infamous could be sending messages from the grave.

Stranger still when he was related to her . . .

Was this real? Or were the Krewe of Hunter units a little unbalanced?

How could *he* ask that question when he talked to Longman, and when he'd finally seen Trey Hardy at the jail today?

He kept his voice level. "Well, see what else you can get her to say."

"It's not a joke, you know."

"I'm not joking."

"Fine," she said tersely. "I'll see you tomorrow."

"Yeah." Then he added, "Go right to the station, okay?"

Jane rolled her eyes. "Sloan, I hardly think this killer is going to wait for me to order pizza."

"Just take care. This killer will know you're an FBI agent," Sloan said.

She nodded, then turned and started to leave.

"Jane," he said, calling her back.

She paused, and he walked over to her. "Please, tell me whatever goes on, will you?"

"All right. If you share with me, too. This

166

is your town. You'll know what I don't."

She studied him with those gold eyes, and he felt the life in them. He wanted to reach out, to touch her. He wished that they'd met at a bowling alley, in a country bar . . . hell, online. He wished there hadn't been a murder and that they were talking about ghosts and solving mysteries because they both saw what others didn't.

He nodded. "Yes. I will . . . with you." He felt a rueful smile tug at his lips. "Even though you're just here as an artist."

She smiled slowly in return. "Good night, Sheriff," she said.

She left him then. He felt uneasy as he watched her go inside. The theater was safe, he told himself. There might be a few ghosts running around, but ghosts didn't shoot people. She was staying in a place with six actors, a theater "mother" and a director. Housekeepers arrived at the crack of dawn and bartenders didn't leave until just a few hours before the housekeeping staff showed up. She was safer here than . . . well, with him, really.

He returned to his car to make the drive back to his house.

It was late when he got home but he went out and checked on the horses and his property. Everything seemed to be in order.

When he went to bed, he was afraid he wouldn't sleep. When he began to sleep, he was afraid he'd dream. Something was happening in Lily. He'd sensed it the day he'd gone to the Old Jail in search of wallets. And now he felt it more strongly than ever.

There were a few hangers-on at the bar when Jane returned, but she didn't see any cast members she knew, and the waiters and waitresses had gone home for the night. She didn't know the young man behind the bar and she was actually glad; she was eager to escape to her room and get some sleep.

The theater seemed quiet as she walked up the stairs.

In her room, everything was as she'd left it. She washed her face, prepared for bed and curled up under the covers. She smiled in the darkness, thinking that at least she now understood why a brush had come flying at her.

She lay awake, wondering what could have happened in the past. Sage McCormick had married a local man, had a child with him — and been suspected of having an affair and running off with that man. Yet her husband had been in the bar below when she disappeared. It didn't make sense.

The fact remained: she *had* disappeared

and so had Red Marston.

And two weeks later, a stagecoach bearing gold had, too.

Now, Sage's skull had turned up in the basement of the theater, another man's body had been unearthed from the sand — and a tourist had been murdered. How did it all connect?

The questions whirled in her mind and, finally, she drifted off to sleep.

She didn't know what woke her; she only knew that she opened her eyes and saw a woman standing over her.

It was Sage. She knew her face now. She had drawn it, and she'd seen the similarities between her drawing and the painting over the bar.

"Hello," she said softly.

The woman straightened without speaking. She beckoned to Jane. Jane stood. Sage McCormick moved to the door.

Jane was dressed in a long cotton T-shirt gown. She wasn't sure whether she should dress quickly. She decided against it. She didn't want to lose the ghost, so she'd venture out barefoot and in a long T-shirt.

There was a chill in the air, and Jane shivered. It was about 4:00 a.m., she thought — just that time when the bartenders had finished cleaning and setting up for

169

the next day. They'd left and the housekeepers had yet to arrive. She wished she'd grabbed a sweater.

The ghost sailed along the upper level hallway, heading for the stairs. Jane followed her down the steps and then into the theater.

Sage McCormick walked down to the dimly lit stage, stepped onto it, then turned and waited. Jane continued to follow her.

Sage led her back to the stage wings and the dressing rooms beyond. Here, it was even darker, as there were only a few emergency lights left on during the night. She could barely see Sage, but the ghost was still leading her forward.

Jane hadn't been back here before; she had no idea where she was or where the ghost was trying to take her.

The apparition seemed to be upset, looking grim and agitated as she stood at a door. She floated through it and then reappeared, waiting for Jane.

Jane opened the door. It was one of the dressing rooms.

The ghost walked to the rear of the small, crowded room.

Jane wished her nightly specter had told her it was going to be so dark and that she'd need a flashlight. She couldn't understand what Sage was doing. There was a table covered with jars and tubes of makeup and several hanging racks filled with costumes. She had to push back the costumes to reach the place where Sage was standing. As she made her way through, her hair caught on a button and she had to untangle it.

She stopped where Sage was, almost on top of the dressing table. Because the ghost was insistent, she went down on her knees and inspected the floor.

At first, she saw nothing. Just old wood, so weathered that the planks seemed to blend into one another. Looking more closely, she realized that beneath the dressing table, there was something that wasn't quite right. She ran her fingers over the floor and under the table. What had appeared to be a dark spot shielded by the costume rack and the dressing table was a metal ring.

Made of tarnished bronze, it had probably been long hidden by the position of the rack and the dressing table. The latter had no doubt stood in place for decades; the feet had worn small indentations in the floor. She gave the table a shove, moving it just a couple of inches but revealing the brass ring more clearly — and an area that, when carefully traced, proved *not* to be a stretch of wood planking.

Jane looked up at the ghost, who nodded

171

gravely, and then back down at the loop. She slid her fingers over the flooring around it and saw that it had to be a knob or a pull and that it opened a trapdoor of some kind. She tugged at the metal ring but couldn't get it to give.

As she worked at it, she heard a noise from the bar area of the theater. She wasn't sure why it disturbed her; there were a number of other people in the building. The scraping sound had an odd, surreptitious quality. As she looked up at the ghost, the apparition of Sage McCormick faded away.

Jane didn't like being where she was. She hadn't dressed — and she hadn't brought her gun.

She held still for several more minutes and listened. Nothing. Then she was sure she heard a faint noise — as if something was being dragged across the floor.

Jane crept silently from the dressing room and tiptoed back to the wings, across the stage and down the side aisle until she reached the point where the red velvet curtains were drawn back. She stayed there, glad that her eyes had adjusted to the darkness and the pale glow of the emergency lights. She used the curtain as a shield and looked out to the dining room. No one was there.

172

Had she imagined it? All of it? The ghost who'd come to her room and the sound from the dining area?

No, she'd heard *something.*

Certain that whoever or whatever it was had gone, she stepped out. She moved quietly through the room, telling herself that perhaps someone had merely needed a glass of water. Or someone who couldn't sleep had come down to get a snack from the refrigerator behind the bar. She still felt uneasy. But a quick run through the bar and the dining room showed her that she was right. No one was there — not then, at any rate.

The kitchen was immediately behind the bar. There was a large oven in the center, two stoves on either side, two large refrigerators, a freezer and two workstations. All were clean and shining, waiting for the next day's business.

She left the kitchen and returned to the bar area. As she did, she heard someone fitting a key into the lock on the outer door.

The housekeeping staff was here.

She turned and raced up the stairs, slipping into her room just as the outer door opened.

She leaned against her own door, breathing hard.

Then she heard another door closing somewhere down the hallway.

Whose?

She couldn't tell. She went back to bed, hoping for a few more hours of sleep.

Sage did not come again that night. Jane closed her eyes and wondered what lay beneath the trapdoor in the dressing room. Tomorrow, she would tell Sloan what had happened. They would get Henri's permission to see what was beneath the floor.

It took a while for her to sleep, but at last she did.

She woke a few hours later and saw that it was 8:00 a.m. It wasn't as though she was on a schedule; she now had a car. She could drive herself down to the station. She supposed, with a sense of wry humor, that she didn't want to look like a slacker. She wanted Sheriff Sloan Trent's respect. *And she wanted him to like her. She liked him. She more than liked him.* She felt a sweet rush of fever when she was near him, the urge to reach over and stroke his hair, run her fingers down his cheek, explore the movement of his muscles. . . .

It had been years since she'd felt so attracted to a man. And now was not the time to feel this way. She loved her work. And she was here for just a short while. . . .

Crazy. This was crazy. Even time itself seemed crazy. Maybe that was it; she'd barely arrived and so much had already happened. Not only that, so much had happened between the two of them. . . .

She walked into the bathroom to start off with a shower. She stepped in, turning the water up to a nice hot level. She leaned against the tile, looking down — and stared incredulously.

Something red was mingling with the water and going down the drain.

Blood.

And it was coming from her feet.

Sloan rode Roo out to the replica Apache village along the trail.

Crime-scene tape still roped off the tepee where Jay Berman had been found. Sloan sank down and inspected the site; the crime-scene unit had been thorough. They were good at what they did, Sloan knew, so he didn't know what he could find. There certainly weren't going to be any useful prints, so he was really hoping, more than anything else, that he might figure out where Berman had been before his murder.

He rose, thinking about their present location and what was nearby. He wasn't even sure how the victim — and his killer — had gotten out here.

They'd probably ridden. He made a mental note to ask about Jay Berman's clothing, although the report would contain any of the information they needed on trace evidence. But if they *had* ridden here, had they come together?

Why come here at all?

There was nothing at the Apache village that could relate to the past; it had been created as an educational site. Yes, it had been created by Apaches, but that was only a few years ago. Before that, it had been a patch of sand with a few rocks and scrub and cacti.

He walked out of the tepee. Someone had dug up a body from the past — and murdered Berman. Why? Why leave the old body to be seen and Berman back in the tepee? To torment the police? Or someone else?

He stood outside looking around. Then he mounted Roo and rode around the village, studying his surroundings.

Not far back on the trail was the sealed entrance to an old silver mine. No one even knew where the one vein of gold had been found, and the silver had long ago run out.

Berman's killing, the nature of it, was something you might expect in a big city, where mob, drug and gang violence existed.

He'd been from the city. One of the biggest cities in the world.

Sloan rode back to the sealed entrance to the silver mine. Dismounting, he moved to the entrance. Years ago, to prevent the unwary from going inside to explore and dying in a cave-in, the entrance had been dynamited shut.

Walking over, he inspected it. At first, all the rocks in front seemed to be as solidly in place as ever. He continued to poke at them and test them.

At the far right of the rock pile, he found a loose boulder. He shifted it — and it rolled free.

He stared into the darkness, wondering if the rock had just worked its way loose with time or if someone had been using the cavern for illicit purposes.

But what?

Silver and gold were part of the past. Lily survived on tourism now. Ranches dotted the area, but everyone needed the tourists.

As he stood there, his phone rang. It was Jane.

He felt a rush of heat as he heard her voice.

"Hey, Sheriff, you coming into the office anytime soon?"

"Yeah, I'm coming in. I asked Betty to let you know I'd be late."

"You're out at the crime scene?"

"Yes."

"Anything?"

"Not directly." He hesitated. "Why?"

"I might have found something, but I'd rather not pursue it until I talk to you."

"Where are you? What did you find?"

"I'm at the station. And maybe nothing. I'll explain when I see you. Meanwhile, I thought I'd work while I waited."

"I'll be there soon."

He wedged the boulder back where it had been. He would need light to go farther into the old tunnel. He was rather fond of living, so he wasn't exploring until he had one of his deputies with him — and until his whole crew knew where he was and what he was doing.

Before mounting up, he looked around again. Someone was running around the desert with a gun and executing people. Well, only one so far, but that could be just the beginning . . .

He wasn't letting anyone take him that way.

Right now, he was damned certain that he was alone.

He rode home and took the car into the

station, anxious now to see Jane and learn what she had discovered.

No, he realized.

He was anxious to see her.

By the time Sloan arrived, Jane had placed half of her clay "muscle" strips over the wooden depth-marker pegs she'd attached to the skull. When she heard him come in, she covered the skull — remembering that it had belonged to his great-great grand-mother. He grimaced.

"I'm a sheriff. I can take it," he told her. But he didn't wait for her to move the cloth. "What did you find?" he asked.

She got up to close the door he'd left open.

"I saw Sage last night," she told him.

He looked at her and arched his brows slowly. She wondered if he thought she might have imagined a sighting — because last night they'd spoken about the dead they saw.

"I woke up because she was standing over me."

"That's what the supposed 'ghost expedition' guy said when he ran out," Sloan told her.

His voice was level. She still couldn't tell if he was skeptical.

179

"She led me out of the room. It was late, in between the bar closing and the day staff coming in," Jane said.

He was watching her with a deep frown but didn't say anything so she went on. "I followed her down to the theater and into one of the dressing rooms. She wanted me to see that there's a trapdoor in the flooring."

"And what was under the trapdoor?"

"I don't know. I couldn't budge it, and then . . . then I left because I thought I heard someone in the bar."

"Who was it?"

"There was no one there, and then I just ran back up to the bedroom because the staff was coming in."

"So, you want me to ask Henri Coque about opening the hatch in the dressing room," he said.

"Yes. I mean, I shouldn't even know it's there. I'm a guest. I have no business being in that part of the theater at all."

He nodded. "I guess I need a reason to prowl around the dressing rooms," he said.

"There's a little more. . . ."

"What's that?"

"When I woke up and showered . . . there was blood on my feet."

"You cut yourself?" he asked in a thick voice.

She shook her head. "No, I didn't have any cuts — not even a scratch. So, somewhere I walked, there was . . . blood. And when I heard those sounds, it was like something being dragged. But I didn't see anything at all, so I don't know if I imagined it. And I was in the kitchen, so it could've been blood from meat they used or . . ." She stopped, shaking her head again in disgust. "I'm not even sure it *was* blood. It had rinsed down the drain before I realized I'd tracked it in."

"All right. Let me call Newsome and check in with my deputies, then we'll head back to the theater," he said.

He left, and she figured she had about fifteen minutes so she could get another few strips placed on the skull. She went back to work and was concentrating so fully that she didn't hear him when he returned. He must have been watching her for a while.

"Muscles make the face," she murmured. "And soft tissue. The mouth is such a major part of a person's expression, but working with eyes and nose can give us a good idea of that person's appearance and demeanor. A skull can tell you about a person's health and development, too. The reconstruction

181

done on the skull of Robert the Bruce clearly showed the leprosy he suffered before his death. And the skull of King Midas revealed that he'd had his head bound as a child to create a longer vault — something considered noble or beautiful at the time." She dusted her hands on her work jacket and covered the skull again. She'd been rambling on about her work.

But, to her surprise, he didn't refer to anything she'd said.

"What you did was really dangerous," he told her instead.

"Pardon?"

"Last night. You took off in the middle of the night to follow a ghost. You were barefoot, so I'm assuming you were still in your pajamas. And you didn't bring your Glock."

She'd never mentioned that she carried a Glock, which she did — a Glock 23. A .40 caliber handgun with a magazine that allowed her seventeen bullets. He'd assumed it either because the Glock 23 was a common weapon among law enforcement personnel — or he hadn't assumed it at all; he'd seen it beneath her jacket. But he'd homed right in on what she'd done the night before.

"Sloan, there are a number of people in that building."

"And they were sound asleep. If they weren't, they should have been. The cast *seems* to be a decent group of people — but someone in there probably dug up that skull somewhere . . . and used a mummified dead man to point the way to a recent murder victim."

"I won't leave my room again without my weapon," she promised him.

He turned and left the room. She quickly threw on her coat and hurried into the kitchen to wash her hands.

As he drove, he was thoughtful. "So, you were in the shower, and you noticed blood going down the drain."

She nodded. "I thought I'd stepped on something and cut myself and hadn't realized it. But the blood wasn't mine." She glanced at him. "I suspect traces of it could be found. And the housekeeper is afraid of my room. I told her not to worry about it, just to bring me clean towels now and then. So, I must have tracked it into bed and . . ."

"And it'll be on the sheets," Sloan finished.

They neared town and he braked, sliding to the side of the road, surprising her. She looked into the yard where they'd stopped. A handsome young man in his late teens was helping an older woman into a house with groceries.

"I need just a minute." Sloan was frowning slightly as he surveyed the teen and the slim, gray-haired older woman.

"Certainly," she said.

Jane got out and stood by the car. The older woman had gone into the house; the young man had a bag in his arms.

"Jimmy," Sloan called.

"Hey, Sheriff," the teen said, waiting. He smiled at Jane and nodded politely.

"Giving a hand here, I see," Sloan said.

The teen blushed. "I, uh, came over here to apologize. I did hit Miss Larson's car the other night. I figured the least I could do was a bit of hauling around for her."

"Your father know you're here?" Sloan asked him.

Jimmy looked uncomfortable. "This was just something I felt I should do."

"Good," Sloan said.

The older woman came back out. She waved to Sloan. "Hello, Sheriff!"

"Hi, Connie. You take care."

"Yes, sir, thank you! Young Jimmy here helped me get in a week's worth of groceries. Tomorrow, a lot of mayhem will be coming down on us, what with Silverfest on our doorstep," she said cheerfully. "Now, I won't have to venture out into the crowds. I can

184

see the parades and such from my rooftop!"

"Great, Connie. Enjoy," Sloan said.

Jane lifted a hand and waved to her. She waved in return.

"Jimmy Hough," Sloan explained, getting back in the car. "Kid smacked the older woman's car with his dad's Maserati the other day. He's actually a decent kid — well, he'd been drinking and I'm not sure what else, but he leaped out of the car to run around and check on Connie Larson. I had him taken in for the night, and his father, Caleb, had a fit. He was in the office to threaten me. I would've thought he'd want Jimmy to learn a lesson — before he killed himself or someone else. I went easier than I could have on Jimmy, not because of his father, but because of him. Like I said, he's a decent kid and I honestly think he learned that you can't drive when you're impaired. I was really glad to see that, of his own voli-tion, he came over to Connie's place to see if he could help her."

Jane grinned. "So, the father is a blow-hard jerk. And the kid seems to be turning out okay, anyway."

"Yeah." He still seemed worried.

"What is it?" she asked.

He shrugged. "Believe it or not, I doubt his father would be pleased. Caleb Hough has a big beefalo ranch about a mile or so past my property. He's one of those people who feels entitled. He'd think his kid was a *pansy* — a word I've heard him use — for helping the woman just because he nicked what Caleb would call her 'shit' car.' "

She was quiet for a minute; she could tell he liked the kid — if not the father.

"He looks like he's about to graduate. He'll grow up and make his own decisions about the kind of man he wants to be."

Sloan nodded. A moment later, they pulled into town.

"What are we going to say to get into the dressing room?" Jane asked.

"You haven't figured it out?"

"No! This is your town, these are your friends. I waited for you because the plan was that *you'd* figure out how we'd get down there. I can't say a ghost led me!"

"Hmm. I was pretty sure the plan was to get me involved because you couldn't get it open last night."

"With time, I could've managed. You're missing the point — on purpose, I suspect." She glared at him. "So *do* you have a plan?"

His grin deepened. She felt a sizzle of fire; he really could assault the senses with that smile of his.

"I kind of have a plan," he said.

"Yeah?"

"We'll get some lunch and come up with a plan. That's the plan."

"They don't serve lunch at the theater."

"We can make sandwiches, can't we?"

"Sure."

"Okay, while we're having our sandwiches, we'll come up with a plan. It'll be easier to do that if we're in there, right?"

"You can't just say you want to check out the dressing rooms?"

"You don't think someone will ask why? Of course, I *could* tell them all that you seem to be friends with the ghost of my great-great grandmother," Sloan suggested, ignoring Jane's groan.

"Let's have lunch — and come up with a plan."

Sloan grinned. "Isn't that what I said?"

6

Jane exited quickly as Sloan parked the car. If she didn't move fast enough, he'd be around to open her car door. It was nice, but not necessary every time.

They entered the theater and she blinked a minute, letting her eyes adjust after the bright sunlight.

Alice Horton, dark hair swept back in a ponytail, in sweats, as unvamplike as could be, was digging in the refrigerator. She looked up and greeted them with "Hey, Jane. Sheriff. Any news on the murder?"

"We're investigating," Sloan said. He walked through to the bar. "But a man has to eat."

As he came up next to Alice, Jane noted that she wasn't the only woman who seemed to flush when he was around. Alice was enough of an actress to behave casually, but Jane got a glimpse of her eyes.

"Salami?" Alice asked him. "Oh, Jane, how

about you?"

"Salami. Do you have cheese, tomatoes, maybe lettuce and mayo?" Sloan was saying.

"I'll eat anything," Jane assured Alice.

Alice plopped paper plates and the various makings on the bar.

"We can do an assembly line if you want," Jane offered. "Make lunch for all of us."

"Great," Alice said. "I'll throw some bottles of water up here and we'll make a few extra sandwiches. I know Valerie is coming down, maybe someone else." She seemed pleased that Jane took a seat at the bar while she stood behind it with Sloan. They got a system going — Jane put out the bread and spread the mayo, Sloan added the meat and cheese, and Alice finished up with lettuce and tomato slices and cut the sandwiches in half.

"Is anything going on this afternoon?" Sloan asked. "Rehearsal for the shows?"

"Rehearsal? Today?" Alice said, shaking her head and rolling her eyes. "Oh, yeah. But not for the show. We're going to take our act out on the street for a trial run with the locals."

"Your act?" Jane echoed.

"Tomorrow's the yearly arrival of the lemmings," she said. "Actually, I mean that appreciatively. We get huge crowds. By the weekend, Silverfest will be crazy. There'll be 'settlers' selling all kinds of things — some antiques, some reproductions, you know, Old West clothing, weapons, belts, buckles, dresses, plus corn cakes, barbecue and beans. Oh, yes, and silver jewelry, of course. Turquoise. A lot of Native American art. We all play a part out there, taking on the roles of old settlers." She paused to grin mischievously. "Sloan gets in on it. He plays Trey Hardy sometimes."

"I always had a soft spot for Hardy," Sloan admitted.

"What's that deal?" Jane asked. "I've heard about him from Heidi. He was sort of a Robin Hood character, wasn't he?"

"Hardy had been a lieutenant in the Confederate cavalry," Alice explained. "He held up trains and stagecoaches, but he'd give to whoever needed it — whites, newly freed slaves, Native Americans. He was finally caught by our local sheriff, Brendan Fogerty, who seemed to like him, too. It was just that he had to bring him in. We had a traveling circuit judge back then, and — do you know this part of the story?"

"Some of it. Go on."

"Okay. I think Fogerty thought he might face his charges and get off — since no one would act as a witness against him. But the deputy at the time, Aaron Munson, had a thing about Hardy. When he was on duty alone, he shot Hardy in his cell. Pumped him full of bullets while he was in there like a caged rat. Well, someone saw him and Munson wound up being dragged out onto Main Street and lynched by the crowd. It was sad all the way around."

"I remember hearing that," Jane said.

"Hardy haunts the jail, Munson haunts Main Street," Sloan said.

"Hey, I don't go to the Old Jail alone, and I don't hang around the street at night, either," Alice said solemnly.

"Was he killed before or after the stagecoach disappeared?" Jane asked.

"About a month before. It must have been a strange time for Lily," Alice said. "First, Hardy's shot down, then Munson is lynched — and four weeks later, Sage McCormick up and disappears, along with Red Marston."

"They disappeared on the same night, didn't they?" Jane asked.

"Yes. According to local legend," Sloan said.

Alice smiled at him affectionately. "Poor Sloan! His great-great grandmother was the scarlet woman of the age! But, boy, according to everything I've read, she was a brilliant actress. She could go from comedy to drama in the blink of an eye. They said her performances could make the toughest cowboy weep."

"Well, I don't think she did run off with Marston," Sloan said.

"Really?" Alice looked at Sloan and then Jane. "Did you finish with the skull? Do you think it belonged to Sage McCormick?"

"It's possible. I haven't finished, but I have done a two-dimensional sketch. Seems like it just might have been Sage." She glanced reproachfully at Sloan. Apparently most people in town knew about his ancestry — something he might have shared with her from the get-go.

Alice shivered. "So, maybe she *has* been haunting the theater. But if she was murdered, who killed her?"

"Who killed who?" Valerie Mystro asked. They all turned around as they heard her voice; she was coming down the stairs.

Alice said, "The skull you found might have been Sage McCormick's."

Valerie shivered. "That was soooo creepy!" she said, taking a seat at the bar. "I mean — *soooo* creepy! But I guess she might've been buried around here somewhere. Under the floorboards. Oh, but . . . she disappeared

you're on Main Street, we'd have a Sage McCormick," Henri said.

"What a great idea." Sloan smiled pleasantly as he leaned on the bar.

So much for saving *his* ass, she decided.

"Wow. That would be cool, Jane," Alice said.

"Really. You could be mysterious — around sometimes and not around other times," Valerie chimed in.

"I don't have a costume," Jane protested.

Henri lifted his hands. "Come on! We're a theater troupe. We have tons of costumes. We even have costumes that were actually worn by Sage McCormick. Of course," he added. "Those are really museum pieces now."

"Valerie, you and Jane are about the same size," Sloan said.

"Sure!" Valerie said. "I have several costumes — not just for the show we're doing now, but other shows, too. A number of them are late Victorian."

"I don't want to take your things. . . ." Jane demurred.

"They aren't mine. They belong to the theater," Valerie said. "Come on. If you have a minute, I'll take you to the dressing rooms."

Jane started and looked at Sloan. She realized that, as he'd hoped, a plan had arisen.

"I'll come down with you, see what's there. We'll need our costumes for tomorrow, so we might as well take care of this now," he said.

"You'll both do it!" Henri clapped his hands. "That's delightful."

"Come on, then. Let's go," Valerie said.

Alice stuffed the last of her sandwich in her mouth and washed it down with water. "Hold on. I'm coming, too."

They left the bar and entered the theater, walking down the aisle and over to the wings and then the area behind the stage, where the dressing rooms were situated against the back wall.

As they paused at Valerie's door, Sloan looked at her.

She recognized his silent question. *This one?*

She shook her head, indicating with a movement of her chin that she'd been in the room next door.

But they went inside Valerie's, and she rummaged through the racks of period clothing. Jane waited for Sloan to take the lead.

He did. "I was just thinking. . . . Alice, you're a little taller than Valerie. I guess it doesn't have to be exact, but Jane is taller than both of you. Maybe something you have in your dressing room would fit better."

"Sure," Alice said, "and if not, we have more in the basement. In storage."

"Except I'm not going down there," Valerie insisted.

"Something here should work," Henri said.

"Might as well try my stuff first," Alice said. "Because it's true. We didn't take Jane's height into consideration."

They moved into the next room. As Jane went through the costumes, Alice perched on her dressing-table chair and Valerie leaned against a prop box. Henri seemed interested in her possible choice of costume.

"The blue! That's a copy of Sage's costume from *The Heiress*. That would be great!" he said.

While Jane pulled out the costume and oohed and ahhed over it, Sloan walked to the back of the room.

"Hey, Henri," he called, kneeling down. "What's this?"

"Huh?" Henri joined him. "I don't know," he said with a shrug. "It's a big brass pull on the floorboard, I guess."

"It's a trapdoor. Where does it lead?"

"Well, it could only lead to the basement

— or to more floorboards," Alice said.

"Do not open it!" Valerie shrieked. "Not if it leads to the basement."

"It might've been a cubby where the old actors and actresses stuffed their valuables," Alice suggested.

"Or it might've been for extra costume pieces, accessories, stuff like that," Jane murmured.

"Let's see," Sloan said.

Jane had never thought of herself as a weakling, so she was glad to see that, at first, it seemed to be sealed tight. But Sloan levered himself against it and pulled harder — and the trapdoor opened.

It didn't lead to the basement. It led to a dark compartment. Something seemed to glimmer.

Sloan pulled out a flashlight and pointed it down into the hole that was about two feet deep.

Valerie let out a scream. "Didn't I tell you not to open anything that might lead to the basement!"

"That — that's not the basement," Alice said.

"Those are bones!" Valerie wailed. "I'm getting out of here. No, no, I'm not. I'm not going anywhere alone. Oh! Lord, what's happening in Lily?"

Sloan looked at her. "It's all right, Valerie. They've been here for a very long time. You can see that the fabric — the dress — is nearly decayed. It looks as if a body was left here and it decayed and . . . it must have smelled like hell. I wonder why someone didn't find it back then."

"Oh, how horrible," Valerie said.

Henri was down on his knees, horrified as he stared into the hole.

"Someone's found it recently," he said, a catch in his throat.

"How do you know?" Alice asked.

"Because this body is lacking something it should have," Henri said.

"What?" Valerie demanded.

"Her head," Jane said softly.

It did seem most likely that someone — playing a trick on the cast at the theater — had found the space beneath the floor, taken out the skull and set it on a wig stand. Despite the fact that he knew the bones had to be as old as the mummified remains discovered in the desert, Sloan called in the county medical examiner to retrieve them.

Alice moved into Valerie's dressing room for the time being. She'd switch with either Brian or Cy after Silverfest had come and gone.

Once the hoopla over the bones had ended, the afternoon was wearing on and Henri, though pensive, was also eager to get his cast out onto the street to start entertaining the locals.

At three o'clock, Sloan and Jane were finally able to leave the Gilded Lily. "Want to go exploring?" he asked her.

"Sure. Where? But should I be working on the skull? I just worry that I'm not accomplishing what you wanted out here."

"Doesn't matter. I know the skull belonged to Sage. And now I'm virtually certain we have the rest of her. As soon as that's confirmed, I'll plan a proper burial for her. We have our own version of Boot Hill here — except ours is called Dead Horse Hill. I would like to see that she's buried and I think that's an appropriate place."

"I'll still finish," Jane told him. "What are we exploring?"

"An old silver mine."

"I thought the entrances were all sealed."

"So did I. But I went by the mine entrance off the trail today and it has a few loose boulders. I hadn't brought a flashlight or anything with me, and I didn't want to go into an old mine shaft with no one knowing what I was up to. Of course, I had my phone, but . . ."

"If we're both in the mine, who will know where we are?"

"Johnny Bearclaw," Sloan said. "I trust him with my life."

"And you don't trust your own officers?"

"I do. But I'm not sure anymore that I want everyone finding out what I suspect until I've had a chance to prove it."

She shrugged. "Okay, I'm game." She turned to him; he didn't dare do more than glance at her. The gold of her eyes could be too hypnotic. "And I'm armed, I'm fully dressed and I'm wearing shoes."

"As I said before, that was rather a foolish thing you did last night."

"If I hadn't followed the ghost when she beckoned, we might not know what she's wanted us to know all along."

"It was stupid," he said decisively. He was being argumentative, but he still had the feeling that something had changed, that a dark cloud remained above them.

"Like going into a long-closed mine shaft?" she said.

"You don't have to go in. In fact, maybe you should stay outside and wait for me."

They'd reached his house by then. He'd already called Johnny so the horses were ready. He noticed that Johnny had one of

Mike Addison's mares in the paddock and asked, "What's Lucy doing here?"

"In case I have to come bail you out," Johnny told him.

"Hopefully, you're not going to have to bail me out," Sloan said.

Johnny offered him a shrug and a wry grimace. "I wouldn't want to lose Agent Everett out there. You, you're going to do what you're going to do."

"You'll know where Ms. Everett is," Sloan agreed. "What did you tell Mike?"

"Nothing. Just that you were taking Kanga and Roo and I might want to ride later," Johnny explained.

"Thanks."

"It's what I do," Johnny said. He smiled, but there was a seriousness in his expression. Sloan wondered about the other night when the cat had hissed as if something was near. He hadn't seen anything on the property, but they did have coyotes in the area. And yet he wondered if someone had been through his place. He'd consider it paranoia — except that a man had been murdered.

He led the way, with Jane behind him, breaking into a canter over the clearer ground and slowing Roo when they reached the rockier area of foothills and outcrops. She followed him wordlessly until they got to the old mine entrance.

He dismounted and she did the same. She walked over, waiting while he moved the loose boulder he'd found earlier. She played the flashlight he'd given her over the black gaping hole he created.

"See anything?" he asked her.

"A hole," she said.

He crawled through, not wanting to dislodge more than the one boulder. If someone was doing something in the old tunnel or shaft and wasn't there now, he didn't want that person knowing the entry had been discovered.

When he was inside, he turned to help Jane, but she was agile and had already come through. They both trained their lights on the old shaft. He checked the sides, where rock was crumbled from the explosion. Shifting his light, he saw that the center of the shaft was clear. Had it been like that when it caved in — or had someone been clearing it?

Jane was behind him as he carefully moved forward. They went about fifteen feet before they had to crawl through another pile of rubble. Past that, they found a second clear stretch. A few feet later, they came across a large room. There, part of the floor had been dug up; pointing his light down, Sloan saw something dazzling. He crouched down and searched for the source.

"What is it?" Jane asked.

"Dust," he said. "Gold dust."

"When was this mine closed down?"

"Years ago. The 1920s, I believe."

"Has the gold been here that long?" she asked.

"I don't know. Look for signs that someone's been in here. I can't find prints, because the stone is so uneven. . . ."

She walked around the perimeter. "I think I've found what you're looking for," she told him.

"What?" he asked, and shone his light toward her.

It was a plastic water bottle.

"I don't think they made these in the 1920s," she said.

He nodded. He wasn't sure what anyone was doing here — other than maybe conducting some kind of illegal trade. He doubted the person or persons in question had found the cache of gold — although he had no idea why there was gold dust scattered near the entrance.

He pulled a small listening device out of his pocket and looked around for a rock with a little crevice.

"How long will that last?" Jane asked skeptically.

"Well, it's motion-activated and the battery will last twelve to twenty-four hours when it's active," he told her. "Come on. Let's get out before the wrong person comes along and realizes that we're in here."

They crawled back out. When they were once again standing in the late-afternoon sun again, he looked at Jane and laughed.

"That's rude," she chastised. "Especially from a man who looks like he's been mud-wrestling with pygmies."

He sobered only slightly. Jane was covered in dust; even her eyelashes were a smoky taupe shade. Her auburn hair was almost gray.

"Come on. You really should see yourself," he said.

"Yep. And you really should see *yourself!*"

They both mounted up. "Let's hope we don't meet up with anyone!" Jane muttered.

"The trail rides don't start until tomorrow, so we should be okay," he said.

Johnny was waiting for them when they returned. He looked them both up and down.

"Nice. May I suggest showers? And you might want to hurry. Chet's coming by with some reports from Detective Newsome at county."

"Shall we?" he asked Jane.

"Yes, thanks, although my clothes will still be covered with this stuff. Remind me next time we're going to crawl through tunnels not to wear a cotton suit."

"I have a washer and dryer," he told her. "We'll be fine. Chet won't stay, I'm sure, but I do have to get you back to town."

They left Johnny whistling as he tended to the horses. "Strange," he told Jane. "The other night, I was convinced someone was on my property. I didn't find anything — but my place is the most direct route when you're riding through to the trail. There's that little gap between those rocky hills once you're off the property line."

"So you think whoever murdered Jay Berman went through your property?" she asked.

"The question is still *why*? Is someone selling illegal drugs? Smuggling illegal aliens? Trying to reopen the silver mine? Or —"

"Or maybe the gold from the heist was hidden in the mine."

"I'd thought of that — except the mine wasn't closed down until almost forty years later. So I can't figure out what anyone's doing in there. For one thing, it's danger-

tered the house, carrying a file. "So you found the whole body, huh?" Chet asked, and Sloan realized that as far as Chet knew, he'd spent most of the afternoon at the theater while the medical examiner removed the bones of Sage McCormick.

"Well, we're assuming." Of course, there was no proof yet, but the skeleton almost *had* to be hers. . . .

"I think you can feel pretty sure," Chet said cheerfully. "DNA testing will prove who she was — that she's Sage McCormick, your *ancestor.*"

"Thanks, Chet. Anyone go through this?" Sloan asked, taking the file.

"Yes, sir. So far, they haven't found the rental car. The bullet was pretty degraded because it went through the hard part of the skull, but it was .45 caliber. It's a nightmare for the crime-scene guys, since dozens of people go through that tepee every day, so sorting anything out is going to be tough for them. They have some hair and some fibers, but . . . those could belong to the guides or to a bunch of tourists. No luck tracing anyone who knew anything about the man coming here. He hopes you're having better luck."

"Thanks, Chet. I'm going through the books the man bought. Hopefully, that will give us some clue."

He couldn't have said exactly why he wasn't telling his own deputy that he'd been crawling around the mine. He trusted Chet and Betty and his entire department. But just for now, he wanted to investigate on his own. Or with Jane.

Maybe I shouldn't even be *investigating,* he told himself.

Chet never knew that Jane was in the house; he was gone before she came out at last in one of his grandfather's beautiful old Native American robes. It was too big for her but she'd tied it around her waist and she seemed comfortable, walking out in bare feet with her hair slick and clean and clinging to her face and neck. She carried her clothing, neatly folded. "Tell me where your laundry is, and I'll manage to get the dust out of these before we head back."

"It's right off the kitchen."

"Thanks." She seemed at ease, but he realized he wasn't. The thought that wouldn't leave his mind was that she was naked beneath the robe.

He went into the kitchen and rummaged in the refrigerator. Johnny had left him a meat loaf. There was a bowl of fruit to go with it, and a note about how long to nuke the food. He took it out and put it in the microwave.

Jane reappeared, smiling wryly as she watched him. "Do you like cooking?" she asked.

"I don't mind it. Problem is, my hours are usually long. Johnny's a decent cook, as well as the best property manager I've ever known. He'd been with my grandfather since I was a teenager, the best friend someone could have. We respect each other, we look after each other. It's good."

"It *is* good," she agreed. She pointed at the folder he'd set on the counter. "So Chet came by?"

"Yes."

"This is what Detective Newsome has?"

"Yep. Not much."

"Aren't you supposed to be sharing with him?"

"I intend to, as soon as I have something to share. You hungry?"

"Well, crawling around in abandoned mine shafts does whet the appetite," she told him.

"It's meat loaf, but don't be too disheartened — Johnny makes a hell of a meat loaf."

They ate, and she swore it was the best meat loaf she'd ever tasted. He explained that it was slightly different because of Johnny's gift with seasoning and because it was made with pork and beefalo. "Emu is popular around here too," he said. "I don't think it ever caught on the way people hoped, but we still have some big ranches around here."

When they'd finished eating, he found himself staring at her. He also saw her staring at him.

Her clothes must be ready by now. They'd eaten, and it had been a long day; he could take her back to town.

But he didn't offer and she didn't say she needed to go. Their silence should have grown uncomfortable. It didn't. He wasn't sure which of them smiled first, but then they both were and their smiles deepened.

"I guess I should ask if you're in a relationship," she said.

"Pretty obvious, I think. You see me living here alone."

"Ah, but I saw the way Alice looked at you today. And then I noticed that Valerie got that touch of awe in her eyes. Of course, you came to her rescue when she discovered the skull, so . . ."

"I guess I've missed those looks."

She glanced down and her lashes swept her cheeks for a moment. Then she raised her eyes again. "You didn't ask me if I'm in a relationship."

He shook his head. "No."

"Is that because you don't care?"

"It's because I don't believe you'd be here now, speaking to me like this, if you were," he told her.

"That's a compliment," she said.

"And it's true, although I'm sure *you've* noticed that many people look at you with appreciation," he said. "There's nothing wrong with appreciation, of course — unless it turns obnoxious."

"True."

"Hmm. I'm going to suggest you were involved not too long ago."

"It's been a while now. Since I joined the Krewe," she said.

"He was intimidated?"

"He was. And you?"

It was such an easy conversation. With every word he felt her voice as if it were a caress. He thought she could arouse him to a greater hunger with words than another woman, naked and twisting and writhing before him.

"It ended when I left Texas."

"She wouldn't move."

"I don't know. I didn't ask her to. I was coming home to take care of someone who was dying. There are different kinds of intimacy. I guess we didn't have enough of the right kind."

Jane nodded, gazing down at her hands. When she looked up, her smile was slightly crooked, incredibly sensual, and her eyes were like the golden fire of a sunrise.

"Well, I suppose one of us should make the first move. . . ."

7

In a thousand years, Jane would never have thought that becoming intimate with someone she'd known a matter of days could be so effortless and natural.

Yes, one of them had needed to make a move, but ever since they'd sat down together, they'd both been making moves. And after she spoke, he stood, and she must have stood, as well, because she was suddenly in his arms.

She wondered just when she'd known that she had desperately wanted that moment to come, and she wondered what made one person so desirable to another. Was it the unique, underlying scent of each human being? The way a mind worked, the sound of a voice, the way one person could reach out to someone else . . . ?

Then all thought left her mind. She felt his fierce heat as he drew her close and as his lips touched hers. For a moment, that first kiss was almost frantic, as if they both feared they had seconds and nothing more, and every taste and sensation had to be seized.

And then it eased into something that was slow and seductive, the feel of his mouth, his tongue a harbinger of everything about him that suddenly seemed necessary for life itself.

When they broke apart, his lips were mere inches from hers, and he whispered softly, "Not that this isn't my house, and not that I have a multitude of neighbors close by, but . . ."

She smiled, and she was almost afraid it was a stupid smile, she felt so deliciously giddy. Then he gathered her up into his arms, and that was easy and natural, too, although he paused and said softly, "May I? Agents of the law can be very finicky when a threat is perceived."

She slipped her arms around his neck. "I'd thought about doing the same to you. I mean, after all, I *am* a federal agent."

"But this is a local situation," he told her.

"Yes, but you did invite me in," she reminded him.

"Because of your artistry."

"I hope it's up to par."

He carried her down the hall. "Agent

Everett, the second I saw you, I became aware that you certainly surpassed par."

"Thank you," she said. "And I do admit, we feds never like to appear as if we can't handle a situation, but I'm not sure that if we'd reversed this, I wouldn't have dropped you."

"Sometimes things just work out the way they should," he said.

They'd reached the bedroom. It was dark inside, the only light coming from the hallway and the rooms beyond. He didn't turn on a lamp, nor did he pause to close the drapes; through the window they could see the dark, moon-draped hills beyond, majestic in the purple shades of the desert.

Cloaked by the shadows that surrounded them, he eased them down onto the bed. Their mouths fused together again, as he opened the belt of the robe she wore. She was instantly aroused by his touch. He rose, removing his holster and the Colt he'd chosen for his work weapon, laying them on the table by the bed. She felt his hands brush her midriff and her breasts as the hot, wet fever of their kiss deepened. She tugged at his shirt, pulling it from the waistband of his jeans. Breaking apart only momentarily, he all but ripped the shirt over his head before joining her again and the feel of his bare flesh against hers was so arousing she was almost embarrassed. Following her career or her "calling" into the Krewe had been all-consuming for many of the past months. But none of her previous relationships over the years had ever had this depth. Sloan *knew* her, as no one she'd met before had; he knew that she saw and felt and accepted a world that existed on the fringes of their own, and he was the same. These were the wonderful reasons in her mind that gave everything about this moment a heightened intensity, and then there were the simple physical reasons, which were like the staggering heat and brilliance of the desert sun.

His touch, his kiss, lips, tongue, flesh — all moved against her. She stroked the breadth of his back, fingers playing his spine. She felt him trying to kick off his shoes and she laughed, playing with his buckle while he removed the shoes and socks. Then he slipped the robe from her shoulders, impatiently pushing all remnants of clothing to the floor. They were locked together in a tangle of limbs, and again, she felt erotically bathed by his caress and the heat and fire of his lips. Her breasts were warmed by that fire. So were her midriff, hips, thighs and intimate areas, and she responded with a passion and abandon she hadn't known she possessed. She twisted in his arms and rolled on top of him, returning the intimacy of his touch. They laughed and teased and whispered, and then words were gone in a flurry of hunger; she was aware of the thundering of her heart, the rush of her breath and the feel of him, moving into her at last, moving with an urgency that appeased and spurred the desperate need that rocked through her.

Each thrust took her higher, each brought another burst of sensation that wiped away the rest of the world. The climax swept through her like lightning in the desert beyond, and she felt the fierce and shuddering movement of his body as he joined her. Then he lay beside her in the shadows, and again, the sound of their breathing, the beating of their hearts, seemed like a rhythmic chorus. They lay with their bodies damp, still entwined, wordless for several minutes. The silence between them in the aftermath was comfortable. For her, making love had never before seemed so miraculous, and maybe it had been new and unique because the intimacy she'd felt with him was deeper than she'd felt with a man before. He knew and understood what she was, what made her different from others, and it didn't stop him from wanting her.

He rose up on an elbow, smiling down at her, and teased, "You *are* an artist, Agent Everett — a true artist."

"Aw, thanks, Sheriff. You're not bad yourself, you know."

She touched his cheek in the darkness, marveling at the shape of his face. He could have been a poster boy for the perfect Western hero, the lawman who was tall and strong and relaxed in his own masculinity.

She almost drew away in that moment, reminding herself that she wasn't here forever. It was one thing to accept the stunning attraction between them and another to feel it shattering her insides; after all, they led separate lives.

He laughed at her remark. "I try, ma'am, I try."

He pulled her close. She wasn't sure why until he murmured, "Are you going to stay?"

She turned into him, her fingers on his chest. "I'd love to stay. I just think it would be a mistake." She saw the confusion in his frown and added quickly, "What I mean is that I think it would be a mistake for me not to be at the theater. There's . . . there's so much going on there."

He nodded, smoothing back a section of her hair. "We've found Sage," he said. "And *she* found someone she could reach. I

220

wonder if she just wanted it known that she was still here, in Lily, that she didn't run out on her husband and child."

"Maybe. And I'm surprised you were afraid to find out it was her. Isn't it better knowing that she was taken from her family, that she hadn't left them on purpose?"

He smiled at that. "I suppose I can look at it that way. I never wanted to believe she'd been murdered. It was easier to tell myself that she was a free spirit who couldn't stay. But I *am* glad she's been found, that we can give her a service and bury her properly."

"You've never seen her?" Jane asked him curiously. "With your abilities, I would've thought that maybe she'd come to you."

He shook his head. "She's never come to me. Even though she's an ancestor of mine and a bona fide legend around here . . . She did, however, come to you."

"Maybe that's the reason — the family connection. Could be that you're just too close to her. Perhaps the love we have for family extends through the generations and she's been afraid of hurting you."

"Maybe."

"Someone obviously found her before she led me to the bones," Jane said. "Whoever it was put her skull on display."

"And was it a prank — or a warning? And does it have anything to do with the murder victims out in the desert today?"

"Well," Jane began.

He placed a finger on her lips. "That was, for the moment, a rhetorical question. If I'm going to bring you back to the theater tonight . . ."

"Oh!" Jane said, and started to rise.

He pulled her back down. "If I'm going to bring you back tonight," he said, straddling her, "we haven't got much time."

She laughed and they made love again. It wasn't until they were in the car and on their way back to town that they returned their attention to the questions at hand.

"Maybe all these things are separate situations." Jane turned to Sloan as he drove. "Sage appeared to me because she wanted the truth known. She wanted her body found. Someone — maybe a cast member who wanted to torment Henri Coque — uncovered the stash of bones in the floor and put the head on the wig stand. Completely unrelated, there's something going on in the desert. Jay Berman didn't come out here just to enjoy the sights. He had a purpose that was illegal, and whoever his partners were, he double-crossed them. And perhaps his death was meant as a lesson to others — thus the 'execution,' and the old corpse dug up to point the way. Do you know who that corpse might be?"

"Who knows? Maybe Red Marston. He disappeared when Sage did. Maybe one of the stagecoach guards or the driver. I haven't heard about any graves being disturbed, so it's most likely someone who'd been buried out in the desert. Especially when you think about the mummified state of the remains. Sand will do that." He shrugged. "The point is, someone's been in the old mine shaft."

"Maybe I'm wrong. Maybe Sage made such a strong appearance to me because we're supposed to know something we don't."

He glanced over at her. "You still going to dress up as Sage tomorrow?"

"I guess. You're going to dress up as Trey Hardy, right?"

He smiled. "Me dressing up as Trey Hardy isn't all that difficult. I wear a plumed hat and an old Confederate cavalry jacket. You, however, will have to walk around in a Victorian dress."

"I can handle it for a day," she said. "But seriously, should I keep working with the skull — sorry, your great-great grandmother's skull? With everything else —"

"Yes, keep working on it. And the medical examiner's office is going to clean up the skull of the old corpse we found. It would be good to learn who he was before we bury him again. And the more I think about it, the more I believe this might have to do with someone — or several someones — figuring they can find the gold that disappeared in the 1870s. Hmm." He slowed the car as they came onto Main Street. "Town's already hopping."

And it was. People were crowding the street. The saloon was overflowing, and although it was almost eleven, people were coming in and out of Desert Diamonds, many wearing old-fashioned garb.

"I'll see you at the station tomorrow," Jane told him. "Don't get out!" she said, suspecting that he meant to stop the car and open her door. "I'll be fine."

He nodded and watched her go.

Jane hurried through the busy downstairs of the theater and up to her room. She stepped inside, closing and locking the door behind her. "Hey," she said quietly. "I hope you're feeling better. We do know the truth, and we'll bury you properly," she promised. "Oh, and by the way, I take back anything bad I said about your great-great grandson.

In fact, I think I'm a little too fond of the man!"

Sage didn't respond. But later that night, when Jane started feeling chilly in the air-conditioning, she was suddenly warm.

Sage might have been Bohemian in her lifestyle; she might have been a great actress, stealing many hearts.

But Jane had the feeling that she'd been a very tender mother, as well.

It was barely six in the morning when Sloan's cell phone rang.

He woke immediately and reached for it, afraid something else might have happened at the theater.

Grabbing the phone he noted the caller ID. Liam Newsome.

"We found the rental car, Sheriff. Want to meet out on the highway?"

"You bet. Where are you?"

Newsome gave him the coordinates, and Sloan told him he could be there in twenty minutes.

He got ready quickly, but before heading out, he went to his at-home office. He turned on the receiver, hoping he might have caught sounds from the cave shaft where he'd left the bug yesterday. He listened, but nothing registered.

Someone was doing something in the old mine. What? If he knew that, he was certain he could solve the murder.

He checked in with Johnny, asking him to monitor the audio and get in touch right away if he heard anything.

When he arrived at the site of the car, he wasn't surprised it had taken so long to find. It was almost off the highway, strategically placed behind and to the side of a hillock of grassy shrub and brush, now covered by desert sand and blended into the landscape.

A tow truck from the county stood ready to retrieve it and bring it in for forensics, but Newsome had halted the recovery until Sloan could reach the scene.

"Thought you'd want to see where it was," Newsome said.

Sloan nodded. "Thanks. I doubt Jay Berman parked it here," he said drily, "which leads me to believe that two people were probably involved in his murder. Someone had to drive the car here, and since we're miles from anywhere, whoever drove it must have had someone come by to pick him — or her — up."

"That's what I was thinking," Newsome agreed. "What still gets me is that there has to be a reason. You only see this kind of thing when gangs, mobs . . . drugs are

226

involved."

"Unless it was made to *look* like a mob hit. In a real hit, the body would usually be found in a scrap yard or such — not in the desert with another dead man pointing the way."

"Yeah. You have anything else? He did come out of Lily," Newsome said.

"I'm working a few angles," Sloan told him. "Combing the area where the body was found."

"Crime-scene tape is still up."

Sloan nodded. "Anything inside the car?" he asked.

Newsome walked him over to it; the doors and the trunk were open. The trunk was empty. So was the car. The glove compartment stood open and Sloan asked Newsome what they'd found in it.

"Maps. Maps of the county — and maps of Lily. One was especially interesting. Copy of a map done by a surveyor back in the early 1870s. I'll get it scanned and over to your office as soon as I'm back in mine," Newsome said. "Your fed artist is still here, right?"

"Yes."

"We'll have the skull of the dug-up corpse ready by this afternoon. Someone will bring it over. I guess you've got a lot on your

227

plate, what with Silverfest, but the medical examiner said he'd be done by then, so we might as well send it over."

Sloan wondered if it was wrong to be glad that they had another old corpse to identify, since it would keep Jane in Lily for a few more days. . . .

He drove back to town.

Main Street was alive with activity. He arrived just in time to see the annual lynching of Aaron Munson. For the past few years, Mike Addison from the Old Jail had taken on the role of Sheriff Fogerty, while Brian Highsmith portrayed the ill-fated Munson. Henri Coque orchestrated the reenactment, and volunteers were drawn from the crowd to play small roles, along with the rest of the theater troupe.

Sloan decided to take a few minutes to watch the spectacle before heading into his office for the day. Betty was handling the desk alone. Chet was in town; one officer was always on Main Street during Silverfest, assuring tourists that law enforcement was concerned about their safety.

Parking, he saw Chet standing on the wooden sidewalk in front of the saloon.

Cy Tyburn held Mike back in his role as Fogerty as he tried to prevent the mob from taking his deputy — even if his deputy had just shot their prisoner in cold blood.

Valerie Mystro and Alice Horton were out to spur the crowd into action, Valerie screaming that Munson had killed their hero, Hardy. Bartenders and waitresses from the theater were all in on the action, encouraging the crowd to join them as part of the lynch mob.

"Our hero! This man — this deputy! — shot down our hero! No trial, no conviction. He shot him down when he was defenseless, cornered, caged! Lynch him!" Valerie cried.

"Take him, take him! Show him that we won't allow even a deputy to take the law into his own hands!" Alice Horton shouted.

"Get rope! Get a horse, get this man dead!" Henri Coque demanded.

Sloan recognized two of the night bartenders as they came down the street from the stables with a horse and a rope. Brian, loudly protesting that he'd killed a heinous, low-down bank robber who just wasn't going to get away with robbing the county blind, was dragged up onto the horse; the noose was slipped around his neck. The rope was then tied to the rafters of the overhang by the Old Jail. Someone slapped the horse's rump and "Munson" swung from the rafters.

Henri Coque crawled up on a podium set to the far side of the road for the reenactment. "And so it was that Deputy Aaron Munson paid the price for his eagerness to kill Trey Hardy in Lily, Arizona. Was Hardy guilty? Beyond a doubt. But he was loved because at a time when the country was healing, when the West was still wild, he was a man of the people. Take care today, friends. The ghosts of Trey Hardy, murdered in his cell, and Aaron Munson, lynched by the crowd, still wander these streets! Just as the ghost of our beautiful diva, Sage McCormick, roams the stage of the theater and haunts her old room — appearing at her window to watch the streets of the town she came to love."

There was a roar of applause, especially as "Munson" — hanging from the rafter but with a safety harness around him — lifted his head. "And come back and see us here in Lily!" he called out. "The Old Jail fills up for Silverfest, so get your reservations in early!"

Sloan applauded with the rest of the crowd. He looked up at the theater, drawn to the window Henri had indicated.

His heart seemed to quicken. There *was* someone at the window. A woman, gazing down.

He glanced around to see if he was imagining things, but he saw a little girl in the crowd tugging at her mother's hand and pointing. "It's Sage! Sage McCormick!"

For a moment, he thought he'd actually seen her at last.

But then the woman raised a hand and he realized she was looking right at him. She smiled.

And he smiled in return.

It was Jane, and she was playing her role, just as she'd been asked.

The crowd broke up after Henri announced that there'd be a gunfight between Mean Bill Jenkins and Savage Sam Osterly on Main Street in an hour.

Chet walked over to him. "Hey, Sloan."

"Chet. Everything going well here?"

Chet nodded. "We've got a heck of a crowd, though. You hadn't left orders, but Betty checked in with the chief over at county. They have a few of their people here, just wandering through the crowd. Hope that sits fine with you. Not that we usually have trouble, but with this many people . . . The boys from the night crew suggested it. The reports are on your desk." He shrugged. "We had a few bar fights last night."

"I think Betty was brilliant and I'm

ashamed I didn't take care of it myself."

"Silverfest is getting bigger every year," Chet said happily.

"Yes, it is."

"And what with a murder in town and all . . ."

"Yep. I'll go in and check the reports," Sloan said. "Then I'll be back here for most of the day, unless something breaks."

As he spoke, Jane appeared on the sidewalk. He thought she did the town's diva and his great-great grandmother proud. Her hair was swept up in a loose chignon and she was wearing a blue period dress with gold cord that seemed to bring out the brilliance of her eyes. She smiled and joined him.

She was stunning. But then he remembered that he knew, as of last night, that she was stunning naked, as well.

Something he shouldn't be thinking about now.

"I was just about to go in and work on the skull," she told him. "Are you sure you want me to finish?"

"I'd like it if you did. We can get her a coffin and bury her. I think she'd like your artistry — for you to rebuild the lifelike appearance of her face, that is. She was reputed to be a little vain, you know."

Henri Coque walked up to them, a smile splitting his face. "It's all going wonderfully. I admit, I was worried. I'm always worried when using nonactors. But the lynching went off perfectly. And have you seen all the vendors? They're set up behind the saloon and Desert Diamonds. We have more vendors this year than ever before, and with what they pay for their licenses, the town will be flourishing!"

"Congratulations, Henri."

"Would you get into your Trey Hardy apparel, Sloan? Next year, we should reenact his shooting," Henri said excitedly. "We've never done that, you know, because we can't fit spectators into the jail. But where there's a will, there's a way! I'll work on it. Come on, Sloan, let's go get your costume."

Sloan started to excuse himself to Jane but saw that a little girl was asking to have a picture taken with her beneath the theater sign. Jane seemed puzzled at first and then realized that her costume made her a tourist attraction. She smiled and posed with the child.

He went in with Henri and made his way down to Cy Tyburn's dressing room, where he could procure a plumed cavalry hat and Civil War butternut-trimmed cavalry jacket.

"You could let your hair grow out," Henri

233

told him. "Then you'd be the spitting image of Trey Hardy."

"I think your chances of the ghost cutting his hair are better than your chances of me growing mine out," Sloan said. "In case you've forgotten — it's hot as hell out here."

Henri shrugged and they returned to the street.

Jane had become a celebrity. She was now with a group of Boy Scouts.

He was surprised when Henri, still standing near him, said, "Good thing you're hanging around today, Sloan. I like Chet, he's a solid deputy. But he's still a kid. What with the stuff going on, I'm glad you're here."

"We're fine whether I'm here or not, Henri. County sent over some men. They're all in uniform, as you can see them in the crowd. Their presence will let any would-be rabblerousers know that we're watching."

"Yeah, but I'm glad you're in town, Sloan," Henri said again. "Hey, the shootout is coming up next!"

Sloan studied the activity in the street. People were pouring in and out of Desert Diamonds, the saloon, the stables — and even the spa. He saw Heidi bringing out a tour group of ten; the stables charged a hefty sum for every tour they took out and he could see from the sign in front that they'd sold out for the day.

Everything was going well.

Jane was now posing in front of the theater sign with Alice, Valerie, Cy and Brian. He smiled slightly. Brian Highsmith had always thought of himself as a lothario. "Bad boys get the chicks, you know?" he'd told Sloan once. He seemed to like having his arm around Jane; Sloan wasn't so sure that she was "feeling the love" in return.

As he watched, his cell phone rang. He reached into his pocket for it.

It was Johnny Bearclaw.

"Sloan," Johnny told him, "your bug has gone off. I heard shuffling. There's movement in the mine shaft."

"I'm on my way out. I want you to ride with me, Johnny."

"I'll get the horses ready."

He hung up quickly and went over to interrupt the "Kodak moment."

"Jane, can I see you, please?"

"Sheriff!" Cy protested. "We've become a sensation! We're better than ever with Agent Everett. She can work tomorrow, can't she?"

"I'm not taking Agent Everett away," Sloan assured Cy, although he didn't understand why Cy was so worried. Brian might play the "bad boy," and "bad boys" might

235

be popular, but Cy did all right for himself. He was tall, blond and built. He had plenty of charm, too — and he knew it.

"Good!" Valerie said happily. "I'm always glad to have a fed with a gun around! Especially since we're missing Jennie today. Where's our stage mom? Haven't seen her yet."

"Maybe she's getting into costume," Cy said with a shrug.

"Yeah, running late!" Brian murmured. He grinned as if they were conspirators. "I think Jennie's been getting it on lately. She crawled up to her room really late a few times in the past week."

"Jennie — getting it on?" Valerie asked. "Seriously? With whom?" She giggled.

"Oh, for a sweet young thing, that was cruel!" Alice told her.

"Not cruel, just . . ."

"Truthful?" Brian suggested.

"Well, let's face it. Jennie isn't going to be the next swimsuit model of the year," Cy commented. "Still, it *was* cruel, young woman," he said to Valerie. "There's someone out there for everyone!"

Sloan shook his head, unimpressed by the actors' banter, and turned to give Jane a questioning look. She wasn't wearing her customary holster.

"Strapped to my thigh," Jane said softly. But she was heard.

"Sexy!" Brian told her.

"Safe," she said, her tone harsh.

"Excuse me. Like I said, I need to speak with Jane for a minute."

"Okay, you're the sheriff. Steal our prize act for the day!" Brian said with mock dismay.

He took her aside. "That was Johnny. There's someone in the mine shaft. I'm heading out there."

"I'll go with you," Jane insisted.

"No," he said firmly.

"I'm an agent. Not an actress. This is fun, but I don't think you should be going in there alone. You —"

"Jane," he broke in. "I know you're a competent law enforcement officer, and that you can use a weapon."

"Well, then?"

He hesitated, about to say something he hadn't wanted to admit before. "Jane, I need you to be the one who knows where I am in case something happens. Jay Berman was from New York, yes. But I still believe he was killed by someone out here. Someone who's aware of the old legends — someone who thinks he can find the gold, perhaps, or someone running an illicit scheme out

237

here." He lowered his voice. "That means I don't know whom to trust. What if one of my staff talks to the wrong person? For the moment, anyway, the fewer people involved, the safer I'll feel. Johnny will ride with me. Just make sure you keep hearing from me every hour or so."

"All right," she said slowly. "All right, but you know I'm going to be a nervous wreck."

"And you know that it's the best way for me to work this."

"I'm not so sure about that," she said. "You could call in Newsome . . ."

"I will," Sloan told her. "But I don't want to cry wolf. I want to have some idea of what's really going on here. And I don't want to scare anyone away from the mine shaft, not when it might be a piece of the puzzle."

"Should I stay here in town?"

"You're making a lot of kids happy," he said. "And you'll be closer to my property and the Apache and mine sections of the trail ride if I do need you."

Jane touched his arm and moved closer. "Ghosts might appear, but facial reconstructions do not complete themselves."

"We'll get back to work soon," he said. He took a deep breath. He couldn't help disliking the fact that his great-great grandmother was a pile of bones and decayed, dried-out tissue and fabric on a slab at the county morgue, while her skull was riddled with markers and clay down at the police station.

Still, that couldn't compare with a man who'd just been murdered, even if he hadn't been the most upstanding citizen.

He was also certain that they needed to establish the identity of the long-dead man who'd been found at the Apache village.

Somehow it all connected. He knew it.

"I'll keep in touch," he told her.

"You'd better."

As he left her, walking around to the rear to get his patrol car, he thought that while it had been far more grueling to be a cop on the mean streets of Houston, being here was disturbing in its own way. A different way. In Houston, it had been easier to recognize the bad guys; here, he was afraid, he was looking for someone who might well be a friend.

Driving out of town, he could see the Silverfest celebrations taking place in the cordoned-off section of Main Street.

People were in high spirits. Most were convinced that a tourist killed in the desert had nothing to do with them.

And most of them were right.

In a few minutes he was back at his place, where Johnny Bearclaw had the horses saddled. Sloan mounted Roo, while Johnny took Kanga.

"We'll probably run into the trail group," Johnny told him.

"Yeah, I know. We'll wait until the group that's out now has moved on to the Apache village. It won't look strange that we're out there," Sloan said. "There was a murder."

"I'm ready for anything." Johnny patted his holster.

Sloan carried a .357 eight-shot Magnum. He saw that Johnny had prepared with his weapon of choice, the 629 six-shot .44 Magnum. He'd had that weapon as long as Sloan could remember, but he didn't carry it often.

Leaving the property and entering the trail, they caught up with Heidi and her tour group about halfway through. He noted that Heidi wasn't alone; her older brother, Lars, just out of the military, was riding second with her. Sam, another of the tour guides, was carrying, too.

When Heidi saw him, she went ashen, so he urged Roo through the riders, saying a friendly hello to the mounted tourists as he did.

"There's nothing wrong, Heidi. I'm just

keeping an active presence all over town today," he assured her quickly.

She let out a sigh of relief. "Thanks, Sheriff. Even though I brought my own 'hired gun,'" she said with a rueful smile.

"I see that."

Sloan waved to Lars, who waved back. Heidi was in good hands; Lars was a serious kid who had done two tours of duty in the Middle East.

"Hey, I'd rather not find any more dead men," Heidi said. "I mean," she added in a hushed voice, "I only found the old dead guy, but . . . that was creepy enough for me."

"You should be fine today."

"Thanks, Sloan. Hi, Johnny!" Heidi said.

Johnny waved, and Sloan urged Roo back to Johnny's position beside the group. He smiled as they passed them.

"Give it five minutes?" Johnny asked.

"Yep. We'll give it five."

The tour group moved on.

They left Kanga and Roo rooting around for scrub grass and walked to the entrance. With Johnny's help, it was easy to move the loose boulder. Sloan crawled through and Johnny followed. There was nothing in the first opening; they climbed over rock to reach the second chasm and then the third.

Sloan directed his flashlight all around.

At first, he saw nothing.

And then he saw the dark pile with the tarp over it on the earth-and-rock flooring. He walked over to it and tore away the tarp.

"Son of a bitch!" he exploded.

8

Being Sage McCormick was fun.

Jane had never thought of herself as an extrovert, but she did enjoy being in this costume, and she enjoyed seeing the children so excited. Thanks to the cast of the dinner theater, she was quickly at ease answering all manner of questions, telling kids and adults alike the history of the theater and how she had disappeared one night. "I was suspected of all kinds of terrible things," she told them, emoting more than she'd realized she could, "but now people know — I was murdered right in the theater and buried under the floorboards!"

Posing for pictures and playing the part of Sage was good; it distracted her from worrying about Sloan.

It was a foolish thing to do, she reminded herself. He'd signed on the line that he was willing to give his life for his work; she had done the same.

She loved her job. She had to go where her work took her and her real home was Arlington, Virginia, where the Krewe units had their offices and where she'd found the town house she loved. Okay, so she could leave a home. But she was an important part of her Krewe, and they solved cases when others couldn't.

Not that Sloan had asked her to do anything, or vice versa; they'd slept together once. She didn't regret it.

No, she really wanted to do it again. . . .

But whatever their involvement, it didn't matter; she'd be worried about *anyone* investigating a murder. Law enforcement officers everywhere signed up for this, and it didn't stop those who cared about them from worrying about it.

"Hey, time for the old shoot-out," Cy said, nudging Brian.

"The shoot-out." Brian grinned at Jane. "I love this part of the show!"

"Well, of course he loves it — he gets to be fastest on the draw," Valerie said.

"The things we'll do for art!" Cy said. "Yeah, sadly, I'm Mean Bill Jenkins and Brian gets to play Savage Sam Osterly. And Osterly outdrew Jenkins."

Henri Coque was back at his podium. "Ladies and gentlemen, boys and girls,

244

make way, if you please! Not long after the lynching of Aaron Munson, the streets of Lily grew even wilder! Sheriff Fogerty struggled to hold on to a deputy, but men were afraid in Lily. He did his best to protect the law, and he turned a blind eye to the men who fought in the streets. On January 17, 1873, two of the meanest, most vicious outlaws ever to come to town met on Main Street, right here, ready to duel it out. They say it was over a chorus girl from the saloon."

As he spoke, Cy walked out onto the street and waved to the crowd.

For a moment, Jane was distracted. She turned to look back at the Gilded Lily.

There was definitely someone at her bedroom window.

"Mean Bill Jenkins fought on the Union side during the war. He was something of a hero when he was with his Indiana unit at Gettysburg, or so the history books tell us," Henri said.

Jane turned back to watch the action.

Cy raised his hat, smiled proudly and bowed to the audience — among them, many admiring women.

"But," Henri announced, "when the war was over, he took up with a group of Kentucky Rebels and Yanks — and they weren't the kind who robbed banks nicely and kept from killing people. Not like our dashing Trey Hardy!"

Cy paused midsmile and frowned at Henri.

"Sorry," Henri said as an aside, bringing a rise of laughter from the crowd. "Mean Bill Jenkins was as mean as they got! Oh, yeah, mean and vicious, through and through."

The temptation to look back was strong. Jane did so. The ghost of Sage McCormick remained. She was staring at Jane. She shook her head; her ghostly hand slammed against the window.

What the hell was she trying to say?

"Yes," Henri Coque repeated, "mean and vicious, through and through."

Cy shrugged, and made fists of his hands.

"So," Henri continued, "on this day, late in the afternoon, after both men were liquored up, Mean Bill challenged Savage Sam to a duel!"

Behind Henri, Valerie raised a sign that told the audience to say "Oooh!"

The audience complied.

"Now Savage Sam . . ." Henri paused as Brian stepped out onto the road, "was a man who kowtowed to no government!"

Brian stood straight and accepted the cheers of the crowd.

246

"No, he was just a vicious killer."

It was Brian's turn to stare at Henri.

"Hey, that's history!" Henri told him.

Brian sighed and his shoulders slumped, but then he, too, straightened and twisted his lips in a sneer.

"Yes, friends, it was over the love of a woman!"

"Me! Me!" Valerie said, rushing forward.

"No, it would be over *me!*" Alice argued, pushing her way into view.

"Sorry, the identity of the woman was never written down in the history books. She was just one of many bawdy-house women plying their trade in Lily," Henri said.

"Oh, let's see — bawdy woman. That *would* be you!" Valerie said sweetly to Alice. Alice drew back her arm as if she was going to throw a punch. Mike Addison slipped quickly between them. "Hey, the duel was between the *men!*"

"No, let's have a catfight!" someone yelled from the crowd.

There was a lot of laughter at that. When it calmed down, Henri said, "The men asked Sheriff Fogerty himself to call the duel. Oh, wait, that's me!" He walked down from the podium and stood between the men on the street. "Twenty paces, men."

247

The duel progressed. As it did, the amusement Jane had been feeling began to fade.

They were actors, she reminded herself. *Playing with blanks.*

"Twenty paces!" Henri called again.

Brian and Cy made faces at each other and turned to walk their paces.

"And now . . ." Henri said.

Both men stood still, forty feet from each other.

"Ready!" Henri called.

They swung around.

Jane looked back at the window. Sage remained there, shaking her head.

She wanted the duel stopped. Why? Did she know something?

Jane was terrified that if the duel went through, someone was really going to die.

"Aim!" Henri shouted.

It was quite possibly one of the stupidest things she'd ever done, but she couldn't stop the abject fear that swept through her.

She burst out into the middle of the road between the men, arriving a split second before Henri could call, "Fire!"

"Wait! Wait!" she shouted. She had no idea where'd go from there, but she started speaking, saying whatever came to mind. "People died back then because they weren't smart enough just to have a conversation.

Now we're living in a new time, a new day — and I'm sure you gentlemen are smart enough to have a conversation and work it all out!"

She looked back and forth between Cy and Brian; they stared at her blankly and then looked at Henri. Henri frowned at Jane, then shrugged.

"Hey, come on, shoot it out!" someone cried from the audience.

"No! Enough violence. We've already had a lynching," Jane said. "Think how cool it would be if Congress actually *talked* with one another."

She was grateful that those words brought more laughter; she was swaying the crowd. "Now you guys . . . neither of you is really mean and vicious. You just need a hug, right?"

She smiled at the laughter she received.

"All in favor of a peaceful discussion, raise your hands!"

She was still afraid she was going to lose. She might be entertaining the crowd, but they'd come to see a duel.

To her astonishment, she got help from an unexpected source. Valerie came bursting onto the scene. "No shooting, gentlemen! How will the play go on tonight if we lose one of you?"

Not to be upstaged, Alice Horton, vamping it up, ran out, as well. "And we all know that a good bad girl loves a bad boy with a story — the strong but silent type, you know?"

"Talk it out, talk it out, talk it out!"

Jane was grateful when the crowd took up the chant.

"Give me your weapons, boys!"

They handed them over. She didn't dare take a chance on looking at them then; she had to make sure her improvised charade went on.

"Now say you're sorry for flying off the handle, Mean Bill Jenkins!" she told Cy.

His blue eyes touched hers with curiosity and a surprised admiration. She smiled at him, silently thanking him for playing his part.

"Oh, all right! I'm sorry, Savage Sam. I think you got you a fittin' girl now, and I'm going to get me one, too."

"Oh, yes!" Valerie said, running to throw herself into Cy's arms.

"Well, there you go!" Henri said. "The gunfight that wasn't. Damned good thing we're not at the O.K. Corral! Hey, everyone, take a gander at all the activities out back. Kids, you can mine sand for silver. Ladies, you can buy some great jewelry. And don't forget that while you're in town, you can catch these fine folks performing for you every night at the Gilded Lily!"

Jane stood still in the street for a moment, feeling grateful on the one hand, ridiculous on the other.

A little boy walked by saying, "I thought there was going to be a gunfight!"

He wasn't happy.

But a cluster of twenty-something young people walked by and the tallest among them was talking excitedly, "See, I told you. It's great to come out here. They're not stupid, they keep changing it up!"

"Who would've figured?" Henri Coque said, walking up to her. He shook his head. "Never saw you as a drama queen, much less someone who'd be so quick with improv."

"Seemed like a fun thing to try. As a law enforcement officer in the twenty-first century, of course," she said.

"And it was good!" Valerie said enthusiastically, coming up beside her. "Jennie still hasn't shown up. She usually screams and cries and falls down in tears, saying she's Jenkins's mother."

"There's something wrong if Jennie isn't here," Henri said, frowning. "Valerie, will

251

you run in there and see if she's in her room?"

"I'm not going in the Gilded Lily by myself!" Valerie said. "Even our staff is all out on the street now. I can't go in there alone."

"I'll go," Jane said. "Which room is Jennie's?"

"She's next to Brian and Brian is next to you," Henri explained. "You don't mind? Thank you! I hope she's okay." His voice was worried.

Jane nodded and hurried into the Gilded Lily. It did seem strange to be in the theater when it was so silent. The main doors behind the old Western slatted doors were open; apparently, Henri wasn't worried about break-ins, but then it was true that everyone who belonged in the theater was pretty much right in front of it.

Jane ran up the stairs and realized she was still clutching the antique guns Cy and Brian had been about to use for the duel reenactment. Before going to Jennie's room, she went to her own and inspected the guns. They were replica Colt 45s, also known as Peacemakers, each with a cylinder that held six metallic cartridges. She opened the cylinders, and the cartridges fell out. The bullets from the one gun were obviously blanks.

From the other . . .

She had learned to shoot; she knew the action of her own gun. She also knew the most important thing about any gun — when loaded and in the wrong hands, it beat brawn every time.

She wasn't sure about the cartridges. She left both guns, emptied, on her bed, and stashed the blanks and the questionable cartridges in tissues and then in one of her shoes.

Then she ran down the hall and knocked on Jennie's door. There was no answer. She called the woman's name. Still no answer. She tried the door — which was open. Hesitantly walking in, she continued to call the woman's name.

Jennie wasn't in the bathroom or anywhere in the room. Jane felt a growing sense of unease and even checked under the bed. Again, no sign of her.

Coming out of the room, she saw Sage McCormick. The ghost was waiting for her on the second landing by the stairs, and as Jane approached her, Sage drifted down the stairs. She walked around to the bar and behind it.

Puzzled, Jane followed her.

Sage went through the door at the far end of the stage. Jane opened the door to a set of stairs that led to the basement, now the costume storage area.

Where Sage's skull had been found.

Jane carefully went down the stairs. It was broad daylight outside, she reminded herself, and when she tried the switch on the wall, the basement flooded with light.

Sage kept moving.

The basement seemed to run the entire length of the theater. From the stairway, Jane could see the rows of wigs that now sat on mannequin heads, old and new. Most of them had faces either carved into them or drawn on them; they were supposed to be artistic, Jane supposed. Mostly, they were grotesque.

She was, however, glad to see no skulls among them.

She walked around the center of the main room.

There were racks hung with costumes, most of them now conserved in cases. There were shoes, canes, stage guns, props and boxes everywhere. She saw no sign of Jennie.

"Jennie?" Jane called out.

No one answered her.

She realized there were three rooms that

led off the main section of the basement; they were separated by foundation walls. There were no doors, just arched separations with handsome wood carved designs as if someone, long ago, had determined that a theater must be beautiful — even in the storage areas.

Jane made her way through crates and boxes to the first of the rooms.

It contained more crates and boxes.

Irritated, she shook her head.

"Where are you?" she whispered aloud.

The ghost had gone through the door — and then disappeared. But Sage had brought her here for a reason.

And then disappeared.

"You could be more helpful," she said. But then again, if she was right and the ammo in the one Peacemaker was live, the ghost had been a great deal of help; she'd saved a man from dying.

But if it *was* live . . .

Then someone here was setting people up to die.

The thought chilled her, and she walked into the last room, the one closest to the Old Jail Bed and Breakfast. In fact, it almost seemed as if she was *under* the Old Jail.

This room was different. The light from the main room didn't seem to reach far enough and she couldn't find another switch. The one bulb down here illuminated the main room and stretched as far as the second room. By the third room . . .

The third room was filled with shadows. As she walked toward it, she stopped for a minute.

It was creepy, mostly shadowed — and crowded with mannequins. Some of them were poor, barely more than two-dimensional, and held theatrical billboards. Some of them were excellently crafted and wearing costumes or cloaks from the many decades the theater had been in existence. Some were old movie props, collected fifty-plus years ago.

Some were headless.

And some had heads with faces that offered very real expressions of anger, fear, hope, happiness — and evil. Some were lined up. Some were falling over on one another.

"Ah, Sage, where are you?" she asked.

At first, there was nothing. Her little pencil flashlight was back in her room; she hadn't thought to stuff that in a pocket with her cell phone.

She wondered if it was better to see — or not see — the mannequins. Coming close to one, she saw that it was a mannequin of

a Victorian woman, carved from wood.

The eyes were huge, made of blue glass. The mouth was a circle, as if the woman had witnessed the greatest terror on earth.

A placard hung from the wrist. Jane stooped to read it. Come One, Come All. Come Scream! The Gilded Lily Brings You *The Strange Case of Dr. Jekyll and Mr. Hyde!*

Turning from the mannequin, Jane bumped right into a mannequin of Mr. Hyde.

She almost screamed but managed to swallow down the sound.

Federal agents don't scream at the sight of mannequins! she chastised herself.

Something swung toward her — an arm. A gasp escaped her and then she laughed softly. Backing away from Mr. Hyde, she'd pushed a replica of King Lear.

"Sage!" she whispered.

She was stunned when, in response, she heard a groan.

So far, Sage McCormick's voice had been silent; it was unlikely that the ghost had suddenly decided to groan.

"Jennie! Jennie, is that you? Are you down here? Are you hurt?"

She began to squeeze her way through the mannequins. In the eerie light, some seemed real, as if they could come to life. Among

257

them were chorus girls and cancan dancers, fan dancers, handsome men in tuxes. And wolf men and grisly zombies and vampires. . . .

She heard the groan again.

That wasn't the ghost, she was sure of it — and definitely not the mannequins.

A deranged-looking figure in a straitjacket held a cleaver high. The cleaver was plastic, although the mannequin was creepy. Out on the street it had probably drawn many to the theater; by day it would be a come-on to those who wanted to be a little scared by their entertainment.

Ignore the mannequins. They aren't real.

"Jennie?" she called again. The mannequins might not be real, but they made it very hard to find someone who was.

"Go ahead. Try to scare me. I am ignoring you," Jane said aloud. She laughed at herself and admitted that the mannequins scared the hell out of her. She determinedly wound her way around some shrieking harpy and a man with a fly's head.

Again, it seemed that one of them, a man in a turn-of-the-century tux, swung around to touch her and knock her in the arm. She almost cried out in surprise, but realized she'd pushed another mannequin into it and the thing had moved.

She heard the groan again.

Another mannequin with a wide-open circular mouth was in front of her, holding up a book. She scooted by it and at last found the flesh-and-blood woman she sought.

Jennie was crumpled on the floor, lying on her back. Her eyes were closed and a trickle of blood had dried on her forehead.

"Oh, Jennie," Jane cried, digging in the pocket of her skirt for her cell phone as she knelt down by the woman, clasping her wrist to test the strength of her pulse.

It was weak.

"Jennie, stay with me. I'm getting help right away," she said.

Even as she spoke, she felt as if there was a tap on her shoulder. She looked up. Sage McCormick was with her again, in front of her, between Jennie's crumpled body and a row of frontier schoolboys.

She had a look of terror on her face and she waved an arm frantically.

It was a warning to turn around.

Jane started to do so. She felt a whoosh of air and briefly saw the twisted face of a madman wearing a pork pie hat, lips pulled back over teeth that were bared and yellow.

It seemed to be coming at her.

She felt the slam of something hard and

heavy against her head.

She crashed down on Jennie's prone body.

Jane didn't answer her cell phone when Sloan called. That worried him instantly; someone like Jane would *always* have her phone handy, ready for any emergency. He called Chet, who was working Main Street, and asked him to find her.

"I don't see her right now," Chet said, "but, boy, did I see her earlier! She got into the action on the street. She was great! She was funny, and she switched the whole scene. They didn't have the shoot-out. She turned it into a totally different scene, with the girls from the show and the guys hamming it up. She's a natural!"

"Chet, I'm glad to hear that, but I need to speak with her *now.*"

"Sure. I'll look for her. Want me to call you back?"

"No, I want you to stay on the line until you find her."

Sloan sat on a chunk of rock that had fallen to the floor when they'd caved in the shaft entrance. He glanced over at the body beneath the tarp, his mind racing. He'd already called Liam Newsome; he and his crime team and the medical examiner were on their way. Sloan rued the fact that there were no real roads back here and nothing was easy once you were this far into the desert.

"What's happening now?" Johnny asked him as time ticked by.

"Chet asked Henri Coque where Jane went. Henri said she's looking for Jennie and he hasn't seen either of them since."

Sloan turned his attention back to Chet. "Where's she looking?"

"In the theater."

"Well, get in there and find her!" Sloan said.

He waited; Chet eventually came back on the line. "I've been to her room, I've been in the theater, behind the stage, back of the bar, in the kitchen. She's not here, Sloan."

Sloan cursed and stood. "I'm on my way in," he said. "Get everyone looking for her, Chet. I mean *everyone.* Tear the town apart."

"We're needed here," Chet argued. "We've got a town full of people and some of them are getting drunk and a little rowdy —"

"Find her," he broke in. "Everyone on it. We've just come across another victim."

"Who —"

"Just find her, Chet. Now," Sloan ordered.

He hung up, feeling so frantic he was ready to crash through the rock walls.

"I will deal with Newsome," Johnny said. "I will tell him that the boulder was loose, and that you suspected there might be mischief going on in here, like you said when you called him."

"Thanks." Sloan had already pocketed his bug.

He cursed himself. He *had* known there was illicit activity in the mine, and he'd wanted to catch someone doing something.

He hadn't expected this.

He paused, glancing down at the body they'd discovered. It was that of Caleb Hough, the big-shot, big-mouthed rancher who thought his son should get away with everything. Sloan hadn't liked the man. But he wasn't happy to see him come to this.

He lay in a pool of blood. He hadn't been shot execution-style. It appeared that he'd taken a knife wound to the gut, and when he'd doubled over, stunned by the attack, a second person had gotten him from behind, slashing his throat with such force that he'd almost been decapitated.

"Go," Johnny told him.

Sloan nodded, backing out the way he'd come in. He whistled and Roo trotted over; he told Kanga that she had to wait for Johnny. People said horses didn't really understand commands, that they responded

262

to a tone of voice, but Sloan thought that his animals did understand him. Kanga whinnied and stayed as he had commanded. She went back to eating grass and, for a moment, Sloan wished he was a horse.

The trail back seemed long, even though he kept up a mental argument with himself — would it be faster to ride to Main Street or get his patrol car?

He opted for the car.

When he reached the theater, he found that whether Chet agreed with his command or not, he'd carried it out. The cast, crew, waiters, waitresses and everyone involved with the theater seemed to be combing it inch by inch. He'd met up with one of the county men outside who'd assured him that his people were searching the campsites, settler tents, saloon and stores.

Sloan went back to Jane's room, trying to discern if she'd been there recently and if she'd left anything that might give him a clue as to her whereabouts.

Her room was empty. Nothing seemed to indicate that she'd been there since her stint as Sage, standing by the window.

He left the room and went down the stairs, almost crashing into Henri. "You

263

checked all the dressing rooms, the stage —"

"Everywhere," Henri swore. "As you know, Jane volunteered to come in and search for Jennie, since we haven't seen her all day. The last time I saw Jane, she was walking into the theater. But she could've come back out. We could've been distracted. There's a lot going on."

"The basement — you looked in the basement?"

"Of course." Henri nodded. "I've been down there. So have Cy and Brian."

"I'll try again, anyway. That place is a mass of crates and boxes and clothing. Anyone who was hurt down there might not be easily seen," Sloan said.

"I went down there," Henri repeated. "But . . . I'll go down again with you."

"I'll go. Keep looking around up here," Sloan told him.

He headed through the door and down to the basement. As Henri had said, when he reached the landing and the main room, he didn't see a thing. He shoved aside boxes and crates, costumes, even the wig stands. Frustrated, he moved into the first room, then the second, and finally he went into the third. Mannequins stood and stared at him from the shadows. They looked like an army of the ridiculous, assembled to protect the interior of the room.

He almost jumped when his cell phone rang. He was surprised that he had service in the basement. The shadows were so deep that he couldn't read caller ID. He answered quickly. "Sheriff Trent."

"Sloan," a voice said. For a moment it sounded as if his name was being spoken by the killer in a slasher movie, the tone was so distorted.

"Yes, it's Sloan Trent. Who the hell is this?"

"Jane. It's Jane."

There seemed to be an echo, and he realized it was because he was hearing her speak in the room at the same time as he heard her speak over the phone.

"Where are you?" he asked.

"Probably about fifteen feet in front of you, since I heard your phone ring," she said "I'm getting up."

He started, jumping back, as theatrically clad mannequins began to topple over and fall against one another.

"Jane!"

He slid the phone in his pocket and began to crawl over the mannequins. One seemed to rise before him; seconds later, he saw that it was Jane.

"What the hell?" he demanded as he reached her.

In the dim light, she might truly have been part of the theater's history. Her hair was coming loose from the chignon she'd been wearing and she seemed very pale in her blue period dress. She wavered as she stood, and he pushed past the creature in the pork pie hat to steady her.

She brought her hand to her head. "Something . . . someone knocked me out," she told him. "I'm all right, but Jennie . . ." She stepped back, and he saw Jennie lying on the floor, and his heart leaped to his throat.

"She's alive, unconscious," Jane said. "I don't think anything's broken. Can you get her out of here? I don't have the strength right now."

"It's not ideal to move an injured person but I'll definitely get Jennie out. Help can't even reach her in here." He paused long enough to hit speed dial and tell Chet to call for paramedics immediately.

He ducked down and lifted the slender woman in his arms.

"You're sure you can manage?" he asked Jane gruffly. He was frightened, and his fear was making him angry, but he wanted to get Jennie to a hospital and have Jane checked out before he let emotion rule his actions.

"Yes," she told him. "And I don't believe Jennie has any broken bones. Someone knocked her on the head, too. Her pulse is decent."

"Go up the stairs ahead of me."

He heard activity at the door to the basement.

"I can hear them! He's found her!" Henri Coque shouted to someone at the top of the stairs.

Sloan was heedless of what he knocked over as he carefully made his way back to the main room and toward the stairs, following Jane. Her first steps were clumsy, but she recovered her balance, and Henri was there to help her up the stairs. When Sloan got to the landing, he saw a group awaiting them, all wide-eyed and worried. He noticed Henri first, and then Valerie, Alice, Cy and two of the night restaurant staff.

"Back off, please," Sloan said. "Let's make sure she has air!"

"Oh, Jennie!" Valerie Mystro cried in dismay.

They moved back, a stricken expression on every face.

"What happened?" Henri asked, sounding lost.

Yes, what the hell had happened? Sloan wondered. As he walked slowly through the bar to the center of the restaurant, Liz, the waitress, rushed ahead, clearing one of the longer dinner tables. Sloan came forward to lay Jennie down. As he did, the swinging doors to the Gilded Lily swung open, and Chet hurried through, leading two paramedics in uniform and bearing black medical bags. They immediately began to work over the prone Jennie, while asking questions regarding her injury.

Sloan listened while Jane replied that no one had known where Jennie was, so she'd gone down to the basement and heard her groaning and finally found her, only to be knocked on the head herself.

"Knocked on the head?" Henri burst out. "But . . ."

"Those stupid mannequins!" Valerie said.

"A mannequin did not knock her on the head," Alice protested, "but those old bastards *can* hurt you. One of them fell on me when I first came to the theater and went to look at them, thinking they were so cool."

"They're evil, Henri! We should get them out of here," Valerie said.

The paramedics started an IV on Jennie. One of them talked on his radio, and a minute later, two other emergency workers joined them, bearing a stretcher. The oldest of the group turned to Jane. "You come to the hospital, too. Head injuries can be dangerous."

"I'm fine, really. I —"

"You need a scan. You could have a concussion," Sloan said harshly. He took her by the arm. "We're going to the hospital."

"Sloan!"

"The hospital!"

"But . . . we don't know what happened!" Henri said.

"All I know is that I found Jennie on the floor. I got my cell phone out to call for help, and the next thing I knew . . . I was waking up on the floor myself," Jane told him.

Sloan was torn; he didn't want Jane going to the hospital without him and he didn't want anyone crawling around in the basement until he'd done the initial investigation himself.

"Chet," he barked, calling his deputy.

"Yes, sir?"

"Stand at that door. No one goes in or out until I'm back."

"Yes, sir!"

"If anyone comes out of that basement, arrest him!"

"Hey!" Henri frowned. "I need to get down there and see what kind of damage has been done. These two might have knocked over mannequins and been knocked out by them. Sloan, this doesn't mean there's some kind of a diabolical plot —"

"Henri, you started all this because you wanted to know who put the skull on the wig stand. By God, I'm going to finish it."

The paramedics had already taken Jennie out. One of them was standing at the door impatiently, waiting for him and Jane. The hospital wasn't quite two miles away; he could easily be back soon.

He narrowed his eyes. "We don't *know* what's going on in this town. The one thing we *do* know is that it involves more than the theater. I just found Caleb Hough dead in an abandoned mine. We've had two murders. You listen to me. *No one* goes down in that basement!"

Valerie gasped and the others stared at him in stunned silence.

He turned. Jane was staring at him, too. He grabbed her arm, leading her to the door.

"Sloan —"

"X-ray or CAT scan — or whatever they do!" His words were a growl; he was acting

like a macho jerk. But he was the sheriff —
and it was going to be done his way.

They went out to the street as the paramedics and county cops cleared a path to
the ambulance.

The sirens blared and they drove to the
hospital.

Jane wished she'd come to long before
Sloan had gotten to the basement.

She was poked and prodded, scanned, put
into a hospital gown and given an IV and
then a serious warning from a young doctor
who said she did have a minor concussion,
and that she needed to be watchful because
of it. "You should be able to resume normal
activity — but nothing strenuous. You were
unconscious for a while. This could have
been severe." He paused. "You were fortu-
nate."

"Can I leave now?" Jane asked him.

"Yes, I'll discharge you." He looked over
at Sloan, who'd been at her side throughout,
except when medical procedure had dic-
tated he wait outside. He'd taken that time,
he'd told her, to talk to Detective Liam
Newsome with county, and that conversation hadn't improved his mood any.

"Yes, just take care."

"She will." Sloan leaned against the wall,

arms crossed over his chest.

Ten minutes later, they were both seated in the back of a county patrol car, being driven to Lily.

The ride was silent. Uncomfortably silent. But apparently, Sloan didn't want to talk in front of anyone else, so she didn't try.

When they returned to the theater, it was open for business, with the restaurant and bar in full swing. Liz came hurrying to the door to meet them. "Jane, you're all right?" she asked anxiously.

"I'm fine," Jane assured her.

"And Jennie?"

"Jennie's still unconscious, but she's being given the best possible care," Sloan said. "Where's Henri?"

"Backstage, setting up for this evening's show. He's getting the cast to help him with everything Jennie usually did," Liz said. "Your deputy's been standing guard at the basement door since you left."

"Thanks, Liz." Sloan waited until she'd hurried off, then turned to Jane. "You should lie down for a while."

"I don't want to lie down."

"I'll take you upstairs," he said.

"Listen to me. I'm *fine*. If there's something to be found in the basement, you'll find it faster with two people looking," she said.

"Jane —"

"Sloan."

He swore under his breath. "Come with me, then. But when we're finished, you have to go to bed."

"We'll search the basement first," she said stubbornly.

"I need to know exactly what happened down there," he said, winding his way through groups of people, one hand on Jane's back.

The crowd in the bar was rowdier and more cheerful — and much drunker. Sloan's mood was like a thunder-cloud, and Jennie had difficulty disentangling herself from the people trying to stop her as she walked toward the door. Most wanted pictures, and she promised to pose with them later. Each time she did, Sloan, scowling fiercely, would step between her and the tourists, and they'd back off.

"I haven't moved, Sloan," Chet said when they reached the door. "Liz made coffee and brought it to me. No one's been down there." He started to smile at Jane, but cleared his throat and shifted awkwardly away from the door.

Sloan managed a brief, "Thank you, Chet."

He walked down the stairs, not turning back as she followed him. He paused to pull a giant flashlight from his belt, using it as he went straight to the third section of the room — the place she'd forever think of as the mannequin's lair.

With the light playing over the mannequins, they seemed far less real.

"So, relive every second of what happened," Sloan said.

"I looked for Jennie upstairs. She wasn't there." Jennie hesitated. "I saw Sage McCormick. She led me to the basement door and then disappeared. I checked every room until I reached this part — the mannequin room — and then I heard a groan. I pushed over a few of the dummies and found Jennie." She stopped for a moment, shivering. "When I went to take out my phone, I saw Sage again. She was warning me to look behind me and . . . and then something whacked me and I went down."

"So someone was in here with you."

"Yes."

"One of the mannequins didn't just fall?"

"I think it's a little unlikely that a mannequin would fall and hit Jennie so hard that she's still unconscious — and then fall

274

on me, too. Don't you?"

"Of course I do. I'm just asking you. Because, apparently, no one saw anyone come down here. Or leave."

"No one was in the building when I came in. Well, except for Jennie."

"Obviously, someone else *was* in the building — and in the basement."

Sloan trained the light over the entire area. Now half the mannequins were on the floor.

"What are you looking for?" she asked him.

He pointed suddenly.

She stared in that direction and saw what seemed to be a partial footprint on the dusty floor.

"It could be anyone's, Sloan."

"Not really. Too big to be either yours or Jennie's, and I'm not wearing work shoes. Walk around it. I'm going to get the crime-scene unit in here. See if you can find anything else."

She tried to search without touching while he went meticulously through the room.

"Found it," Sloan said.

"What?"

"The weapon." He pulled gloves from his pocket and reached into the fallen pile of mannequins near the spot where she'd discovered Jennie.

He carefully lifted something out.

It was a cane, a Victorian walking cane with a snarling wolf for a handle.

"Grab the light," he told her.

She did, shining it on the cane. On the handle, almost as if the snarling wolf had just bitten flesh, was a bloodstain.

"I imagine that's going to be Jennie's blood," he said tersely. "You could have been hit a hell of a lot harder."

"Yes, and like the doctor said, I'm very lucky I wasn't." She sighed impatiently. "Are you going to get that to a lab?"

He took out his cell. He spoke briefly but she could tell that he was speaking to Liam Newsome. "Yeah, I'll be here until you send someone," he said, and hung up.

"Newsome isn't coming himself?" she asked.

"Newsome is still at the morgue with the body we found this morning," he told her.

She felt dizzy and fought the sensation. *Concussion. She had to be careful.*

"You found someone — in the mine shaft?"

"Yes. I didn't want to talk about it earlier. Not until we knew you were okay. You didn't need anything else to worry about."

"Who . . . who was it?"

"Caleb Hough, the rancher. His throat

276

had been slit."

Jane stood watching him. "Sloan, can all of this be related? A skull here, the bones . . . Jennie and me being knocked out in the theater? These may be entirely separate. No one was killed here."

"Jennie is in a coma, still unconscious. Maybe one or both of you was meant to die."

She was almost afraid to tell him about the guns. She had to, she knew. "Sloan, I stopped the duel today —"

"Yes, yes, I heard about it," he said. "I'm told you gave the day a whole new meaning."

"I stopped it because of Sage McCormick — and I stopped it because I was afraid someone had tampered with one of the guns. Which, as far as I can tell, turned out to be true."

He stiffened and scowled. She hadn't thought he could look any more like a powder keg about to blow, but he managed it.

"You *know* this? You found cartridges that weren't blank?"

She felt her cheeks burn. "I'm not a hundred percent sure, but the cartridges in the two guns were different."

"Where are the guns now?"

"On my bed."

"No, they're not."

"I left them on my bed!"

"I went into your room when I arrived, when I was looking for you," he said. "There are no guns on your bed."

Lock your door. Jennie had told her to do that.

And she hadn't.

"I still have the bullets," she told him.

"You do?"

"Unless someone ransacked my whole room. They're in the toe of one of my boots."

He still looked as if he could bite those bullets in half.

"I know you're worried about me, but you'll have a heart attack if you don't control your temper," she said mildly.

He stared at her, incredulous, but he didn't have a chance to respond. Chet called down the stairs. "Sloan? You okay?"

"Fine, Chet. Stay there, will you? I'm waiting for the county crime-scene people."

"Yes, sir."

But behind Chet, Henri had a different opinion on the matter. He came running downstairs. "Sloan, what are you doing? This is one of our two biggest nights of the year! You're going to have crime-scene

278

people in the theater *now*?"

"Henri, someone viciously smashed in the head of your stage manager with a cane — and then used it on a federal agent. On Jane. You're damned right I'm having crime-scene people down here!" Sloan informed him.

Henri was at the foot of the stairs now. He shook his head. "What are you talking about? This place is a mess! Jennie must've fallen — the mannequins, look at them! They've all fallen over. Nothing evil was done here, it's just —" He paused, turning to Jane. "Oh, Jane, I'm so glad you're okay. I don't mean to sound as if I don't care, I'm just running around like a crazy man. And now . . . you're saying this was done on *purpose*?" he asked.

"Yes, Henri, someone purposely bashed Jennie and then Jane. So crime-scene people will be coming down here. You're lucky I don't close the whole theater. But while we're on the subject . . . No more duels, no hangings, nothing violent — even as playacting."

"But the outlaws were supposed to come riding into town tomorrow, shooting it all up!" Henri protested.

"Think of something else. No guns, no knives, no ropes, nothing."

"I'm the mayor, Sloan. I can fire you!"

"Fire me, but the county is coming in, and the county can trump you, Henri, and you know it," Sloan said. "Henri, did you hear me? Jennie is really hurt. She's in the hospital, in a coma."

Henri went silent and hung his head.

"And there's been another murder, Henri. This one, a townsman. Caleb Hough."

Henri looked up. "Sloan, I'm sorry. I'm truly sorry. But he was a bigmouth and a bastard, and I'm not surprised he got into trouble. But —"

"He was murdered in the mine shaft."

"It can't have anything to do with the theater!"

"The crime-scene investigators will come down here, and you'll get to keep your theater open. For now. Something is going on, and I'd think you'd want to make sure a body doesn't suddenly fall on your stage in the middle of a show."

Henri glowered at him. "Hah! Now that's being overly dramatic, Sloan."

"Henri, get back upstairs. We're coming, too."

"What's that?" Henri demanded, pointed at the cane.

"It's the weapon that bashed people's heads, and it's going to the crime lab,"

Sloan said.

Henri let out a groan of frustration and marched up the stairs. Sloan turned to Jane. "Go up to your room and get those bullets. See if the guns fell somewhere, although I doubt it. When the county crime-scene unit arrives, I'll be up. And then, tonight, you'll stay at my house."

She moved closer to him. "Sloan, if something's happening, I should be here."

"So you can get your head bashed in again?" he asked. "You have a concussion. You're off for the night. Either do it my way, or you're uninvited," he said bluntly.

Jane straightened her shoulders. She was tempted to tell him to take his whole haunted town and shove it.

But now she'd seen Sage McCormick — a ghost trying to communicate.

And people were dying.

"Fine," she snapped, and left. Chet tried to pretend that he hadn't heard everything as she walked by him. "Jane," he said, nodding politely.

"Chet," she said in return, and kept going.

As she passed through the bar area, she was accosted by many people in the crowd again. She posed for pictures. Too bad if Sloan didn't like it.

While she worried about poor Jennie, Jane could also understand Henri's position. She couldn't begin to calculate the amount of money the theater would be making that night.

When she saw the crime-scene techs walk in, she quickly begged off doing more pictures. She heard people whispering, wondering why the officers were heading for the basement.

She didn't see anyone running out in fear.

But the forensics people were there; Sloan would be along any minute. She excused herself and ran up to her room.

In front of the mirror, she studied her reflection — no one had acted as if she looked strange. She gingerly touched the top of her head. She had a knot there, but she felt all right.

It could have been worse. But she hadn't done anything stupid, not then. Rushing out to stop the gunfight when she was afraid there might be live ammunition — now, *that* had been stupid.

As Sloan had said, the guns weren't where she'd left them. Neither were they on the floor — or anywhere she could find.

She moved quickly, packing a small overnight bag and digging the cartridges out of the toe of her boot. When Sloan came to her room, she was ready.

He stepped inside for a moment and closed the door behind him.

"The bullets?" he asked.

She handed them over. All twelve were there. He glanced at them and then at her.

"Do you know which of the actors was holding the gun with the live ammunition?"

She shook her head. "I just took them — fast."

She thought he'd accuse her of being the worst law enforcement officer ever; to her surprise, he didn't.

"You saved someone's life, that's for sure," he said. He didn't look fierce anymore; he looked tired and worn.

"Let's go," he said dully. "I have two county men staying through the night. Whatever's going on, I know damned well that the theater's involved. I should close the damned thing down."

"If you do, you'll never know."

He shrugged. "Let's pray the county guys are as good as you are." He took her bag. "Come on," he said. "I'm tired enough to drop and we've got a stop to make before we get to my house."

"Where?"

"I have to go to the Hough ranch. Tell his wife and boy Caleb's dead."

"Okay, then you'd better give me a hand getting out of this Victorian get-up," Jane told him.

He looked at her helplessly, and she sighed.

"Just unlace the bodice at the back," she said. "I'll need a few minutes to change and we'll be on our way."

9

The Hough ranch was massive. Barns, paddocks and stables far to the east of the property, while the main house sat on a hillock. A stone patch, surrounded by an attractive cacti garden, led the way to the house, which could have graced many a magazine cover.

Jane stood on the porch with Sloan as he rang the bell. He was glad she'd come along with him. He'd always hated having to tell someone that a loved one was dead — but he hated the idea that they'd hear it on the news or through another source even more.

She touched his hand. "It's been hours since you found his body. Do you think they know already?"

"Liam Newsome came by to speak with the family," Sloan said. "As much as you seem to think I don't play well with others, I keep him up on what I've discovered — and he's a detective. I haven't even actually seen Liam yet. Johnny Bearclaw and I were waiting for him to arrive with someone from the medical examiner's office when I called, but then you went missing. Johnny waited at the scene, while I drove to town. Newsome came out here right after."

"Then why are we here now?"

"Liam couldn't get an answer. They've called a couple of times. Apparently, Caleb took Jimmy's cell and Zoe, Caleb's wife, is notorious for never knowing where hers is. So, Newsome had an officer come out, but he still didn't find anyone home."

"It doesn't seem that we're finding anyone at home, either," Jane said. "Maybe they're out of town. Jimmy was in trouble, wasn't he?"

Sloan frowned. "Sometimes Jimmy works for the stables." He pulled his cell phone from his pocket. Heidi answered breathlessly.

"Lily Stables."

"Heidi, it's Sloan —"

"Oh, yeah, your name's on caller ID. What's up?"

"Did Jimmy come into work today?"

"No, the little dweeb was a no-show, and he didn't answer his phone all day, either. That's why I can hardly breathe. I'm hauling hay all by myself for the hayride. Is something wrong — something else? Wow. I went by on my third trail ride today, and an area near the old mine shaft was cordoned off. A guy in a county uniform told me just to take the trail group on by. What else has happened? Oh, God!"

Heidi was going to get hysterical and he couldn't afford to listen right then. "Thanks, Heidi," he said, and hung up.

Watching him, Jane stepped gingerly into the garden to look inside the house. She pressed her nose to the picture window.

"Sloan," she said.

"What?" he asked, joining her.

"I see a handbag and a shawl on the little table in the foyer. There are keys lying next to it."

Sloan figured someone had to be out by the stables and barns. It was a massive ranch. But the house was also set apart from the work buildings.

He tried the front door; it was locked. It was a solid wood door — slamming his shoulder against it for the next ten years probably wouldn't break it in. He hesitated a bare half second, then drew his gun and shot the lock. If Jane was surprised, she didn't say so. They entered the house.

"I'll take the upstairs," she said.

Sloan walked through the dining room,

the kitchen, Caleb Hough's office and cigar room, the pantry. Nothing seemed to be out of order. Maybe his instincts had been wrong. Explaining why he'd shot through a lock to get onto private property — when he'd gone there to tell a woman that her husband had been murdered — wasn't going to be easy.

"Hey, Sloan!" Jane called. "Up here."

He ran up the stairs. She was in Jimmy Hough's bedroom. It looked as if there'd been a scuffle. Pillows were on the ground and the sheets were halfway ripped off the bed.

"But where is Jimmy now?" Sloan asked rhetorically. He felt ill; Caleb Hough had been a blowhard, but no one deserved to die the way he had. Jimmy was a good kid with the potential of becoming a fine man.

Jane set an arm on his shoulder. "This doesn't mean he's lying dead somewhere. Maybe he's been kidnapped."

"But the father is dead, so why would someone hold Jimmy?" Sloan asked. He turned on his heel.

"Where now?" Jane asked.

"The garage."

He ran down the stairs and back to the kitchen. A door opened out to the garage. It was locked, but it was a thin wooden door

288

and, that one, he did slam his shoulder against. The door gave.

"Carbon monoxide," Jane said.

He swore. There were three cars in the garage. While he could smell the gas, it had faded, and he couldn't see anyone. He strode quickly to the Mercedes Benz at the far end of the garage while Jane started with the Acura SUV closest to the house. They reached the '57 Chevy in the center together. He yanked open the passenger side while Jane opened the driver's door.

There they were, Jimmy and his mother — both looking as if they were dead. Covered in sheets like children playing at being ghosts.

They ripped the sheets off the pair.

Zoe Hough was in the driver's seat and her son was in the passenger seat.

Sloan felt for Jimmy's pulse. He found a flicker of life in the vein at the boy's neck. Glancing at Jane, he was relieved when she nodded.

"Weak — but she has a pulse."

Sloan pulled out his phone and called in an emergency.

"I'll open the doors, get air," Jane said. She rushed to the garage doors and, even as they slid up, Sloan saw cop cars coming down the drive. One was from his office and two were from county.

No one could have answered an emergency call that fast, but he was glad they were there.

Declan McCarthy, his managing night deputy, was the first to reach him. "Sloan — wow, you're here. What the hell happened now? I heard about Caleb Hough, and that, so far, we hadn't found his wife and son," Declan told him.

"We need an ambulance. It's on the way," Sloan said. "How did you get here so quickly?"

"The house alarm went off. The security company called county, and county called me," Declan explained.

"Let's get them out of the garage," Sloan said.

The two officers from county didn't pull their guns, recognizing the situation before they reached the door. Jane had Zoe Hough halfway out of the car; the county men assisted her. Declan helped Sloan maneuver Jimmy out from the other side. They got them into the driveway. There was no real grass on the lawn anywhere, but Declan got a blanket from the back of his patrol car and Jimmy and Zoe were placed on it. "Mrs. Hough is breathing," he said. "Jimmy, he's got a pulse, faint . . . but I'm not feeling his breath."

Sloan fell to his knees by Jimmy's side, and began mouth-to-mouth resuscitation, breathing into his lungs. Declan went into emergency mode with him, counting, pressing on the boy's chest.

Jimmy choked, then he started breathing on his own. Sloan felt the tension ease from his body. The kid was going to live. He didn't know how long he and his mother had inhaled poisonous gas; he didn't know how Jimmy would be when he woke up, what brain damage he might have sustained. But he would live.

The ambulance arrived, and the emergency medical technicians took over.

One of the officers from county introduced himself as Sergeant Johnson. "I was here earlier today," he said. "Never occurred to me to break in. Thank God you decided to do it, Sheriff. I'll let Newsome know." He shook his head. "It's a real miracle those two are still breathing."

"I'm not the reason for the miracle," Sloan said. "One of those two got the car turned off. They saved themselves, really."

"Yeah, but if they'd spent the night in there, they might not have come back from it," Johnson told him. "You want to cover this scene, Sheriff?"

"Officer McCarthy will stay here, repre-
senting the town," Sloan said. "I know this
kid. I'd like to ride with him."

"I'll hang in with the mother," Jane said.

As the emergency med techs began work,
Sloan noted that three men were coming
from the stables. They were obviously ranch
employees — they wore boots, jeans and
cotton shirts that showed signs of sand and
mud. The Hough ranch was one of the few
places in the area that had a stream and a
steady water supply; Hough had paid a great
deal of money for the water rights so his
place would be a viable location to raise
beefalo in the middle of a desert.

A burly fellow came forward, his ranch
hat in his hand. There was deep concern
wrinkled into his face. "I am Inego Garcia,
one of the managers," he introduced himself. "What has happened here?"

"These two were apparently attacked,"
Sloan said. "Sometime earlier today. Did
you see anyone here, anyone who could
have done this?"

Sloan was sure the man was sincere when
he shook his head. "We've been working,
moving the herd. We've had a dry spell and
needed to get the animals to the second
pasture. Mr. Hough — he doesn't like us
around the house. He says the house is his

home and the ranch is where we work. Mrs. Hough, now, she's a nice lady. She doesn't mind dirt and mud. She sometimes brings us cupcakes or cookies. She is a fine lady. Is she —"

"She's alive right now," Sloan told him.

"And Jimmy — the boy?" Inego asked, tears glistening in his eyes.

"Alive, too," Jane said, gently touching his arm.

"Have you been able to reach Mr. Hough? I have tried to get him several times during the day. I can keep trying if you like."

Sloan took a breath before answering him. "Mr. Hough is dead, Inego. I'm sorry to tell you this. We've been trying to get hold of the family all day to tell them, and now, of course, we know why we couldn't. Inego, we'll need your help. We need to know who might have had an argument with Mr. Hough. We have to find out who did this — who killed him and tried to kill his family."

Inego Garcia worried the ball cap he'd removed and held between his hands. He glanced at his fellow workers. "Well, Sheriff, he had a major argument with you. Said you were going to ruin his son's life — and turn the boy against him."

Sloan felt the county men look his way.

Yes, he had really disliked Caleb Hough.

293

And now, he'd been the one to find him in the mine shaft — and he and Jane had found the family in the garage. He imagined he wasn't looking so good.

"Anyone else?" Sloan asked.

Again, the workers glanced at one another. Inego coughed. "Well . . . everyone," he said.

"Everyone?"

Another of the men stepped up. "I'm Lee Cho," he told Sloan. "I was in the barn the other day when he came in swearing about the man who owned Desert Diamonds. Grant Winston. He said that Winston was —" He paused, clearing his throat as he fixed his gaze on Jane.

"Please, repeat what he said. I'm a federal agent, Mr. Cho. I've heard some pretty nasty language in my time," Jane said.

"Mr. Hough was saying that Mr. Winston was a grade-A, motherfucking stupid asshole who had no appreciation for the fact that without his ranch, Lily was a godforsaken dust pool," Lee Cho said, staring at the ground as he spoke.

The third man cleared his throat, as well. "He hated the theater, too. The Gilded Lily. He was ranting and raving about Henri Coque being a womanizing —" he paused, but continued quickly "— a womanizing small-peckered fuck-face," he said. "I don't know what his fight was with Mr. Coque. He never said. Mr. Hough didn't mind ranting in front of us, but he didn't consider us his friends. We kept our mouths shut."

Sloan felt a tap on his shoulder. It was one of the emergency med techs. "We're ready to roll, Sheriff."

Sloan turned to Declan and the county officers. "You'll get statements from these men?"

He received solemn nods in reply.

"And we'll get the crime-scene folks out here, too," Johnson said. "This is the busiest they've been in a hell of a long time!"

"You ready to go?" Sloan asked Jane.

"Ready," she said.

Only one of them could ride in the ambulance, and Jane felt it should be him. "I'll drive behind in your patrol car," she said.

"No, you get in there," he insisted. "You were diagnosed with a concussion a little while ago. I'll drive the car. Stay with them for me."

She didn't argue. As he followed, he realized she was just about the perfect agent. She was a listener, not butting in when others were questioning people, responding when she needed to respond and keeping quiet when something more might be learned.

She was a talented artist, too. He had the feeling that she worked well with her Krewe, handling the street work and the action, as well as the office work.

She'd never leave her job.

But what about him?

He hadn't known how much Lily, his home, meant to him until someone had brought murder to it.

Not something to think about now, he told himself.

But he felt numb, like someone other than himself. So much had happened in Lily, and so fast. Lily, Arizona — where all the violence had been in the past.

Until they'd found Sage McCormick's skull.

In the hospital, Jane dozed off, exhaustion taking its toll while they sat waiting. She woke with a start when Sloan nudged her; she'd fallen asleep on his shoulder.

"I'm going in. They said I could go in," he muttered. He sounded weary. Beyond weary.

She nodded. "I'll be here."

He smiled briefly and joined the doctor, who was allowing him to see the patients. She started when her phone rang. Logan.

She winced; she should have reported in already. Glancing at her watch, she realized it was almost 1:00 a.m. on the East Coast.

"News services have picked up reports about a second murder in Lily," he told her.

She reported in on the day, glossing over her own experience in the basement of the theater. When she'd explained it all, she paused.

Sloan seemed fine working with the county police. She didn't know what his concern seemed to be when it came to his own people — other than that they were all from Lily.

"Sloan thinks that everything's connected. And I believe it's more than possible. He also doesn't seem to trust his own people. . . ."

"Sloan is probably right about a connection. And if Lily *is* the source of all these crimes, he might just figure that his own people are too close to too many of the players," Logan said.

It wasn't her place, but she decided she should make the suggestion, anyway. "Maybe you and Kelsey could head out here."

"I'll talk to Sloan," Logan said. "See if he'll issue an invitation."

"Jay Berman crossed state lines to get

murdered here," Jane pointed out.

"We'll see." He must have been sitting at the computer. "We can catch an 8:00 a.m. direct flight that'll get us out there at about eleven tomorrow. Do you think the facial reconstruction started all this?" he asked.

"No." She thought for a minute. "I think it started before the skull showed up on the wig rack. Something major has to be going on. Two men don't die out in the desert — one shot, one with his throat slit — because of some minor disagreement. Men who shouldn't even have known each other. And now we have three people hospitalized — Jennie in a coma from head trauma, and Hough's son and wife with carbon monoxide poisoning."

"And a skull and two corpses removed from their graves," Logan said. "Sloan and I were friends. I'm sure he'll be fine with us going out there."

"He's in with the wife and son of the murder victim now," Jane told him.

"Have him give me a call," Logan said.

"You should call *him*," Jane began, but Logan didn't reply. She heard a dial tone and realized he'd already hung up.

Jimmy Hough was conscious but drowsy. He looked at Sloan through glazed eyes when Sloan came and sat by his bed.

"My dad is dead," he muttered.

"Yes, I'm sorry," Sloan said.

Jimmy's jaw tightened. "He was such a jerk. He was a bully. He beat me up with a spoon when I was a kid. He stopped doing that, though. Once he figured I could be a football star. Then he started telling me that . . . that I should seize the world. I'd have everything, money, women, anything I wanted. The bigger a jerk I became, the better he liked me." He paused and tears welled up in his eyes. "I know he was a jerk, but he was my *dad.*"

"Yes, he was your dad and you should mourn him, Jimmy," Sloan said quietly. He waited a minute and then leaned forward. "Jimmy, who attacked you and your mom?"

Jimmy shook his head. "I don't know. We were getting ready to leave. I was going to help Heidi out at the stables. And my mom . . . she loves all the Silverfest activities. Dad's never gone with her and she gets to . . . she gets to kind of be herself. She watches all the stuff the actors do, she shops at all the vendors' booths . . . she has a beer at the saloon. She doesn't drink — that's her big thing. A beer at the saloon during Silverfest." Tears welled in his eyes again.

Sloan put a hand on Jimmy's and

squeezed it. "Can you tell me what happened today? If I can find the people who attacked you, I can find the people who killed your dad."

Jimmy shut his eyes. "I didn't see anything. I didn't see anything at all. Mom had just called me from downstairs, telling me she was ready. I was opening the door to leave and when I did a sheet came down over my head. I fought. I fought like crazy. But whoever it was . . ." He stopped for a minute. "There were two of them. There had to be. Because when they dragged me downstairs to the garage, my mom was already there. I kept trying to struggle but they knocked me on the head with something, and the next thing I knew, I opened my eyes and I smelled the exhaust fumes and the car was running. It was horrible. . . . I couldn't make myself move. I knew we were dying and I couldn't move. I wasn't tied up, but . . . I don't know. Somehow I managed to reach over and turn the car off . . . and then I passed out again."

"Jimmy, did the person speak?" Sloan asked.

"He grunted a few times," Jimmy said. There was a touch of pride in his voice when he added, "I got him in the ribs. He seemed to be about my size . . . but he was strong. Really strong. I'm in good shape, Sheriff. But this guy had it all over me." He paused again. "The other one, though . . ."

"What is it, Jimmy?"

"The other one was a woman, I think."

"What makes you say that?"

"Because my mother's a fighter, too. And I think she hurt the woman, because I heard her say something to the guy when they were leaving. Sounded like, 'Bitch hurt me. I'm not in on crap like this anymore.' "

Sloan stood and set his card on the table next to Jimmy.

"If you remember anything else, call me, Jimmy."

Jimmy nodded. "My mom's going to make it, isn't she?" he asked.

"Yeah, I think so. You saved her life. You saved both your lives when you managed to switch off the ignition."

At the door, Sloan found himself called back one more time.

"Sheriff?"

"Yeah?"

"You're not a bad guy. My dad thought you were a puffed-up dick who'd spent too much time in Houston to be an Arizona lawman. But I never believed him. You were right to say I had to be locked up. And I'm lucky that you didn't kill my record. I learned from that."

"You're going to be fine, Jimmy. You're going to be just fine," Sloan assured him.

He left Jimmy and the nurse directed him down the hall to Zoe Hough's room. She hadn't come around yet, the nurse said, but she was breathing easily and all her vital signs were good.

Sloan stepped in, anyway. Zoe Hough was a pretty, blonde woman. Her hair was always impeccable, her nails always manicured; she worked out every day in her home gym and often visited the spa in the old town. Caleb Hough would have expected his wife to be perfectly put together at all times.

As he stood there, her eyes opened. She blinked, and he knew it was taking her a minute to realize where she was.

"Sloan?" she said. His name, her single word, was a raspy whisper.

"Let me get you some water," he said, pouring her a cup from the plastic dispenser. "Take it easy. You've been out of it. They're feeding you fluids through that IV, but your mouth must be dry." He helped her take a sip of the water. She lay back, gasping, eyes fluttering closed. Then they opened again. Her eyes were blue, usually a pretty color; tonight, they had a dullness about them.

"Jimmy?" she asked anxiously, trying to rise.

"Jimmy's recovering. He's right down the hall," Sloan told her. "He's a good kid, Zoe. He got the car turned off. Saved your lives."

"What about Caleb?" she asked.

He took a deep breath, wondering how much she could handle at the moment. Despite what Jimmy had said about her being a fighter, she'd always seemed to be such a fragile woman.

"Caleb was killed in the old mine shaft off the trail today," Sloan said.

She didn't act shocked. Nor did tears spring to her eyes. She stared at the ceiling, and then her gaze slid to meet his. "You're going to think I'm horrible, Sloan. I just feel . . . numb. I was so in love when I married him. He was big, he was confident. . . . He seemed to rule the world. Then my life slowly became endless days of fear. Fear that he wouldn't like dinner, fear the house wouldn't be clean enough, fear he wouldn't like the clothes I'd bought for Jimmy. Later on, I just wanted Jimmy to grow up so I could leave, you know? And then I was praying I'd have the nerve to get out of there."

"So what happened, Zoe? What was he involved in?"

She flashed him a rueful smile. "Do you

303

think he would ever have told me what was going on with his business or anything else?" she asked. "I was there to cook, clean, have babies and keep my mouth shut. I didn't do so well on the babies — we only had the one. But Jimmy was such a great kid . . . and then I saw what Caleb was doing to him."

"Jimmy will grow up to be a good man, Zoe."

"Now that his father is dead." She suddenly appeared to be furious. "Whatever he got himself into this time, he nearly killed Jimmy and me, too. What kind of father does that?"

"I'm sure Caleb didn't know you'd be at risk. He loved his son, Zoe, even if he misdirected that love sometimes. Caleb's killer probably thinks you knew something about what was going on."

"Sloan, they could try for us again."

"I'm going to have an officer watch over you two while you're here," he said.

"And then what?" Zoe asked.

"Then I'll have an officer watch over you when you're out," he said. "I promise, Zoe. I'll see to you and Jimmy."

He bade her good-night. He was the only one in the hospital by then. Newsome still had people at the Hough house, and he had people in town.

He called the county detective and told him he needed an officer at the hospital.

"You really think whoever's doing this would risk trying to kill the Hough family in the hospital?" Newsome asked.

"I think we'd be irresponsible if we don't keep guard over them."

"Yeah," Newsome said wearily. "We're getting stretched pretty thin here, but this kind of thing requires the county to be in on it. I've got men on overtime as it is, but you're right. I'll get someone over there."

"Do we have any news yet?" Sloan asked him. "From forensics?"

"About the basement at the theater? They'll be going through what they lifted from that place for weeks. We haven't gotten a damned thing from the mine shaft, and I had those men try everything. It's blocked by solid rock about fifteen feet from where you found Caleb Hough's body. They sifted for anything they could find, but the place was clean. What he was doing in there when he was murdered is a total mystery to me."

"What about the old corpse in the desert?"

"The medical examiner's office cleaned down to the bone. No identity yet. Ms. Everett could give us a likeness of the man, although I imagine he was dug up as a scare tactic. I wish we had more, Sloan, but we just don't."

"Maybe finding out who the dead man is will be important," Sloan said. "Anyway, I'll wait until you can get someone down here."

He went to tell Zoe that an officer was on the way, but she was sleeping again.

He returned to the waiting room.

He figured Jane might have fallen asleep on one of the chairs. She hadn't. She was sitting very straight, looking beautiful and composed as always. He smiled when he saw her. "Ready?"

"Yes. By the way, I checked in with Logan. He asked for you to call him." She was look-ing at him strangely — almost as if she expected him to tear into her for some reason.

"He's still awake?"

She nodded.

He called as they left the hospital.

"Jane's kept me up on events in your town. Seems it hasn't been easy for her to get the work done."

"She's done it already, for all intents and purposes. We know who the skull belonged to." Sloan went silent for a minute. Logan, he thought, was going to ask for Jane to come back. He winced inwardly. She was

306

only on loan. He'd been a fool to get used to her being there, on both a personal and professional level.

"But, yeah, it's kind of rough here right now," he said.

"I wondered if you could use some help. I have some of the team working at a historic hotel in the capital now, but I can bring Kelsey, and the two of us can come out. Are you willing to let us give you a hand?" Logan asked.

Sloan looked at Jane and then he understood. She'd been afraid that she'd stepped over the line by bringing in more federal help.

He smiled slowly, shaking his head.

"I'd be delighted, Logan. I was just talking to the lead detective at the county force. We're stretched thin, so if you can get here by tomorrow, that would be great."

Logan said he'd make it by eleven.

Still grinning — almost stupidly, but he was dead exhausted — he told Jane, "I don't know who said what and I don't care. We can use the help. Come on, let's get some sleep."

He was surprised that at his house he suddenly felt awkward. Their day had included the hospital for Jane and another dead body, and two attempts at murder. And they were no closer to solving the mystery.

Cougar appeared as soon as they entered the house, demanding attention. As he'd already discovered, Jane was an animal lover. She crouched down to play with the cat.

Johnny had left food, a pot of goulash, in the refrigerator. They sat down to eat, but neither was very hungry. When they'd finished, he said, "You can sleep in my grandfather's room. There's actually a bell on the bedside table in case you need anything."

"Why?"

"Pardon?"

"Why would I sleep away from you?" she asked. She offered him a rueful grin. "I thought the sleeping-together part went really well."

He stood and came over to her, kneeling down and taking her hands. "I thought it went more than well," he said. "It's just —"

"If you need to be alone, that's okay. I understand. But don't do it for me. The doctor said to take it easy. He didn't say that I had to stop any kind of physical activity. Although, frankly, I wouldn't mind a long hot shower first."

He rose. "You know where it is. Although you did have a concussion. You could fall in the shower or . . . I can wait to have mine until you're finished."

"Or we can just shower together," she suggested.

In a matter of minutes, she'd undressed. Her thigh holster and gun were placed in the bedside table in his room; he brought his into the bathroom. After today, he wanted it within arm's reach — no matter what. Jane didn't question the gun on the towel rack. She stepped into the shower, turned on the water and they both took a minute to luxuriate in the hot steam before finding the soap.

The day seemed to evaporate with the steam and with her touch. Her fingers moved dexterously over his body while he returned the sensual ministrations. Soap bubbles slid down her breasts and they were slick to the touch. It was incredibly erotic.

And yet, he realized, she only had to smile to arouse him.

Her fingers ran down his back and curled around his growing sex, and he knew it was time to leave the water.

"We need to get out," he said thickly.

"I'm not going to fall," she told him.

"I am!"

Jane turned off the water. They got out of the shower and picked up towels, drying each other, pausing for deep, wet kisses that increased his desire to the breaking point. They started to leave the bathroom; he went back for his gun.

He laid it on the bedside table, then pulled her to him and they fell on the bed together. Their bodies were silky clean, caressed by the cool sheets. She straddled him, damp hair trailing over his shoulders and chest as she stroked him and delivered more wet kisses to his naked flesh. He took her in his arms, fascinated again by the scent and feel of her, his lips straying along her arms, her thighs, her sex. She rose against him and he felt her warmth envelop him. Her eyes were on his as she moved slowly and then with a sensual rhythm that sent his libido soaring. They switched positions so that he stared into her eyes as he moved over her. Far too soon, he felt the urgency of his climax overtake him. Then he felt her shudder in his arms and they lay together, trembling, seeking breath and still entwined.

In the same position, he slept.

But in his dreams he saw Longman again, up high on a plateau. Jane was talking to him, and he could see the dark cloud, evil rising around them.

And heading for Jane.

He awoke with a start. She still slept

peacefully at his side.

He rose carefully, dressed and took out a notepad. He had all the pieces, he thought. He just had to put them together.

He started writing down a timeline, including everything that had happened, everything he knew.

Then he went to get the books he'd bought at Desert Diamonds to read through them.

Caleb Hough hadn't been a nice guy. He'd argued with just about everyone. Including Grant Winston.

And he'd gotten the history books from Grant Winston's Desert Diamonds. Jay Berman had the same books.

There had to be something in the books. Something to do with the infamous gold heist?

Two people — one a man, one a woman — had attacked Zoe and Jimmy Hough.

A stranger, Jay Berman, had been killed, and so had a local, Caleb Hough.

Just how many people were involved in what was going on?

10

Jane came out of Sloan's room, wearing the same robe she'd worn before, to find that he'd already brewed coffee and had apparently been working for several hours. He had the books from Desert Diamonds on the table, along with sticky notes, a poster board and a long list of notes for himself.

"As we started to discuss earlier, I think there's a clue in the books," he said. "I've skimmed them both. The one by Sheriff Fogerty talks about the town around the time the stagecoach filled with gold disappeared. So, I'm beginning to suspect that Sage knew something about the robbery — and that's why she was killed. She charmed everyone who came to the bar after her performances. And while a lot of the rougher clientele preferred the saloon, I'll bet Sage had her share of admirers who came to the theater. She might have heard something from one of them. And I don't

312

believe she was having an affair with Red Marston. From what I've been reading, they were friends from back east and he came to town with a reputation for being a playboy."

"Why did she visit Trey Hardy in his cell?" Jane asked.

"The same reason — simple friendship. Sage was a charmer and so was Trey Hardy. They might've seen each other as kindred spirits. I gather that most people liked Trey, just as they liked Sage."

"So why kill Red? If we're right about that . . ."

"I think both Sage and Red were killed because they knew too much — just like I think Zoe and Jimmy were attacked because someone thought *they* knew too much. And I'm convinced that Jay Berman came here because someone he knew was in on the situation, and that he was murdered because he got greedy — or because someone thought he'd spilled the beans."

Jane poured herself a cup of coffee and sat down across from him. "But if this is all about gold, why would these murders be taking place now? It's not illegal to look for gold lost over a hundred years ago."

"I don't know," Sloan said, sounding frustrated. "I'm assuming the state would weigh in on the gold, since it was stolen, but there'd have to be an enormous finder's fee. Maybe the people involved have no intention of handing it over to the state. And everyone's always assumed that the gold's around here somewhere. The stagecoach never made it to Tucson. It just disappeared. It would be easy enough to make a stage-coach disappear in the desert. The horses were probably let loose and could have been adopted by Apaches in the area. This book — the one by Brendan Fogerty — suggests the driver and guards were murdered and buried in the desert, and the gold was hid-den somewhere, secreted away."

"What would the silver mine have to do with it?"

"Again, I don't know — unless it was be-ing used as some kind of cache or even a meeting place. The mine didn't go out of action until long after the stagecoach dis-appeared."

"So you really think this is about gold?"

"I can't figure out anything else. It's almost as if digging up the corpses from the past is like a warning to someone who's involved. One of the conspirators, if you will. That's why I'm not sure the theater is safe."

She nodded in agreement.

"Let's get going. Logan says he'll rent a

car in Tucson. He and Kelsey will be in town sometime in the midafternoon. Before then, I want to start on a few things. I'll ask Johnny Bearclaw to bring that water bottle you found in the mine to the lab. We must be able to get a DNA hit off it, and that could at least send us in the right direction." He shook his head. "I should've done that right away. But now I want to get to town and question everyone at the theater about the live rounds in that gun — and when they last saw Caleb Hough."

"I'll get dressed," Jane said. "And the bottle is tied to the saddle I was using." She shrugged.

"Good. I'll let Johnny know," Sloan told her.

Twenty minutes later, they were on their way back to town.

As they drove, she flipped through the books Sloan had gotten at Desert Diamonds. Both were well-written and did an excellent job of recreating the past; it was still the wild, wild west. Everyone carried a gun. Ladies were ladies, whores were whores — and actresses were looked on as little better than whores, though a woman like Sage McCormick would be admired, desired and placed on a pedestal.

By all accounts, Sage loved her husband

and child, but was known as well to frequent the bar of the Gilded Lily. She even smoked a cigar upon occasion and was a good poker player.

She frequently visited Trey Hardy, once he'd been taken to jail, and was disconsolate when he was shot down in his cell. Trey Hardy, being an outlaw who'd often held up stagecoaches — but let the driver and guards go — could have learned during his time in jail that a stagecoach bearing the last of the area's gold was leaving town. And maybe he knew who might have gone after it. So if Sage McCormick had been spending time with him, it was logical that he'd told her about the intended heist.

"I'll bet she did know something," Jane murmured. "But *what*?"

"And will we ever find out?" Sloan responded. "Hey, take my phone. The number for the hospital should be in the contacts. See how Jimmy, Zoe and Jennie are doing."

Jane dialed, putting the phone on speaker so that Sloan could identify himself. He was told that Jennie remained unconscious. Zoe and Jimmy were doing well.

"There's still a county officer watching the halls?" he asked.

The nurse giving the report assured Sloan that an officer was on duty. He come in to spell the night man just an hour ago.

Sloan thanked her, then said, "One more. Find the number for Newsome's office. And please put it on speaker again."

Newsome was at the morgue, but one of his officers told Sloan that all they'd heard so far was that the blood on the cane found near Jennie Layton belonged to Jennie Layton. The cane itself had been wiped clean.

Sloan sighed, disgusted that they couldn't seem to get any solid evidence. He turned to Jane. "When we get there," he said, "we'll play along with the street theatrics again."

She glanced at him, surprised.

He offered her a crooked smile. "I can force a county investigation, but that won't help figure out what's really going on here. I may even find that people are more willing to talk when we're in costume. Anyway, a costume isn't all that different from a uniform."

"You know this is kind of crazy, don't you?"

"Everything about it is more than a little crazy," he agreed.

It was still early, not quite 8:00 a.m., when they arrived. But the doors to the theater were unlocked. As they entered, they saw Henri sitting at one of the tables with his cast.

"Jane!" Valerie cried, running over and giving her a hug. "How are you? You poor dear. Do you have any idea what happened to you yesterday? Should you really be up and walking around?"

"I'm fine," Jane assured her.

"But . . . do you remember anything more?" Alice asked. "I mean, could you have tripped?"

"No," she said flatly.

Valerie looked at her anxiously and then at Sloan.

"Oh, my God! Sloan, haven't you found out anything? It's all so horrible! Caleb — *Caleb Hough* — was murdered!" Valerie said. "Sloan, he's not a stranger. He's one of us! Please tell us you found out what happened to him."

"No, I don't know yet," Sloan said. "And someone attempted to murder Jimmy and Zoe, as well. There's something going on here in Lily — and everyone's in danger until we find out what it is."

"Someone tried to kill Jimmy?" Brian repeated. "Jimmy Hough? The kid's decent. He used to come by a lot. He loved the show. And his mom! What a doll. Why would anyone hurt her?"

"But they're okay? The family's okay? They were . . . attacked?" Alice asked.

"They were knocked out and left in the garage to die of carbon monoxide poisoning," Sloan said.

"But they survived?" Henri asked.

"Jimmy managed to turn the car off," Jane told them.

Alice let out a little sound and Cy groaned softly.

"Sloan, Caleb was an outspoken jerk. I'm surprised he didn't get killed long ago," Henri muttered.

"Henri!" Alice chastised.

"Well, it's true. So maybe Caleb was in collusion with that tourist who got shot in the desert. Caleb was probably running drugs or illegal aliens — or maybe he was even into human trafficking," Henri said. "It's a crying shame the bastard got his family involved. But, Sloan, come on. It's your job to find out what the hell's happening here, but it has nothing to do with us in the theater. You didn't come in to suggest we shut down for the day, did you? Lord, the town's still full of tourists. None of them have been scared off by this."

"No, Henri, I'm not suggesting you shut down. However, the same rules apply as yesterday. No knife fights, no shoot-outs, nothing with weapons."

"Oh, come on!" Henri said again.

Sloan reached into his pocket and let the cartridges spill out on one of the tables.

Everyone stared at them and then at Sloan.

"What? What is that? What are you trying to say?" Henri demanded.

"These are from the guns Cy and Brian were going to use for the duel yesterday," he said. "You'll note that one set is live rounds."

"Shit!" Brian said, jumping to his feet and backing away, as if the bullets could take aim at him from where they lay scattered on the table.

Cy stood, too. He swallowed, frowning at Jane. "You!" he said. "You knew. *How* did you know?"

"Yes, how *did* you know, Agent Everett?" Henri asked.

Jane felt all eyes on her — accusing eyes. "Intuition," she said. "Something just seemed wrong."

"Who handled the guns?" Sloan asked.

"Before we had them on the street?" Brian looked at Henri.

"Jennie Layton," Henri told them. "Jennie was always responsible for props. They were in the prop room — right where they were supposed to be — before I went to get them for the duel."

"But none of you saw Jennie all day. That's why I had to go search for her," Jane said.

Henri waved a hand in the air. "She had all the costumes ready, plus the prop guns and the rope and rigging we used for the lynching, the night before."

"We can ask Jennie." Valerie's voice wavered.

"Hard to ask her if she's unconscious," Alice snapped.

Sloan ignored them. "Who had access to the props besides Jennie?" he asked.

"It's not locked," Henri explained. "Anyone could've gotten into the prop room. But like I said, Jennie got them ready the night before. She came to tell me we were all set for the first of our big Silverfest days."

"You do realize that while anyone might have gotten into your prop room, not many people would know the guns would be there — set for a shoot-out," Sloan said.

"Oh, my God!" Valerie cried. "Sloan You're accusing one of *us!*"

"Cy is my best friend out here," Bria said. "I'd never shoot him — and he'd nev shoot me. I mean, on purpose."

"This theater is my life!" Henri announ — theatrically — getting to his feet.

"Jennie did prepare the guns." B frowned. "But then . . ."

"Then she accidentally bashed her own head with a cane?" Sloan asked.

"We have housekeeping staff. Cooks, servers and bartenders," Henri said.

"Yes, and I'll get to them all one by one," Sloan told him.

"But — but . . . it's Silverfest!" Henri protested. "Sheriff, I *am* the mayor of this town —"

"I know that, Henri. I told you, I'm not going to close anything down. Jane and I will get into costume again and be part of it. I'll keep an eye on everything all day."

Henri nodded, his bald head shining in the light of the chandeliers. "All right, Sloan, all right, that's good."

"Oh, and two of Jane's coworkers are on their way. Henri, I thought you could put them up in Jennie's room for the next few days," Sloan said casually.

"Jennie's things are all in her room. It's not like an empty guest room, Sloan."

"They'll be very careful of her personal belongings."

"Who are these agents?" Alice asked.

"Logan Raintree and Kelsey O'Brien. They work together but they're a couple, as well, so just one room will be fine," Sloan replied. "They'll be protection for you. I still believe you're all in danger."

"Bring them in, bring them in," Valerie said.

"I agree," Alice added.

"Of course, Sloan, if you think it's necessary," Henri agreed.

"I'm all for it!" Brian said. His face ashen. "One of us — Cy or me — almost bought it yesterday." He looked at Jane, but not with the same rakish *I'd love to pick you up* stare he usually gave her. He looked at her as if she'd suddenly become an oddity.

"Instinct. Or . . . maybe it was the ghost. I glanced up at the window and I thought I saw a woman there. Sage McCormick. It was like a warning that something was going to happen," Jane said.

"Oh, no, please . . . I don't want to believe there are really ghosts here," Valerie moaned.

"I say thank God for a ghost if she saved my life!" Brian said.

Cy lifted his coffee cup. "Hear, hear."

"Time to go," Henri said suddenly. "We need to open our doors and be out on the street. So, Sloan, you two will costume up again?"

Sloan nodded. "Yes, we'll be part of it."

"I'll take you down to the dressing rooms," Alice offered.

"Agent Everett," Henri asked. "Where's

the blue gown? It's an important part of our costume department."

"It's safe," Jane assured him. "It's in my room, but after everything that happened yesterday . . . it'll need to be cleaned."

Henri sighed dramatically. "Then we'll have to find you something new for today."

"Before we get our costumes, I have one more question," Sloan said. "Did all of you see one another early yesterday morning?" he asked.

They were silent for a minute. "How early?" Alice shrugged. "I didn't get up very early. We have late nights here, you know."

"Brian and I were both up. We had coffee together at about eight," Valerie said.

"I . . . slept in," Cy murmured.

"And I had a meeting with Mike Addison," Henri said impatiently. "Are you suggesting one of us attacked Zoe and Jimmy Hough?"

"I have to ask, Henri. You know that," Sloan said.

"Well, you've asked." Henri was evidently angry. "We're theater people. We entertain — we don't hurt others. We sure as hell don't kill them!" he ended indignantly.

"Let's get our costumes, shall we?" Alice suggested. "There's way too much testosterone flying around this room!"

Better testosterone than bullets, Jane thought.

She wasn't sure what else Sloan had planned for the day, but at the moment, it was time for costumes.

"Yep, let's do that," Sloan said. But he looked sternly around the group. "Don't be anywhere alone. Make sure you're on the street in a crowd or with someone else at all times. I'm not making accusations — I'm just trying to get answers. And I don't want to find any more bodies."

Silence followed his words.

Those in the room exchanged glances.

"Don't!" Henri warned. "Don't go getting suspicious of one another, please! An ensemble cast must work together. Sloan, see what you've done?"

"They have to be careful, Henri. This group may be entirely innocent — but this group is in danger. Someone put Sage McCormick's skull on that wig stand, and someone got into the basement and struck Jennie and Jane. And someone shot a stranger in the desert and slit Caleb Hough's throat and tried to kill his family. Everyone needs to be watchful. Someone in this town is a murderer."

They all looked at Sloan in silence as he spoke.

"We'll be careful, Sloan," Valerie said in a small voice. "Honestly."

He nodded. "It's your lives," he reminded them. "Take that very seriously."

Jane set her hand on his arm; he had gotten his point across.

Henri didn't seem happy. "Come on, then. If you're going to be breathing down my neck, get into costume." He paused, glancing around. "Has anybody seen our housekeeper, Elsie, come in?"

"Yes, she's upstairs cleaning the rooms with one of the local girls," Valerie said.

"Valerie, run up and ask her to make sure Jennie's room is clean so the other agents can stay there," Henri told her. "Alice, you come with me and Jane and the sheriff."

"What do you want Brian and me doing?" Cy asked.

"Go ahead and start entertaining the tourists as they show up on the streets." Henri looked over at Sloan. "They're allowed to do a little trick-riding, right?"

"Trick-riding is great."

"Good. I'm glad you don't think the horses are in on it!" Henri said with a sniff.

That, at least, made them all smile — even Sloan.

"No, Henri, I don't think the horses are in on it," he responded drily.

They rose to do as asked. Behind the stage in the dressing rooms, Henri selected clothing for Jane and Sloan to wear. Sloan just had to change into a period cotton shirt, jacket and plumed hat. Jane told them she'd change into her new costume upstairs.

She ran ahead before any of them could protest. Up in her room — or Sage's room — she spoke out loud while she changed. "We could really use some more help here, Sage. Something was going on — and you knew about it, didn't you? I wish there was a way you could tell me what you found out. Because people are dying again, Sage."

If Sage was there, she wasn't speaking at the moment.

Jane walked into the bathroom. As she brushed her hair and arranged it into a loose chignon, she wished she had time to take a shower; Sage seemed to like writing on the mirror.

She bent down as she dropped a bobby pin. When she looked into the mirror again, she seemed to have double vision — and then realized that the ghost was standing right behind her.

Jane spun around. The apparition didn't disappear. Instead, she reached out as if she could touch Jane, and then her hand fell.

"I know it can be hard, very hard, to appear and communicate. I also know you've been here many years, and I'm not sure why. Do you watch over your family or have you been waiting for this all these years — someone killing people because of the past? I realize you'd never hurt anyone, that you want to help people, but we need to know what you know," Jane said.

She thought of the different apparitions she'd encountered, and she knew that some were present and never appeared, some were like mist . . . and some had become so experienced at showing themselves that they could cause a great deal more than cold drafts or whispers in the night.

"Sage, we really need your help," she said again.

The ghost seemed to step through her. Sage touched the mirror, but of course there was no steam. Jane quickly closed the door and ran the hot water in the sink, creating a vapor.

The ghost wrote, "Trey Hardy."

It seemed to take all her effort. She wrote the name and faded away.

Trey Hardy, gunned down in his cell. *Jane had to get to the Old Jail and into that cell.*

Chet Morgan and Lamont Atkins were in town, in uniform, patrolling the streets on foot, making their presence known.

Sloan spoke with them both. They were worried, aware that Lily needed Silverfest even though the town had been plagued by murder.

"Bad days, Sloan, bad days," Lamont told him. "But we're watching everyone. And Newsome over at county has done his part. There are three officers, two men and a woman, keeping up with everything. So far, I'm feeling like a tour director, but that's all right. No trouble happening here as I can see."

Sloan started into Desert Diamonds next, but the place was overflowing with people and every step he took drew another question from a tourist or someone wanting to pose with him. He went back to the street and called Grant Winston, asking him to come out for a chat.

Sloan leaned against the post by the Old Jail Bed and Breakfast, playing his part as Trey Hardy. He didn't mind being Hardy — he actually felt a certain kinship with the man. But his main goal that day was to interview everyone in town about Caleb Hough.

His call to Grant Winston had ruffled the man. He was extremely busy and delighted to be; these days let him stay open for the rest of the year. But Sloan was insistent, and Grant promised he'd go over to the Old Jail as soon as he could get his staff functioning smoothly.

As he waited, Sloan watched people move along the street and he listened to their conversations.

Some talked about leaving Lily then and there, despite all the festivities planned for the day; the news services had carried information about the murders that had occurred in the desert. But someone in the party would usually argue that the murders had taken place out in the desert and in a mine shaft, and had nothing to do with anyone in Lily.

"Drug-related, obviously!" one person said.

"We're not that far from the border! It's all about human trafficking!" another woman suggested.

Then they would stop to chat with him.

People asked him about the outlaw Trey Hardy, and he played his part whenever they did, telling them he wasn't a bad sort at all. There were those who'd profited by war and those who'd been impoverished by it, and he just didn't think it was right for people to make money on war.

"Still happening. It will always happen," a

man said.

He posed for pictures with kids, with young women and even the men — many of whom were walking around with the replica Western gunslinger pistols they'd bought at Desert Diamonds.

He studied every gun he saw that day.

As he'd promised, Grant Winston came out of Desert Diamonds, wearing the kind of apron an old-fashioned shopkeeper would wear.

"Sloan, what the hell? It's the busiest day of the year!" Grant was obviously flustered and annoyed.

"I would have come to you," Sloan said.

"I don't want to talk in the store!" Grant protested.

"Because I want to ask you about a dead man?"

Grant's ruddy face grew even redder. "Caleb Hough got himself murdered. I'm surprised his wife didn't kill him long ago."

That was a common assertion. "I heard you and Caleb had a big argument. Want to tell me about it?"

Grant Winston frowned and seemed truly perplexed. "First off, the guy never came to my shop. The wife and kid did — Zoe loves a cappuccino, and the kid came with all the other kids, bought pizza, looked through the magazines and books — but Caleb Hough never darkened my door. Then all of a sudden about a month ago he comes in and asks about my history books. I showed him where they all were, although a numbskull could've found them on his own. Then, about two weeks ago, he's back, telling me I'm holding out, that I've got books I'm not selling. I told him I owned collectible books that no, I didn't sell. He wanted to see them. I said no. Then I come in one day and he's just let himself into my office in back and he's going through my private collection! I told him to get the hell out — that everything I have has been republished over the years. He told me he'd pay me some ridiculous sum of money for my collection and I said, 'No!' I collect books because I love them. He told me that if I had any sense, I'd accept his offer or he'd see that I wound up being closed down. I said he could take his money and stuff it where the sun don't shine and that I'd take my chances. That was the last time I saw him. And if you think I'd go crawl into a mine and kill someone because he was an idiot, you're crazy!"

"What books did he buy?" Sloan asked.

"The same books that stupid tourist did — and that you took the other day. You had a worse argument with the bastard than I did, Sloan. You told your deputy to keep his kid in jail overnight. He exploded over that!"

"How did you know?" Sloan asked. "Thought you hadn't seen him."

"I *haven't* seen him," Grant said, exasperated. "This is Lily — you sneeze and everyone knows it!"

"All right, Grant, thanks." Sloan paused. "But I'm going to need to see your collectible books sometime soon."

"Sloan, you can read through the night if you want. I have the original of the book Fogerty wrote after it all happened and he'd retired, and I have some of the newspapers from the day, but I don't know what you're going to get out of them."

"I don't, either. But I appreciate the opportunity to go through them."

"You got it, Sloan. Whenever you want. Just so long as you don't stop me from working today. The place is hopping!"

As Sloan let him get back to work, Mike Addison came outside, grinning.

It was bizarre that a local had been killed — viciously murdered, his throat slashed — and that no one in town seemed to mourn him.

But then, neither did his wife.

"What's the smile for, Mike?" he asked.

"I just had some people check out of the B and B," Mike told him.

"And that's a good thing?"

"The wife was all freaked out. She said she saw the ghost of Trey Hardy sitting in the chair by the bed when she woke up. She made her husband get them a room at the chain hotel down the highway."

"But don't you *want* people staying in Trey Hardy's cell?"

"Sure, but the more haunted the cell gets, the more I'll have people clamoring to stay there. The wife is some kind of big blogger. Now I'll have reservations for every night of the year!" Mike said happily.

It was while he was talking to Mike that Sloan saw Jane walking on the raised sidewalk from the theater to the Old Jail. Her costume today was crimson, and the color of her hair and eyes seemed to be enhanced by the color. She looked more beautiful than ever; he wondered if the ghost of Sage was pleased. She waved and made her way over.

"Wow," Mike murmured. "Wow. You know her?"

"That's Agent Jane Everett," Sloan said, realizing that Mike and Jane hadn't met.

"She's a fed?" he asked incredulously. "Oh, but she's an artist. She doesn't . . . I mean, she doesn't have a gun or anything like that, right?"

"She has a very big gun," Sloan assured him.

"Hi," Jane said to them.

Sloan performed the introductions. Jane was pleasant as she met Mike, but then she glanced at Sloan, a silent question in her eyes. He shook his head slightly, letting her know he hadn't learned anything new.

"Mike is all excited. His guests ran out of the Trey Hardy room," Sloan said.

"Oh?" Jane asked.

"Double income!" Mike said happily. "As soon as people hear, I'll have someone else in. Double income — oh, yeah!"

"Hey, don't rent it out for tonight," Jane told him.

"Are you kidding me?" Mike asked. "Don't you understand? This is a great thing for me. I can make double! The couple who left had paid ahead for the next few nights. I'll rent the room out again, and I'll be in good shape. That's a rule when renting here — if you leave early, I keep the money!"

"I'll take it for the night," Jane said.

Mike looked at her in surprise. "You like ghosts, huh?"

"I love them."

"I heard you were staying at the theater."

"Oh, I am, but I'm here for a bit longer. I'd love to have the haunted Trey Hardy cell for a night."

"Um, sure, but . . ." He glanced at Sloan and then asked her, "You, uh, wouldn't shoot up the place or anything if you freaked out?"

"Believe me, Mike. I don't freak out," Jane assured him sweetly. "And I've almost never had to shoot anyone."

"I'd feel kind of badly taking your money," he said next.

"Oh, I'm here working. You'll be paying for it in a way, too. Your federal dollars at work."

"Well, then, what the hell! The room is yours," Mike said.

"May I see it now?" Jane asked.

"Sure. Come on in!"

Sloan looked at her curiously, and she smiled. "I'd love to get to know Trey Hardy," she said lightly.

Mike opened the door. The three of them passed the old sheriff's desk — the check-in area — and the deputy's desk, where the concierge sat; it was empty at the moment. Sloan saw that the "concierge" was busy serving breakfast to a number of guests in the old gun room. He watched the way Jane studied the place as they entered. She commented to Mike on what a great job he'd done turning it from an old jail into a bed-and-breakfast, while keeping its historic integrity.

"It wasn't me, really. I mean, I've made some improvements, but the guy I bought it from had all the ideas. I've made a point of improving the bathrooms, though!" Mike said. "Guests these days expect that."

They went through the barred wooden door that led to the rows of cells, which were now guest rooms. "There it is!" Mike told her proudly. "The Trey Hardy room. Right where Aaron Munson gunned down the poor guy. Take a look."

"Thank you." Jane walked into the room and slowly looked around. There was a towel on the floor and the bed needed to be made. A water glass was knocked over — it seemed evident that the last guests had departed quickly.

"It needs to be cleaned, of course," Mike said.

"Don't worry, I won't be going to bed for hours." Jane dug into her crimson velvet wristlet — a perfect match for her costume — and produced a credit card. "Would you please charge me now? I don't want to lose the room, knowing how popular it is."

"Anything for you!" Mike said, and Jane smiled pleasantly.

After the arrangements had been made, Sloan walked Jane down the street. "What was that all about?" he asked as they posed together by an old watering trough for the pleasure of a few tourists.

"Sage wrote 'Trey Hardy' on the mirror. I thought we'd have to wait until this whole Silverfest thing was over to get in there."

Sloan was silent. She spoke so naturally to him, and he wondered what it was like to be comfortable with seeing things that others didn't. He'd wondered far too often himself if he wasn't crazy, if Longman wasn't a being his mind had invented, a sort of device to help him figure things out.

"Trey Hardy was dead before the stage-coach disappeared," he reminded her.

"But . . . there's something connected to this that has to do with him. I'm positive. Sloan —" Jane stopped to smile and say, "A pleasure!" to the people thanking them for posing. "So, have you spoken with Grant Winston?"

He nodded.

"What was the fight about?"

"Grant's collection of rare books. He caught Caleb Hough in his office. Hough told him he'd ruin him if he didn't sell him

338

his own books."

"Oh. But is that a motive for murder?"

"I don't think so. I'm more concerned with what Caleb was looking for. I'm going to get back into Grant's office before the end of the day," he said.

His cell phone rang as they walked, and he answered immediately. It was Liam Newsome.

"My officer just called from the hospital," Liam said. "Seems there was a woman in some kind of period costume there. She was bringing a basket of food to Zoe and Jimmy Hough."

"Who was it?" Sloan asked.

"He didn't know. When he stopped her in the hallway, she took off. He couldn't go after her and still guard his patients, so he called to tell me about it."

"Thanks, Liam," Sloan said, and hung up. "I'm going to borrow a horse from the stables and ride out to the hospital. With all the traffic, not to mention the street closures, that'll be the fastest."

Jane had heard the conversation. "That woman — it could be anyone, Sloan. Could genuinely be a friend. Half the people here are in costume, or wearing old hats and skirts. She could be heading the other way now, you know."

"And she could be heading this way," he said. He hesitated, then suddenly took her by the shoulders. "Be careful."

"I will. And Logan and Kelsey are due soon," she added.

He started to walk off, but then turned around. "No basements!" he warned her.

"Not unless someone screams blue blazes and I'll be ready if that happens," she promised.

"Jane —"

"I'll get backup, don't worry."

He left her on the street and hurried over to the stables. Heidi was just getting a group mounted for the trail ride to the Apache village.

"I need a horse," he told her.

"Sure, Sloan, but why? Your horses are better than anything we have in our hack line."

"I'm going to the hospital and I'd rather take a horse than a car right now. Don't want to waste time going back to my place."

Heidi looked at him wide-eyed. Her eyes brimmed with tears. "It's about Jimmy, isn't it? Is he all right? I should've known when he didn't show up yesterday that something was wrong."

"Jimmy is doing well, Heidi. Now —"

"Take Bullet. He's saddled and he has

340

some spunk in him," Heidi said.

Sloan mounted the horse and rode out of the stables.

He heard a loud cheering and realized people thought that he was part of the festivities. He tilted his hat to them — and set out on the road that led from Main Street to the hospital.

He took the trail at an easy lope until he was a good mile past all the hoopla. Then he slowed Bullet and moved to the side of the road, watching for cars.

People were driving slowly, even this far from town. He was glad to see it; they needed to be careful with the number of people moving around on foot.

A car carrying what appeared to be parents and three children passed him, followed by a car with three young women. He lifted his hat to them all. They waved in return.

More parents, more kids, went by. More young people.

And then he saw the car he was waiting for.

A young woman was driving. She wore a prairie bonnet.

She frowned, concentrated on her driving, clearly irritated that she had to slow for a van filled with school-children.

Sloan moved Bullet back onto the road, behind the van and in front of the car.

The driver looked up and saw him. For a moment, he thought he saw surprise and dismay on her face.

Then it was gone.

For a frightening few seconds, he was afraid she was going to hit the gas and try to run him over.

She didn't. She smiled. "Sloan! What are you doing out here? Oh, my God — nothing else happened, did it?"

11

At one o'clock, Cy Tyburn and Brian Highsmith dazzled the crowd with feats of
derring-do on horseback.

They rode at each other almost as if they
were jousting; they were supposed to have
ridden with reins between their teeth, guns
blazing, but Sloan had outlawed the use of
weapons.

Cy stood in his saddle and leaped for
Brian. The two flew from their horses and
staged a brawl right between the theater and
the saloon. Jane watched the action anxiously, but they put on a good show and
when it ended — with both of them "dead"
on the street — they leaped to their feet
and took a bow.

Jane applauded with the others.

After that, she slipped into Desert Diamonds and found Grant Winston, whom
she hadn't officially met. He seemed har-
ried and harassed, but he was cordial to her,

343

and he offered her a chance to look through the books in his office.

"Terrible thing about Caleb, but . . . not totally unexpected. Okay, well, his throat slit in the old mine — that was unexpected. This is Arizona, and a lot of people carry weapons. Me, I keep a shotgun behind the main checkout counter. He pissed me off so much I might have shot him if I actually carried a weapon. I'm sorry. I know I sound terrible. But you won't find many people here who are crying over the man," he told her. "Go into my office, Agent Everett. I told Sheriff Trent he was welcome back there anytime." He suddenly frowned at her. "Wait. I thought you were an artist."

"I am."

"Oh." He still seemed confused. "Well, make yourself at home. I can't help you, I'm afraid. Busy, busy, busy. And, of course, you know —"

"I know that the items you're letting me see are the real thing — collectible and priceless. I'll be very careful with anything I touch," Jane promised.

He nodded. "Cappuccino? Espresso?" he offered.

She shook her head. "I'm fine, thanks. And I wouldn't risk spilling anything."

That pleased him. She wondered if the offer had been a test.

He walked her past rows of pamphlets and souvenirs to his office. It was a large room with a plush swivel chair behind the desk, which held memo boxes on one corner, plus a computer and printer. Behind the desk and along both sidewalls were rows and rows of books carefully placed in glass-covered wooden shelves. "Behind the desk — that whole shelf is on Arizona history and Lily."

When the door closed behind him, she turned to look at the shelves. She saw the original of the republished book she'd been reading by Brendan Fogerty.

Carefully, she removed it from the shelf and sat behind the desk. The book was in excellent shape for its age. She was surprised that the original had a dedication she hadn't seen in the replica edition.

"To Sage, wherever in this world or the next she may be."

Apparently Brendan Fogerty had thought it possible that Sage was dead.

But who had killed her? Not her husband. First, he'd been in the bar waiting for her when she'd gone to her room. And then, it was unlikely that he could have gotten away with burying her in a dressing room. Or had she been buried elsewhere first? Jane could only imagine that even in the Old West, the smell of a decomposing body would have alerted someone to Sage McCormick's presence under the floor.

A man named Eamon McNulty had been owner, manager and artistic director of the theater back then. His actors had been more transient; only Sage had won so many hearts that she was hired to play role after role.

Jane kept flipping pages.

Most of what she read she'd already seen.

A "rancher" named Tod Green had been in town for several weeks before the deaths of Hardy and Munson and the disappearance of Sage, Red Marston and the stagecoach. Fogerty stated that he'd been suspicious of the rancher, since no one had known him until he started moving cattle. He'd checked with friends in Texas, Oklahoma, Kansas and other states, but the man had no background that he could discover. Fogerty openly voiced his dislike and suspicion of Green as far as the robbery went, while saying at the same time that he had no proof against him. Nor would he ever learn anything — because Tod Green had died in the streets just days after the stagecoach had disappeared. He'd been staying at the Gilded Lily and gotten into a huge dispute with Eamon McNulty; the two had taken it to the streets and Green had died in the dirt, shot to death by McNulty.

"So," she murmured to herself, "if Fogerty was right, Tod Green took down the stage-coach, murdered everyone and hid the gold. Where?"

She turned another page. As she did, a fragile piece of old paper fell out. The ink was barely legible. " 'I will see that he is brought to justice. My word to you, old friend,' " Jane managed to make out. Her fingers trembled slightly. The writing was full of flourishes and very pretty — a woman's hand, she thought.

Sage McCormick's?

She pondered whether that could be the case when there was a tap on the door. Before she could answer, it opened. Heidi was there. "Agent Everett, I've found your friends!" she said happily.

Jane quickly stood, closing the book.

Kelsey O'Brien and Logan Raintree entered the room behind Heidi.

"I'm so glad you're here," Jane said, stepping around to greet them both.

Of her Krewe, Jane knew Logan the best. They had often worked together in Texas when he'd been a Ranger and she'd been called in to do facial reconstructions. He was the perfect Texas Ranger, steady and strong, simply there to do what he was called upon to do. He always used reason and negotiation before brawn and bullets. He'd had a horrible time when his wife was murdered, but a couple of years had gone by and during the San Antonio case, when they'd all been brought together, he'd been paired with Kelsey O'Brien — a U.S. Marshal back then.

Kelsey had known that she wanted to be in law enforcement all her life. Despite the fact that she'd already been a Marshal, she'd had to go through the academy at Quantico to become part of the Krewe.

She'd been tougher than Jane from the get-go, but she'd taught her a great deal about inner strength; Jane thought she'd gained a great deal of her own confidence with Kelsey's help. Jane was also proud of being a very good shot — if not quite as good as those in their Krewe who'd been practicing at the range much longer.

She was grateful to have them here. She'd never worked any case without at least another few members of her Krewe before. It had just been days, of course, since she'd left them, but it felt like a lifetime.

Then again, she'd only come here to do a facial reconstruction.

"Lily is pretty interesting," Kelsey said.

"I've never been anywhere quite like this. And may I say that you've, uh, managed to fit right in?"

Jane remembered that she was in period attire and grimaced. "Just being part of the theater crowd." She turned to Heidi. "Thanks for finding Logan and Kelsey and bringing them here."

"My pleasure." Heidi smiled. "Well, back to the grind. We're all doing double shifts today — so many people in town. I would've thought . . . well, that these events would've scared off more people. I mean, after I found that old corpse out by the Apache village . . ." She gave an elaborate shudder.

"I'm sure you're safe with your trail rides, Heidi," Logan told her.

"With another guide and parties of up to fifteen . . . yeah, I hope so," Heidi said. "Anyway, I'll see you around."

They all said goodbye. "You've found something?" Logan asked Jane.

She confirmed that the door was closed and then showed them the note. "It's not addressed to anyone, but I believe it might be from Sage — written to Trey Hardy." She glanced at Kelsey. "I've tried to keep Logan up on what's going on —"

Kelsey nodded. "He's filled us in on what he knows."

"I was honestly surprised that Sloan was okay with bringing you in. But as we've discussed, he doesn't seem to entirely trust his own people. Logan suggested he's afraid that one of his deputies might have — inadvertently or not — shared information. There's also the possibility that someone in town instigated whatever it is going on, and I suppose it could be over the gold."

"From what I understand, that shipment was about a hundred pounds of mined gold, but at about fifty dollars a gram . . . someone could consider it enough to kill for. But we're talking about *millions* today. Trey Hardy was dead before the gold was stolen, so what would Sage have meant by this — if she *was* writing to Hardy?"

"I don't know," Jane said. "I just don't. Trey Hardy might have suspected something about what was going to happen. And even though he wasn't a killer, he might have been condemned to death once he stood before the circuit court. He was a gentleman outlaw, so he might've been ready to tell what he knew, to see that people weren't killed."

Logan remarked, "Maybe Hardy's legend made too much of him being a good guy. Jesse James, for instance, comes out looking like Robin Hood, but if you were the one

350

being robbed by him it probably wasn't so great."

Jane shrugged. "I don't know. I *want* to think of Hardy as being a good guy."

"Well, legends are based on real men and women, and none of us is all saint or sinner. I'll leave you two to your reading. I'm going to go into the county station and see if they can give us anything from forensics. I'll keep in touch."

"Where should I start?" Kelsey asked Jane.

"I'll keep going with this. Why don't you go through the old newspaper clippings and see if there's anything new you can discover."

Valerie Mystro stood by the car staring at Sloan. She appeared completely bewildered. She batted her lashes and played the betrayed heroine to the hilt.

"I don't understand why you're here, Sloan, why you'd be waiting for someone who simply wanted to be friendly and bring a basket of goodies to the hospital. Everything that's happened is terrible, but your fixation on the theater is ridiculous! Yes, I went to the hospital. Jimmy Hough was a nice kid, although Caleb was obnoxious to everyone — insulting Alice and me when he wasn't trying to pick us up or bribe us to have sex. I thought I was doing something good!"

"Valerie, this is one of the two busiest days of the year for the theater — but you had time to drive out to the hospital?" Sloan demanded.

"I felt bad! Caleb was murdered — and those two almost died, as well. Give me a little credit here, will you? Sloan, you think it all has to do with the theater because of the skull. Don't forget, I'm the one who found the skull and was nearly scared out of ten years by it!"

"Why didn't you stay at the hospital?" Sloan asked.

"The guard frightened me! I was just going to drop off the basket, ask Jimmy and his mom how they were doing and rush back before anyone knew I was gone. But the way he barked at me and asked what I was doing — well, I just turned around and left."

"Let me see the basket."

"You got a search warrant?"

"You don't want to let me see the basket?"

"Sure, you can see the basket — if you ask nicely. I watch TV. I know I could make you get a search warrant!"

He rolled his eyes. "All right, all right!"

She leaned into the driver's window to lift

the basket off the passenger seat. It was a little straw basket with a bow and a card that said "Feel Better Soon." She handed it to Sloan; he went through the contents and found cookies and candy.

He didn't want to admit it, but he felt a little foolish as he handed it back. "Valerie, I'm sorry. But it looks suspicious for you to leave when you're supposed to be playing your role for the town, and more suspicious when you run out because a guard wants to know who you are and what you're doing when you're visiting people who barely escaped attempted murder."

"Sloan, I was just trying to be friendly, like I said. And," she added, "even though he was a total prick — and probably because it looked good — Caleb Hough donated to the Theater Restoration Fund. I wanted to make sure his wife continued to do so."

Sloan was silent for a minute.

"Sloan, please — can I get back to town before they notice I'm gone?"

He walked away from the car. "Okay. But do me a favor. Be a friend by *not* going anywhere near the Hough family right now, okay?"

"You're being paranoid, and you need to be out there finding out who really did this, not persecuting good citizens!" Valerie said angrily.

"Trust me, I'm trying," he said as he turned away.

"I'm learning about gold mining. It wasn't found on the surface or in the streams here. It was an accidental discovery when they were expecting to find silver. But once they came across the gold vein, they created a processing station right by the mine, and they used fire and chemicals to melt the gold and mold it into bars. While the gold was being processed, it was protected by Pinkerton guards," Kelsey told Jane.

Jane looked up at her and smiled. "I'd wondered about that. I mean, I know it wasn't going to be like a pirate cache of gold coins."

"No, but they were pretty sophisticated. So, the gold would have been formed into bars before shipping and it would've been relatively small in bulk, and thus easy to carry on a stagecoach. There were guards the whole time it was loaded. And there were actually two armed guards on board, and the driver was armed, as well. I sincerely doubt that one person could have been responsible. And then the dead men had to be buried, the stagecoach dismantled and made to 'disappear' and the gold hidden somewhere. It was a pretty complex operation."

"One they must have been planning for a long time," Jane agreed. "Two guards and an armed driver. So, maybe a party of three?"

"And someone in the know," Kelsey said. "Only someone working for the mine, someone involved in its administration, would be aware of exactly when the gold was due to leave the mine."

Jane glanced down at her book. "Well, this is like looking for a needle in a haystack. It could have been almost anyone living in the area at the time except . . ." She paused. "The administrators at the mine would have known — but local enforcement must have known, too."

"Yes, I imagine they would alert the sheriff's office."

"Okay," Jane said, thinking it out as she spoke, still and staring down at the pages in front of her. "We know that Hardy was shot *before* the stagecoach was attacked. What if Hardy suspected something concerning the sheriff and the deputy — something he'd picked up in jail because he could hear them when they talked? So Aaron Munson was afraid Hardy would blow the whistle on them before they got the gold. He went in and shot Hardy — never imagining that the townspeople would react so violently."

"That's possible. But it would mean Munson was dead when the stagecoach was robbed — and disappeared from the face of the earth."

"But not Fogerty!" Jane said. "His book points at a man named Tod Green, a man claiming to be a rancher, who was in town at the time. A guy called Eamon McNulty was the director at the theater. McNulty and Green got into a huge argument and they had a duel in the street. Green died."

"What happened to McNulty?" Kelsey asked.

"I don't know. I haven't found another reference to him, other than the fight."

"Okay, say the sheriff, his deputy and McNulty were in on it together. They set this Tod Green guy up to take the fall. Munson was lynched before the robbery, so he was no longer a player. But Hardy suspected what was going on and he told Sage McCormick about it. Sage disappears. We're virtually certain she was murdered because her body was found in the theater."

"Then there's Red Marston, who disappeared the same night as Sage," Jane said. "He might have been part of the conspiracy.

356

People thought Sage ran off with Red Marston, but if Fogerty was involved, the rumor makes sense — Fogerty is the one who implied that Sage had gone off with Red. So, let's say Red *was* part of this, and he did care for Sage. Maybe he didn't want her killed, and because he wouldn't take part in the murder, he had to go, too." Jane wrinkled her nose. "This is getting really complicated."

"No kidding." Kelsey frowned. "But if Fogerty and McNulty came out of it alive, why didn't they take the gold and get out of town when it all blew over?"

"I don't know. That *is* a dilemma. And I doubt Fogerty admitted anything in a book he wrote himself," Jane said.

"No. I wonder about Eamon McNulty, though." Kelsey pulled out her phone. "I'll look for him on Google."

Jane waited, watching her.

" 'Eamon McNulty, renowned actor, director, theater manager,' " Kelsey read. " 'Born April 2, 1833, in New York City, New York, died June 4, 1873, Lily, Arizona, of a suspected aneurysm.' " Kelsey looked up at Jane. "It goes on to talk about his start as a poor Irish kid working in the bawdy houses of Five Points, getting a leg up in legitimate theater, staging some of the hits

357

of the day. After critical success and financial failure, he accepted a request to manage the infamous Gilded Lily, in Lily, Arizona, where he brought in artists like Sage McCormick and Daniel Easton, known for their brilliance on the stage."

"What if McNulty was the one who stashed the gold — maybe lying about where it was or keeping it a secret. And then he up and dies of natural causes!" Jane said. "That would mean Fogerty had to spend the rest of his life looking for the gold. But since he didn't find it — and he'd gotten rid of all witnesses — he wrote a book!"

"Why would he do that? Although he wasn't a half-bad writer."

"I guess he wanted his version of Lily's history to be the one future generations accepted as truth," Kelsey said. "But how does that affect what's happening now?"

"Someone else knows what we know. And they're determined to find the gold."

"If that's the case, they must have some idea of where it might be. Hidden in the old shaft of the silver mine where Caleb Hough was killed?" Kelsey suggested.

"Maybe. But I still don't understand why Sage McCormick's skull was found on a wig stand, and why the body of an old-timer was dug up to point the way to Jay Berman's corpse," Jane said. "Unless, of course . . ."

"Unless it's a warning to all the players to stay with the program," Kelsey said.

"And Jay Berman somehow became a liability, just as Caleb Hough did. Whoever killed them thinks Jimmy and his mom knew what was going on, that Caleb let something slip," Jane said. "Someone's pulling the strings here. We know that at least two people, one of them a woman, are involved, because two people put Jimmy and Zoe Hough in the car in the garage and left them to die. Jennie was attacked in the basement. I was, too. Someone attempted to kill either Cy Tyburn or Brian Highsmith around the same time as Jennie was hurt. And the skull was found in the theater. Two things — the theater has to be implicated in some way . . . or someone's going to a lot of effort to suggest it is. And, second, I think we're looking at something similar to what happened all those years ago. There are partners in this, and a few of them are warning the others — or killing those they're afraid might be on to something."

"And the ghosts aren't talking?" Kelsey asked.

"Sage . . . leaves messages. I've yet to meet Trey Hardy, but I'm hoping to make his

359

acquaintance this evening."

Sloan had just gotten Bullet back to the stables and was dismounting when Logan called him. He was glad to hear his old crime-fighting partner's voice, glad he was in town.

"I'm at the morgue," Logan told him. "With Liam Newsome. He's brought me up to speed. We're expecting some lab reports any minute."

"Where are Kelsey and Jane?" Sloan asked.

"Reading at Desert Diamonds."

"They should be safe enough there," Sloan murmured.

As he spoke, Heidi came up to him. "I'll take Bullet, Sloan, unless you still need him."

He gave Heidi a quick smile, handing her the reins. He realized Logan was silent at the other end.

"Logan?"

"Yeah, I'm here. They're both good at what they do," he said.

"But I found Jane with a concussion down in the basement of the theater. We're lucky our killer didn't finish her off. Or Jennie."

"You're going to need to have faith in Jane. This is what she does. Trust in her training," Logan said. "You, me — anyone out there — can be taken by surprise, especially when we're not on alert."

That was true; he'd seen massive sharpshooter cops brought down by junkies because they weren't prepared to be attacked, because they were trying to help.

"I know you're right," Sloan said. "I'll stop in and see what they're doing and then head over to join you," Sloan said.

"You've got men in town, right?"

"Both my day guys, and the county has men in."

"Yeah, Newsome told me. See you when you get here."

Sloan walked over to Desert Diamonds. Seated on a fake boulder in front of the theater, Brian Highsmith was regaling the crowd with the story of Lily, proudly boasting that the Gilded Lily was older than Tombstone's Birdcage.

Alice Horton was beside him, dressed in full vamp attire, handing out fliers.

Sloan walked on, to the store. There were long lines at the pizzeria and the coffee bar. People were shopping, spending money — everything was going as it should.

He passed Grant Winston, who was at one of the counters, cheerfully instructing a cashier to return a man's money; the man had purchased the same book twice. Grant saw him and smiled, then motioned toward his office. Sloan nodded.

He entered the office. Jane was standing with a tall, pretty woman whose reddish blond hair was tied back in a ponytail. They were going through a book slowly, page by page.

She looked up at Sloan. "Well?" she asked. "Who was it?"

"Valerie Mystro."

"Valerie? What reason did she give?"

"She likes Jimmy and Zoe Hough. She brought cookies and candy. And Caleb Hough donated to the theater. Apparently, she wants to make sure his wife likes theater, too."

"You believed her?"

He shrugged. "We'll see what else happens. What about you?"

"Oh!" she said with excitement. "We think we've got it!"

"You know who killed Jay Berman and Caleb Hough?" he asked cautiously.

"No," she said, her smile fading. "But I think we've figured out the past. Brendan Fogerty wasn't such a good guy — and he fooled the world with his book. He was in on the stagecoach robbery with his deputy, Aaron Munson, and the theater manager,

Eamon McNulty. But Hardy heard them talking — and that's why Munson shot him in his cell. He hadn't expected the mob to go crazy and lynch him. Oh, and I forgot about Red Marston. I guess he was in on it, too. Sage must have found out from him or her friend, Trey Hardy. We think she was killed because she was trying to find a way out of town so she could tell the truth. She couldn't go to the law in Lily, because the law was involved. Marston cared about her and wanted to protect her, which meant Fogerty and McNulty had to kill him, too."

"Why didn't they get out with the gold?" Sloan asked.

"Because McNulty dropped dead of an aneurysm — and he'd either been the one to stash the gold or he'd moved it, not trusting his partners!" Kelsey said. She flushed, offering him her hand. "Hi, Sheriff, I'm sorry. We haven't met. Kelsey O'Brien."

"Good to meet you," Sloan said. She had clear eyes, a steady handshake and a lovely manner. He hid a smile; he'd expected no less from the woman who had finally lifted Logan Raintree from his pain. "And glad to have you here. Logan is at county, getting lab reports from Newsome. I'm going to drive over and see what he has."

Jane nodded. "I'm going to suck up to

Grant Winston and beg him to let me borrow this book for the night. Then I'll ac-
quaint Kelsey with the theater, and be Sage
again for a while until we hear back from
you."

"Keep an eye on each other," Sloan said.

"Of course. We've been doing that for a
long time," Kelsey said.

He nodded and left them.

On the street, Henri was giving a history
lesson on the theater with each of his cast
members popping up to illustrate a different character. People thronged around
them. Others stood just outside the saloon,
some of the men with plastic cups of beer
raised high as they leaned against the
sidewalk support posts, like old-time cowboys.

The drive took him about forty-five minutes. As he neared his destination, he
received a call from Logan telling him
they'd meet at the morgue. He arrived at a
lab and offices that made his little place look
like a ma-and-pa operation. But he was
grateful that he had the county for backup;
it was impossible to have the manpower and
technical and forensic support in a town as
small as Lily.

A receptionist met him and instructed him
to follow a hallway. In an outer room, a man

who introduced himself as Dr. Madsen's assistant gave him a paper lab suit and mask, and he entered the room.

"Sheriff Trent, just in time," Madsen said.

"Glad to hear that, Doctor," Sloan said, nodding to Logan and Newsome.

"I was explaining to Agent Raintree and Detective Newsome that because of the way the throat was sliced, I believe the killer was right-handed and that the knife used was about six inches long and two inches wide."

"Something like a Bowie knife?" Logan asked.

"Yes, something like that. I'd also say the killer came up behind his back, grabbed him around the chest and attacked immediately — he didn't have time to fight back." He shook his head. "There are no defensive wounds on the man anywhere. It must've been a lightning-bolt attack."

"By someone Caleb didn't think would kill him," Logan said.

"Probably. If I understand the circumstances correctly, whoever was in the mine shaft with him had to be known to him. You don't just walk into a place like that. You crawl in through an area the size of a two-by-four boulder. Is that about right?"

"That's right," Sloan agreed.

"Can you say anything more about the

blade?" Newsome asked.

"It was very sharp. And jagged."

"What about any trace evidence on him?" Logan asked.

"Just the sand and dirt you'd expect from the mine shaft," Madsen said.

"What about our other dead man? Jay Berman?" Logan asked.

"He was kneeling. There were powder burns, so he was shot point-blank," Madsen said. "The bullet fragmented and the lab's still piecing it together. You found no shell casings, right?"

"Right," Newsome glanced at Logan. "My people went over the tepee with a fine-tooth comb."

"Why would a man kneel down to be executed? Why wouldn't he fight?" Madsen wondered.

"Maybe he believed he'd be let up — that he was just being taught a lesson or . . . well, people go on hoping while they're still breathing," Logan said.

"One more thing. Both of our victims ate not more than two hours before they were killed," Dr. Madsen said. "Mr. Berman had nachos and beer. Mr. Hough dined on steak, potatoes, spinach and wine. Oh, and Mr. Berman was suffering from liver disease, while Mr. Hough had an artery that was almost completely blocked. I suspect he would've suffered a massive heart attack within a week. His killer really needn't have bothered."

They left the morgue soon after and spoke on the sidewalk.

"You feel my men are doing well by you in Lily?" Newsome asked Sloan.

"Yes. Other than the murders and the attempted murders, we've had remarkably little trouble during Silverfest," Sloan said. "Thanks, Liam — I needed your help."

Newsome nodded, looking at Logan. "Are the feds taking over?"

"No. We're just here to lend assistance," Logan said.

Newsome smiled. "I'm not resentful, Agent Raintree. If you decide you can better manage the investigation, feel free. This one has me grasping at threads, and I'm sure Sheriff Trent feels the same way. We've got nothing on Berman. We can't get anything other than that he was down here on vacation. He didn't have a home phone, and we couldn't find any connection to anyone in Arizona on his cell. What he became involved in — I don't know."

"I don't know anything, either," Sloan said. "But the angle we're working is that someone's after old gold."

367

Newsome frowned. "Old gold? You mean from the stagecoach that disappeared over a hundred years ago?"

"Yes."

"Hmm. Interesting," Newsome said. "By the way, the skull of that old corpse you found in the desert has been brought to your station. Maybe your artist can work with it. If you find out it was one of the old stage robbers, maybe you *are* on to something." He sighed. "Except that no one knew who they were."

"I suspect Red Marston might have been in on it," Sloan said. "If it proves to be him, we just might be on the right track."

Newsome removed his glasses and studied Sloan. "So . . . that would mean one of the citizens of your fair town is involved. What tourist would have the connections and the know-how to research what happened in the past?"

"Yep," Sloan said. "That's why I figure I've got a local involved. Has to be. Jimmy and Zoe Hough were attacked by people who obviously knew the house, knew the distance from the stables and barns and knew the family. They were familiar with the garage. So, that's why I'm really grateful for county help."

Newsome frowned. "You think one of

your own deputies —"

"No," Sloan broke in. "Or, at least, I couldn't begin to point a finger at any one of them. And it could be a question of talking to the wrong person, of being careless. But don't —"

"Trust anyone," Newsome finished. "That's kind of a given in law enforcement sometimes, isn't it? Sad, but true," he said. "Oh, we got DNA off your bottle. The bottle from the mine shaft. But there aren't any matches in the system."

"But if we know who to get DNA from, we could have a match, right?"

"Of course. However, that only proves a particular person was in the mine shaft at some time. I don't think you can prove murder with it."

"Hell, Liam, I just need a solid suspect!" Sloan told him.

"If you can get me DNA — the right DNA — I can get you a suspect."

They parted ways. When Newsome was gone, Sloan turned to Logan.

They'd been excellent coworkers from the start. While Logan carried all the traits of his Native American ancestry and Sloan didn't, they still shared something of that past. They'd also quickly realized that they both worked on instinct.

And heard voices.

Sloan smiled slowly. "Good to see you, old friend," he said. "I wish it were under different circumstances."

"Yeah, well. I'm not here to take over. I'm here for support. What's your plan?"

"How do you feel about stealing a few glasses, cups, mugs, tissues — whatever we can find?" he asked.

"Sure. Where are we going?"

"The Gilded Lily."

"Great. I've gotten accustomed to living back east. I'm feeling mighty parched. I could go for a beer," Logan said.

"Me, too," Sloan seconded.

"Sounds like a plan to me."

Jane headed out to the street with Kelsey following. She'd barely reached the sidewalk when she heard Brian Highsmith call out with a deep Western twang, "There she is! There's my girl now!"

Brian jumped down from the "boulder" that had been set up for performances and came striding toward her. "Ladies and gentlemen!" he said, taking her hand, "I give you the esteemed, the one and only, indeed, the *adored* Sage McCormick! I was madly in love with the lady — I adored her from afar, of course, because she was already

He slipped through the closed door, disappearing as she wedged her way through the crowd to reach it.

12

Sloan and Logan made their way through the crowds on the street to the Gilded Lily. When they arrived, Valerie was perched on a bar stool singing a Civil War ballad to an appreciative audience of drinkers.

Liz came up to him. "Sloan, want me to get you a table? Hello," she said, smiling at Logan.

"A table would be great, but it doesn't look like you have any," Sloan replied.

"Give me a minute. I know how to squeeze people."

She did; Liz managed to get one couple to join another, freeing up a table. Sloan thanked her and introduced her to Logan.

"You're FBI, too?" she asked.

"He works with Jane," Sloan told her.

"That's good. We're glad you're here." Liz bent low to the table as if listening closely to get their orders.

"Thank you," Logan said. "I hope we can

be of some help."

"I'm sure you will be — and just having more officers around . . . well, that's good." Liz shook her head. "I can't afford to quit, but I don't feel great when I come into work anymore."

"Has anything else happened?" Sloan asked.

"Besides Jennie being attacked and still in a coma?" Liz responded. "And someone digging up Sage McCormick's skull? Or the murders? Or the attack on the Hough family?"

"Sorry. I meant here at the Gilded Lily," Sloan said.

"No. I mean, not that I've heard. I don't come in now until I know someone else is with me. Never bothered me before to be the first one in for the night. The actors and Jennie and Henri live here, so there was usually someone around, and it never bothered me to hear noises from upstairs or the theater or even the basement, but now . . . anyway, I'm terrified of the place. I wouldn't be alone in here for the world!"

"Did you hear noises from the basement a lot?" Sloan asked her.

"Well, sure. Old buildings creak. Oh! Maybe we have rats or something down in the basement? Or ghosts. This place is haunted. We all think so. But the ghosts always seemed to know I'm a complete coward — they never gave me any trouble. I should move along. What can I get you two?"

"For now? Draft?" Sloan said, looking at Logan.

"Yeah. We'll call Kelsey and Jane in a few minutes. I doubt they've eaten," Logan said. "How's the food?"

"The food here is good," Liz assured him. "I'll be right back."

She returned swiftly with the drinks. As she did, Cy Tyburn came into the bar; he walked up to Valerie where she was singing and stood, hat in hand, sighing. She smoothly switched songs, and he joined her in a sweet duet. The heroine and the hero, singing together. When the song was over, Cy slipped away, coming to their table. "Sheriff. How's it going?" he asked anxiously.

"Sit down," Sloan said. Cy glanced at Logan and smiled awkwardly. "Hey."

"Cy, this is Logan Raintree, an old friend of mine who now runs Jane's FBI unit. Logan, you've seen him perform already. This is our hero in residence, Cy Tyburn."

Cy and Logan shook hands. "Glad to have you here. Have you learned anything else?"

Cy asked, turning nervously from one man to the other.

"We're working on it. Hey, you need to calm down some," Sloan said. "How about a beer?"

Cy glanced at his watch. "Yeah, sure, one before the show and I'm actually a better performer. Thanks. That would be great."

"Your day went well?" Logan asked him.

"Everything was fine. Had so much fun acting out the stories and doing improv with people that I forgot someone might've been trying to kill me yesterday," he said.

Before either could respond, Valerie made her way over to the table. She immediately offered Logan her hand. "Hi. You have to be another officer, right?"

Logan nodded and stood, taking Valerie's hand, then pulling out a chair for her. She sat, lowering her voice as she spoke. "Have you found out anything? Your friend here —" she nodded at Sloan "— nearly bit my head off today for going to visit people at the hospital."

"You went to the hospital?" Cy asked her. "Why?"

"Well, I *tried* to see Zoe and Jimmy — but a muscle-bound suit came after me, and then Sheriff Suspicious here stopped me on the road coming back," Valerie said indignantly.

Sloan lifted a hand and smiled at Liz. "Can we get two more here?"

"Of course," she called back.

"Is one for me?" Valerie asked.

"Yes, I'm sorry. Didn't you want one?"

"Sure. But I would've ordered a double Scotch."

"We do have a show, Valerie," Cy reminded her.

"Yeah, one that could wind up putting us in a hospital, too," she muttered.

"If you're afraid to perform, I can close this place down," Sloan said.

Valerie sniffed. "If you closed it down, we'd have nowhere to go. And no money to get someplace else, anyway." She leaned into the table. "I don't think *anywhere* in this town is safe, so it doesn't matter, does it?"

Liz delivered two more glasses of beer. "You could get out of town," Logan said politely.

"Do you know how hard it is to get acting jobs these days? If I were in L.A., there'd be a million girls like me trying for one role. I have a great character to work with here, and I want to stay with the ensemble for another year. That'll help my résumé . . . I *can't* leave here now," Valerie told him.

"I could," Cy said thoughtfully.

"Stop it, Cy!"

"Hey, *you* weren't told that there were live rounds in guns that should have held nothing but blanks!" Cy protested.

"Oh, Lord, Henri's coming in." Valerie stood instantly and raised her glass. "Three cheers for the Gilded Lily bartenders and servers!" she called, and moved away from the table, starting another song.

Sloan arched his brows at Logan. *There goes our beer glass!*

"Well, that girl sure knows how to suck up!" Cy stood, as well, following Valerie around the room, adding his voice to hers in harmony.

"They *are* good," Logan commented. "Those two definitely know when and where to pick up on each other's moves."

"They do," Sloan agreed. "I want to keep an eye on those beer glasses, though."

Henri Coque saw Sloan and Logan and immediately came over to join them. He seemed as eager as anyone else to greet Logan and welcome him, expressing hope that he could help solve whatever was happening to their formerly peaceful town of Lily.

"Sit, Henri, have a drink with us," Sloan invited.

"Should you be drinking?" Henri asked. "Being on duty and all."

"I think I'm fine with a beer," Sloan said, nodding slowly.

"Do you have any information about what's going on?"

Same question they were all asking, Sloan thought. That made sense, although at least one person — and as yet he didn't know who — had a private agenda.

"No, but we're expecting more information back from county anytime now," he said.

"Oh?"

"Trace evidence. You've heard the old theory that you take something and you leave something everywhere you go. They'll find some evidence that will pin the killer," Sloan explained. The theory was solid; it didn't always work. Fingerprints could belong where they were found, and dozens upon dozens of prints could be lifted from any one place. DNA was great — as long as you had a sample for comparison. Legally obtained, of course.

"So, let's get you a beer," Sloan said.

"If you're buying, I'll have a bourbon," Henri said. "No ice. My usual."

Sloan waved a hand to order as Logan asked Henri where to find the restrooms.

Henri gave him directions.

As Liz brought Henri his drink, Sloan saw that Logan had casually slipped his hand around the beer glass Cy had left on the bar.

"So, Sloan," Henri said, "today seems to be going fine. The actors are working. The theater is open!"

"It's a great day . . . so far," Sloan agreed pleasantly. He watched Valerie glide around the room. When he saw Logan on his way back, he nodded toward the glass she'd just placed on the bar. Logan nodded in return.

Henri sipped his drink.

The spirit of Trey Hardy had disappeared when Jane and Kelsey entered the Old Jail.

Mike Addison was behind the sheriff's desk, giving directions to a couple who wanted to ride out and see the old cemetery. His "concierge," a woman of about twenty, was serving complimentary wine to guests in the old gun room, along with nachos and cheese.

When the couple moved on, Jane approached him and introduced Kelsey, then asked for the key to her room.

"Calling it a night, Agent Everett? It's still early."

"I'm just showing Kelsey what a wonderful bed-and-breakfast you have," Jane told him.

Mike beamed. "I do love it," he said with enthusiasm. "Silverfest days are great. Halloween is great. But sometimes . . . well, Lily is off the beaten track. So if you want to go on any travel sites and rave about the place, I'd be very grateful! Oh, and, ladies, it's wine and snacks time in the gun room."

"Thanks, but we're going to my cell for a few minutes. Then we'll head back out, of course. We'll probably catch the show tonight."

"Are you in it tonight?" Mike asked her. "I saw you outside when Brian Highsmith grabbed you and dragged you into the action. You'd think — especially as an actor — that he wouldn't be so obvious in his attempts to accost a pretty woman. I had half a mind to walk up and say something to him!"

She kept forgetting she was wearing the Sage costume. It was almost unnerving, since she spent most of her days in very practical business suits. But she'd learned to move easily in the Victorian attire and forgot about it . . . until she walked in front of a mirror.

"I'm not in the show. I've enjoyed playing Sage out in the streets, but their show's

382

almost abutted the Gilded Lily. From the bathroom area — closed-in now — there might have been a barred window that looked onto the Gilded Lily. Had Trey Hardy believed he was going to hang? He probably hadn't expected to be gunned down in his cell, but he might well have expected that his life was about to end.

She rose and walked into the bathroom, glancing into the mirror above the sink. She was sure that, at one time, barred windows had hung where the mirror was now. Trey might have paced the room and looked over at the Lily. Right here, she stood only about twenty feet away from where the audience would be sitting at the Gilded Lily tonight.

And if the jail had a basement, the basement here would adjoin the room in the basement below the Gilded Lily, the one that held all the props and old mannequins.

She opened her eyes. Trey Hardy was there.

He stood behind her. He seemed as real as flesh and blood. His eyes were dark brown, his hair was dark, too, and he had a handsome, weathered face. The lines in it were attractive, as if he'd spent more of his life smiling than in anger. But now he looked grave as he stared back at her.

"Help me," she said. "I'm trying to help you."

He slammed a fist against the wall, his expression bleak, frustrated. She jumped. "You can speak," she encouraged him. "You can speak if you try."

His mouth moved; a sound escaped but it was like a groan. . . .

He slammed the wall again and stamped his foot. He was certainly practiced at causing bangs and bumps, even if his speech was nothing but a groan.

Suddenly she heard a knocking on the outer door.

"What the hell?" Kelsey cried, leaping up.

Trey Hardy disappeared in a flash.

"Agent Everett!" Mike Addison called. "Agent Everett! Are you all right in there?"

Kelsey was already at the door by the time Jane reached it. Mike was standing outside. "Your neighbors were worried. What on earth are you two doing in here?" he demanded, looking suspiciously from one to the other.

"I'm sorry," Kelsey said, shrugging. "I was zoned out."

"Well, they heard a tremendous thump and a bang," Mike said. "This is a wooden building, you know. Sound carries!"

"Whatever they heard must have been

from outside," Jane said, meeting his eyes. "Kelsey was sleeping. I was just fixing my hair. I dropped my brush and hit my head when I bent down to get it. Maybe that was it?"

"Well, keep the noise down, please. Forgive me, but I do have other guests."

"It wasn't us, Mike, honest," Jane said sweetly. "Maybe it was the ghosts — but the noise was probably because of whatever's happening at the theater."

"Yeah, sure. That's what I'll say," Mike said, turning to leave.

Kelsey closed the door, rolling her eyes. "Honestly . . ."

Jane looked at her. "It was Hardy. He kept banging on the wall in the bathroom. He was trying to tell me something, but he can't speak. In all these years, he hasn't learned how to speak to those who can see him."

"Where is he now?" Kelsey asked.

"I don't see him. When Mike started pounding on the door . . . he disappeared."

Kelsey angled her head. "I hope I can get one of your ghosts to speak with me, or at least make an appearance. You can't be in two places at the same time."

"A number of people have seen both of these ghosts. Most of their friends, of course, assume they're crazy. Even a ghost-busting TV guy went running out of the Gilded Lily. But I'm sure they'll eventually communicate with us. I just don't know what they can tell us." She paused. "Sage sent me some fairly general warnings, but aside from that . . ."

"Like you said, they're definitely trying to tell us *something.*" Kelsey's phone rang and she quickly picked it up. "It's Logan," she murmured a few seconds later. "He and Sloan are next door. They thought we should eat."

"Yeah, food sounds great," Jane said.

Kelsey shook her head and slowly smiled. "You're sleeping with him, aren't you? Logan told me that he's a good cop and an all-around good guy. He wasn't afraid to quit his job and come home to take care of his grandfather who was dying of cancer."

"I'm that obvious?" Jane asked.

Kelsey shrugged. "Not to someone else. I work with you. I went through the academy with you. We see ghosts together and have rational conversations about them. That gives us a bond, you know?"

"Yes, it does," Jane agreed. "And yes, I'm sleeping with him."

"Fast worker," Kelsey teased.

"It was . . ."

"The circumstances. Believe me, I know. Who instigated it?" Kelsey asked.

"Me."

"Wow. I am impressed." Kelsey laughed.

"Kelsey —"

"Sorry! But does this ghost talk to him?"

"I'm not sure."

"We should find out," Kelsey said. "For now, let's eat."

As they left the Old Jail, Jane waved to Mike at the desk where he seemed to be going through paperwork. He smiled at her. "Out to enjoy the evening? Oh, I guess you're working, what with everything going on here. Shame about Caleb Hough — although I doubt anyone in town is really surprised."

"I wonder if that's why no one wanted to shut down Silverfest," Jane watched Mike's reaction. "I mean, I guess he was universally disliked."

"Pity about the kid and his wife being hurt, though," Mike said.

"Interesting that no one seemed to be deterred from coming here, despite every-thing that's been going on," Kelsey said.

Mike shrugged. "In big cities, you some-times have a murder a day. No one leaves a city because of a murder. Now, I'll grant you, our population is small in comparison, but, heck, we haven't had a murder since before I moved here. I have faith in the sheriff. He'll straighten it all out. Especially with the county — and you feds — working on it, too."

"Actually, it was two murders in less than a week — and four assaults," Jane said.

"Four?" Mike asked.

"You mean Zoe and Jimmy Hough and —"

"Jennie and me in the basement of the Gilded Lily," Jane finished.

He gave her a patient smile. "The basement — it's a death trap, you know. You should stay out of it. Those mannequins are unstable. Jennie probably fell. You just got whacked by one of those fake people."

"Wow." Jane grimaced, looking at Kelsey. "Imagine. Jennie fell — right on the rough end of a walking cane."

"I'm always warning you about those mannequins," Kelsey said jokingly.

Jane didn't laugh, responding to Mike instead. "Mike, I'm not part of the theater — *and* I'm not known for overreacting!"

Mike frowned at them.

Kelsey took up the conversation. "Well, it's really great to hear that you have faith in your law enforcement system, Mike."

"Town, county — and federal!" he said

pleasantly.

"See you later, Mike," Jane told him.

"Take care now," he said, returning to his paperwork.

They left the Old Jail and walked the few steps to the entrance of the Gilded Lily. Country music was playing on the stereo system when they arrived. The bar area was busy but they quickly saw Logan and Sloan at a four-top table.

They slid into seats to join them.

"Anything new?" Jane asked Sloan.

"A bit of an interesting twist," he said, leaning close. "You know the mummified corpse in the desert? Well, it's been stripped down to the bone for you to do a reconstruction. But the M.E. found something interesting — or rather, something lacking — in the skull when he removed the rest of the soft tissue."

"What?"

"The tongue," he replied. "Whoever our mystery corpse might be, he had his tongue sliced out before he was shot in the chest."

"Gruesome." Kelsey shuddered. "But that's a classic punishment for talking too much, isn't it?"

"Heretics sometimes had their tongues cut out," Logan said. "I guess you could say they talked too much — against the establishment or the church. It's beginning to look as if whoever we found in the desert was killed to prevent him from talking."

Kelsey shook her head. "That was cruel and brutal, since they obviously meant to kill the victim, anyway. What difference did it make if he could talk. They were going to kill him. It doesn't make any sense.

"Some people *are* cruel and brutal," Logan said, "and we've all learned that cruelty doesn't have to make sense. Sloan, I know Jane is still working on the skull you've already determined to be that of Sage McCormick, but if she did up a quick two-dimensional drawing from photos and scans of the second corpse, do you have old photographs or paintings we could make comparisons with?"

"Over at Desert Diamonds Grant's got several books written by historians through-out the years, plus replica editions of books written at the time. There are pictures of Brendan Fogerty, Aaron Munson, Red Marston, Eamon McNulty — and, of course, Sage McCormick. But there's also a nice painting of her over the bar, just behind you. Jane's two-dimensional sketch was really all we needed to see that the skull had belonged to Sage. I'd asked her to finish her recon-struction for sentimental reasons, really."

He paused. "You've probably heard that she was an ancestor of mine." When everyone nodded, he went on, "I believe the skeleton we dug up in the desert is going to prove to be Red Marston, but . . . that's a theory at this point, nothing more. And I think if that body *is* Red Marston's, then we just might be right about the gold."

"I'll get on it first thing in the morning," Jane said. "So what's your plan for the evening?"

"Have you gotten settled yet?" Sloan asked Logan and Kelsey.

Before either could answer, his phone rang, and he excused himself to answer it. Jane watched as first a frown and then an expression of relief came over his features. "I don't want anyone else knowing," Sloan said. "If she does have something to tell us, I don't want her to be a target."

He hung up and told them, "It's Jennie, Jennie Layton. The stage manager — they call her their 'stage mother.' She's conscious now. She's doing well, and the doctor says I can speak with her."

He got to his feet. "I'll call you," he said. "I don't know what she'll know. Maybe, just maybe, she'll remember some of what happened."

Jane set a hand on his arm. "Sloan, this

may sound strange, but I'm not sure the person — or persons — who attacked Jennie and me can be the same as whoever killed Berman and Caleb Hough."

"Why do you say that?"

"Because Jennie and I are alive," she said quietly.

"Jennie got a pretty good hit on the head with that cane," he argued. "And you were knocked unconscious."

"But Berman was killed with a bullet. Caleb Hough had his throat from slit ear to ear," she said.

"I'll see what Jennie has to say," he said. "I'll call when I'm on my way back."

"I take it you're going to stay with Jane over at the Old Jail tonight?" Kelsey asked Sloan blandly. "If something's going on in that room, two pairs of eyes would be better than one."

Sloan seemed confused for a minute. Kelsey had left him a nice opening, though, Jane thought, lowering her lashes to hide her amusement.

"Certainly. Of course," he said. He paused to talk to Liz and then walked out the door.

"We'll eat first, and then you can show Kelsey and me where we're sleeping," Logan said. "And, if you don't mind, you can show us the infamous Sage McCormick suite."

"Of course. We can catch some of the show and I'll give you a tour of the place — with Henri's permission."

"Charm him," Logan suggested. "What's good on the menu?"

"Everything I've had so far," Jane said.

They ordered their meals. There was enough activity and noise in the bar so that Jane could really talk to them, put events in chronological order and get their feedback.

"People kill for different reasons," Logan said. "Revenge, sometimes for presumed injustices. They kill for passion. Or because they're mentally ill. And they kill out of greed. Lily's past victims seem to have died because of the greed of others. And maybe the same thing is going on today. How many of the people in the town have ancestors who were here at that time?" he asked.

"Well, Sloan. As he mentioned, Sage McCormick was his great-great grand-mother," Jane said. "And I'm not sure who else. The actors working in the theater came from other places, and I believe Henri Coque came here from elsewhere, too. I don't know about the others. We'll have to ask Sloan."

When they'd finished the meal, Jane found

Henri. She requested a key for Kelsey and Logan, and asked if, after the show, he'd mind if she showed them around the theater. Henri agreed, smiling. He told her he liked her even better in the crimson dress than in the blue. "I've heard from a number of our audience members. They say you've been quite entertaining on the street. Thank you! Feel free to take your fellow agents around the theater."

While Kelsey and Logan went out to retrieve their overnight bags and settle into Jennie's room at the Gilded Lily, Jane decided to go to her room there. She was feeling strangely divided. She now had two of her Krewe with her, and yet she still felt it was important to be in both places — the Gilded Lily and the Old Jail.

And talk to the ghosts there.

She gathered a few things to put in a small bag to take over to the Old Jail later that night, then sat on the bed.

"Sage, I wish you'd talk to me," she said.

She stood swiftly, feeling something cold but gentle and . . . yearning sweep by her. Walking into the bathroom, she closed the door and turned the sink faucet on hot until steamy water poured down the drain and a mist rose to cover the mirror.

"Sage? I don't know why you won't speak

to me. We're really trying to help. Trying to solve all this and prevent more deaths."

She felt the air shift around her. The mirror was clouded with steam, but it was through the steam that she'd found the way these ghosts communicated.

Sage was behind her. Jane didn't turn around; she spoke to the mirror image of the beautiful ghost.

"Help us. If you speak to me, I will hear you," she said.

Sage stared back at her.

With a slight stirring of the air, the ghost moved around her . . . and began to write. She clearly saw the words.

SPEAK NO EVIL

A second later, the words were furiously erased.

SPEAK NO TRUTH!

Jane turned slowly around. The image of the ghost remained. Sage McCormick opened her mouth, and although she was a ghost, there was something Jane could clearly see.

Sage McCormick had no tongue; it had been sliced off at the base.

"Oh, God!" Jane said softly, "I'm so sorry, so, so sorry!"

13

The county officer on duty at the hospital acknowledged Sloan as he came in. "The doctor was just in with her. One of the nurses was the first to realize Ms. Layton was coming to. I haven't spoken to her. She went from being in the coma to dozing on and off, but they say it's all right if you speak with her."

Sloan went in. When he entered the room, Jennie's eyes were closed. She looked small and frail as she lay in the hospital bed. He noted the veins in her hands where they lay on the white sheets.

He just sat there for a minute, waiting. After some time, her eyes opened. She blinked, disoriented.

"Sloan," she said weakly.

He leaned close to the bed and took one of her thin, delicate hands. She offered him a shaky smile.

"You're awake," he said, smiling. "They

say you're going to be fine."

She nodded. "When I first opened my eyes, I didn't know where I was. I didn't know what had happened. I had no . . . memory."

"And now?"

"Now, I remember that I went down to the basement. And I woke up here."

"Why did you go down to the basement, Jennie? Do you remember? You were in the room with all the old props and mannequins. Why?"

Jennie was silent, and then she looked at him, hesitant.

"They were talking," Jennie said at last.

"The mannequins?" Sloan asked in a carefully even tone.

"Oh, Sloan, don't be silly! I got hit on the head, but I know mannequins don't talk!" she told him.

He smiled again. "So someone was down there?"

"Yes, someone was in the room. Or more than one person, because I'd heard talking down there several times over the past week. I couldn't figure out what the actors would be doing down there. I'm responsible for storage, props, costumes. . . . I wanted to know what was going on."

"So you didn't recognize anything about

the voices?"

She shook her head. "But, Sloan, I heard them late at night, and once, very early in the morning. Yet whenever I went down, no one was there."

"Did you tell Henri about it?" he asked her.

"No." She ran the fingers of her free hand over the sheets, glanced at them for a minute and then back at Sloan. "I didn't want Henri to think I was too old for my job — too old, or too crazy."

"You're not that old, Jennie," Sloan said firmly. "And Henri likes your work very much. So you'd go down but not see anyone."

"Yes. Of course, the light is pretty dim. All you're getting is the overflow from the main room," Jennie reminded him. "But no, I didn't see anyone, and the only way out is the stairs that lead to the door by the bar. So I thought I was crazy myself."

"But when you were attacked, did you see anything? Do you have any idea who swung that cane at you?"

"The clown," she said suddenly. "It was a clown mannequin. I saw it! Sloan, maybe there *are* ghosts down there."

Again, she was quiet. He didn't press her; he realized she wasn't sure how to say what

400

she wanted to say.

When she spoke, it was in a rush. "There are spirits of all the people gunned down or murdered in or near the theater, and now those spirits are possessing the mannequins."

Sloan felt disappointment streak through him. She'd sounded as if she'd come out of it with all her senses. Now he was worried.

Not that spirits didn't exist. Not that people wouldn't think *he* was crazy if he ever told the truth.

He just didn't believe that spirits were possessing the mannequins. People were down there doing something. He wanted to know who and what. And why . . .

"Jennie, maybe someone pushed one of the mannequins at you," he said. "Maybe one of those people, whoever they are, were in the midst of the mannequins, talking. And that's probably why it looked like the clown mannequin came after you."

"Yes, maybe . . . It can be so dark and shadowy down there. It's funny. The theater's always had that feeling. Of being haunted. Maybe being haunted is the same as being steeped in history. But I always felt good before. Now, I don't."

"You're right not to feel safe — but it

wasn't ghosts of the old theater doing bad things."

Tears stung her eyes. "*Am* I too old, Sloan?"

"No, Jennie. You're not. You walked in on someone's secret meeting. Listen, you do everything at the theater and you do it well. That has nothing to do with the fact that you stumbled on someone who's killing people, and that someone needed to silence you."

"But . . . I'm alive," she said.

"Yes, you're alive, and we're keeping an officer in the hospital, so you'll stay alive. I've given orders that no one else be told that you're awake," Sloan explained. He squeezed her hand. "Jennie, you're going to be okay."

She nodded. "I love that theater, Sloan. I was never an actress. But I love working with the actors. I love fixing the costumes, fixing the props."

"That brings me to another question, Jennie. Henri told me you loaded the guns for the annual duel."

"I did. With blanks."

"One of the guns had live ammunition, Jennie."

"Sloan, I did *not* load a gun with live ammunition. I don't even have live ammuni-

tion!" she said indignantly.

"When did you load the guns and where did you leave them?"

"I always prepare for every day's performance the night before," she told him. "It might have been an hour or so before I went down to the basement."

"Where did you leave the guns?"

"On the prop table. It's backstage left, in one of the theater wings. Even if we — or the actors — are performing outside, we stick to protocol with the props and costumes."

The prop table. Not helpful. Anyone could've gotten to them. But no, that wasn't really true; it had to be someone who could move through the theater unnoticed. The cast and crew had been working outside most of the day, but they certainly went in and out. The housekeeping staff went in — and anyone might duck their head in. But only someone who knew the theater would know where to look for the props.

"Sloan, I would never, ever hurt an actor! Please, you have to believe me," Jennie begged.

He squeezed her hand reassuringly.

Maybe Jennie wouldn't, but *someone* would.

He stood. "Jennie, anything you can think

of, please call me."

"It was the clown, Sloan. I'm telling you. It was the clown."

"Thanks, Jennie. Now rest. Get better," he said, and left.

He reiterated to the staff and the officer on duty that he didn't want anyone else knowing that Jennie was conscious. He checked in on Jimmy and Zoe Hough, but both were soundly asleep. The resident told Sloan that the Houghs were both doing fine and could be released; Sloan asked that they be kept at least one more night, giving him time to talk to Newsome about arrangements for their protection.

He finally walked out of the hospital and headed for his car. The moon was high, the landscape glowing with its silvery light. But as he drove out, the desert seemed cast in shadow and mystery. The sand, he knew, hid many secrets of the past. Not some of humanity's finer moments, he thought drily. Moments of brutality and bloodshed.

He was eager to get back to town.

The show had let out when Jane returned downstairs from her room at the Gilded Lily, her bag stuffed with an oversize T-shirt for the night and the few toiletries she'd need.

She hadn't heard from Sloan yet, and she knew Kelsey and Logan would remain at the theater, alert to all possibilities, so she called Logan and told him she was going over to the Old Jail. He gave her his customary admonition to be careful; she promised she would be.

One of Mike Addison's night managers was on duty when she entered the Old Jail. He greeted her cheerfully, but she felt she was being watched. She wondered if Mike had warned that the "agent" who had rented Trey Hardy's cell had already caused trouble.

There were Do Not Disturb signs on the other cell doors she passed; she was obviously the last one in for the night. Turning her key in the door, she stepped in, then sat on the bed. "I'm here. I wish you'd talk to me. I wish I could understand what you want me to know."

There was no response. She stood, brushed her teeth and prepared for bed. She left only the small night-light on in the bathroom and lay down in the bed. Everything was quiet. She waited. Lack of sleep took its toll and she dozed off long before she intended.

She became aware of a weight settling by her side. Half-asleep, she assumed that

Sloan had returned from the hospital and decided to join her. When she rolled over to touch him, she felt as though she'd slipped her hand into something thick and icy, and she jolted awake, barely managing to suppress a scream.

He was back. Trey Hardy.

He was at her side. He watched her gravely for a minute.

"I see you," she told him. "I see you clearly."

He reached out a hand, as if he wanted to stroke her face. She felt the sensation of something there — and not there. But the room was dark, and he suddenly seemed as solid as any breathing, *living* human being. He got up, waiting for her. She did the same. He walked back into the bathroom.

"Please!" she whispered urgently. "Don't bang the walls!"

He placed his hand on the wall by the sink, then leaned against it. He moved his lips to speak.

"Here," the ghost said. It was a croak — dry, brittle. It was the rough, sandpapery whisper that others sometimes heard, and when they did, they'd get that eerie feeling that a place was really haunted.

"In the wall," she said softly.

He nodded.

She started, hearing a knock at the door. Hardy wavered and was gone.

She hurried to her door, expecting Sloan. She was surprised to see Mike Addison. He hadn't even been at the desk; she'd assumed he'd gone home for the night.

She opened the door. "Mike. What's the problem?"

"I came to make sure you're okay — and ask you to be quiet again," he said.

She frowned at him, startled. "Mike, I haven't made any noise. I don't know what you're talking about." She realized that beneath his Western denim jacket he was wearing a holster. He was armed, while her Glock was on the bedside table.

"That pounding. The guest two cells down called me about it," Mike said.

He was just standing there, a little belligerently, talking to her. She didn't know why he suddenly made her nervous.

"Let me see what's going on in here."

She wanted to slam the door, which would have been ridiculous. But she didn't want to let him into the room. She wished she'd gotten her gun before opening the door.

"Mike, there's nothing going on in here. I'm alone," she told him. "If any of the guests are hearing things, the sounds have to be coming from the theater."

"The theater is closed."

He seemed to be moving toward her. She assured herself that the man couldn't possibly be enough of a fool to offer harm to a federal agent, especially when it was known that she was at the Old Jail.

Thankfully, she didn't have to let him in *or* slam the door. She heard a creak, and the barred door separating the office from the cells opened and closed.

Sloan was coming down the hallway.

"Hey, Mike. What's up?" Sloan asked. "What are you doing here so late?"

"I was over at the theater — thought I'd stop in," Mike said. "And I got here just in time. The guests are complaining about the noise Agent Everett is making."

"I'm *not* making any noise," Jane said with exasperation.

Sloan stared at Mike. "If Agent Everett says she isn't making any noise, I certainly believe her."

"But I had a complaint," Mike protested.

"Tell the complainers the ghosts must really like them," Sloan said.

Mike's eyes narrowed and he cast his head at an inquisitive angle. "You gonna be here, Sheriff?"

"I'm going to be here. I'll see that nothing is going on," Sloan told him.

408

"Oh. Oh!" Mike said. "Okay, um, fine. Well, then. Just, uh, keep it down!" He turned and left abruptly.

Sloan looked at Jane, amusement in his eyes. "What was that all about?"

"I don't know. There really wasn't any noise coming from the room. But I did see Trey Hardy. And he put his hand on the wall again — right by the mirror. But, more importantly, how is Jennie?"

"She's doing well."

"What did she say?"

"She said the clown did it," he told her wearily. "She kept hearing voices from the room in the basement. She started to think that the spirits of people murdered in Lily had inhabited the mannequins. I think someone goes down there to talk and plot or . . . I don't know. But I *do* think we need to get in that room and find out what's down there. Anything happen here?"

"Happen? Not really. But, Sloan, we're getting closer. In the morning, I'll do a two-dimensional sketch of the skull from the desert. I'm willing to bet it's Red Marston. I'm almost positive Red and Sage were killed because they knew too much — and the same with Trey Hardy. I saw Sage tonight and . . ." She paused.

"And?"

"She'd had her tongue cut out. And just like we discussed earlier this evening, you have your tongue cut out when you've said too much or spoken against someone — or when it's a warning not to talk."

"Or if you want to make sure your victims suffer before they die."

He walked past her into the bathroom and ran his hand over the painted plaster of the wall. "So, the ghost insists there's something back there?" he asked.

She nodded. Sloan raised his brows, hands on hips. "I think your agency's budget is bigger than mine."

"Meaning?"

"Tomorrow, we'll dig out that wall," he said. "We'll just have to replace it. Logan and Kelsey are at the Gilded Lily, right?"

"Yes."

"From now on, one of us is at both of these places every night. But for now, we really need to get some sleep."

"I agree."

"I'll take that chair," he told her.

"Why would you do that when we've been sleeping together?" she asked.

"Ghosts."

She smiled. "Just because we're in the same bed doesn't mean that we have to fool around in it."

"If we're in the same bed, I'd *want* to fool around. I'm great at sleeping in chairs."

"That's ridiculous, and you're going to make me feel bad."

This time he smiled. "So, you're saying you can keep your hands off me?"

"With ghosts in the room, I can."

"Get in there. I'll be fine."

Sloan was determined. He pulled the chair up, stretched his legs out on the bed and settled in. Jane crawled into the bed and tossed him a pillow. "You know, I'm going to worry about you all night."

"Don't. I'll be sleeping."

He was stubborn and Jane could tell she wasn't going to change his mind, she crawled into bed. Sloan's head was thrown back; his eyes were closed. For a moment, she thought he'd already drifted off.

"Ironic," he said.

"What's that?"

"Our relationship is going to be all over town tomorrow — because of the one evening we slept apart."

She curled her arms around the remaining pillow. He was in the room with her and she let herself fall into a deep and peaceful sleep.

If Trey Hardy came again that night, she didn't know it. When she woke, Sloan was in the bathroom. The door was open; he'd showered and he was frowning at the mirror.

He turned to her. "He's here. Trey Hardy is here. And there *is* something in that wall."

"I've been looking up the history of mannequins," Kelsey told Jane as they drove to the station. "Great stuff. They found a torso carved out of wood in King Tut's tomb, which shows that the use of mannequins goes back thousands of years. Kings and queens gave them as gifts to fellow royals and to inform other countries of the latest fashion trends. In the 1700s they were often wicker, and a lot of them had no heads, but by 1870 — right around the time all the trauma was going on here — the fashion-conscious French started making them elaborate again and you know how it goes with the world imitating French fashion."

"Whenever I've finished this drawing," Jane said, "we'll get down into that basement."

"Didn't a whole crime-scene unit go through it?" Kelsey asked.

"Yes, but I think we're looking for something a crime-scene unit isn't going to find."

"Such as?"

"I don't know — but that's what we do,

right? Find what we don't know we're look-ing for," Jane said, adding, "in a way."

"Yeah, in a way. We could really use physi-cal evidence against someone, too."

They reached the office. Chet Morgan and Lamont Atkins were still working in town; Betty greeted them at the desk. Kelsey fol-lowed along behind Jane and helped her set the skull on the Franklin plane, take the photographs and do the scanning. Betty came in now and then to see how they were doing. "Wow!" she said, watching Jane work first with the computer and then do her sketch from the overlays. "I'm impressed."

In fact, Betty was in the room when she'd almost finished. "It's him, all right. It's him!" Betty said excitedly.

"Him?" Kelsey asked. "You mean —"

"Red Marston. The man who supposedly helped Sage disappear — and who suppos-edly ran away to Mexico with her. That was the rumor. So poor Sage was murdered at the theater. And Red was found out in the desert . . . so sad!"

"Well, it proves our theory," Jane mur-mured. "Or part of it."

Why had he suddenly shown up in the desert to point the way to a newly murdered man?

"It's brilliant. Your work is really brilliant."

Betty sighed. "If only you were working with the dead people from today — but then we know who they are, don't we?"

"Unfortunately," Kelsey said wryly. "That's not as much of an advantage as you'd hope."

"I still don't get why someone would kill a tourist no one knew in Lily," Betty said. "But Caleb Hough . . . well, you must be tired of hearing this, but the man didn't get along with anyone."

"And, of course, they might have been killed by different people," Kelsey pointed out.

A phone buzzed in the outer office, and Betty went running out to answer it. She reappeared as Kelsey was helping Jane pack up her personal art supplies and printing copies of Jane's sketch. "That was Sheriff Sloan. He wants you to know that he and Agent Raintree are still at the Old Jail."

"Thanks, Betty. Did he ask us to join him there?"

"No, he said to finish whatever you're doing. He also needs to meet Detective Newsome out at the old mine shaft. But you two just stick with your program," Betty said. "You're still busy here?"

"Not really. I have the two-dimensional likeness — enough to know what we wanted to know," Jane said.

"Lunch," Kelsey said. "We're going to go find some food."

"Well, if you need me at any time, just call," Betty said.

They thanked her and walked out of the station. "You were acting a bit strange," Kelsey murmured to Jane. "As if you didn't want Betty to know exactly what you're doing."

"Betty certainly seems helpful and legitimate," Jane said. "But Sloan's been more communicative with Newsome than his own deputies about all this. I'm not sure it's a matter of mistrust so much as a certain wariness, since everyone in this town talks to everyone else. Or maybe it's because we know that Brendan Fogerty — who came out of the whole gold heist all those years ago looking like a hero — was probably behind the whole thing."

"Hmm. So what's our plan?"

"I figure we'll get back into town, see what's up at the Old Jail, maybe get something to eat there," Jane told her.

When they arrived, Mike was at the desk. He gave Jane an angry glare when she arrived.

"You looking for Sloan? Well, he just left. Ripped up my room — and took off."

"Oh," Jane said, disappointed. "Did he leave me a message?"

Mike nodded, not at all happy. "He said for you to keep looking." He glared at Kelsey in turn. "He said between the locals and the feds, they'd get my place back in shape. He *promised!*"

"Mr. Addison, I know we'll see that your place is better than ever," Kelsey told him.

Mike sniffed. "You like throwing those tax dollars around, do you?"

"We can do a lot of the work ourselves," Kelsey said. "Honestly."

"Mike, I'm going to see what he was up to, okay?" Jane asked.

Mike frowned. "He told me not to let anyone back there. But I guess he didn't mean you. Go on. You'll see what he's done!"

Jane made her way through the door to the cells and then down the hall, Kelsey right behind her. They entered the Trey Hardy cell.

"Well," Kelsey said. "I can see why Mike was so upset."

The plaster in the bathroom looked as if it had been attacked with a sledgehammer — which it clearly had.

Jane bit her lower lip, smiling. "I'm pretty sure this is my fault," she told Kelsey. "Trey

Hardy keeps banging on this wall, so . . ."

"Do you think he found anything?" Kelsey asked.

"I don't think he had a chance to get very far," Jane said, brushing at the wall, knocking away first the new plaster and then the old plaster to get down to the wooden beams beneath. Those beams had once been strong and sturdy; when the jail was restored, thinner plywood had been used along with the plaster. She tried poking her fingers through to see if she could find anything.

"I'll call and ask him what's going on." Kelsey pulled out her phone.

Jane thought she knew how Sloan had felt while digging. The more she worked, the more she wanted to get done. She tried to imagine the jail as it had been with no nice modern bath built into the side. She'd already guessed that the barred window would have been just about where the mirror was now, and Trey Hardy might have leaned against the wall right here, staring out at the world. He might've been doing that when the door to his cell burst open — and Aaron Munson had walked in, guns blazing.

"They're at the mine," Kelsey said to Jane. "He'll call us back later."

Just then, Jane's fingers touched something. She wiggled them deeper between the boards. What she touched felt like metal.

"Need help?" Kelsey asked.

"I got it, I got it!"

"What is it?"

"I don't know, but . . ." She managed to extract a little metal tube. It might have been the muzzle of an old gun, sawed or cut off to create a cylinder. Or perhaps it had been fashioned from the leg of an old bed. It seemed as encrusted as something taken from a shipwreck.

And inside, rolled up, was a piece of paper. It was old, fragile, but the metal tubing had done its work.

Jane looked at Kelsey and carefully unrolled it.

The bones were in the mine wall.

They'd been undetected for over a hundred and forty years because they'd been shored up against the stone of the mine wall when work was done to support the structure to protect the miners from cave-ins.

"We found them," Newsome told Sloan and Logan, "because one member of our crime-scene unit noted a little crevice in the rocks in the second set of openings. If she hadn't seen that crack and been determined to go farther . . ."

There was something infinitely sad about the bones in the wall. They were attached to bits and pieces of fabric; time and heat had worn away the tissue and flesh, and they were heaped in a confusing pile. It appeared that the stagecoach robbers had brought them here, dug out the support structure, covered them with dirt and rock, then built up new "support beams" and a new wall around them.

The robbers — the *killers* — must have moved quickly, at night, because miners were working there at the time.

In fact, miners had come to work for years. Maybe, especially in the months afterward, they'd wondered at the smell.

But maybe they'd been so conditioned to the stench of heat and one another that they'd never noticed, and maybe decay had happened fast. . . .

Three skulls lay in the pile of remains. Femurs stuck out, rib bones seemed strewn about.

It no longer seemed tragic, not the way finding the newly dead could be. It was still terribly sad.

"I'll see that they're removed," Newsome told Sloan. "I'll take all the proper measures, do what we can to identify the remains and arrange for burial. I just thought you should see this."

"Yeah, I'm glad to see it," Sloan said. "I think we've managed to solve the past, and what a kick in the ass to oral history and legend. Brendan Fogerty wasn't a good guy at all. He was probably the mastermind pulling all the strings. Just his bad luck McNulty up and died without letting his partner know how to find the gold." He looked at Newsome. "But we have no clue as to where the gold did wind up, right? And what about the stagecoach?"

"The stagecoach might well have rotted to nothing over the years. And bones of dead horses have been found in the desert throughout time," Newsome reminded him. "Or they could've been rescued by ranchers or Apaches."

"Let's hope so," Logan muttered.

Sloan nodded. "Yeah, but that gold is somewhere," he said. "And I believe someone is after it now."

"Your men are still searching here?" Logan asked Newsome.

"Yes, but it's not an easy task. I don't want my people risking their lives in a possible cave-in."

"I know, and we don't want to see anyone injured, either."

"You believe there are a number of people involved in this?" Newsome asked, turning to Sloan.

"At least two. There were two people in the Hough house," Sloan said. "According to the son."

"Later today I'll have DNA results back from those glasses you pilfered from the theater the other night," Newsome said. "Just remember, unless any of them show up in the system, I need something to check them against. I have the bottle you found in here, but that's all I have."

"Appreciate it," Sloan told him.

"It's my job. But you know your town way better than I do, Sloan."

"I *thought* I knew the town," Sloan said. "Now —" He broke off and shrugged. "We'll find out what's going on. I was a lucky bastard in Texas. I was never part of an unsolved murder case. I'm not going to be part of one here, either." As he spoke, his phone rang. To his surprise, it was Jennie Layton.

He stepped back. "Jennie? You okay?"

"I'm improving and they say I can leave. Maybe tomorrow. But, Sloan, I'm afraid to leave. I keep remembering things."

"You do?"

She lowered her voice. "Sloan, can you

421

come see me? I'm feeling uneasy."

"I'll come over right now, Jennie," he promised. "I have to ride back in and get a car, but I'll be there as soon as I can."

"Thank you. There's just . . ." Her voice fell to a whisper he could barely make out. "There's something going on here, Sloan. I can just feel it. Something's going to happen. Something bad."

14

Jane sat on the floor with Kelsey, carefully reading the note left behind by Trey Hardy.

They know, I'm sure, that I overheard them talking. I don't believe they will let me come to trial. They suspect that I will use what I have overheard to save my life before a circuit judge. I *know* this just as I know what will transpire. They leave the jail and speak to one another about their intentions in the alley between my window and the theater, and they have seen my face when they look at me.

There is nowhere to turn. The sheriff and the deputy are both involved. I have lived hard and recklessly; I have seen the fall of the South — and known that we were often wrong. What becomes of me will not be just, and yet it will be deserved because I took the law into my own hands. May God help me. I practiced no cruelty. I killed during the war in the name of a Cause, but never killed at any other time in my life. What comes my way I will accept.

But I fear now for Sage; she has been to see me many times, a dear friend, a skilled actress, and mother and wife. They will kill me before my trial. I pray that someone else might find this letter, stop the crime those conspirators have planned, and see to her safety.

Their plan is that they can surprise the stagecoach. A sheriff and his deputy riding up will not cause alarm. They will murder those on the coach and hide their bodies in the desert; they have no fear of reprisal. They will hide the gold and let time go by, let it be forgotten. Then they will remove it from its hiding place, divide it and make haste across the border. The robbery will remain a legend, and they will invent some story to explain the disappearances of so many — including themselves.

God help us. Pray for all sinners.

Trey Hardy

Jane looked at Kelsey. "This is so tragic. I'm halfway in love with this poor dead outlaw!"

Kelsey nodded, trying to shove a piece of plaster back onto the wall.

It wasn't going to work.

"Yeah, it's sad. It's terrible. But where's the gold?"

Jane was thoughtful. "It's in the theater."

"Why the theater? It could be anywhere. We just dug out a wall and found the note. And here's another question — why kill Berman? He was a stranger as far as we know. Berman, and then Caleb Hough. Hough is probably involved. But . . . why kill people, when the gold hasn't even been uncovered?"

"They both had to be in on it," Jane insisted.

"You seem convinced," Kelsey said. "I'm going to call Logan again. If the county cops are handling whatever they just found in the mine, Logan can come back and get started on figuring out the connection. There *has* to be a connection."

"I think I know," Jane said slowly.

"Know what? The connection?"

Jane nodded. "How do you best hide anything?"

"Um, in a deep hole?" Kelsey suggested.

Jane laughed. "No. In plain sight. I think one of these conspirators found some of the gold, maybe a piece. He brought them all in on it, but the hiding place must be so obvious that no one's seeing it."

"Right. No one — like any one of us."

"So, call Logan and tell him about the note. Meanwhile, we'll go check out the theater."

The county officer on duty at the hospital, a conscientious man in his late twenties, was distressed when Sloan arrived at Jennie Layton's room.

He started to move a few feet from the door to greet Sloan, and Sloan smiled as he heard Jennie calling out, "Don't you leave me, young man!"

He grimaced as he saw Sloan, speaking softly. "I keep telling her I have to keep an eye on three people here and she's just one of them. She doesn't want me to leave her, not for a minute."

"It's okay. Go see Jimmy and Zoe Hough. I'm here. Do you know what got her so upset?"

He shook his head.

Sloan went in to be with Jennie. "Hey," he told her. "You have that young officer all in a dither, Jennie. What's up?"

"They're going to find me now, and they're going to kill me!" she said, her voice hushed. She glanced at the door as she spoke.

"Who are *they* and how are they going to find you?" Sloan asked.

"They know I'm here. Maybe they didn't mean to kill me at first, but they do now," Jennie said decisively.

He sat for a minute, wondering if — despite her job or perhaps because of it — she was still essentially a lonely aging woman with no family of her own.

"Jennie, we haven't let it out that you've even regained consciousness."

"There's someone in here, watching me," Jennie said stubbornly. "One of the nurses, I think."

"None of these nurses has anything to do with the theater." He took her hand. "This is a county hospital. We're from the little town of Lily. Honestly, a lot of county people hardly know we exist."

"No," she muttered, shaking her head. "You're wrong. Someone is here, Sloan. Watching me — waiting for an opportunity."

Sloan was torn. Jennie obviously felt afraid, certain of her own conviction. He didn't want to sit at the hospital and worry about her imagined fear. Just as he began to tell her that he couldn't stay with her, he noticed a nurse hovering in the doorway.

"I'll come back," the woman said in a husky voice. She had long dark hair with bangs and wore glasses with large green plastic frames.

"No, no, come in, we're just talking," Sloan said.

"It's all right. I can, uh, check Ms. Layton's vitals later," the nurse said, and turned quickly to move down the hall.

Sloan stood, frowning. He wouldn't say that the nurse had been ugly, but she had a strange, rather masculine look to her.

He lit out of the room.

"Sloan, don't leave me!" Jennie cried.

"Stop!" Sloan commanded in the hallway, watching the nurse all but run away. "Stop!"

He was completely ignored. He didn't want to threaten to fire or shoot off a warning in a hospital. With Jennie's voice fading in the background, he tore after the nurse.

The nurse looked back and then forward, running, pushing a work cart between the two of them. It flipped onto its side, and Sloan hopped over it as paper cups filled with medications flew into the air and onto the floor.

He caught the nurse about twenty feet past the overturned cart. Tackling the buxom brunette from the rear, he brought both of them down. He finally straddled his madly scrambling prey.

The brunette wig fell off, so did the glasses. He found himself staring down into the face of Brian Highsmith — easily recognizable now despite the eye makeup and bright red lipstick.

"Brian, you're under arrest for the murder —"

"No, Sloan, no, please! This isn't what it looks like," Brian wailed.

By then, they had an audience. Patients, some dragging their IVs, had come out to the hall. Nurses, doctors and orderlies, as well.

Sloan got to his feet, dragging Brian up with him.

"Sloan, honest, I swear to you! I would never murder anyone! You have to believe me. I'd never hurt Jennie. Not on purpose. No —"

"Really? It looks like you're pretending to be a nurse in order to see Jennie Layton. And since someone put her in a coma to get her here —"

"Yes, yes, I was trying to see Jennie. I thought — hoped — she might have recognized me," Brian said quickly. "I never meant for anything bad to happen to her — I love her like I love my grandma!"

"What were you doing, dressing up so you

could slip in that door?" Sloan demanded.

"I had to see her!" Brian answered.

"Mommy!" one of the patients cried out. "That lady is . . . a man!"

"It's all right. Let's go back to your room," the mother said.

"Hey, man, there's meds all over the floor!" A skinny fellow who looked like he should be in detox said happily.

Another nurse came up. "Mr. Wilson, get back in your room!" she told him.

One of the doctors approached Sloan. "You need to take this out of here, Sheriff. You're upsetting my patients."

Sloan spun around on him. "Well, you're going to have to explain to me how an actor got into your hospital dressed as a nurse and was moving among your *upset* patients!" he snapped.

He spun Brian around, snapping plastic cuffs onto his wrists. "I will remove this man that *you've* let in," he said, glowering as he marched down the hall. The county officer was standing in front of Jennie's room, trying to watch Sloan and trying to watch the hallway. Both Jimmy Hough and his mother had come out of their respective rooms. Zoe Hough was standing behind her son, a protective hand on his shoulder.

"It's okay," Sloan told them.

"He got in here!" Zoe said with horror.

"Did you kill my father?" Jimmy demanded, scowling at Brian.

"What? No!" Brian shouted. "I didn't kill anyone! Won't anybody listen to me?"

Sloan pulled his phone from his pocket and called the office. Betty answered. "Betty, get Chet or Lamont down here. I need someone to pick up a prisoner. I want him held at our facility until I can get back there myself. And warn whoever's coming not to take their eyes off him for a minute. You understand?"

"Yes, Sheriff, of course. Who's being picked up? Did you —"

"It's Brian Highsmith. I want this man in our lockup, and I don't want him getting out. No mess-ups. Get someone here now!"

"Yessir, yessir!" Betty said.

He hung up his phone. Jimmy Hough, fists clenched, looked as if he was going to hit Brian with a hard right hook to the jaw. Sloan quickly stepped between them. "Jimmy, stop. We have to get to the bottom of this. Please, go back into your rooms. Everything's under control."

"Sheriff, you're not leaving us, are you?" Zoe asked, her eyes wide and frightened.

"Not right now. I'm here until I can get more help in."

431

"Do as he says, please, Jimmy!" Zoe told her son. Jimmy continued to stare at Brian but he moved back as his mother pushed his chest. "Jimmy, the law will take care of it."

"He killed my father," Jimmy said dully.

"We don't know that yet," Sloan said.

"I swear I just came to see Jennie!" Brian insisted. "I was, uh, fooling around in the basement when she came down and I didn't want to get into trouble. I didn't mean to hurt her — or that nice agent, Jane. I didn't want them to know I was there. . . . I accidentally hit Jennie too hard and I need her to forgive me. I was trying to . . . I was trying to talk to her, to beg her forgiveness. I — I was worried about jail, but I love Jennie. I need her to forgive me."

"Shut up for now, Brian," Sloan said. His phone was ringing. He flipped it open; Logan was calling.

"I found the connection," Logan said without preamble.

"Which connection?" Sloan asked.

"Jay Berman. He did some work for Caleb Hough about a decade ago. I'm pretty sure he put a few ranch workers in the hospital. He'd been out in Arizona on another so-called vacation. That was right around the time two of Hough's workers —

432

who'd demanded higher pay — ended up injured. So, I'm not sure who the hell killed Hough, but I'll bet Jay Berman messed up, so Hough was the one who might've killed him."

Sloan looked at Brian. "Can you get down to the hospital?"

"Right away."

He hung up. Brian was shaking his head. "I'm not a killer, Sloan. I'm an actor! I was just going to plead with Jennie not to give me up so I didn't go to jail or lose my job!" he said.

"Brian, people just 'fooling around' in the basement of the building they work in don't render old women unconscious because they're afraid of being caught."

"No, you don't understand. I could have lost my job."

"Brian, you *should* lose your job for nearly killing people," Sloan said.

"But I didn't mean to! Hey, Sloan, I'm a good guy. Really. Sure, I wanted to look for the gold. That's all anyone talks about now. But I never — I swear I *never* meant to hurt anyone."

Jennie came into the hall then and confronted Brian, her face twisted in a mask of fury. She pointed a finger at him. "You tried to get in before. There was another nurse in here and she sent you to tend to another patient. God help that patient! How could you, Brian? How *could* you?"

"Jennie, please, believe me! I came to beg your forgiveness!"

Sloan was relieved to hear the sound of a siren. "Jennie, go back to bed. Brian, move!"

He prodded Brian to the front, pulling him through reception where stares and whispers followed his every move.

As he drew Brian outside with him, he was surprised to see Betty getting out of the car.

"Hey, what are you doing here? I told you to send Lamont or Chet."

"Lamont was breaking up a bar fight and Chet was dealing with some kid who was higher than a kite. He'll probably be in here in a few minutes. Talked to Scotty and he was on his way in. It sounded urgent when I talked to you," Betty said.

Sloan nodded. "Betty, get him back to our offices, put him in lockup, make sure he's secure. And stay there. Scotty will be manning the office alone, since the other night guys will be back in town. It won't be that long. I'll be back as soon as I've gotten the Hough family and Jennie calmed down enough for me to leave."

"If he calls an attorney —" Betty began.

"I don't care if he calls in all the gods on Olympus, I can have him for twenty-four hours and I want him there when I get in," Sloan told her.

"I've got it, Sloan. But . . . Brian? Brian Highsmith? What the hell were you doing, young man? And to think I enjoyed your performances!"

Brian groaned. "Yes, I knocked Jennie out by mistake. Okay, and the agent. But I didn't kill anybody. Honest to God, I'm not a killer! I just thought I'd look for gold, too. I mean, I hear so much about it!"

"Betty, get him out of here," Sloan said, irritated. Betty took Brian by the arm. "Wait!" Sloan said, accosting Brian head-on. "What about the bones? The skull? Did you put the skull on the wig stand?"

Brian turned red and pursed his lips, nodding. "Sheriff, I . . . found the trapdoor, the body. I should have reported it, but . . . I set up the skull. You weren't supposed to come. When Valerie screamed, I was supposed to save her. I was just trying to get lai—" He broke off, looking at Betty. "I was trying to make Valerie see me more as a date than a coworker. The woman in the floor had been dead forever. Yeah, I figured it might be Sage McCormick. Sheriff, I know she was . . . that you're like her great-great-

whatever grandson, but come on, she'd been dead for years. More than a century. I didn't kill anyone, I swear it."

"You never went near Caleb Hough? Or his wife or son?"

"Never! I'm here because I had to try to tell Jennie I'm sorry!"

"In a nurse's uniform — dressed up as a woman?"

"I *am* an actor!" Brian reminded him with wounded dignity.

"Whether you did or didn't hurt anyone else, you almost killed Jennie and you assaulted Agent Everett. You're in it deep, Brian, and when I get back, you're going to tell me everything — step by step. Betty, get him out of here!"

He watched while Betty put Brian Highsmith in the backseat of her patrol car. Then, trying to get a grip on his anger, he walked back into the hospital. He called Newsome and told him what had happened, then called Logan to give him the latest and was glad to hear that Logan was nearly at the hospital. As soon as he'd finished that conversation, he phoned Jane.

"So that's it?" she asked. "Brian — Brian Highsmith — knocked me out and put Jennie in a coma. And he claims he didn't want to *hurt* anyone?"

"That's his story."

"And he started the whole thing by putting Sage McCormick's skull on the wig stand?"

"He said he was trying to scare Valerie into sleeping with him when he became the hero who saved her. Apparently, I ruined that by showing up."

"What about Jay Berman — and the corpse in the desert? Do you think Brian killed Caleb Hough?"

"He denies it — but as he just reminded me, he *is* an actor."

"Well, there's also the fact that two people went into the Hough house and attacked Jimmy and Zoe Hough," Jane said.

"I'm going to talk to Jennie and the Hough family — calm them down, calm myself down." He sighed. "I was pretty sure that Jennie was being paranoid. Once Logan gets here I'll go back to talk to Brian."

"Kelsey and I will hang around the theater," she told him. "Mike Addison is breathing fire over the fact that we've ripped up his wall." She was quiet for a minute. "You'll want to see this letter. Kelsey mentioned it to Logan."

When Sloan acknowledged it, she went on. "Trey Hardy managed to file down some metal tubing to make sure his note

437

was preserved. He'd hoped somebody would find it if he was killed, and if so, see that his killers didn't get to Sage." She paused. "Or, in the event that it wasn't found until later, I guess he wanted to set the record straight. About the gold heist. And about Sage."

Sloan felt a little numb. He wasn't used to being sentimental, but this did involve his family. Or, at any rate, an ancestor.

"Yeah, I'd like to see that note," he finally told Jane, and realized his voice was a little husky. Maybe it meant something that Trey Hardy and Sage McCormick had stayed around as ghosts all these years — and were here to help out when he'd needed them.

"And while we're at the theater, we're not going to be destructive. We're going to look for the obvious," Jane assured him.

"Hey, did you make a likeness of our mummified corpse?" he asked.

"From the pictures I've seen, I'd say we definitely found Red Marston. I honestly believe he was trying to save Sage, too, and died for his efforts," Jane said.

"Maybe. We know that Trey Hardy was gunned down in a conspiracy. And I'm guessing Sage and Red were killed because of possible interference — or because they might talk. Since Brendan Fogerty was in on it all along, the law never caught anyone. I suspect Caleb Hough discovered that the gold was still here. He brought Jay Berman in on it and then killed Berman. The only possible reason for all these murders is that someone found some part of that gold already — and means to keep it."

"We're going to start looking, Sloan."

"Keep in touch. And be careful."

"Of course."

Sloan rang off and went back into the hospital. Jennie was still upset, but she was in bed again and she'd been given a sedative; she clung to Sloan when he walked inside the room. "You're going to be okay now," he said.

"I don't feel right, Sloan. I don't feel right. Brian! And I cared about that boy."

"He claims he loves you, too, Jennie. That he never intended to hurt you."

Jennie sniffed at that. "He'll go to jail, won't he?"

"That was a serious assault. Yes, I imagine he'll do time."

"What if I don't press charges?"

"He attacked a federal agent, as well." Sloan hesitated. "He might have murdered other people, too. We don't really know the truth yet. We only know what he's willing to admit."

439

"Brian Highsmith," Jennie said. "He played a villain, Sloan, and he was an atrocious flirt, but I always felt he was a good kid at heart."

"He put you in a coma," Sloan said.

"But I believe he didn't mean to," Jennie argued.

There seemed to be no arguing with her; she was still charmed by Brian.

They were both startled when they heard a sound of disgust from the doorway. Sloan saw that Zoe Hough was standing there.

"How could you say such a thing?" she demanded. "That man is a killer!"

"Zoe," Sloan said, rising to walk over to her where she stood in the doorway. "Zoe, we don't —"

"He crept in here dressed like a nurse! He could've come and killed Jimmy or me!" Zoe said, obviously shaken.

"Zoe, he admits to what he did as far as Jennie and Jane are concerned, but denies killing anyone," Sloan told her.

"But he came into the hospital!"

"Zoe, we think that whoever killed your husband also attacked you," Sloan said. "Do you remember anything about him? The sound of his voice? Any details at all?"

"Well, of course I remember him! I've seen him perform."

"I meant on the day you were attacked," Sloan said.

Zoe swallowed hard. "I was attacked by a woman. I think. I mean, it's hard to be sure, but there was something about the scent . . . like perfume."

Bingo. This aligned with what Jimmy had said. It was also the first time Zoe had recalled that particular detail.

Sloan was glad when Jimmy appeared behind her, holding her shoulders. "Mom, come on, you're going to upset Jennie." He looked at Sloan. "He's not the man who attacked me."

"How do you know?" Zoe asked aggressively.

"I just do," Jimmy said. "I would know. . . . I feel I'd know. I wasn't completely out at any time. I'm sure I'd recognize a voice if . . . if I heard it right now."

Sloan was glad to see Logan as he came around the bend in the hallway. He was wearing a tailored denim shirt and jeans and an air of authority that suited him well. He approached Sloan and the small group in the hallway with a query in his eyes.

"I'm heading back to the office," Sloan told him.

"You can't leave us! Even with an officer in the hall," Zoe protested.

441

"It's all right, Mrs. Hough. I'll be here with you," Logan said. "I promise you I'll see to your safety and that of your son. So will the officer in the hall. The sheriff has work to do."

"This man — he's going to watch all of us?" Jennie asked.

"Yes, ma'am, I'll be here. With all of you," Logan assured her.

Sloan tipped his hat to Logan, smiling — and grateful that Jane had called her Krewe and that Logan had come.

"We'll find the truth." He met Zoe's eyes. "I guarantee it."

"Now, don't you hurt that boy!" Jennie called as he turned to leave.

"No torture, Jennie. I promise," Sloan said, making an effort not to smile.

At last he was out the door. He called the office and Scotty, the night desk deputy, picked up.

"I'll be there in about ten minutes," Sloan told him.

"Okay," Scotty said. And then, "Why? What's up?"

"To interrogate Brian Highsmith. He's there, right?"

"No. In fact, no one's here. I came into an empty office, which was pretty surprising, but I chalked it up to the end of Silver-

442

fest. There was a note from Betty saying she'd had to run out. But she isn't here now."

"Call in our troops. Tell them to start looking for Betty's patrol car. She left the hospital with Highsmith. Find her car. Find Betty — and Highsmith!" he said. "I'm on it myself —"

He broke off, swearing. He was still about a mile from Main Street in Old Town.

And there was Betty's car, run off the road.

He pulled his own car to the side and wrenched open the door. There was no sign of Betty in or near the patrol car.

Nor was Brian Highsmith in back.

A trail of blood trickled through the sand. Sloan followed it, his heart pounding, until it disappeared.

15

Silverfest had quieted down. There were still a number of vendors around and Desert Diamonds seemed to be doing a decent business, along with the saloon and the spa. There was a group heading out for a night ride, Jane noticed, but Heidi wasn't leading it — two young men of about college age seemed to be doing it. The haunted hayride was getting ready to roll, as well.

Jane saw Henri Coque in front of the Gilded Lily, out on the street giving a lecture on the history of the theater in the United States, while Cy Tyburn and Valerie Mystro — dressed in hero and heroine attire — were chatting with people on the street. She didn't see Alice anywhere . . . and she wondered if any of them knew that Brian had been arrested.

"Best time ever to sneak in," Jane told Kelsey.

The bar and restaurant had yet to open.

There weren't even any kitchen workers in the old theater; there was nothing but dead silence when Kelsey and Jane walked in.

It felt strange, almost eerie.

"Want to check out the rooms upstairs while everyone else is outside?" Kelsey asked.

"Sure," Jane agreed. "If they aren't all locked."

"The master key is in Jennie's room. I found it last night," Kelsey said. "I'll grab that."

"Good find!"

They didn't need to search the Sage suite, nor Jennie's room, since Logan and Kelsey had stayed in it. They entered Brian's. Anything he might have taken — such as the dueling pistols that had disappeared from Jane's bed — wasn't there.

But they were equally disappointed as they went through the rest of the rooms. The pistols didn't turn up, nor did any notes, remnants of gold, hidden gold — or even gold jewelry.

"Let's try the theater," Jane suggested.

Downstairs, Kelsey admired the stage. "It's a remarkable place, really," she said.

"We should move quickly. The company will be coming in soon," Jane warned.

"What's Henri going to do? He'll be miss-

445

ing a villain tonight," Kelsey said. She was sorting through the props on the table, then looked at Jane. "Hey, I think I just found your dueling pistols."

Jane walked over to the prop table. The pistols were there, in plain sight. She picked up one and then the other, handing both to Kelsey.

"Blanks," she murmured.

Kelsey nodded. "You're *sure* there was live ammunition in one of them?" she asked Jane.

"I'm sure — and Sloan still has the live rounds."

"So, I guess Brian was trying to kill Cy. But . . . why?"

"Because he's the hero? Because he gets the girl?" Jane shrugged. "Although, while he admits he set up the skull, he denies wanting to hurt anyone. According to Sloan, Brian was just trying to get out of the room without being seen."

"Should we check the dressing rooms?" Kelsey asked.

"Let's go." She led Kelsey through the various rooms, showing her where Sage McCormick's body had been found.

As they walked to the next room, Jane saw something on the floor. Bending down, she touched the fresh, wet stain.

She looked up at Kelsey.

"Blood," she mouthed.

Kelsey drew her gun and Jane did the same. Kelsey counted silently to three, then nodded at Jane. Jane threw the door open.

On the floor, as if he'd fallen while clutching the rack of costumes, lay a man in a pool of blood and fallen fabric.

Jane quickly fell to her knees at his side and rolled him over . . . and recognized Brian Highsmith.

She put two fingers on his throat to check for a pulse. It was there but weak. "He's still alive."

As she spoke, Brian's eyes flew open. He stared at Jane but couldn't seem to focus. "She's dead . . . she's dead, too. They knew . . . they knew . . . they killed her."

His eyes closed.

Jane felt for his pulse again. "Kelsey, I think . . . the bullet is in his shoulder. He might make it."

"I can't get a signal down here," Kelsey said urgently.

"Go out to the street. Get an ambulance over here!" Jane begged. "I'll stay with him."

Kelsey left her, running upstairs and out to the street. As Jane tried to staunch the flow of blood, she heard something behind her. She looked up, assuming Kelsey had

447

returned.

But it wasn't Kelsey.

It was one of the mannequins. An old one, from the late 1800s. She'd seen it downstairs. . . . Jennie had claimed that a clown attacked her, but they'd figured out that it had been Brian, that he'd pushed a clown figure toward her. . . .

This clown was moving — alive and moving.

It lifted its arm; it held a gun and took aim at Jane.

She rolled to a corner of the room just as the bullet exploded against the dressing-table mirror. The sound of the mirror shattering was what she heard, and she realized there was a silencer on the gun.

Someone had tracked Brian down. Someone had tracked him to this room. That someone meant to kill him.

And now her.

Sloan searched up and down the road, seeking a trail of blood. While he walked, he called the office and reported that Betty and her prisoner were missing. Then he called Newsome and asked for officers to scour the streets in town, the hell with Silverfest.

He got into his car and drove slowly, searching the road for any sign of either

Betty or Brian Highsmith.

He was five minutes from town when his phone rang.

Logan said, "Got a call from Kelsey. She has an ambulance rushing to the theater. She and Jane found Brian Highsmith, shot and bleeding to death, in his dressing room at the theater."

"I'm almost there," Sloan told him. "Any word on Betty?"

"None. I've got another officer coming to the hospital. I'll be there as soon as he shows up."

"Thanks. Whatever's going down seems to be going down *now*," Sloan said.

He stepped on the gas.

As he reached the outskirts of Lily, he was forced to slow down. There was some kind of Silverfest event happening on the road.

He left the car on the edge of Main Street and started running in.

As he did, he nearly ran by a heap on the ground. He recognized what it was — a body — and stopped himself.

He turned and fell to his knees.

It was Betty.

His heart thundered as he carefully examined her for an injury.

"Betty!" he said softly.

449

She groaned and looked up at him. "Sheriff!"

"Betty, what the hell happened?"

"There was someone flagging me down . . . I veered off the road. Next thing I knew, someone was in front of me, spraying something in my face . . . I can't remember. My head . . . my head is killing me. . . . I . . ."

"Stop talking. I'll get an ambulance out here."

Betty sat up. "No, no, I'm fine. Go . . . after him. Whoever it was . . . took Brian. He took Brian. . . ."

"Betty, who the hell was it?"

"I . . . don't know."

"How can you not know?"

"He — I can't even say if it was a man or a woman — was dressed up. Dressed like a . . . like a Plains Indian . . . like an Apache in buckskin . . . with a dark wig and makeup and a black mask. I don't know who it was . . . but —"

He'd reached for his phone. She set her hand on his. "No, Sloan. I'm all right. Go — get to the theater!"

"Betty, you're injured —"

"I'm fine! I'll call for help. Go."

He didn't trust her. Betty — who'd been his right hand since he'd returned to Lily.

450

He rose, suddenly very afraid — for many reasons. On many fronts. He crouched down again and pretended to make sure she wasn't shot or injured, hoping his sleight of hand was successful.

"All right, Betty," he said, and rose.

She might be innocent; she might be telling the truth.

But he didn't know.

Cops would be crawling all over the theater any minute — but he felt a growing urgency to get there himself.

"Go!" Betty insisted.

He did. He ran. As he raced through the streets, he looked for people he knew. He didn't see anyone. He paused just long enough to pull out his phone and call Logan. "Found Betty on the road. I left her there. I'm at the theater."

"You see Kelsey? The ambulance?"

"No."

"I've called for backup. Was Betty shot? Dead, alive?"

"Alive. I don't trust her, Logan. I don't trust anything right now."

"I'll be there in a few minutes. You've also got county cops moving in. Maybe you should wait for backup."

Maybe he should.

"I can't," he said.

451

He burst in through the slatted doors of the theater.

Jane scrambled to get her own gun. She managed to fire a shot at the clown, but then the clown was gone. She jumped to her feet and moved carefully to the door — just in time to see the clown run across stage right. Ever wary that a bullet could come tearing at her again, she pursued the clown.

She got off a shot when the clown passed ahead of her in the bar area, but he threw open the door to the basement and tore down the stairs. She walked to the doorway, determined to guard the one entry until someone could come.

Then she realized that someone was behind her. She turned, ready to fire.

Her gun went off just as she was slammed in the head. As she went tumbling down the stairs, she heard someone cry out; she might not have killed her attacker, but at least she'd injured him.

It did her little good. She landed in the basement, staring up at the clown.

She hadn't released her grip on the Glock.

She lifted her gun. The clown dived to the floor, knocking the wig stand on top of her. She struggled to free herself from the hair and heads with sightless eyes.

Footsteps were heading her way down the stairs. The clown, too, was trying to get free from the wigs. She fired again; the clown rolled across the floor and into the mannequin room.

Someone was nearly on top of her, coming down the stairs — and swearing in fury. Jane managed to get up and tear across the room, plowing into the rows of mannequins.

Once she was there, she went as still as she could . . . and she listened. Someone was breathing near her. And someone else was walking into the room.

In the near-darkness, Victorian madams stared at her, along with Mr. Hyde. A vampire held his cape above his eyes and in the dim light seemed real.

Why not? The clown was real.

And then she heard a voice she'd come to know well. "Agent Everett, you're harder to kill than I'd thought! But you should just give it up. Those bullets won't last forever, and quite frankly, you're outnumbered. Give it up!"

She didn't move, didn't breathe. When she felt movement beside her, she turned and fired. She heard a gasp and a scream and then cursing.

She knew the voice. A woman's voice. She

hadn't even begun to suspect that it could have been this woman!

Who was not alone.

Just how many people were involved?

Suddenly, the mannequins were shoved at her. They all seemed to be coming at her, their faces grotesque in the shadows.

Painted faces, wooden faces, laughing faces and the leering eyes of a Dracula . . .

She tried to remain steady, but tripped and fell. One of the arms struck hers, and the Glock fell with her in the chaos. She hit the floor.

And something soft.

A body.

Kelsey.

She managed to keep quiet.

"Have you found your friend yet, Jane? Such a conspiracy! And so easy to figure out. I mean, Sloan was friends with Logan. They sent you in, and then Kelsey and Logan showed up. So easy when lawmakers get involved. Just like before!"

Jane felt for Kelsey's pulse. She was still breathing. In the darkness, Jane patted her holster. They'd taken Kelsey's gun.

She realized they'd never been alone in the theater.

"We're going to get you, Agent Everett! Oh, don't go thinking it's like the play —

that the good guy's going to save you. We've been waiting for him, and in a few minutes, well . . . the gang will all be here! And the gang will all be dead!"

Sloan let his eyes adjust to the darkness. He raced to the stage and was startled to run into Cy Tyburn, who seemed to be practicing a monologue.

"Cy! Where is everyone? Has the ambulance come? What the hell is going on?"

"Damned if I know! Everyone's supposed to be in here. What did you say? Who needs an ambulance?"

"Brian. Brian Highsmith," Sloan said. He started to go backstage. As he did so he heard the familiar click of a gun.

He spun around. Cy had a Colt aimed at him. "Yes, go on back."

"You are not going to shoot me, Cy."

"Oh, yes, I am. But . . . play your cards right, and you can hope for escape in the next few minutes."

"What?"

Sloan moved toward Cy, itching to reach for his own weapon.

Cy shot the stage floor in front of him — barely missing his foot.

"Turn around and walk. We're going down to the basement."

"This place'll be crawling with cops in about two minutes," he said.

"I don't think so." Cy indicated the aisle along the side of the seats.

Someone was coming — and he knew who it was. Betty. His trusted deputy. Sweet, older, gray-haired.

And lethal.

"No, I just talked to Scotty and I called Newsome," Betty said. "On your behalf, of course. I assured him that no ambulances were needed. You're here, and everything is under control."

"Kelsey called for the ambulance. Not me. A federal agent," Sloan said.

"And you know how those feds are, always trying to take control. No, I assured him that I'm all right. We've got Brian Highsmith again . . . and it's all good."

"Until they find us all dead, of course?" Sloan asked.

"You've figured out the old story — you and your so-called *artist*. So, figure *this* out. When we're done, it'll look like you — the sheriff — and Agent Jane Everett got together and plotted to take the gold for yourselves. You were going to shoot Brian and me and the others, but we're not idiots. We shot you first."

"Seriously? Who the hell is going to

believe that?"

"We have our story down pretty well," Betty told him. "So, do you want to die alone or see your pretty agent one more time before you go?"

"Well, of course I'd like to say goodbye," Sloan said. "And if we're going to die, I think I'd like to hear how this all started. Brian wasn't involved, was he? Cy, you were the one who put live bullets in the gun, but when Jane did her little charade in the street, you really had no choice but to go along with it. But why start this whole thing? Why kill people over gold when you didn't even have it?"

"Caleb Hough found some of it. Didn't you know? He had it — and he was acting like a big shot. He called in that enforcer of his to keep the rest of us in line. Can you believe that? Caleb knew Jay Berman and probably thought we'd all be afraid of him, that we'd keep our mouths shut and obey his every edict. But I think Caleb felt that his own enforcer got greedy — and that's why he shot Jay Berman out in the desert. Then, well —"

"Shut up, Cy. Quit being such a drama-tist!" Betty snapped. "Get him downstairs."

"Not fair. Not fair if I don't know the whole story. So, let me see — Caleb was

457

holding out on you. That's why he wound up dead?" Sloan asked.

"Get him moving!" Betty shouted.

"I'm moving, I'm moving." Sloan turned, hands held high, and started walking toward the front of the room as Betty indicated. She had her gun trained on him.

"Go on. Go on!" Betty urged, nudging him with the muzzle.

"To the basement?"

"You got it, smart boy!"

He walked slowly. Betty might have stopped the county people from coming, but not Logan. Still, he didn't want Logan taken by surprise — as he'd been.

He didn't waste a lot of time cursing himself; he'd made a mistake. Now he had to fix it.

"Why were you out at the mines?" he asked.

"That bastard, Hough!" Cy said. "He had us all convinced the gold was in the mines. But it wasn't. And he admitted it."

"So, if you knew where it was, why didn't you just get it and take off?" Sloan asked. "And, by the way, where *is* it?"

Silence was his answer.

He chuckled softly. "You still don't know, do you? Let's see, Caleb showed you a sample because he was going to need help getting it. He needed a cop on his side, so he got you, Betty. And then he created a little gang of thieves, but you were so afraid of being double-crossed that you did him in. Of course, he *was* trying to double-cross you, wasn't he? He actually cared for his son, so that probably got in his way, didn't it? And let's see — one of you was supposed to torture the truth out of him, but you lost it. Or else he fought back and you had to kill him."

"Get down those steps!" Betty yelled.

"Cy," Sloan said. "Why you? Ah . . . you don't really have what it takes. But you were dissatisfied and Caleb saw that in you. Betty, you, too. You hated playing second fiddle."

"Shut up!" Betty shouted. "You think you're so smart. You think you're right about everything."

"I'm sure I *am* right. You needed a cop for protection, and you needed the actors because . . . well, because, of course, you searched the mine shaft — no luck — and realized the theater was the most likely place. The gold —"

"Get down the stairs!"

"I'm going. I'm going!"

"Watch it!" someone called from below.

Jane was down there, just as they'd said.

But she wasn't alone.

"She's in with the mannequins," the voice said.

Damn! He'd never suspected.

"Heidi," he called. "You weren't making enough on the trail rides, huh? But working the trail rides, you were able to set up Jay Berman's body with the corpse of poor Red Marston pointing at it. Caleb didn't leave the body there. *You* dug it up and put it there so Caleb would know you weren't just a bunch of country hicks. You left Red pointing at him to scare Caleb, but then you killed Caleb, anyway. This is really pathetic — because you still don't know where the gold is."

Sloan reached the bottom of the stairs. He tried to judge their firepower. They hadn't taken his gun, and he'd seen to it that Betty's was worthless; that was what his sleight of hand had been about. But Heidi and Cy were armed — and he didn't know who else might be in the basement with them.

"*She* can find it. She knows where it is," Heidi said. "Sloan, come on over here."

He walked around the fallen wig stand. The basement floor looked gruesome — with the wigs and heads everywhere, it seemed to be a floor full of decapitations.

He was about four feet from the first of the mannequins in the third room. He judged his chances.

"Agent Everett!" Heidi called out. "I'm going to suggest you show yourself. You might live if you tell us where the gold is. Oh — and let's see. I'll start by shooting Sloan in the foot, then the calf — maybe a shoulder. Don't want to hit an artery until you come out."

And she would come out, he was afraid.

They were too confident. Heidi wasn't even looking at him. Cy was by the stairs, peering into the mannequin room. Sloan saw that Betty had her gun on him.

He reached for her in a swift movement.

She fired.

Nothing happened; he'd emptied her gun.

He pulled her in front of him and pushed her toward Heidi just as Heidi fired. Heidi's bullet hit Betty, who screamed and choked.

"Shit, Heidi, you killed Betty!" Cy cried. "She was our cop. We needed a cop!"

"Shut up, Cy!" Heidi fired again.

She missed Sloan.

He'd plowed into the mannequins.

They seemed to embrace him. They were everywhere.

"Mike, get out here!" Heidi shouted. "Get the hell out here and we'll just shoot until

461

we get them all."

Mike! Mike Addison made up the last of their little club — or so he hoped.

He heard a scrambling near him; he could have fired. But he didn't know if it was Jane or Mike.

He tackled the moving creature.

A clown went down before him. *Mike Addison as a clown.* Maybe it was fitting.

Mike had a gun. They struggled for it; it went off, but then flew across the floor and disappeared in the pile of mannequins.

When he ripped off the clown face, Mike stared up at him furiously.

Sloan didn't bother speaking. He slugged Mike with the hardest right to a jaw he'd ever wielded in his life. Mike was silent. Lights out.

"Damn you!" Heidi shouted. She began firing. She was going to hit one of them if he didn't draw his own gun. He returned fire.

Heidi screamed and ducked behind a wall. Cy Tyburn sprinted across the room, taking cover by the wall. He fired into the mannequins.

Sloan fell to one side, trying to use a Victorian lady to shield him. Then the door burst open and he heard someone shouting.

"What the hell is going on down here?"

It was Henri Coque.

Jane had to force herself to keep silent. At first, she was afraid they had Sloan, that they'd kill him or torture him if she didn't move.

But then Sloan had gotten into the mannequin room, as well.

And she'd had to keep silent — because she couldn't defend herself.

She scrambled in the darkness, trying not to show herself, desperate to find her gun in the commotion. Then she heard Henri Coque.

"Henri! Get down here, too. You know, Henri, you're really good at keeping this place afloat — and the shows are terrific!" Heidi said. "But we need you now. Come out, Sheriff. Come out, come out wherever you are, or I will kill this innocent man. And you'll have to go your whole life knowing he died because you were a coward. Hmm. Maybe we'll have to run and I can leave Henri alive. I wouldn't mind doing that. He's not a bad guy."

Jane heard movement near her. Sloan.

"I'll kill him, Sloan. It'll all be on you!" Heidi said.

She was still behind the wall. Sloan had been returning fire; she had to know approximately where he was. Heidi wasn't taking any chances. She had Henri in the center of the room. She fired — and Henri screamed.

Just then, Jane felt movement among the mannequins again — but not from Sloan's direction. She turned. For a moment, she thought she was looking at another mannequin.

Then she realized she was seeing Sage McCormick.

And Sage was desperately trying to push something at her.

Jane frowned. Whatever it was glittered in the dim light. She reached for it, but Sage shoved something else at her.

Her Glock.

Jane nodded her thanks and grabbed the gun.

She had one chance.

She shoved all the mannequins toward the wall where Heidi was taking cover; Henri had been knocked over and Heidi raised her gun to shoot.

Jane fired, and Heidi went down. She heard Cy Tyburn curse.

And then saw that he'd taken aim at her.

But he never fired.

Sloan stepped from the mannequins and fired first.

Cy went down like a log.

Henri sat on the floor, sobbing. "My foot! She shot my foot!"

The door burst open and Logan shouted, "You're surrounded in here! Nobody move!"

Jane saw Sloan's shoulders sag slightly. "I think they're all dead, Logan."

"Get some light!" Jane shouted. "Get light, quickly. Kelsey is in this mess."

She heard Logan swearing and Henri crying. In the darkness, she made her way to Sloan as he made his way to her. He took her in his arms and held her, and they were both shaking.

She wasn't sure what happened next; suddenly there were officers everywhere. An ambulance came for Henri, who was completely dazed.

"We'll have to close the show tonight. I've never closed a show. Oh, my God, I've never closed a show. My theater. . . ."

Kelsey refused to go to the hospital. She let the ambulance driver tend to the knot on her forehead. She was humiliated that they'd managed to surprise her right after she'd called the ambulance and come back in to tend to Brian Highsmith.

The rest of the night involved a great deal of paperwork. And because they were law

officers who'd exchanged fire and killed, they had to go through additional hours of questioning. Even though there was no doubt they'd been justified, it was protocol.

Not until late afternoon of the next day did they return to the Gilded Lily.

Jane and Sloan didn't talk about the case after that. They took a long shower together, one filled with tender kisses and whispered words of gratitude that they were together and unharmed. Afterward they made love with an energy and passion neither had thought they could muster.

Then they slept.

Then they made love again.

And at last, when Logan called for a team briefing, they showered once more and dressed and came downstairs.

The Gilded Lily, according to the county, could open the next day.

For that night, Logan had ordered food from across the street. They got drinks from behind the bar and sat and ate in the empty room. They talked and tried to make sense of it all, even though they'd talked about it for so long already.

"The killing spree is what gets me," Sloan said. "Somehow, Caleb Hough found *some* of the gold."

"Where?" Logan asked.

"I think he did find it in the mine, though, at this point, we'll never know for sure. Then he must have realized that it had to be hidden somewhere in plain sight — but I think he felt he couldn't get to it himself. Seems he engaged Betty first, and then Heidi — and then Mike and Cy. But one of them did something that made him distrust them. Maybe it was when Brian foolishly put that skull on the wig stand. They all thought they were betraying one another. Caleb led them to the old mine because he wanted to make sure he could trust his partners after that. He seemed to think they were after him. Brian had no idea he'd started the whole rash of mistrust with that skull on the wig stand," Sloan said. "I heard people creeping around my property because Mike Addison was involved — and he owns the land next to mine. He was probably supposed to be keeping an eye on me, as well."

"How is Brian?" Kelsey asked.

"They shot him and Betty left him for dead. But he caught up with her and gave her a good knock on the head. She really was injured when I found her. And luckily, she was a lousy actress, so she was so busy playing possum she wasn't aware I took her bullets," Sloan said.

"Who killed Caleb — and tried to kill Jimmy and Zoe?" Jane asked.

"I believe it was Heidi. Heidi had been here all her life, and all her life, she'd watched Caleb act like a rich man while she took out hayrides and shoveled manure. So far, according to Newsome, all Mike Addison is doing now is swearing that he didn't kill anyone and didn't mean to be involved with killing anyone."

"Could have fooled me!" Jane muttered.

"Anyway, I'm convinced it was Heidi and Cy who went to the Hough house. Heidi seemed to have the upper hand in everything. Betty was at the station — keeping an eye on me, trying to find out everything I might know," Sloan said.

"I guess I was semiconscious when Heidi claimed you knew where the gold was, Jane. Do you?" Kelsey asked her.

"I didn't know. Not until last night," Jane said.

They all stared at her.

"Sage showed me. She wasn't *trying* to show me. I'm not actually sure whether she knew. I'd lost my gun and she helped me find it. But when she got it to me . . ." She let her voice trail off.

"Where is it?" the other three demanded in unison.

468

"Well, the stagecoach was never found because it was broken up — and used to make mannequins. The gold was stuffed into the ones that were made out of wood that was part of the stagecoach. I only saw a glint of metal in the leg of one that had fallen. The leg broke on it, and you could see the gold. I'm willing to bet that if they're all dismantled, the gold will be recovered."

They all just stared at her.

Sloan reached over and took her hand. "Secretive, aren't we, Agent Everett? You knew that last night, and you didn't say a word."

"Last night, our lives mattered. I hadn't even thought about it again — didn't want to." She paused. "What will happen to it now?"

"I assume most of it will go to the state," Logan said.

"But what's left would go to keep the theater open, right?"

"Yes. Brian will have to do some jail time, but that won't kill the theater," Logan said.

"And," Sloan added, "Valerie was innocent of everything that went on, as was Alice. Henri had no clue. He called us in because he was really indignant about the skull. But . . . he will need to rethink the show."

"So why was Valerie sneaking around the hospital?" Kelsey asked.

"She wanted to talk to Jennie. She was afraid the theater was haunted or that someone really was after the people here," Sloan said.

Logan cleared his throat. "Actually, Henri *is* in trouble. Valerie's heading back to L.A. She says that as far as she knows, no one ever killed anyone over a toilet paper commercial. Alice says she'll come back — but she wants a two-week paid vacation. Cy is dead and Brian . . . Brian won't be working for a while."

"Henri will be all right," Jane said confidently. "Directors have done new shows or recast old ones since the day theater began."

"He gets to reopen tomorrow," Sloan murmured. "I wonder what he plans to do."

The next night, Sloan couldn't believe he was standing onstage. Or rather, lying on the stage. He and Jane were now staying together at his place, and she'd talked him into doing this.

Jane was a natural. She was playing the vamp who sang most of the songs and had the most lines. She was carrying him through the song they did as the vamp and the hero — just as Logan and Kelsey covered him at other points.

They'd done a reversal in the show; Kelsey got to save him from the train. That way, he had fewer lines.

Henri had talked Jane into persuading the rest of them. But Henri was halfway in love with Jane himself. The others had thought it would be fun; they'd give Henri three days to find a new cast. They'd warned him they couldn't possibly learn the lines, but he'd told them it didn't matter. Ad-libbing was better than no show at all.

They did their performances for a week.

Meanwhile, Sloan had placed Chet in charge of the sheriff's office, and he and Lamont were interviewing for a new deputy.

Sloan wanted Chet to get in a lot of experience, because Logan had broached Sloan with a job offer.

He and the higher-ups at the Krewe center — men named Adam Harrison and Jackson Crow — had decided to create a third Krewe. Logan wanted him in on it.

It was a big decision.

On the day they finished the show, he went out to his house alone. Out back, he stroked Kanga and Roo and talked to them. He told Johnny Bearclaw about the offer, and Johnny assured him that he'd stay at the Arizona ranch and care for it, no matter where Sloan might be.

In the end he sat in his living room with Cougar on his lap. When he looked at the chair by the fire, he saw that his ancestor, Longman, was sitting with him.

"What should I do, Longman?" he asked.

"Make your own decision," Longman said. "You came here when you needed to come here. You can't go back, but you can go forward. Maybe you came back for many reasons. But it's time to bury the past, all of the past. And then, as men must, go where your heart leads you."

He smiled and leaned back. He still wasn't convinced Longman was real. Longman had said what Sloan felt in his own mind.

In the next few days, Jane finished the reconstructions of Sage's skull and she did a quick job with Red Marston's.

He wanted a quiet service for the two of them, but the whole town showed up at the chapel by the cemetery.

The dead were put to rest.

He lingered when the others left the graveyard; Jane stayed with him. She'd never once tried to influence him to accept Logan's offer, but they were together every night — as if they'd always be together.

She squeezed his hand suddenly. "Sloan. There they are."

He looked up. The day was dying; red streaked a darkening sky. But he could make out three forms and they slowly became clearer.

Red Marston, Trey Hardy and Sage McCormick. He stood and Jane rose with him.

One figure broke away. It was Sage. She moved among the wooden crosses and the occasional stone marker to reach them. She set a hand on his face. He felt it, like the caress of a soft and gentle fog.

Then she turned away and rejoined the others. They started walking into the darkness as the sun fell lower and lower.

Someone else was walking toward the three friends, someone who seemed to shimmer with light.

"Your great-great grandfather?" Jane whispered.

"Maybe," he said.

Then they were all gone. Neither he nor Jane spoke as they left the cemetery.

"There's beautiful land in Virginia," she told him. "Not far from Arlington. Beautiful horse ranches, too."

"Virginia. There's a lot of horse country there."

"Yes, there is. And cats are happy just about anywhere."

"Yeah?"

473

She smiled. "Home is where the heart is, you know."

He whirled her around and kissed her as the red drained from the sky and soft shadows surrounded them.

He smiled, because she looked at him a little anxiously when they separated.

"So I'm going to be a fed," he mused.

"They'll make you go through the academy," she warned.

"Well, they taught you to shoot!" he said.

"They did."

He kissed her again.

"When do we leave?" he asked.

And with those words, she threw her arms around him.

ABOUT THE AUTHOR

New York Times bestselling author **Heather Graham** has written more than one hundred fifty novels and novellas, has been published in nearly twenty-five languages, and has over seventy-five million copies in print. An avid scuba diver, ballroom dancer, and mother of five, she still enjoys her south Florida home, but loves to travel as well. Reading, however, is the pastime she still loves best, and is a member of many writing groups. For more information, check out her Web site, theoriginalheathergraham .com.